KATIE JENNINGS

things lost in
THE FIRE

a novel

Sapphire Royale
publishing

Cover design by Katie Jennings

Cover design consultant, interior book design,
and eBook design by Blue Harvest Creative
www.blueharvestcreative.com

THINGS LOST IN THE FIRE

Published by
Sapphire Royale Publishing

ISBN-13: 978-0692333402
ISBN-10: 0692333401

Visit the author at:
www.katieajennings.com
www.facebook.com/authorkatiejennings
www.twitter.com/dryadquartet

Purchase other books by Katie Jennings in print,
eBook, or audio by scanning the QR code.

To Brandon,
who makes me thankful every day
that I fell in love with my best friend.

prologue

THE FIRST thing she noticed was the stinging scent of smoke. It trailed off cigarettes and hand-rolled joints and wafted up the stairs in heady plumes, beckoning like an invitation to the madness coalescing below.

Sadie breathed in and out of her mouth in soft huffs, immediately regretting her decision to come downstairs. Already her head hurt from the blaring music—Three Dog Night's *Mama Told Me*—and her eyes burned from the smoke. People flooded the living room, sprawled over sofas and chairs or gathered in intimate social circles. Others wandered lazily, drifting into the kitchen for another drink or a hit of something darker. Like always, her mother permitted party guests to indulge their vices, no matter how vulgar.

At fifteen years old, Sadie had witnessed her fair share of her mother's extravagant parties. They were always the same—packed with Hollywood stars, industry wheelers and dealers, perfect strangers, and of course, her mother's personal entourage of musical geniuses. It was a life she'd been born into, a world more chaotic and privileged than most could ever dream of.

It was also a life she despised.

Her hand skimmed over the wooden railing as she descended the last few steps, hoping her presence went unnoticed. The craving for a glass of milk to help her sleep was too powerful to resist, even when it meant facing the freaks her mother called friends.

She slid like a covert ninja through the sea of guests, careful not to make eye contact or welcome conversation. Some of them knew who she was, and the others couldn't give a damn. All she needed was to slip into the kitchen then back upstairs to safety.

Though her mother's five thousand square foot home nestled in the Hollywood Hills boasted an open floor plan, with the party in full swing Sadie felt suffocated. Strangers brushed and bumped against her, releasing the scent of musky perfume and alcohol. Laughter and voices rose over the din of electric guitar and drums. Somewhere in the chaos, she heard her mother's legendary bell-like laugh.

Sadie squeezed into the kitchen and went straight for the fridge. She ignored the guests crowded around the marble island behind her, knowing without looking that her mother was among them. Valerie Ryan had the voice of a goddess, and not just when she sang. That voice was giddy with gossip now, breathy with elation as she divulged some sordid secret she likely concocted out of thin air.

Sadie poured milk into a glass, trying hard not to stare at the half-empty bottles of her mother's treasured Grey Goose littering the countertop. After replacing the milk in the fridge, she nearly made it out of the kitchen before her mother called to her.

"Lovely child, sweet baby Sadie. Isn't she beautiful?" Valerie crooned, beaming at her friends with glazed eyes and a serene smile. The women giggled and gushed while the men cracked sarcastic jokes. Valerie tossed back her mane of silken blonde hair, gazing upon her daughter with relish. "Doesn't she look just like me? Ben *hates* it."

"That's because Ben's an asshole," the gangly man beside Valerie drawled, leaning in to press a sloppy kiss to her forehead. She patted his length of dark hair, winking at her friends.

"This little angel is your spitting image, Val," a striking brunette said, tipping back her martini. "I bet money she sings one day too."

Valerie laughed brightly. "Imagine us doing a duet. Ben might shit himself."

"You've been divorced for four years and he's already remarried. He needs to stop bothering you," another skeleton-of-a-woman argued, puffing on a cigarette. "Surely he has better things to do."

"You'd think so, but no." Valerie lifted her chin, honeyed eyes glittering. "When he sings our songs I can tell he's never gotten over me. Albatross isn't the same since I left and he knows it."

"Whatever, who gives a shit what Ben thinks?" The man grunted with a cocky grin, downing the last of the vodka tonic in his glass. "Today's about you and your birthday and I say we're long overdue for a hit."

He dug into his jeans pocket and pulled out a small, clear bag of white powder. As he dumped some onto the marble and divided it into lines with a tattered business card, Sadie flushed. She knew adults did cocaine, had witnessed it before. That didn't make it any easier to see her mother give in to the substance like the rest of the weirdos parading around their home.

Sensing an opportunity to slip away, Sadie ducked out of the kitchen, milk in hand. The second she turned there were warm hands on her shoulders and a toothy grin beaming down at her.

It was Tommy Barnes, the bassist for her father's band, and at that moment he was like a life raft in the middle of a sea of sharks. "Hey Sadie-bug, what're you doing down here?"

"Hi, Tommy." She attempted a smile in return, though she couldn't help but glance back at her mother. Valerie was laughing hysterically and brushing at her nose.

Tommy followed her gaze and frowned. "C'mon, kid. Let's get you back to bed."

He draped his arm over her shoulders and led her through the crowd, stumbling a bit and laughing as he told her a joke he'd just heard. She knew he'd been drinking and likely smoking pot, but she didn't mind. Even under the influence he was the kindest, gentlest person she'd ever met.

They stopped at the staircase and she looked up at him. She took in his messy cap of chestnut hair and bright blue eyes and smiled. "Can you take me to the Pier tomorrow?"

"Sure thing. Sleep tight, kid." He wandered off, cracking jokes to random guests and inciting bouts of laughter. Tommy was always the life of the party.

Sadie ascended the steps, eager to return to her room. Out of the corner of her eye she spotted a man dressed in black trailing behind her. When she reached the top of the stairs, she realized he was following her.

Thinking he was looking for a bathroom, she ignored the instinct to run and continued down the hall. Even from up here, she could hear the thumping of the bass and the wail of Robert Plant. If she needed help, no one would hear her.

He was closer now, mere steps behind her. She didn't have to look; she could sense him. He reeked of cheap cologne, and his footsteps were heavy on her mother's powder blue carpet.

Her hand shot out the second she reached her bedroom door and she threw herself inside. She attempted to close it but he shoved her back, forcing his way in. She threw her milk glass, barely missing his face, and attempted to push past him into the hallway. Instead, he caught her and wrestled her back, his hand flying to her mouth.

"Shush, sweet babe," he murmured, gritting his teeth as she continued to fight him, a muffled scream bursting from her throat. "I said quiet!" He released her and struck her hard across the face, sending her spiraling back onto her bed. Tears of pain and horror fell from her eyes as she lay stunned from the blow. Through the throbbing on her cheek, she felt the warm drip of blood.

He stripped off his coat, tossing it to the floor. She spotted the small handgun he carried tucked into his belt. When he lifted it out her heart sank with dread, but he set it aside on her dresser and slowly closed the door.

As he approached, she was able to get a good look at him. He was her mother's new drummer, Lee Walker. He hadn't been around for more than a month, but she knew he was dating Georgina, another ex-member of Albatross. Rumors had circulated about his drug use, and she'd noticed him watching her before.

His hand swiped through his untidy length of brown hair as he stared at her, madness widening his eerie dark eyes. His tongue slid along his teeth as if he contemplated what to do with her.

In desperation she tried to slide off the bed and run, only to crumple on the floor, reeling with dizzying pain. He tossed her back onto the bed and pinned her beneath his body, his right hand holding her wrists over her head, fingers digging into her skin. His other hand clamped over her mouth again when she attempted to cry out. She sucked in quick gasps of air through her nose, breathing in the scent of tobacco and sweat as sobs built and exploded in her throat.

"They won't hear you." His eyes bored into hers as a sick smile twisted his lips. "Just relax now. I know you want this."

She closed her eyes and turned her face into the blankets. The more she tried to fight, the tighter his grip became. Pain shot through her as more tears fell.

When he released her mouth to glide his hand under her nightgown and over her inner thigh, she shuddered in disbelief. The weight of him on top of her was crushing, suffocating. She knew what sex was, she wasn't ignorant. But she also knew this was very wrong.

"Please, don't," she begged, trembling as he forced her legs apart. She couldn't look him in the eye, couldn't bear it. There was something wrong with him, something manic and evil that seemed almost inhuman. She heard him fumble for the zipper on his jeans and the horror of what he was about to do set in.

She made another attempt to get free, only to have him backhand her across the face again. The blow sent sparks flying behind her eyes as she reeled from the hot, intense wave of pain. She knew then she had no chance of escaping. Her only option was to lay back, accept, and pray it would soon be over.

A dark haze swept in, her body's instinctive defense numbing her to the horrors of what was happening. She felt herself slipping into a cocoon, retreating away from the monster as he tore aside her nightgown. In her head she sang one of her father's songs, trying to picture his face. Instead all she could imagine was her mother, drunk and laughing like a hyena at someone else's slaughter. Her mother had let this happen. It was all her fault.

Somewhere far away she heard her name. Someone shouted, followed by a release of pressure from her chest. She felt the monster rise away from her, a rush of cool air replacing the heat of his body. Still unable to open her eyes, she hovered in a daze, slipping in and out of the darkness.

An echoing pop thundered through the room. She felt it down to her very bones seconds before a mountain crashed beside her.

Her eyes flew open, dilated and confused, only to land upon the empty gaze of the monster. The bottomless pits of his evil stared back at her as crimson streams drained from a gaping hole in his chest.

It was the last thing she saw before the world upended and turned to black.

SHE REMEMBERED the voices. They swam just out of reach, vibrating hollowly in the distance. Then arms came around her and lifted her away, away from the darkness and coppery scent of blood. The pungent smell of death.

Tommy assessed her injuries. She thought he asked her if she'd done it. If she'd killed the monster. Had she? She didn't think so.

Then her mother's shrieking cries had filled the air, useless and obscene. They had blended with the roaring sound of music and the startled faces of strangers as Sadie was carried to the ambulance waiting outside.

She wasn't hurt. At least not in the way everyone feared. The nurse had treated a cut above her right cheekbone and there'd be bruises on her wrists and legs, but nothing more. She'd been spared a horrific fate, though she had no idea how. Why couldn't she remember?

Who killed Lee Walker? Who saved her?

Tommy insisted he heard the gunshot from downstairs but when he got to Sadie's room, there was no one. The gun was on the floor, Walker was dead, and Sadie was out cold. The police were scrambling to find witnesses, to find an explanation. They'd found out little from her, convinced she'd remember in time.

But she hadn't yet, and she knew she wouldn't. Whoever had shot Lee Walker didn't want to be found. Though she'd never believed in such things, part of her imagined a guardian angel sweeping in to save her. It made more sense than anything else.

As she sat on the edge of the hospital bed the following morning, she heard furious shouting beyond the closed door of the room. Her mother was arguing with the police in the hallway. Though Sadie couldn't hear everything that was being said, the sound of it made her feel sick to her stomach. She hugged herself, staring down at the holes in the faded jeans Tommy had brought her. With it she wore an old Albatross T-shirt, the black fabric and white logo faded from years of use.

Moments later, her mother got quiet. Sadie's eyes shot to the door, hearing footsteps just outside. Valerie called out the instant before Sadie's father, Ben, swept into the room.

It had been nearly three months since Sadie had seen him. Three months since he'd bothered to notice her. She hadn't expected him to make the trip from Boston for her now.

He went straight to her without speaking. No words of comfort, no relieved hugs, nothing. Ben McRae was notoriously cold as stone and impatient. And as always, Sadie felt like nothing but an inconvenience to him.

His hand clamped around her arm at the elbow and he lifted her to her feet, pulling her from the room. Sadie chanced a look at his face, saw it creased with anger as he squared off with his ex-wife. His crystal blue eyes frosted with livid fury.

"Yet again, I have to clean up your goddamn mess," he snapped at Valerie, shaking his head with disgust.

Valerie cocked her chin defiantly and matched his frost with molten fire. "Maybe if you hadn't moved to Boston she could've been with you last night."

"Maybe if you hadn't hired a fucking rapist to be your drummer none of this would've happened," Ben fired back. "What the hell is wrong with you, Val?"

Sadie winced, finding herself trapped between the two of them. It was always the same. Accusations, bitterness, rage. Her mother shed some tears for dramatic effect, and her father balled his free hand into a fist, as though wishing he could use it.

For years they'd used their aggressive passion for each other in their music. They fed on it as much as the audience did while watching them. It had been electrifying, dramatic, and the stuff of legend. Albatross had long been known for its explosive lead singers and their volatile relationship. And when they'd split up at last, unable to survive the heat any longer, Sadie had been left to wither away in their oppressive shadows.

A police officer approached. "Ms. Ryan, we'll need you to come with us down to the station."

Valerie whirled around, indignation darkening her voice. "Excuse me?"

"I'm afraid you're under arrest," the officer continued, reaching instinctively for the handcuffs on his belt. "We can keep this civil and not give the press anything to gawk at, but that's up to you."

"What the hell am I being arrested for? I didn't do anything!" Valerie threw up her hands dramatically. "My baby is in the hospital and you people want me to just *leave* her?"

"You don't have a choice, ma'am. We found drugs at your residence and have witnesses who claim you were using. We have to take you in for child endangerment." The officer nodded to his partner, who reached for Valerie's arms.

She struggled against his grip, shrieking at the top of her lungs. "*No!* You can't take me! Don't you know who I am?"

Sadie watched with wide eyes as the police arrested her mother. So they *were* making her pay for what she'd let happen. She was going away. A sliver of hope glittered through her at the prospect, mingling with the childish satisfaction of revenge.

A vindictive smile twisted her father's lips. His gaze was set on his ex-wife as the cops dragged her out of the room, kicking and screaming. He didn't bother to hide the pleasure he got from seeing it.

"Come on. Let's go." He nudged Sadie and led her in the opposite direction, keeping his hand locked tight around her elbow. She stumbled along as they came up to the glass entrance doors of the hospital. Outside, she could see dozens of people gathering and the black town car that would take her away.

Ben grimaced at the sight of the crowd but said nothing. Instead he slipped on a pair of Ray Ban sunglasses and kept Sadie close. His bodyguard waited by the door for them.

As they emerged into the morning sun, the mob of people swarmed in like buzzing hornets. Cameras flashed all around them. Voices clamored all at once—questioning, shouting, salivating. Sadie instinctively burrowed into her father's chest as he led the way through the chaos.

"Sadie, what happened?"

"Ben, can you tell us if Valerie has been arrested?"

"Were you raped, Sadie?"

"What was his name?"

"Did you kill him?"

Ben ignored the paparazzi and guided Sadie into the backseat of the town car. He slipped in after her, closing them in while reporters continued to snap off pictures and shout questions from outside. Once the bodyguard settled into the passenger seat, the driver pulled out and took them to freedom.

Sadie watched the hordes of nosy passersby and reporters as they drove off, hating them all. Soon everyone would know what had happened to her. Her friends at school, her teachers, her piano instructor. The maids would gossip behind closed doors and her mother's friends would pity her.

And Georgina...she'd completely forgotten about her. How would she take the news that her new boyfriend was not only dead, but that he'd attempted to rape Sadie?

Because the thought made her uncomfortable, she forced it from her mind and turned to her father. He was staring out the window, seemingly lost in thought. Her eyes swept over his russet curls of hair, cropped neatly around his head. The style accentuated the sharpness of his cheekbones, refining a face that was infamously handsome. Women had always thrown themselves at him. Even at forty-six, he was in his prime.

"Am I going to Boston with you?"

"No. I'm sending you to my parents."

"In Lake Tahoe?" Sadie shook her head. "But I want to go with you."

He sighed, then cast an impatient look at her. "I'm leaving this weekend to go on the road for a few weeks. I'm not going to be around to take care of you."

"That's okay. I can hang out with Isaac." She brightened at the idea, missing her younger step-brother.

"It isn't going to work," Ben insisted, looking out the window again. "Paulette is very busy. She doesn't need the added stress of you staying under our roof."

Sadie bristled at the mention of her step-mother. Paulette had never made it a secret that she wished Ben just forget Sadie altogether.

She stared at her hands bundled tightly in her lap. Bruises were forming on her wrists, marks made by the man who'd tried to hurt her. She could still see his face, contorted with evil, and the image made her shudder.

Ben slowly turned back to her. He watched her silently for a few moments, as though wondering if he should try and comfort her or leave her alone. When he spoke, his voice had softened with a regret he rarely showed.

"I'm sorry this happened, Sadie." He kept his hands on his knees, though she wanted nothing more than to be held by him. "You won't be seeing your mother for awhile. I'm going to see to it that she loses custody. After this fiasco, I can't imagine any judge will take her side."

Sadie chewed on her lower lip, unable to meet his eyes, unable to speak. This was what she wanted, wasn't it?

He continued. "You'll be safe in Tahoe. That's the best thing I can offer you right now."

"Safe," she whispered, tears stinging her eyes again. She clung to the word like a life vest, soothed by it despite everything.

Maybe he was right. Getting out of L.A., away from the spotlight and the press was the best thing. Maybe then she could escape the horrors of the night before and pretend it never happened.

She'd leave the image of that face behind, along with the life she was meant to live.

Chapter *one*

INCLINE VILLAGE, NEVADA
JUNE 2013

H ER FINGERS trailed over the silvery surface of the lake, creating ripples in the glass. In the light of early morning, her heart
absorbed every last drop of peace the water had to offer.

Sadie lost herself in it, gazing into the clear depths to view the
rocky floor below. Occasionally she'd spot a slender fish darting in and
out of the rocks, or hear the perky cry of a seagull in the distance. If
she listened closer, she could hear the throaty roar of a boat engine,
the sign of a fisherman setting out to take advantage of the lake's
peaceful morning. Within hours, tourists would flood the area and the
lake would be filled with jet skis, swimmers, and summer fun.

Until then, though, the lake was hers. She often found herself
setting out in her grandfather's old wooden canoe at the crack of dawn,
needing time alone. It was in these moments that her creative juices
flowed best, and lyrics poured like rain from her fingertips. Here, in her
quiet cove of beautiful Lake Tahoe, she was farthest from the life she'd
once lived. And up until three days ago, she never imagined she'd want
to leave. Want to go back to the place where everything fell to pieces.

Sadie removed her hand from the chilled water and lay back in the canoe, folding her arms behind her head. Her long waves of golden hair spilled around her, framing a face of softly honed feminine beauty. Sea foam green eyes gazed up at the colorless sky, lost in all that early morning gray. Beneath her, the collection of multicolored blankets and pillows made the boat feel like a floating bed, like something out of a dream.

But this was no dream. Her mother was dying.

She closed her eyes on a long sigh, feeling that sting of pain hit her again. Once the disbelief and shock had worn off, the sorrow had replaced it. Directly in her heart, in the one place she'd always assumed Valerie Ryan couldn't reach. But somehow the woman had a hold over her, even after everything she'd done.

It had been three years since she'd last seen her mother. There were the occasional phone calls, Christmas cards or birthday wishes, but the two were largely estranged. Sadie preferred it that way, and could only assume Valerie did too.

Then the call had come. Not from Valerie herself, but from Sadie's father, Ben. He'd heard through the gossipy grapevine of Albatross that Valerie had been diagnosed with stage three ovarian cancer. The chances of her surviving were lower than thirty percent. He'd wanted to tell Sadie before the press got a hold of the information.

Now she was faced with a choice: stay away and ignore it, or go back to L.A. and confront her demons head-on.

Part of her wanted to pretend that nothing had changed, but she couldn't. As distant as they may be, the woman was still her mother. And all Sadie could think about was how scared and alone Valerie must feel, how lost and hopeless. It would take a colder heart than hers to ignore the only mother she'd ever have in the final days of her life.

So she'd be making the drive in a matter of hours, destined for that horrific city she'd long ago escaped from. Every time she returned there she felt smothered. There were too many people, too many scars of the past. Worst of which being the nightmare she'd experienced at fifteen.

Sadie's eyes opened to avoid the image of his face. It tended to creep up on her, catching her off guard in moments of peace and quiet.

Lee Walker would always plague her memories and dreams, even though her experience with him had lasted less than five minutes. He was the monster she'd spent the last eleven years running away from. Despite being dead he was always there, hiding in the dark corners of her nightmares, ready to strike back and take what he'd been cheated out of the first time.

The police had never solved the mystery of what happened to her. There had been no fingerprints on Walker's gun other than his own and there were no witnesses. Except for Sadie, of course. But to the dismay of the police, she never remembered anything that could help.

Though they'd rounded up her mother, Tommy, and some house guests to test for gunshot residue, the majority had fled in the chaos. With hundreds of people, many who were friends of friends or even strangers, the likelihood of recovering them all and finding the shooter was near impossible. The police were left to give up and concede that the evidence supported Lee Walker assaulting Sadie, resulting in his albeit deserved death.

It'd taken weeks for the media coverage to die down, and even then the mystery of who shot Lee Walker remained one of L.A.'s greatest and most infamous scandals.

Unlike in Los Angeles, Sadie felt safe in Lake Tahoe. It was her quiet haven away from the notoriety that came from both the scandal and from being the only daughter of a pair of legendary musicians. While her parents continued to perform—her father with his band Albatross and her mother as a solo artist—Sadie stayed hidden. Stayed *safe*.

She couldn't ignore the music in her blood, though. Nothing could ever stop that hunger, even fear of the spotlight. So she'd done the next best thing: she'd created a YouTube channel and performed under an alias.

Her grandfather had helped, understanding her need to release the music in her heart while preserving her anonymity. He'd seen what a lust for fame had done to his only son. With a video camera and a clever disguise, they'd created a mysterious, brilliant artist the world knew as Piper Gray. Sadie was shocked to see her videos garner hundreds of thousands of hits and pleas by the public for shows and an album. They adored her without having a clue who she really was.

If they knew they'd probably want her even more. But she preferred to see how far she could get on her own, without the names Ben McRae and Valerie Ryan behind her. Unlike her parents, it wasn't the fame she desired. It was the joy of pouring her heart and soul into lyrics, into music, and sharing it with anyone who cared to listen.

That was why she'd turned down offers by record companies and agents who'd offered to make Piper Gray a household name. She didn't need the money they promised, and she certainly didn't feel comfortable performing in front of a crowd. The thought of being recognized terrified her. And all the publicity that would come with it, both good and bad, scared her even more.

She released a deep breath, knowing all of that would need to be put on hold for now. Who knew how long she'd be in Los Angeles—a week, a month, a year—whatever it took to fulfill her final duties as a daughter.

Then she could return to Tahoe and the peace she enjoyed there. Life would go on, and at least she would know she did all she could to help her mother.

The sun crested over the mountain range, spilling light across the water. Sadie sat up and reached for the little spiral notepad she carried with her everywhere. She jotted down a few song lyrics, inspired by the moment, then closed the pad and reached for the canoe's wooden oar.

As she paddled her way back home, her vision blurred with unshed tears. By nightfall, she'd be in Los Angeles. Home to her greatest nightmare.

"DID YOU pack your cell phone charger?" Sadie's grandmother asked, helping lift a guitar case into the back of the car. Her grandfather was busy trying to load a large suitcase, as usual too stubborn to admit his age.

"Yeah, it's in my purse." Sadie grabbed the guitar from her grand-mother and placed it in the trunk of her green Suburu Crosstrek, then reached over to assist her grandfather. He swatted her hand away with a stubborn sniff.

"And the car charger too?"

"Yep." Sadie gave up on helping her grandfather and faced her grandmother, offering a reassuring smile. "You know me. I'm the orga-nized one in the family."

Jo Beth McRae laughed, her vibrant blue tunic shifting to reveal her wooden beaded bracelets as she patted Sadie on the arm. The sun lit up her wild waves of salt and pepper hair, which she wore long and free of bonds. "That you are. Now, Walt, don't hurt yourself."

Walter McRae grunted as he finally shoved the suitcase into the trunk, shooting his wife a smug look. His dark eyebrows lifted with his smile. "Yes, dear."

He was a tall, well built man with a deep voice and an even deeper heart. Though his coffee brown hair had gone gray over the years, he retained a sense of youthfulness and humor that could charm even the toughest cynic.

He'd married his Jo Beth when they'd both been eighteen, two country kids shuffling through the dust of nineteen fifties Oklahoma. They chased their dreams to a little town called Burbank, California, where they started a family and dug in roots. It wasn't until the city closed in on them and the chance to retire from his job as a fireman came that they escaped to the sheltered forests of Lake Tahoe. By then, their son Ben had wandered into the sights of Valerie Ryan while living in Boston with Tommy Barnes, and history was made.

Sadie knew she was the product of that troubled, tormented history. Valerie had been, in the opinions of many, the best and worst thing that ever happened to Ben McRae. But without her, Albatross would have never soared to the same heights it did with her. Her goddess-like voice and Ben's husky, soulful tone were a match made in music heaven.

Jo Beth let out a soft sigh, glancing around to make sure they'd gotten everything. "Well, it looks like you're ready to go."

Sadie nodded. "I won't be gone that long. Maybe a month or so."

"If I know your mother, she'll live another ten years just to keep you in L.A. out of spite," Walt said, earning a snicker from his wife. Neither of them had ever made a secret of their distaste for their son's ex-wife.

Sadie shrugged, feeling that ache in her heart again. "Odds are she won't have the option. And I'm all she has left. She needs me."

"We know, honey." Her grandmother pulled her in for a tight hug, patting her on the back. "You always were such a gentle soul. We're so proud of you."

Sadie met her grandmother's cornflower blue eyes as she broke the hug. "I'll miss you guys."

Her grandfather rested a hand on her shoulder, squeezing it. "It takes a lot of courage to do what you're doing."

She faced him. "Does it? It just feels like something I should do."

"Just don't let her or anyone else in that hellhole of a city get you down. If at any time you want to come home, you know we'll be here waiting for you."

She nodded, unsure what to say in response. Instead, she wrapped her arms around his tall frame, breathing in the scent of Old Spice and pine needles. "I'll call you when I get there."

"I'm grateful you'll be staying at Ben's old place," Jo Beth put in as Sadie gave her another hug. "I wouldn't want you at Valerie's. Too much bad energy in that old house."

"I'll be happier having my own space, anyway," Sadie replied, reaching for her keys in her colorful patchwork purse. "Though it did take some convincing to get Dad to say yes."

"Not like he's using the place," Walt said with a knowing grin. "He avoids going to L.A. like he'll catch the plague."

"I don't blame him." Sadie sighed, feeling anxious. "Is it bad that all I can think about is someone recognizing me?"

"You'll be fine." Jo Beth offered her a warm smile, the laughter lines around her eyes deepening. "Now go on before the traffic gets nasty."

"Right. I'll call you guys later. I love you." Sadie hugged them both once more for good measure, then rounded her car and hopped in the driver's seat. As she buckled in and started the car, she waved goodbye. Her grandparents stood together, arm-in-arm, to watch her leave. She offered them both a smile, hoping to portray more confidence than she felt.

Her heart started to race as she put the car in drive and headed down the long, sweeping driveway. It carried her downhill, out of sight of their wooden home surrounded by towering pine trees. She watched it disappear in the rearview mirror, battling the urge to turn around and flee to safety. The decision was made. She was going to L.A. There'd be no turning back now.

Feeling a little more positive, she turned onto the main road that would carry her through North Lake Tahoe toward the freeway. From there, it'd be smooth sailing down the mountain.

Her cell phone vibrated, signaling a text. As she came to a stoplight she read her best friend Tess's words of excitement, promising bottles of wine for a long overdue girls' night. A smile lit Sadie's face at the idea.

After shooting off a quick reminder to Tess to use the spare key hidden under a rock by the front door, she programmed her iPod to play her 'going home' mix. The soulful voices of The Mamas & The Papas rang out of her car speakers, dreaming of California. Singing along, Sadie continued down the road.

She didn't know what awaited her in L.A., but it was sure as hell going to be an adventure.

Chapter *two*

A COCKY GRIN lit Brody Odell's face the second before the punch came. He ducked not a moment too soon, dodging the blow with a nimble sidestep and a wild laugh. Exhilaration raced white-hot through his veins, his hand surprisingly steady as he held up his camcorder, recording every second.

His opponent tried again, only to be wrestled back by his own beefcake of a bodyguard. Being that it was midday on the busy streets of West Hollywood, witnesses were starting to gather. A scattering of paparazzi swarmed in like ants, eager to capture controversial rapper DeShawn "Murda" Williams in a raging mood.

"You goddamn son of a bitch," Murda snarled, baring his teeth as he struggled against the hold of his guard. His rail-thin super-model girlfriend rolled her eyes and scoffed, obviously annoyed at yet another of her boyfriend's outbursts. She tried to grab his arm only to be swatted away like an annoying fly.

Brody continued to smile, swiping his free hand through his crop of dark hair. His brown eyes honed in on the rapper with eager intensity. "Do it again. I dare you."

Murda gritted his teeth and Brody could tell he was struggling against the temptation to beat him into a bloody pulp. He was also probably debating if the satisfaction would be worth an assault charge.

Never one to fear risking life and limb, Brody gave a brisk nod. "So what'd you think of that SNL skit last night? I thought it was pretty funny, myself. Though I have to say, they might've downplayed your temper little a bit."

"I don't give a shit—"

"C'mon, baby. Let's go," the girlfriend interrupted, her ebony eyes sweeping over Brody like he was a moldy piece of garbage. She hooked her spidery arm through Murda's muscled one, urging him onward.

"The best part was when they parodied your new song. I was laughing my ass off," Brody added, keeping the camera directly in Murda's face to capture every detail.

Murda bit back a retort and flipped Brody off for good measure, shoving his middle finger into the camera lens. He turned around and let his bodyguard and girlfriend lead him away, grumbling obscenities under his breath.

Brody shut off his camera as he watched them go, pleased with himself. "TMZ thanks you!" he called out, laughing like a hyena. Murda shot him a venomous look, barely restrained from jumping into attack mode once more.

A few of the other paparazzi nearby burst out laughing while a couple of them trotted after Murda to get more footage. Brody merely lifted his aviator sunglasses from the neck of his white 'I Make Stuff Up' T-shirt and slid them over his eyes.

"Well, ladies and gentlemen, it's been a pleasure." He bowed to his fellow reporters and to the crowd that had gathered, earning more looks of disgust than appreciation. "Until next time."

Camera in hand, he took off in the opposite direction. He dug into the back pocket of his jeans for a pack of cigarettes, shaking one out of the case and into his mouth. Seconds later he lit it and smiled into the bright California sun, smoke dancing around his face. The worn-out Chucks on his feet slapped against the chewing-gum smeared concrete, taking him east down Sunset Boulevard.

He knew he should be grateful he'd narrowly escaped a beating, but the blood rush had been worth the risk. There was a time not long ago when he'd dodged bullets and laid awake at night with the sounds of sirens and bombs exploding in the distance. *That* had been a real rush, he recalled, the sentiment bittersweet. He'd had a real job back then, a respectable one. Now he was stuck chasing celebrities all across the greater Los Angeles area to exploit them in their weakest moments. Moments of adultery, anger, inebriation, violence—whatever the tabloids were willing to pay him for. Sometimes it paid big, but most times he was stuck begging for scraps.

Either way, it was a life he'd earned. He knew that much. He held no delusions that he deserved anything better than what that bitch Karma had bestowed upon him. In the end, he was right where he belonged.

His mouth twisted around his cigarette in a cynical grin as he approached his car. It was a white '95 Thunderbird, beat to shit and barely functional. He reached for his keys and unlocked the door, slipping onto the faded red seat with a grunt and tossing the camera onto the passenger seat. As he coaxed the car to life, he wheeled the driver's side window down to let the smoke from his cigarette escape.

The radio kicked on, the snarky wisecracks of Jack FM preceding one of his favorite songs. His smile widened as he cranked up the sound of Guns N' Roses singing about Paradise City, instinctively bobbing his head in time with the beat.

Shoving the car in drive, he whipped out into traffic and joined the mad rush of Hollywood.

He let his arm hang out the window, smoke drifting from the tip of his cigarette. Without working air conditioning in his car, he had no choice but to embrace what little breeze there was on the hot streets of the city.

He'd lived most of his twenty-nine years in L.A., except for that glorious time when he'd roamed the darker, more grotesque cities of the world on the hunt for a story. Those had been the best years of his life. When he'd lived for something meaningful and pursued truth the way a hound hunts down a slippery fox. Back then, even his father had to admit that he'd been worth a damn to the world.

Brody sucked on his cigarette and tapped ash out the window. Bitterness wallowed in his gut but he forced it back. His pride wouldn't allow him to suffer under the weight of the old man's judgment anymore.

His father, the lawyer. Not just any lawyer, but the most powerful defense attorney in all of Los Angeles. Everyone who could pay the price tag sought out the services of Max Odell of the Odell & Son law firm. His reputation was spotless, his intellect and knowledge of the law impeccable, and his ability to win cases legendary. He could whittle even the most reliable witnesses offered by the prosecution down to sputtering uncertainty. And the power he held over wobbling juries was the stuff of legend.

If only he'd been half as good a father as he was a lawyer, maybe things would have worked out differently. Brody scoffed at the idea, knowing he'd be the black sheep of the family even *if* his father wasn't such a righteous bastard.

The 'son' in Odell & Son was Brody's younger brother, Chase. Mr. Perfect. Brody's opposite in nearly every way.

Where Brody had the dark, sharp featured looks of their mother, Chase had the chestnut brown hair and bright blue eyes of their father. While Brody lived on his toes and let impulse rule his every move, Chase was a successful family man with a baby on the way. And where Brody had made every bad, rebellious decision in the book, Chase was as straight-laced as apple pie on a Sunday afternoon.

The offer had always been open for Brody to join the family law firm, or to let his mother help pay rent, but he couldn't lower himself to accept charity. He made his own way in the world, even if it wasn't flashy or pretty. He'd seen bad times, but he'd seen some damn good times, too. At least it had always been on his terms, on his back, and with his own sweat dripping down his face. His life was *his*, and he'd live with the choices he made, good or bad.

And boy, had there been a lot of bad ones.

When his thoughts drifted to that godforsaken desert on the other side of the world, he grimaced. He forced the demons away as he snuffed out his cigarette in the car's ashtray. He was paying the price, wasn't he? Every goddamn day he was paying for that stupid, horrible, *fatal* mistake.

After releasing a heavy breath to clear the guilt from his system, he swerved into a faster lane of traffic and gunned the engine. What he needed was some food and most definitely a cold beer. He dug into his pocket, only to discover a measly twenty dollar bill. Well, it'd be cheap take-out and even cheaper beer. Until he got his next check from one of the many tabloids he submitted to, he was strapped for cash.

The irony of it never ceased to amaze him. There had once been a time when he'd had more money than he knew what to do with. Now he was lucky if he could afford a couple containers of second-rate Chinese food.

Oh, how the mighty have fallen.

BRODY HAD chosen the third floor apartment in the heart of Venice Beach not for the water stains on the ceiling or for the late night sounds of muffled Gangsta rap coming from his teenage neighbor's bedroom, but for the fact that it had a month-to-month lease at a price he couldn't afford to pass up.

It may not have been a castle, but he was satisfied. The threadbare brown carpet could use replacing and the walls were more gray than white, giving the quaint one-bedroom an outdated look. He'd tossed up some 1980s movie posters to add splashes of color and let the rest of it be what it was.

Brody perched on the edge of his sagging navy blue sofa, tapping away at the keyboard of his laptop. It rested on the maple-colored Ikea coffee table he'd dragged out of a dumpster a year or so before. A fresh cigarette hung from between his lips as he typed, not yet lit. In his distraction he'd forgotten all about it.

In the corner of the living room an old box TV was set on the Dodgers game. Occasionally he'd glance up and grunt at the score. He scratched his head beneath his prized Dodger blue baseball cap, irritated to see his team losing. Ignoring the game, he turned back to the email he was writing to his contact at TMZ.

Scattered around him were stacks of newspapers and magazines, many containing images he himself had captured. A Corona bottle now wet with condensation lay forgotten on the table, lost in the clutter of fast food napkins, month-old mail, and matchbooks.

At the knock on his front door, he tossed the unlit cigarette aside and shot to his feet, digging deep into his pocket for what remained of the twenty dollars after he'd bought the beer. When he opened the door the delivery man grinned ear-to-ear.

"What's up, bro?" the man asked with a quick nod, hoisting a white plastic bag filled with Chinese takeout containers. He was in his mid-twenties and dressed more like a Latin hip-hop artist than a delivery man, but at least he was punctual.

"*Nada mucho*, Juan." Brody handed over the cash and accepted the bag, sniffing inside hungrily. "I'll have to get you next time for a tip. That's all I got right now."

One of Juan's eyebrows lifted as he shook his head. "Man, you always say that shit. If you're that poor maybe you should go get a real job or something."

"What, like you?" Brody snorted, their eyes meeting. His mouth twisted in a wry smile. "Then I'd be the sucker not making tips."

He closed the door against Juan's threat to blacklist him from the restaurant. Chuckling to himself, Brody carried the bag into the kitchen and set it on the cheap laminate countertop. Grabbing a single box of chow mein and a pair of chopsticks, he returned to his seat on the couch and dug in.

He mindlessly watched the game as he ate. A few moments later, his cell phone rang on the table beside him. When he read the caller-ID he rolled his eyes.

"Yeah?" he answered, his words muffled by the food in his mouth.

"*Hey, how's it going?*" Chase, Mr. Perfect himself, asked cheerfully.

"Just peachy, you?" Brody swallowed and set aside his food. He leaned back against the sofa, rubbing his face with his free hand.

"*Good. Abby's due in a couple of weeks. She's so calm somehow, I don't know how she does it. I'm a freaking mess.*"

"Having babies is a scary business," Brody drawled, toying with his lighter. He flicked it on and off, his eyes honed in on the flames. "If you're looking for brotherly comfort you'd have better luck with a shrink."

Chase laughed. *"Probably. Hey, I wanted to remind you that Dad's sixtieth birthday is coming up and we're throwing him a big party at the house. He'd love for you to come."*

It was Brody's turn to laugh. "You're kidding, right?"

"No, not really—"

"The last time I attended one of these *parties* of yours, Dad and I nearly went to blows across the punch table. Trust me, he doesn't want me to come."

"Brody, please," Chase began. *"I know you guys don't always get along, but it'd mean the world to me if you could just try for once."*

"You make it sound like *I'm* the problem," Brody fired back, feeling bitter. "Don't forget that Dad's a part of the equation here, too. That stubborn old piece of shit just never really liked me. It's okay, I accept that. You should too."

"It doesn't sound like you accept it." Chase's voice went cold, a sure sign that he was at his wit's end. *"You can keep trying to push me away, but I don't give up so easily. Even when you're an arrogant ass, you're still my brother."*

"Gee, thanks."

"Anytime."

The line went dead as Chase hung up. Brody held the phone to his ear for another long moment. Eventually he set it aside, shutting his eyes tight against the guilt.

His brother had a way of making him feel selfish when he was pretty sure avoiding the family was in everyone's best interests. There was no reconciling with his father, so why bother trying?

No longer feeling hungry, he packaged up the chow mein and tossed it and the rest of the boxes into the fridge. He swiped his gym bag off the floor of his closet-sized bedroom and slung it over his shoulder, eager to sweat out his frustrations. A good session kicking the shit out of a boxing bag would do the trick.

He grabbed his keys and left the apartment, locking it behind him. As he trotted down the stairs, he passed his elderly neighbor who was headed up. She scowled at him, muttering something in Spanish under her breath. Like many of the residents in the complex, she knew who he was and what he'd done. There was no escaping it.

"Hello to you too, you old bag." He clenched his teeth around the words with a fake grin as he passed.

He ignored whatever else she grumbled and headed for his car, shaking off what remained of his guilt.

Chapter *three*

S HE DROVE down the 101 and watched the city come alive with light. It was impossible not to admire the beauty of it—all the glittering buildings and billboards and headlights. It was somewhat ethereal, maybe even magical. But most of all, it was a world away from the quiet mountain forest she called home.

Sadie wondered what it looked like from the air, where she'd be a spectator rather than a participant. After only a few minutes the city was already closing in on her, giving her the impression of being caught in the middle of a wild stampede. If she didn't pay attention, she'd get trampled underfoot and never make it out alive.

A hot red Camaro shot out from behind, exploding past her going nearly 90 MPH. Sadie sucked in a quick, startled breath, her hands squeezing the steering wheel so tight she thought she might break it. More cars darted in and out around her, making her wonder why everyone was in such a hurry. Then again, this was Los Angeles. The entire *city* was in a hurry.

She had no idea why anyone in their right mind would want to live in this chaos. Her blood pressure was already through the roof. She'd been cut off, honked at, almost clipped, and on one memorable occasion nearly driven off the road by a teenager texting on her cell phone. It was amazing anyone survived.

Once her heart settled, she checked her GPS to confirm the exit she needed to take. Hollywood and Highland, which would take her right past the Hollywood Bowl and into the heart of Hollywood.

She rolled her shoulders, her body aching from the tension of a long drive. Eight hours on the road wasn't easy. She'd only stopped one time to grab a burger and use a questionably clean restroom at a fast food restaurant, which meant she was starving and desperately needed to stretch her legs.

Her eyes caught the sign for her exit, and she quickly merged into the far right lane and followed a few other cars smoothly up a sloping hill flanked by trees and then back down again, curving into Hollywood. She hit the usual bumper-to-bumper traffic, and tried to comfort herself that at least she was off the perilous freeway.

All around her, the streets were a flurry of lights and sounds and people. After a moment's hesitation, she dared to roll her window down a crack just to get the full experience. She could hear the blast of techno music from a nearby Honda Civic, and caught a whiff of someone's bad exhaust and cigarette smoke. Her nose wrinkled as she rolled the window up again.

After nearly twenty minutes of sitting through traffic, she finally turned onto Hollywood Boulevard and made her way toward the Hollywood Hills.

When she made a right onto Laurel Canyon, her heart began to race again, this time with excitement. Soon she'd be able to settle in and relax, enjoy some wine with Tess, and catch up. Plus, she was in desperate need of a long, hot shower and nothing sounded better than a pizza with everything on it. Her mouth watered at the thought.

She cruised up her father's street and arrived at the very top in a cul de sac, spotting his ranch-style home with its tropical landscaping and Spanish tile roof. In the driveway was Tess's sparkling silver BMW Coupé.

Sadie pulled her car in beside Tess's. Her friend burst out the front door, a wine bottle in each hand and a bright grin on her face.

"Welcome to L.A.!" Tess greeted. Her straight chocolate-brown hair bounced just above shoulders covered by a slim and stylish black dress.

Sadie opened her car door, taking a second to admire her oldest friend. Tess had the tall, well-built body of a super model, with a brain sharply honed from her years of climbing the ranks at the top real estate development firm in Los Angeles. She was successful, single, and ferociously independent—a true modern woman. Sadie couldn't help the rush of envy she felt at seeing her.

"Did you miss me?" Sadie vaulted into her friend's arms for a swaying hug.

"Hell yeah, I did," Tess replied, pulling away. Her tawny eyes inspected Sadie from head to toe. "Honey, you look like you need a bottle of wine and a straw, STAT."

"Yes, yes I do." Sadie accepted one of the bottles, not bothering to read the label. Instead, her eyes remained fixed on Tess as she took a steadying breath. "God, I'm back."

"You're back." Tess patted her on the shoulder, a sympathetic look crossing her face. "I'm sorry to hear about Valerie. Though this feels a lot like karma coming back to bite her."

Sadie shrugged. "Let's not talk about it now. I want a shower, wine, and pizza."

"Wonderful. Calories don't count when you're on vacation, so eat up," Tess reminded her, sliding an arm around her shoulders to lead her inside. "Then again, you're such a twig. Maybe you could use a pizza or two. What're they feeding you up there in the boondocks, anyway? Berries and nuts?"

Sadie snorted and dug an elbow into her friend's ribs. "We occasionally eat a squirrel or two," she joked.

"Ew. You better just be messing with me." Tess paused before the open front door, motioning for Sadie to enter first. "Go on. Don't be scared."

Sadie laughed, giddy with excitement. The last time she'd been to the house was back when her father lived there, which was right after the divorce. For some reason he'd kept it all these years, even though she knew he'd never move back to L.A.

She let Tess take the bottle of wine from her hands and took the first few steps into the house. The living room was high-ceilinged and open, spanning out into a dining area and a stunning kitchen complete with amber granite and white cabinets. A stone fireplace roared to life to her right, an enormous flat screen television above it set to a music station. Aretha Franklin's soulful voice crooned out about feeling like a natural woman. Surrounding the fireplace was an expansive beige leather sofa with neutral-toned throw pillows that Sadie itched to spread out on.

Beyond the dining area straight ahead were glass patio doors that led to the backyard. Even from the front door, Sadie caught a glimpse of the view.

"Oh, wow," she murmured, her feet carrying her forward. She stopped at the glass, her fingertips rising in an attempt to touch the lights that were so far beyond her reach. How could she have forgotten about that *view?*

The skyline of towering buildings and the surrounding city glittered in the night. They cast a glow that blew up into the heavens, extinguishing any chance she had of seeing the stars. At that moment, she didn't care. She'd spent the last eleven years admiring the stars. Now she wanted nothing more than to enjoy man's rebellious attempt at creating his own starlight.

She could see the freeways curving in and out of the city, a million cars seemingly a million miles away. Here was that feeling she'd wondered about before, only now she *was* a spectator, enjoying the city at its very best. From a safe, comfortable distance.

The popping of a cork startled her. She turned to see Tess pouring two glasses of burgundy wine.

"Have a glass of wine first before that shower. You deserve to relax." Tess brought over the glasses and motioned for Sadie to open the patio door. She did, and the two stepped out into the night.

"Great view, huh?" Sadie asked, taking a seat on one of the cushioned outdoor chairs. She accepted the wine glass and took a sip.

Tess nodded, sitting beside her in a matching chair. "As my boss would say, it's a one-in-a-million-view worth all the millions in the world."

Sadie smiled. "I guess the city's not *all* bad."

"You'll be back to hating it in the morning."

"Yeah, you're right." Sadie sighed, settling into the chair. "It really is pretty from up here, though."

"You know me, I love this town," Tess said with a wink before sampling the wine. "It's home."

"I wish I felt that way," Sadie admitted, her eyes fixated on the city lights.

Tess reached for her hand, urging Sadie to look at her. "I know you don't like to talk about it, but I'm sure just being here brings it all back up again. You survived, Sadie. You got lucky or saved or whatever you want to call it, and then you survived every day since. Not many people would've been strong enough to do that."

"I ran," Sadie replied, irritated with herself. "At the time I had no choice, but I could've come back. I was—am—just too afraid."

"Well, maybe this is one of those 'everything happens for a reason' things," Tess suggested. "You kept your distance for a long time, but then Valerie gets sick and you make up your mind to come back. And maybe while you're here, you'll discover some reasons to stay for good this time."

"I don't know about that." Sadie laughed, nervous at the thought. She took her hand back and drank more wine.

"Hey, you never know," Tess mused. "Maybe you'll wake up tomorrow and feel brave enough to try out the stage."

Sadie coughed and shot her friend a horrified look. "No way. Absolutely not."

Tess chuckled, her shoulders lifting in a shrug. "Just a thought. You know, you really are good. People love you. Well, they love Piper Gray."

"What if someone recognizes me?" Sadie asked, mortified by the thought. "My cover'll be blown. I'll have to shut down my page, get rid of all my videos. I'll never be able to sing again."

Tess looked at her for a long moment. When she spoke, there was curiosity in her voice. "Why do you think you can't sing as Sadie McRae? Why can you only sing as Piper?"

"Because then my parents will find out, and the press will be crawling all over my grandparents' house, demanding interviews and pictures of me. My life will be over. I don't want the spotlight. It scares me more than anything else in the entire world."

Tess nodded. "I get that. But I really don't see the harm in doing a couple shows as Piper Gray. No one's going to think twice about you being anyone other than who you say you are. It'll be fun for you, and it's a risk I think you're ready to take."

Sadie's lips parted in a silent retort, though she couldn't find the words. She turned away and sipped her wine instead, draining the glass. She shook her head. "I don't know."

"You're thinking about it though, aren't you?" Tess pushed, eager now. "C'mon, I know the guy that manages The L.A. Rock Lounge. It's just down the street and it's not that big of a place, so it'll be a low key show. I bet we'd sell out the second we made the announcement. People have been *begging* for a Piper Gray live show."

"I know." Sadie bit her lip, her heart galloping at the thought. "I'm scared, Tess. What if I mess up? What if they hate it?"

"You won't and they already love you, so don't worry about it. You have talent, girl. It's in your freaking genes." Tess rose to her feet and slipped Sadie's empty wine glass from her hand. "Now go take that shower while I order pizza and pour us more wine."

"Yes, ma'am." Sadie teetered to her feet, buzzed from the wine and giddy at the thought of performing. She carried the nerves with her into the shower, surprised she couldn't wipe the silly grin off her face.

SHE DRIFTED over the lake in her grandfather's canoe. Her arm stretched out over the side, her fingertips desperate for a taste of the calm, cool water. It should have been so close, and yet it seemed to fall away, almost like a mirage.

Sadie kept her balance with her other arm, her weight causing the side of the boat to drop deeply into the water as she reached. Tendrils of her honeyed hair spilled over her shoulders, caressing the skin of her arms.

Almost there. Almost…

Beneath the waters she could see nothing but a haze of murky blue. It only frustrated her more. Had she floated too far from her cove? Where was she?

The sound of pealing laughter ripped through the silence. Sadie pulled her arm back and turned, finding herself in her mother's kitchen with its white cabinets and marble counters. It was like being dropped into the middle of a circus. The contrast of it dazed her, until she realized she was no longer sitting in the canoe at all. She was standing in that kitchen, a naïve, barefoot teenager. Looming over her were the monsters with hunger glazing their dark eyes.

Valerie draped over Lee Walker's right shoulder, her fingertips tracing the collar of his black leather jacket. Other nameless, faceless horrors hovered behind them, mere shadows in the chaos. Their presence sent a quivering hum of dark energy over her skin.

Though her lips were moving, Valerie's words were nothing but dull vibrations. She tipped her head back for a laugh, releasing an odd, echoing sound. Lee Walker smiled, his teeth eerily sharp and white as snow.

Sadie realized she held a glass of milk in her hand. She stared at it dully, trying to remember if it had worked. Had it scared him away last time?

She wanted to throw it but found her arm immobile. Her entire body was frozen in place, making her a mere witness to the circus before her. Just like before, she had nowhere to run. And when Lee lunged forward with bloodlust in his eyes, all she could do was cower and scream.

Sadie exhaled sharply, forcing her eyes open. Her mind spun from the dream, lost and dazed. It took a moment before she realized she was safe. Lee Walker wasn't there.

She was no longer fifteen, and Lee was no longer alive. None of it had been real.

Rubbing her face, she choked back a sob that rose in her throat. It'd been years since she'd had a nightmare so vivid, so extreme. Years since she'd let his face rule her imagination.

She forced herself to stare at the ceiling of the guest bedroom in an attempt to clear her mind. The room was dark except for the soft glow of moonlight that filtered in from outside. For a few moments, she basked in the comforting calm of silence.

Once her heart settled, she sat up and wandered into the kitchen for a glass of water. It was just after two in the morning. As she poured water from the faucet into a glass, she released a burdened sigh.

She couldn't deny she blamed her mother for what happened. She probably always would. And Lee Walker was still the monster hiding under her bed, even after all these years.

No matter how much time passed, the pain didn't fade. It never got easier to bear. Instead, it hung around her shoulders like a hundred pound weight, dragging her to the ground. Keeping her rooted within the confines of her own nightmare.

Words and sentences suddenly formed like rapid fire in her mind. Try as she did to refuse them, she couldn't. With her breath held in her throat, she grabbed her notepad from her purse and jotted down the lyrics in her heart.

When she had them on paper, she exhaled in relief. She abandoned the water and, taking the pad with her, grabbed her guitar and went outside.

The cool night air welcomed her, as did the sparkling lights of the city. She admired them, oddly calmed by their presence. In the distance, she could hear the soft chirping of crickets and the faint hum of tires on asphalt. One sound was as familiar as the feel of her own skin, while the other more foreign than she cared to admit.

She settled into a chaise lounge with her feet up and the guitar in her lap. As she began to play, her eyes drifted upward to drink in the endless expanse of sky.

She let the song begin organically, running off the emotions that flowed through her veins. As her fingers strummed, the words tumbled from her lips in an effortless harmony.

"It won't go, I can't make it. These shackles, they bind for good. This monster isn't leaving, I can't outrun it. Why did I think I ever could?"

Her heart ached with a bittersweet longing, a cherished misery. This was her burden to bear, her albatross, the one thing she carried with her everywhere she went. Long ago she'd accepted that she would never be rid of it.

"Who says the pain heals? That the memories fade? Not ours, not yours, not mine. Instead we're stuck in these flames, until there's nothing left but ash…"

With a sad smile, she jotted down the additional lines and their corresponding notes. Encouraged by the healing power of music, she continued to shape and perfect her song as night gave way into morning.

Chapter *four*

S ADIE JOLTED awake at the sound of a lawnmower starting. She glanced around the backyard in a daze, wondering where she was. When she spotted the gardener pushing a lawnmower over the grass, she jumped.

They made eye contact and he nodded politely, tipping his hat in apology for waking her. She smiled sheepishly, knowing she was bright red with embarrassment. Grabbing her guitar and notepad, she retreated back into the house and locked the door, feeling stupid.

The need for caffeine distracted her from the awkwardness she felt. She tore open the box of basic kitchen supplies she'd packed and dug out the coffee and her favorite mug. Within minutes, she was seated on the sofa in the living room, enjoying a hot cup of relief.

She flipped on the television and watched some *I Love Lucy* re-runs to distract herself. Already the nerves were starting to swim in her belly, bringing on waves of nausea.

Today she was going to visit her mother. She didn't know what they'd talk about or what they'd do, but it was happening whether she felt up to it or not. And God, did she feel terrified. Terrified of what shape Valerie might be in, both physically and mentally. How would she cope with her mother's notorious mood swings that had likely gotten worse since the diagnosis? How was she going to comfort and soothe someone she barely even knew?

She breathed a heavy sigh, trying to calm herself. It would be okay. It had to be.

Her cell phone rang on the coffee table. Seeing Tommy's name on the caller-ID chased away most of her nerves.

"Hey stranger."

"*I hear my Sadie-bug is in L.A.,*" Tommy replied, sounding cheerful as always.

"I drove in last night." Sadie downed the last of her coffee and set it aside, curling her legs beneath her. "Speaking of, people out here suck at driving."

He laughed. "*It's a competitive sport, kid. You'll get used to it.*"

"I don't think I'll ever get used to L.A. Period."

"*You won't be there long enough to worry about that.*" Tommy's voice softened. "*You been by to see Val yet?*"

"No. I'm going over there today."

"*Good luck and give her my best. I know she'll be happy to see you.*"

"I hope so. I'd hate to have come all this way for nothing."

"*You didn't have to do this, we all know that. Val knows it, too.*"

She snorted. "Please. I'm sure she's loving all the extra attention. Even if it *is* over something so scary."

"*That's our Val. Though when it comes to you she's never expected much. She knows how you feel about her. You never even had to say it.*"

"Well then she must be really surprised that I offered to come visit," Sadie retorted. "If she knows the hell she caused me, it'd be nice of her to apologize for it."

"*Apologies have never been her thing. Don't take it personally.*" Tommy chuckled. "*I'm actually surprised how well-rounded you are, being the offspring of the two biggest assholes I know. I mean that in an affectionate way, of course.*"

"Thank my grandparents. They saved me from becoming someone I don't even think *I'd* recognize." Sadie's heart felt heavy as she said the words, knowing just how true it was. "Getting away from this place was the best thing that ever happened to me."

"It had to happen, kid. We all thought so. When I remember that night and how tightly you held onto me when I carried you out of that room…"

"If someone hadn't shot him, you would've found me with more damage than just bruises," Sadie said, darkness washing over her. "I wish I could remember. I wish I'd seen who it was. I owe them my life."

"It doesn't matter now, anyway. Dwelling on it won't solve the mystery, it'll only frustrate you."

"True." She sighed, brushing her fingers through her hair. "Well, I should probably take a shower and head on over to see her."

"Make sure to say hi for me. And if she's in a mood, don't let her bring you down. You stay positive, kid. That's what you're good at."

"Thanks, Tommy."

She hung up the phone and pressed it to her lips, feeling more anxious than before. Shaking it off, she stood up and wandered into the guest bathroom to shower.

THE NAVY blue skirt draped over her legs, nearly brushing the floor. She'd paired it with a white and blue striped blouse and delicate gold jewelry that hung around her neck and on her wrists. Taking in her own image in the bathroom mirror brought on a wave of nostalgia she couldn't fight.

God, she did look like her mother. The same long, golden waves of hair. The soft, feminine bone structure and slender nose. The only difference was the eyes. Valerie had the rich, bronzed eyes of a gypsy, while Sadie's resembled the blue-green waves of the ocean.

No wonder her father rejected her. She really was the spitting image of the woman he despised above all else. Knowing it filled her with a sadness she thought she'd gotten over years ago.

Pushing it to the back of her mind, she left the room and grabbed her purse from the kitchen counter. Keys in hand, she made her way out to the car and slipped on her favorite pair of round, silver rimmed sunglasses.

The five minute drive to her mother's house went much too quickly. Before she could prepare herself, she was pulling into the private driveway overgrown with fuchsia bougainvillea flowers and rolling down her window to tap the buzzer.

As the gates split open to invite her inside, she found herself holding her breath. She struggled to release it as she drove in and parked behind her mother's prized electric blue '69 Corvette.

She shut off the car and sat in silence, trying to steady her heart. Nerves tickled over the skin of her arms and danced in her belly. She gazed out the windshield and looked up at the grand, two-story Victorian mansion she'd once called home.

It looked just as it had when she'd been a child. White siding broken up by countless tall windows. Steeply sloped roof with Medieval-castle-inspired details. The landscaping was carefully maintained, but gave the impression of being untamed with its abundance of colorful wildflowers. Boston ivy climbed up the walls of the home and bougainvillea bloomed around the front door. Hanging from the trees were white Chinese lanterns, swaying in the breeze.

Sadie swung open the car door, purse in hand. As she shut it behind her, she lifted her chin in an attempt to bolster her confidence. She walked up to the front door, surprised by her own smile as she looked upon her mother's various fairy statues, each holding colorful glass orbs that shimmered in the sunlight. Valerie had always cherished fantasy over reality.

When she pushed the door bell, the first thing she heard was the yapping of a tiny dog. Its barking grew louder, then was accompanied by the sound of little claws scratching against the wooden door.

The door opened to reveal a harried looking maid, who scooped the excited white Pomeranian into her arms. "Miss Sadie. Come in, please."

Sadie smiled and reached out to pet the dog, only to jolt back as it nipped at her.

The maid chuckled. "Coco's not so friendly to strangers. My name is Carla."

"Nice to meet you." Sadie waited for Carla to set the dog down before extending her hand. The Pomeranian scampered off down the hall and out of sight.

Carla accepted the handshake and paused, her dark eyes drinking their fill of Sadie as she smiled. "Ms. Ryan is taking a bath. Why don't you wait in the music room while I let her know you are here?"

"Okay." Sadie followed her past the high-ceilinged parlor and the sweeping staircase into a large, airy room to the left. The far wall was covered by windows, exposed to let in the brightness of daylight. Beyond, she could see the expanse of her mother's prized garden, flowers in full bloom. A kidney-shaped swimming pool sparkled in the sun, giving way to a view of the surrounding Hollywood Hills.

"Make yourself at home," Carla said before leaving her alone.

Sadie's eyes fell from the view outside to the white and gold grand piano in the center of the room, flanked by French revival sofas and chairs cloaked in soft pink fabric. They were for the adoring audiences that Valerie craved like a bird needs the open air. That, at least, hadn't changed.

She stepped farther into the room, her feet trailing over the cherry-wood floor. Before she realized what she was doing, she was seated at the piano, her fingers hovering over the keys.

Her eyes closed as her flesh met the ivory, absorbing with it all the emotions that had been played out over those keys. All the memories, dark and light, morbid and fantastical, that lay embedded within. She imagined her mother slaving away at those same keys for hours on end, pouring her wild emotions into song.

Inspired, she launched into one of her own creations. One of Piper Gray's songs. She lost herself in lyrics that spoke of losing childhood innocence, the softness of her voice poignant with emotion and an old, deeply rooted heartache.

Moments later she heard a sound and froze, her eyes darting to the entrance of the room. Her mother stood there, still as a statue, her face unreadable.

Sadie let her hands fall from the keys, embarrassed. As she tried to find something to say, her mother saved her the trouble.

"I thought I was watching myself for a moment, only thirty years younger." One of Valerie's brows slid up as she walked into the room. The sweeping crimson skirt she wore fluttered around her legs, accompanied by a lacy white blouse that tied in the front with ribbons. Her long mane of blonde hair spilled over her shoulders and down her back, the once vibrant color dulled by age.

Sadie blinked, then rose to her feet awkwardly. "I'm sorry. I should've asked first."

"No need. I would've been shocked if you hadn't been drawn to my piano." Valerie came to a stop before her daughter, holding her gaze. A smile teased her carefully painted lips. "It's where the magic happens, after all."

Sadie nodded for lack of something better to do. Her hands twisted together as she debated whether or not to hug her mother.

Valerie saved her the trouble yet again. "Come here. You look like a bunny caught in headlights. I'm not going to bite."

Sadie let her mother hug her, keeping it safely distant. When she pulled away, she tried to smile. "How are you?"

"Right as rain, like always," Valerie replied, her goddess voice light and carefree. She patted Sadie's cheek. "Why don't we have tea in the garden? I'll have Carla make up this fabulous Rooibos tea I picked up the other day. It tastes like oranges and vanilla, you'll love it."

Within minutes they were settled into comfortable armchairs beneath a flowering magnolia tree. They faced the pool and the view of the mountains, sipping iced tea from tall, slender glasses. A plate of strawberries and grapes sat on a little table between them. Coco lazed in Valerie's lap, licking the condensation from her glass.

"So was that song you were playing something you wrote yourself?" Valerie inquired, jostling the ice in her glass with her straw.

Sadie blushed. "Yeah. Just for fun."

"It was lovely," Valerie complimented. "And very sad."

"Life is lovely and sad."

"Very true. Have you played it for your father?"

Tension bunched in Sadie's shoulders, a defensive reaction. "No."

"Ah." Valerie sounded pleased. She sipped her tea and cast her eyes upon the view. "Isn't it beautiful here? I don't know why I ever go back inside the house. I should just bring my bed right here beneath this tree and never leave."

"There's a spot back home that overlooks the lake…" Sadie began, only to feel awkward at the thought of Lake Tahoe. Her mother had always held a distaste for any place north of Santa Barbara. "Anyway, it's beautiful."

"Not as beautiful as this, though," Valerie preened, smiling at her. "You can't beat L.A., darling."

Sadie fought back the urge to roll her eyes and said nothing.

"Georgina just bought this amazing beach house down in Dana Point and hosted the most fabulous party last weekend. If you'd been here you could have come." Valerie nibbled on a strawberry, then fed the rest of it to her dog. "I know everyone would love to see you again."

"It's been awhile," Sadie replied, thinking of Georgina. The woman had never looked at her the same after what happened with Walker. "I talked to Tommy this morning. He says hi."

A wicked grin lit up Valerie's face. "I'm sure that's not all he said."

"No, it wasn't."

"He probably told you how surprised I was when you called to let me know you were coming to visit. I couldn't help but call him right after and find out if this was some elaborate trick Ben was setting up."

Sadie frowned, shaking her head. "Why would my dad do something like that? I just wanted to come see you."

"And that's what Tommy said. But I had my suspicions at first." Valerie smiled knowingly as they met eyes. "If you'd lived under his thumb as long as I did, you'd understand."

Irritated, Sadie turned away and downed the last of her tea. They sat in silence for a few moments, giving Sadie time to bury her anger.

"So how are you feeling, really?" she asked again, glancing at her mother. Despite her worst fears, her mother looked as healthy as always. There was very little evidence of the deadly cancer that had taken home in her body. "What have the doctors said about your—"

"I don't know what you're talking about, Sadie," Valerie replied, her fingers tensing over her dog's fur. "I'm doing just fine."

"You can't seriously sit here and pretend like nothing's happening," Sadie retorted, confused. "I want to help you, but I won't be able to if you won't admit you're sick."

"You sound just like your father," Valerie said, dark amusement in her tone. "Always so *pragmatic*."

Sadie frowned. "I'm not him. And I'm not you, either."

"No. If you were like me this would be so much easier. I know perfectly well what's wrong with me. I just choose not to dwell on it."

Emotion caught in Sadie's throat and froze there, making it difficult to breathe. Guilt spread over her body and sank its teeth in. "Fair enough," she murmured, unable to say more.

Her mother smiled again. "Forget it. Why don't we go shopping? I think some new shoes will cheer me up."

Before Sadie could agree, Valerie had risen to her feet. She swept off for the house, leaving no room for discussion.

"SO, WHEN are we going to record your first album?"

Sadie blinked in surprise, glancing up from her mixed greens salad. "Excuse me?"

They sat together in a corner booth at a high-end Italian bistro nestled in the heart of Rodeo Drive. Sadie glanced around nervously, as if someone might overhear. The last thing she needed was a rumor to get out that she might be recording an album with her mother.

Valerie smiled indulgently. "Just think of the publicity we would get. We could even do a duet together. Something upbeat and fun. Oh, it'd be fabulous."

Sadie winced at the thought. "Um, I don't really want to…"

"Sure you do. You're just nervous. That's fine, I understand," Valerie pushed, her eyes bright with excitement. She reached across the table for Sadie's hand, grasping it in her own. "I always wondered if you'd be able to sing. I'm just glad I got to you before Ben did. God knows he'd be dying to produce an album for you."

Sadie doubted very much that her father would lift a finger to produce anything for her, much less an album. "This isn't a competition."

Valerie rolled her eyes and laughed, releasing Sadie's hand. "With Ben and I, everything is a competition."

Sadie digested the statement, hating how true it was. "I just write music for fun. I'm not that serious about it."

"Why not?"

I don't want to turn out like you. Sadie sighed. "I don't know."

"Are you scared? I'll make sure you're a success, darling. You don't need to worry about failing." Valerie took a sip of sparkling water, seemingly oblivious to Sadie's discomfort. "With your name and bloodline, everyone will be clamoring for a taste of you. I can just see the headlines now...*Daughter of Rock Goddess Charms Sold Out Crowds.* We'll make history!"

Sadie felt a little sick at the thought. "I don't think—"

"Oh, have some spine for once, Sadie," Valerie snapped, getting impatient. "Fate brought you back to L.A. so we can make music together. Don't you see that?"

"No, I don't." Sadie shook her head. Her hands were trembling as she lifted her fork to push arugula leaves drenched in balsamic dressing around her plate. "I'm not doing this with you."

Valerie huffed. "I don't understand why not."

"I don't want to." Sadie lifted her eyes to meet her mother's, unprepared for the hurt she saw in them. Anger she'd expected, but pain?

Valerie sniffed. "Okay. I can take a hint. You still hate me, I get it. I guess I can see why you feel that way, though I think it's completely unfair of you."

Sadie tensed and focused back on her salad, bitterness souring the taste of her tongue. Words she wanted so badly to say just couldn't seem to make it out of her mouth. *If I hate you so much, then why am I here?*

She waited for her mother to say something more, to launch into one of her emotional tirades. When it didn't come, Sadie tore her gaze away from her food. Her mother's face had a pale sheen to it, alarming her.

"Are you okay?" Sadie asked.

Valerie rubbed her temple, her eyes closing. She winced as if she were in pain, her other hand pressed against her abdomen. "I think I...oh, I'll be right back."

She fled from the table, bee-lining for the restroom. Sadie sat, helpless, wondering if she should go help her. After a few tormented minutes of deliberation, she rose to her feet and started after her mother.

Valerie appeared from the restroom, still pale but with a shaky smile on her face. She waved her hand when she saw Sadie approaching.

"I'm perfectly all right." Valerie laughed, though her hands were visibly shaking. She looked like she was on the verge of collapsing.

"I'll drive you home," Sadie said, tossing some cash onto the table and retrieving her purse. She looped her arm around her mother and led her from the restaurant, noticing a few people staring curiously as they passed.

Valerie held her head high and smiled, ever the performer. If she felt like dying, she certainly didn't show it. Sadie found herself feeling grateful for that, at least. Making a scene was something they both abhorred.

By the time they got back to Valerie's home, Sadie felt sicker than her mother looked. Concern filled her as she helped her mother out of the car and into the house.

Valerie swatted her hand away with a light laugh. "I'm fine, darling. No need to fuss."

"Are you sure?" Sadie followed her inside, shutting the door behind her.

Valerie smiled. "Of course. Though I do want a nap and maybe another bath. Carla can make you something to eat."

"No, that's okay." Sadie crossed her arms, feeling hollow. Scared. Never in her life had she felt the helplessness of a child seeing their parent broken and weak. That feeling of suddenly having to be the protector instead of the protected. Nothing could have prepared her for it.

"I'll see you soon, then." Valerie started up the stairs, her hand tight on the railing to keep her balance. She hid her concentration under another vibrant smile. "You go practice that song of yours. Surely your father has a piano in that house."

Sadie nodded, unable to speak. She watched her mother disappear upstairs, then released an unsteady breath. She heard Carla approaching from down the hall and quickly turned to leave. The last thing she wanted was to make small talk or excuses on why she needed to go.

When she made it back to her father's home, she retreated to the backyard. She took a seat in one of the armchairs, pulled her knees up to her chin, and tried desperately to forget that look of weakness on her mother's face.

Chapter *five*

BRODY GRINNED, delighted at his good fortune. Well, it was half luck and half damn good investigative journalism, but he'd take it. Why did it matter *how* he'd gotten the images? The point was, he was about to be a hell of a lot richer.

The payday from the photos of vixen actress Kyla Gold locking lips with her director Hugh Lovett would stave off the bill collectors for a good three or four months. He couldn't ask for better than that, even if he did have to pay Kyla's supposed best friend thirty-percent for the tip on where he could find the cheating lovers stealing a kiss. Lovett's wife wasn't going to enjoy seeing the pictures, but what did that matter? He was doing her a favor, really. The bastard had it coming and if she was smart, she'd divorce his ass and take half his money.

Brody had hidden out of sight in the bamboo that bordered a little public park off a low key sushi restaurant the two preferred to rendezvous at. He'd waited nearly two hours for them to show up, which put a crick in his back but he'd beat it out at the gym another day. Right now, all he wanted was a cold beer and to get the photographs uploaded onto his computer so he could bask in all the adulterous glory.

He cruised through the streets of Venice, making his way home. The sun was setting, basking the whole world in a vivid orange glow. With the windows down, he felt like he was soaring through the sky and coasting on the wind.

On the radio, Steven Tyler wailed about being back in the saddle again. Brody sang along, tapping his hands on the steering wheel to the beat. When he turned onto his street, he spotted his brother's shiny black Mercedes. His mood immediately soured as if a switch had been flipped.

"Well, shit," he grunted, pulling into a spot across the palm-tree-lined street. He saw Chase exit his car and walk toward him, waving with a smile.

Brody sighed and rested his head against the steering wheel, proceeding to beat his forehead against it. He could hear Chase approach, but didn't stop his defiant act of self abuse.

"Hey," Chase greeted. "Everything okay?"

"It was," Brody lifted his head and eyed his brother with a sarcastic grin. "What're you doing here?"

"I was in the area—"

"Liar. You never leave the Beverly Hills bubble except to come bug me."

Chase frowned. "Bubble?"

"Never mind." Brody grabbed his camera and pushed out of the car. He started for his apartment complex, his brother trailing behind him.

"So did you decide if you're coming to Dad's birthday party?"

Brody grumbled something rude under his breath as he took the stairs two at a time.

Chase followed him, his smile faltering. "What's that?"

"Sure. Yeah. Unless something better comes up." Brody stalked to his front door and hastily unlocked it. When he stepped inside, he left the door wide open. Chase paused before entering, eyeing the clutter inside curiously.

"That's great. I'm glad."

Brody set his camera down on the coffee table, then went to the fridge for a beer. He grabbed two Coronas, lifting one up. "Beer?"

Chase shook his head, looking sheepish. "No, thanks."

"Suit yourself." Brody closed the fridge door with his hip and popped off the top on the Corona. As he took a long swig of beer, he made his way to the couch and settled in.

"So…what are you working on?" Chase asked, venturing inside and closing the door. Brody caught him staring around the room again with his hands tucked in his pockets.

"Come here. I'll show you." Brody tapped into his computer, uploading the photographs he'd taken of the actress and her director. He clicked open the best one, admiring it as it filled the screen. "Beautiful, isn't it?"

Chase frowned as he peered down at the image. "Is that—"

"Kyla Gold. Yep." Brody sat back against the cushions, sipping his beer. A proud smile lit his face. "You know how much these photos are worth?"

"I can only imagine…" Chase murmured, straightening as he turned to his brother. "I don't know if you know this, but Hugh Lovett is a client of ours."

"No shit?" Brody laughed, honestly surprised. He looked back at the image, shaking his head. "What a delightful coincidence."

"I can't in good conscience leave here without convincing you *not* to release that photo." Chase crossed his arms, standing firm as they met eyes again.

"Consider your duty fulfilled, then. Nothing you say will change my mind," Brody told him, offering up a cocky grin. He lifted his Corona with a nod. "Maybe I shouldn't come to that party after all."

Chase rubbed the back of his neck. "No, it's important for you to come."

"Why?"

"Because we're family," Chase said simply, as if it was obvious. "Anyway, I gotta run. I'll see you next weekend."

"You gonna tell Dad I took those pictures?" Brody asked, not sure why it mattered to him that his father know. Maybe it was the rebel in him wanting to defy the man, just one more time.

Chase shrugged. "I suppose he'll find out eventually."

"Yeah. Maybe I'll brag about it a bit and he'll use it as an excuse to kick me out of the party."

"I'll convince him not to talk about it."

"Like you convinced me not to release the images?" Brody chuckled. "Admit it, your persuasive skills are a little rusty."

Chase cracked a smile. "I still convinced you to go to the party. So there's that."

Brody raised his beer in another toast. "*Touché*."

"Take care of yourself, buddy." Chase looked around the apartment once again. "And get a damn maid with some of that tabloid cash, okay?"

Brody laughed as his brother left, amused despite everything. He downed the last of his Corona, then set out to email those photographs. Maybe a maid wouldn't be a bad idea, he thought as he gazed around at the empty take out boxes and stacks of newspapers. Then again, he didn't have anyone to impress.

DOLLAR SIGNS danced in his mind as he did a solitary toast to success. He'd been right about the pictures. That payout would keep him sitting pretty for a solid three months.

Brody sipped champagne and lounged in a plastic outdoor chair on his tiny balcony, feet propped up on the railing and his eyes on the sunset. Shades of yellow and orange blended with the blue of a cloudless sky, framed by silhouetted palm trees and buildings. As the evening wound down, he absorbed the sounds of people talking and laughing across the street, of the nightly news being played directly below him, and of a dog barking a few streets over. He could smell someone barbecuing and also caught the distinct skunky aroma of pot.

TMZ had wasted no time getting the pictures online. He hadn't checked in an hour or so, but he imagined the internet was exploding with the scandal. Outraged fans would be jumping to Kyla's defense. Soccer moms would be lambasting Lovett for being unfaithful with a woman half his age. Other celebrities would be weighing in on Twitter, both in favor and against. It was very possible he'd initiated one of the sauciest scandals of the year.

Oh, how proud his father must be.

At that very moment the old man was likely getting a dinner-interrupting phone call from Hugh-the-adulterer-Lovett, demanding a solution. There was none, though. The damage was done and Lovett could kiss his reputation goodbye.

Funny how easy it all was. Those who live in the public eye are often ruined by the very press that made them stars. They're only human, after all. They make mistakes—they cheat or get drunk or start bar fights. And all of it can break them if caught in the flash of a camera.

It was a vicious circle he knew all too well. Though his mistake had been more than just a poorly timed adulterous kiss. He'd gotten men killed. And not just men, but warriors. Honorable, well-intentioned patriots.

His heart panged at the memory, souring his mood. He closed his eyes and let his head fall back, losing himself in the past.

It'd been a Tuesday. Not really a day he'd ever thought his life would change. The temperature neared one hundred degrees in the Helmand river valley of Afghanistan. He distinctly remembered wondering how the soldiers could stand wearing so much clothing. He'd taken to wearing a T-shirt, jeans, and a bullet proof vest, and even then sweat cloaked his entire body.

He'd been sent to photograph the realities of life in Afghanistan in the midst of the war against the Taliban. The mortar shells buried in the sides of buildings, the poor state of the civilians, the courageous efforts of the American soldiers.

It wasn't the first time he'd been sent to a hostile location by his then employer. As a photojournalist, he'd been all over the world. But there was something particularly dangerous about this assignment. Not that he'd realized it at the time. He had a tendency to skim over the fine print and throw himself into the fray with no regard for his safety. It was what made him such a successful photographer. He captured images most others wouldn't dare attempt.

But in this case, he should have prepared himself.

The day was spent following a group of Marines patrolling the dusty streets of Sangin. After a few days in the town, he'd started to get loose about the whole idea of danger. So far he hadn't seen much worth taking a picture of. In fact, in all honesty he was getting downright bored.

Perhaps it was boredom that had him hunting for danger. Something, anything, to drum up a little action and make the trip worthwhile. Unfortunately, he was about to get exactly that.

While the Marines stopped briefly in the middle of a busy marketplace, Brody hung around on the sidelines, camera hanging from a strap around his neck. He peered through his aviator shades at everyone who passed by, looking for trouble. When he saw a suspicious looking man with a bulky pato shawl wrapped over his body in the middle of summer, his heart began to race.

First he took a series of photographs of the man, who was walking discreetly in the direction of the platoon and the Humvee they rode in on. Then when he realized the guy might actually mean business—suicide bombers were commonplace in the area—he shouted the word "bomb" to the soldiers and pointed.

Maybe it was careless. Hell, it had been damn careless. But at the time all he'd been able to think about was protecting the guys he'd come to know as friends. When they turned on the man and pointed their rifles at him, the man dropped to his knees, his shawl falling open to reveal nothing but fruit he'd just stolen from the market. Brody then spotted two men surface from the crowd with AK-47s, and realized his mistake.

They fired on the soldiers and chaos exploded in the marketplace. Women and children ran screaming as gunfire rang out into the thick afternoon air. Brody dove behind a nearby cart and cowered, mortified at what he'd done. Anger pulsed through him, bringing on an urge to fight back. Gritting his teeth, he reached for the small pistol he kept in his boot. He would have drawn it if one of the soldiers hadn't grabbed him by the arm and dragged him to safety. By then, both of the Taliban insurgents were dead and the sound of gunshots faded with the dust.

Three soldiers had been hit. Two fatally. Brody remembered numbly approaching the Humvee and seeing the blood. He hadn't even known a body could bleed so much.

He'd been flown back to the States that night. After the witness testimony came out about the incident, it was suggested that he resign from his position.

Then the media storm hit.

It was bad enough to have the mothers of the two slain Marines blaming him, saying that if he hadn't distracted their sons then they would've seen the danger in the crowd. He understood their grief just as much as he respected it. But to have his colleagues, his friends, his family, all look at him in disgust was more than he could bear.

He lost everything. Lawsuits and unemployment meant bankruptcy was his only option. It was an option he knew he wholeheartedly deserved. Hell, he was still alive, wasn't he? While those two soldiers were dead. What did any of what he lost matter when he still breathed and they didn't?

He opened his eyes and forced himself back to the present. He tossed back the last of his champagne, though it tasted bitter on his tongue. He wished for something stronger, something that could chase away the guilt. But he knew from experience that turning to hard liquor never solved anything. All it did was intensify the pain the next day.

It'd been two years since the incident, and still his reputation was in tatters. The only job he'd been able to get was freelance, and the only work that paid well enough was through the tabloids.

His life had changed forever that fateful Tuesday afternoon. Maybe it was meant to be that way. He'd lived too good for too long, recklessly selfish without a care in the world. This was karma, serving up a whopping slice of retribution.

His phone buzzed in his pocket and he considered ignoring it. But when he saw it was his brother, that guilt crept in again.

"What's up?"

"I saw you submitted those photos."

"Yep." Brody toyed with his champagne glass, rubbing smudges off it with his thumb. "I told you I was going to."

"I know. Hey, so when you come to the party next weekend, this topic has to be off-limits."

A wry smile lifted Brody's lips. "You mean the old man isn't proud of me?"

"I hope that money is worth it, Brody. I mean, you pretty much just ended a marriage."

"A marriage that was a sham anyway," Brody argued. "All I did was expose the truth that he was cheating."

"And you made a pretty penny off it, too. Good for you."

"If you just called to give me shit then I'm going to hang up."

Chase sighed. *"I'm sorry, I'm just on edge. Look, why don't you come over for dinner tonight? We can have a couple of beers like old times."*

Brody could hear Chase's wife Abby protesting quietly in the background. Why did that not surprise him? "I'm busy, buddy. Sorry. But I'll catch you at the party next weekend."

"Oh, okay. All right. See you then." He could hear Abby launching into a lecture with Chase right before the phone went dead. He tucked it back into his pocket and sighed.

Why Chase tried so hard to be his friend was a baffling mystery. The man had every reason to disown him just like everyone else already had, and yet he still hung on. It was getting to the point where he was almost a goddamn pest.

Though Brody knew that if Chase ever gave up on him, he'd lose the only real friend he had left.

Chapter *six*

SADIE PILED lunch meat onto a couple of slices of rye bread and sang along to Journey's "Girl Can't Help It" on the radio. She danced as she moved about the kitchen, not caring that Tess was giggling at her from the dining table.

Sadie pointed a butter knife at her friend and grinned. "Shut up and drink your margarita."

"No judgment here." Tess toasted with her drink before taking a sip, licking salt from the rim. "Just don't tempt me to sing back at you. Then we'll both be embarrassed."

"You're not allowed to have it all, Tess," Sadie chided. She sliced the sandwiches then brought them to the table. "You can't be hot, smart, *and* a good singer. That's just not fair."

Tess snorted. "You're right. How cruel of me to imagine the possibility."

Sadie sat down and took a long sip of her own margarita. "Hey, maybe you could be the face of Piper Gray. You could lip sync for me."

"You're just trying to get out of what I told you earlier."

Sadie pouted, picking at her sandwich. "No…it was just a joke. I don't know how I feel about that yet."

"So just say yes and fuck it." Tess laughed, waving off Sadie's concerns. "Life's too short. Take a chance."

Sadie shot her a strained look. "Take a chance and *perform* in front of people under my alias? You know me better than anyone, does that sound like something I'd do? I'm too nervous to buy new shoes because they might give my feet blisters."

"Okay, now that's just sad."

"Shut up."

Tess grinned. "Honey, do you honestly think I'd push you like this if I didn't think you could do it?"

Sadie wrung her hands together. "I don't know."

"You're tougher than you think. And trust me, you need this. You need this almost as bad as I need to get laid."

"What happened to Mr. Hot-Shot Lawyer from New York?"

"Turns out he was married with two kids. Bastard." Tess scowled, tossing back the last of her drink. "Whatever. Point is, The L.A. Rock Lounge has a cancelled show and they need a fill-in for next Saturday. I told Leon I'd get back to him by tomorrow morning if you're willing to do it. He's chomping at the bit to host the first Piper Gray show."

Sadie bit back a smile. "I can't decide if I'm excited or terrified. Or nauseous. Maybe I'm a little of all three."

"So you'll do it?"

"I don't know." Sadie took a few deep breaths to try and settle her heart rate, warring internally. "Should I? Oh God. Don't answer that. Okay. I'll do it."

"Good girl. Now let me give Leon a quick call to lock it in and then we'll figure out your wardrobe. You did bring your wigs, right?"

"As a precaution, yeah," Sadie admitted. She felt dizzy as she watched Tess wander off to seal the deal. Oh God, what had she just agreed to?

Unable to sit still, she shoved aside her uneaten sandwich and went into her bedroom. She'd placed most of her clothing into the cherry-wood dresser, neatly folded and organized by color. The costume elements she'd stored in the bottom drawer. Wigs, stage makeup, fake eyelashes—she had it all just in case she needed a disguise at any point while in L.A. Maybe it was paranoid of her, but she felt better being prepared. And now with the show Tess had booked, she was even more relieved to have packed it all.

When Tess came into the room a few minutes later, Sadie was admiring a jet black, shoulder length wig in the mirror. It had a razor sharp line of bangs and a faint bluish tint to it, giving her the appearance of a gothic doll.

Their eyes met in the mirror and Sadie smiled awkwardly. "What do you think?"

Tess began to slow clap, beaming with pride. "Now *that's* Piper Gray."

"Yeah? I just need to darken my eyebrows and put on the makeup, but I think it's a good disguise. It's the one I liked using the most in the videos, though my full face was never really shown. I may need heavier makeup this time."

"Agreed. I think that wig paired with a shimmering silver dress…" Tess trailed off, walking into the closet to rifle through the clothes Sadie had brought. "Kind of 1920s flapper meets Emo-goddess. We may need to buy you something. Don't worry, I'm on it."

"Okay." Sadie turned back to the mirror and ran her fingertips over the dark strands of the wig, overwhelmed by it all.

A few hours after Tess had left, Sadie called her step-brother. She set up her laptop on her father's upright piano in his music room and phoned Isaac using Skype.

"So you're doing a show, huh?" Isaac asked, looking impressed. His black curls of hair had their usual messy look and his poetic hazel eyes were lit with excitement. "What're you going to sing? Or should I say, what is *Piper Gray* going to sing?"

Sadie shushed him. "Don't let Dad hear you."

"Right. Sorry. I think he's asleep anyway." Isaac lifted his guitar and grinned. "How about 'All These Flames'? That's my favorite."

"It's my favorite, too. Okay, let's try that one." Sadie's eyes fell to the keyboard as she placed her fingers on the keys and began to play. Isaac joined her, softly strumming his guitar.

When she began to sing, he softly mimicked her words for the chorus, giving the song a haunting, lonely echo that so perfectly mirrored the lyrics. It was a song she'd written for her parents, a song that bled all those old wounds dry. Relief rushed through her as she sang the words she'd never been brave enough to say to them in person. To, in her own way, call them out for all the damage they'd done.

"These flames destroyed us. These flames made us. These flames are all that remain. When the ashes fall, will you remember my name?"

As she wrapped up the song, she felt a single tear fall from her eye. She smiled at Isaac as she wiped it away. "I wish you could be here to perform with me. The song is so much better with you playing acoustic like that."

"I wish I could, too. Maybe I'll drop out of school and we could hit the road," he joked, earning an appreciative laugh from her.

"Don't you dare. You're going to be a doctor someday and I might need to you to save my life."

She watched Isaac suddenly turn his head, then spotted her father entering the room. He came up behind her brother, then noticed Sadie's face on the computer screen.

"Oh, I didn't realize you were…what's that called? Skipping?"

"Skyping, Dad." Isaac chuckled, shooting an amused look at Sadie. "Old people."

Ben angled down so his face was in view of the camera. He managed a tight smile. "Hi, Sadie."

"Hey." She felt her face burning and hoped he couldn't tell. "How's Boston?"

"Fine." Ben cleared his throat, as if unsure what to say. "How's, uh, your mother?"

"Fine."

"Good. Well, I'll let you kids get back to your…"

"Skype, Dad. Skype." Isaac shook his head and sighed. "Why don't you go call Tommy on your rotary phone and talk about the good ol' days of eight tracks and big hair?"

"Ha ha, very funny." Ben waved at Sadie before disappearing from the room.

Sadie let out a heavy sigh. "Awkward."

"Yeah…" Isaac ran a hand through his hair. "Anyway, wanna do another song?"

"I think I should get some sleep. I'm heading over to see my mom again tomorrow."

"Fun," Isaac replied sarcastically, though there was humor in his eyes. "Call me next week before the show and we'll practice some more, 'kay?"

"Okay." She blew him an affectionate kiss and smiled. "Night."

After she turned off the computer, she continued to sit at the piano and sulk. It was always so awkward every time she talked to her father. It was like they were both holding back from saying something that so desperately needed to be said, yet they were too scared to say it. Or too stubborn, or proud, or who knows what.

She'd never felt like herself around him, not the way she did with Isaac or Tommy or Tess. With her father she always felt the need to put on a show or pretend to be anything other than a replica of Valerie. Which was why the thought of him discovering her performing under an alias worried her. What would he do if he knew she was following his path into music? Would he be proud of her, or would it bring back all those horrible memories he seemed so hell bent on forgetting? Memories of Valerie, the woman who'd been both a blessing and a plague in his life.

Thinking of her mother had her returning her fingers to the keys. She closed her eyes and imagined herself onstage, under those bright lights and basked in the glow of adoring fans. Excitement filled her at the thought, knowing she was born to perform. For years she'd denied herself the pleasure, but God knows she wanted it. Like Tess said, she *needed* it.

And soon she would have it.

Chapter *seven*

HE'D CHOSEN the black slacks and matching button up shirt out of pure defiance. He could've been compliant and shown up to his father's birthday party in the white-tie apparel his brother suggested, but where was the fun in that?

Brody pulled into the driveway of his parents' several million dollar mansion in Bel Air. He was promptly greeted by the valet, who gave him a suspicious look upon seeing his car.

"You better be careful, buddy. She's worth more than your job," Brody joked, patting the valet on the shoulder with a cocky grin. He covered his eyes with his favorite pair of aviators despite it being nearly eight o'clock at night. Again, why not?

As he sauntered up the cobblestone pathway to the front door, he tucked his hands in his pockets and took a good look around. It had been a year since he'd been invited back to his parents' home. A year since the last blow out fight had caused a fissure no one in the family dare try and repair. Except Chase, of course. He was the only one who ever tried to keep the family in one piece.

He was welcomed through the front door by a formal looking butler and immediately thrust into a crowd of fancy guests. A few people cast looks of judgment in his direction, but for the most part they ignored him. Some even purposefully edged out of the way to avoid him, just in case he tried to strike up a conversation. He supposed he didn't blame them.

A server approached him carrying a tray of champagne and offered a glass, which he gladly accepted. He tossed it back with relish and set it back on the tray before the server could walk away. Grabbing another glass, he continued through the house, enjoying the scene he was causing.

Chase emerged from the kitchen and bee-lined straight for him.

"Hey, you made it." He attempted a smile but it didn't quite reach his eyes.

"Yep." Brody sipped more champagne and glanced around disdainfully. "You know none of these people actually give a shit about Dad's birthday. They're just here out of obligation."

"They're not all business associates or clients," Chase replied, though he looked bitter. "So, Dad's kind of in a bad mood."

"Let me guess, it's because you told him I was coming." Brody tilted his sunglasses down to eye his brother. "You should've listened to me when I said—"

"Brody." A deep, emotionless voice said from behind him.

His entire body stiffened as he turned around to face his father. Beside him stood Brody's waif-like mother, Laurie. "Well, if it isn't the birthday boy."

Max Odell scowled, his pale blue eyes never leaving his oldest son. He stood tall at nearly six foot four, his frame trim and rigid. Neatly combed white hair topped a long, hard-lined face that was always more intimidating than it was inviting. "Chase said you'd be coming."

"I wouldn't miss it," Brody said, turning to his mother. He leaned in to give her a cheek kiss. "Mom."

She smiled serenely, clinging to her husband's arm. Her dark hair curled in soft waves around a tired face, her brown eyes that matched his own hazed with whatever anti-anxiety drugs she was on these days. Brody bit back the pity he felt at seeing her in such a mindless, compliant state.

"Take off those glasses, sweetheart. Let me see you." Laurie reached for his face after he removed the glasses, touching his cheek lightly. "So handsome. Why do I never see you anymore?"

"You know why, Mom," Brody replied. His eyes shot to his father as his mouth curved in a cynical grin. "I'm the prodigal son, minus the repentance."

"Indeed," Max drawled. He lightly tugged on his wife to edge her away from Brody. "Dinner's in an hour. I expect you to keep your mouth shut."

"Oh, you mean you don't want to talk about Hugh Lovett?" Brody blurted out on impulse, earning a pleading look from his brother and a furious one from his father.

Max leaned in close to Brody's face, meeting him eye-to-eye. He spoke in a low, dangerous voice, one that only the two of them could hear. "I promised Chase I wouldn't let that little spectacle of yours ruin the party. But so help me God if I won't nail you to the wall in court the second I get the chance."

"Sounds like you've got quite the grudge, Dad." Brody knocked back his second glass of champagne as his father turned and left, his mother in tow.

Chase shook his head and placed a hand on Brody's shoulder. "This is all my fault."

"No, it's not," Brody countered, looking his brother in the eye. "You're the only person here who gives a flying fuck about this family."

He stalked off in search of something stronger to drink, sincerely considering ducking out of the party. If it hadn't been for his brother, he likely would have. Only a fool sticks around when he's so clearly unwanted.

WITH HER first show just over an hour away, Sadie began to panic.

"What am I doing? Tess, you bitch, what did you talk me into?" She fought to catch her breath, her heart racing a mile a minute. The bright lights above the dressing table in the back room of The L.A. Rock Lounge had sweat beading on her forehead.

"Calm down." Tess chuckled, dabbing powder onto Sadie's face to hide the shine. "You're going to be wonderful."

"I'm going to be sick." Sadie started to put her head between her knees, only to have Tess catch her and force her upright.

"None of that. You'll mess up the hair." Tess adjusted the wig, fixing a few black strands that had sprung loose. "Now, I want you to repeat after me: 'I rock, I'm worth it, and I so deserve this.'"

"I rock, I'm worth—oh God, let's just cancel it. I'm having a panic attack. I'm seeing spots in my vision."

"No, you're not." Tess grabbed her by the chin and looked into her eyes. "Now repeat it."

Sadie took a deep breath, let it out. "I rock, I'm worth it, and I so deserve this."

"Damn right. Okay, it's time to look in the mirror and meet Piper Gray."

She spun Sadie around to face the mirror. Sadie blinked, staring at the perfect stranger looking back at her.

"That's not me."

"Well, duh. It's Piper Gray, silly." Tess brushed the wig a bit more, a big smile on her face. "I don't think I've ever been so proud in all my life."

"How nice for you," Sadie replied weakly. Tess had done some fancy work with her eyes, giving them a smoky, hazy look framed by glorious lashes. Her skin tone was lightened and her lips painted a sultry, shimmering burgundy. When she reached up to touch her new hair, Tess swatted her hand away.

"You mess up the hair and I won't fix it again."

"Yes, ma'am."

"Tess?" The manager and Tess's old friend, Leon, leaned into the tiny dressing room. He had black dreadlocks, skin the color of warm caramel and a million-watt smile. "We have less than an hour till we open the doors. We'd like to do sound and lighting checks once more with Piper if that's okay?"

Sadie gave a frail squeak at the thought of the crowd that would be lining up outside. Tess nodded confidently. "Got it, Leon. We'll be there in a few minutes."

As Leon left, Sadie tried to regulate her breathing as best as she could. Tess helped her out of the chair, admiring her outfit.

"I knew silver would look stunning. You're going to light up the stage like the star you are."

Sadie tugged at the hem of the dress. "It's a little short."

"You have rockin' legs, girl. No need to be shy. Now c'mon. Just like we rehearsed."

"I walk out on cue, sit at the piano, and try not to vomit," Sadie recalled, wishing her heart would slow the hell down.

"Oh, I almost forgot." Tess opened the mini fridge stocked with bottled water and pulled out a bottle of champagne. "Some bubbly for the nerves."

"You're a lifesaver." Sadie grinned as Tess grabbed two plastic cups and popped open the champagne. She poured and then handed a cup to Sadie.

Tess lifted her own cup for a toast. "To Piper Gray's Coming Out Party."

Sadie snorted a laugh and clicked her cup against Tess's before taking a sip. She gulped down about half the cup then set it aside. "Okay. One more sound check. Then more champagne. And then I think I'll have enough courage to do this."

"You're doing it whether you have the courage or not," Tess reminded her. She wrapped an arm over Sadie's shoulders and led her out of the room. "You're going to kill it tonight."

"Kill it," Sadie repeated, feeling a little more confident. She lifted her chin up and tried her best to stay that way. "I rock, I'm worth it, and I so deserve this."

Tess pulled her in for a side hug. "Yes, you do."

WHEN IT came time to sit down for dinner, Brody was a couple of shots of tequila in and feeling much better. He wandered out to the backyard and surveyed the crowd.

Dozens of round, six person tables were grouped on the expansive lawn, topped with royal blue tablecloths and stunning white orchid centerpieces. Strings of lights draped over the trees and across the yard, giving the area a celestial glow.

Chase came up from behind and led him to the head table perched in front of the stage, where a band was set up playing soft music. Brody plopped down into a chair across from his father. Though he was tempted to say something, he bit back the urge and focused instead on nursing the Corona he'd swiped from the kitchen.

Chase settled into the chair beside him, along with his heavily pregnant wife Abby. She sent Brody a polite, albeit strained smile, as she lowered herself into the chair.

"Do you need anything? Water? Juice?" Chase offered his wife.

She patted his hand. "I'm fine."

"You sure? It's no trouble."

"I'm sure." Her hazel eyes went to Brody, quietly measuring. "I'm surprised to see you here."

"Join the club." He nodded at her rounded belly. "You have a name picked out yet?"

"Charlotte." Abby brushed strands of strawberry blonde hair out of her face, unable to hide her smile. "After my grandmother."

"That's nice." Brody grinned at his brother and patted him on the back. "Nothing beats family tradition."

Chase started to say something, only to be interrupted as a trim older man with a smooth pelt of white hair walked onstage and tapped the microphone.

Brody sat back in his seat and sipped his beer as the man rambled on about Max's stellar career as a defense attorney. From his meager beginnings just out of law school, working as a state appointed attorney for the drug addicts down in East L.A., to the creation of his firm and its steady rise to the top. And most notably, when his talented son joined him just a few years earlier, ready to carry the torch for the Odell name.

There was widespread applause at the mention of Chase. Brody's eyebrows rose as he glanced around at the crowd, then back at his brother, who was smiling sheepishly. Chase got to his feet, champagne glass in hand, and went to the stage. He shook hands with the previous speaker, then took the mic.

"Hi, everyone." Chase smiled as he looked out at the crowd. His free hand dove into his waves of chestnut hair out of habit. "I just want to thank you all for coming. I know it means a lot to my dad, who, though he doesn't like to show it, is actually really excited today. Excited to be surrounded by so many great friends, colleagues, family members. Surrounded by the people he loves." His eyes fell to Brody as he continued. "When my brother and I were young, my dad taught us to be competitive. He taught us to never give up, to never quit. We both ended up stubborn as a result of it, but I think that's a good thing. We're too stubborn to give up on life when it has so much to offer. Just like Dad was too stubborn to let the firm fail when we went through hard times. So thanks, Dad, for instilling in us that stubborn streak you used to change the world."

He lifted his glass in a toast, prompting the crowd to follow suit. Brody lifted his beer, his gaze drifting to his father. Max caught his eye, his mouth twisting in what was probably meant to be a smile but came out looking more like a grimace.

After the toast Brody drained the last of his beer, realizing he'd had enough. Any longer in this hell hole and he'd do them all a favor and shoot himself in the head.

Before Chase could leave the stage, Brody stood up and walked back into the house. He didn't even bother to see if his father was watching. More than likely, he wasn't. He didn't make it to the front door before Chase caught up with him.

"You're leaving?"

Brody opened the door and handed his empty Corona bottle to his brother. "Yep."

"But—"

"I said I'd show up. I never said I'd stay," Brody began, tucking his hands into his pockets. "Nobody wants me here. I don't want to be here. So just let me go."

"So that's it, then?" Chase shot back. "You're just going to leave?"

Brody nodded. "In case it wasn't obvious, yes."

Chase's hands tightened over the beer bottle, disappointment clear on his face. "You love meeting everybody's low expectations of you, don't you? And the second someone tries to make you a better person, you do all you can to make sure it doesn't happen."

He turned and walked away before Brody could reply.

Brody cursed under his breath. Shaking his head, he slipped out the front door and shut it behind him. After retrieving his car from the valet, he drove off into the night and tried not to dwell on the damage he'd caused.

As he emerged from Bel Air and headed east on Sunset Boulevard, he cranked up the music on the radio to tune out his own thoughts. He drifted through Hollywood on autopilot, not even knowing where he was going or what he'd do when he got there.

When he came to a stoplight in front of The L.A. Rock Lounge, he noticed a horde of people flocking inside. An old college buddy of his worked as a bartender there and could probably get him in. A few more beers and a live show, whatever it was, might be exactly what he needed to take his mind off his brother. It was at least better than going home to sulk.

He pulled down a nearby side street and miraculously found a metered parking spot. Within minutes, he was meeting his friend at the door and entering the venue feeling much better than he had before.

"Thanks, man." He nodded to his friend as he paid for a beer at the bar and settled in to wait for the show to start.

"PIPER, YOU'RE on in two minutes."

Sadie paled, squeezing Tess's hand so tight she thought bones might break. Her friend winced and pushed through the pain.

"Remember to *smile*. Be nice. You don't have to say too much. Play off the mystery of Piper Gray. No one expects to know you. They just want to hear you sing."

"Okay." Sadie tried to breathe as Tess led her to the edge of the stage, just hidden behind the curtains. She chanced a peek at the crowd just as the lights dimmed. Her stomach rolled when she saw it was a packed house.

Leon walked onstage and a spotlight zeroed in on him. He smiled as he lifted a mic to his lips, waiting for the onset of applause and excited cheers to die down. "I have to say, it's a special honor and a privilege tonight to host arguably the most mysterious and brilliant artist on today's music scene. She came out of nowhere with lyrics and a voice that has touched millions. History is being made here tonight, guys. And all of us here at The L.A. Rock Lounge are proud to be a part of it. Give it up for Piper Gray!"

The lights went out as Leon walked from the stage, the crowd buzzing with excitement. It was Sadie's cue.

"Go on." Tess nudged Sadie from behind the curtain. She struggled to keep her knees from giving out and barely managed to make her way to the piano without tripping over her own feet. She huffed out little breaths as she sat down on the bench, her hands shaking.

For what felt like an eternity, she waited with bated breath for the lights to come on.

When they did, her entire world was bathed in blue. She felt like she was floating, suspended in this bubble of anticipation. The moment the crowd saw her, she was greeted with an explosion of cheering and applause. It brought a nervous smile to her face, which she hid behind her hair.

Focusing her attention on the piano, she launched into her first song.

The crowd settled down and seemingly fell into a trance, lost in the sound of the piano and her voice. She found she forgot they were there completely. Instead, she felt like the loneliest person on the planet, singing about a childhood she never had, missed opportunities she never took. The heartbreak in her voice was real, and she felt its pain as she gave all she had to the music. Her eyes closed and she felt parts of her dying with each and every keystroke, only to be rebuilt again by the power in her lyrics.

As she sang the final, heart wrenching note, her head fell back, revealing her face to the light.

Her body felt weightless, her mind in a state of euphoria, the second before the crowd soared to their feet with praise.

It took her by surprise, shocking her from her reverie. Her lips curved as she faced her fans, unable to see them clearly with the lights in her eyes. But they were there, and they adored her.

"Thank you," she spoke into the mic, laughing at the sound of whistles and cheers coming from the back corner. She felt her confidence blooming as she took another deep breath and faced the crowd. "I don't know what to say. This is all kind of new for me. Anyway, this next song is about coming home. I hope it speaks to you the way it does to me."

Chapter *eight*

B RODY WAS stunned. The only thing he could think was, holy shit, that's Sadie McRae.

At first he thought he was hallucinating. It couldn't be. The guy said the woman's name was Piper something. It had to just be a trick of the light.

But when he slipped from the barstool and made his way closer to the stage to get a better look at her, he knew he was right. She had different hair, but that face, those eyes, that voice. She even had the same self-conscious, nervous smile that brought out a dimple in her right cheek.

How long had it been? Eleven years or more, he realized. Eleven years since she'd all but disappeared. She hadn't even said goodbye.

At the time he hadn't blamed her. After what she'd been through, how could he? But they'd been friends once, students together at Harvard-Westlake in Beverly Hills. Though he was two years older than her, they'd been thick as thieves for nearly four years before *it* happened.

He sipped his beer, watching her intently. Years had passed since he'd last thought about her or the scandal involving her mother's drummer, Lee Walker. Back then it was all anyone could talk about, which was why he assumed her father sent her away. Somewhere up north, he recalled, though he couldn't remember where. So what brought her back here, to a stage in Hollywood under a fake name?

It was just the kind of mystery he lived to solve.

He smiled to himself as she sang, marveling at the sight of her. She looked so confident, so mysterious and sexy. Such a radical change from the Sadie he once knew. He was curious to find out if it was all an act, or if she really had changed. Part of him hoped she hadn't. He'd gotten a kick out of the girl he once knew. It'd be a shame if the woman wasn't the same.

When she switched into a more up-tempo song, he gazed out at the crowd and watched the people dance and sing along with her. He'd never seen The L.A. Rock Lounge so packed before, especially for an artist he hadn't even heard of. Clearly she had quite the devoted fan base.

He wondered if any of them realized they were being fooled. This Piper person didn't exist—it was only a clever cover for someone who had a good reason to avoid the spotlight. What would happen if they *did* know who she really was? Would they love her even more?

She was the only daughter of two of the greatest rock gods to ever grace the stage. The progeny of legends. He was curious to find out why she hid behind the alias. Was it out of a need to prove herself without her parents' reputations? Or was it something else altogether?

Either way, he enjoyed knowing her secret while everyone else was fooled. It amused him to watch her and know her, even though she had no idea he was there.

Soon she would. And then he'd have his answers.

SADIE KEPT her cool until the second she was offstage. She crumpled into Tess's arms, her knees finally giving out.

"Oh my God. Did I just do that?" she breathed, trying not to hyperventilate as her lips spread in a wide grin. The crowd was still roaring with praise for her as she met eyes with her friend.

"I'm so proud of you." Tess hugged her tightly, tears in her eyes. "You were fabulous."

"I was terrified," Sadie admitted, her entire body quaking with the thrill of victory. She'd conquered her biggest fear and lived to tell about it. There was no greater high than that.

"Well, you barely showed it. Now c'mon, you deserve a few minutes to rest those lovely vocal cords of yours."

Sadie nodded, still fighting to catch her breath. She let Tess take her back into the dressing room, where she collapsed into a chair and closed her eyes.

"That was…incredible."

"I know." Tess busied herself removing Sadie's stage makeup, a permanent smile plastered on her face. "You rock, girl."

"I do, don't I?" Sadie laughed giddily, her entire body relaxing as relief swam through her.

"So…would you be willing to do it again sometime?"

"Yes," Sadie blurted out, only to second guess herself. Her eyes flew open. "Wait. I don't know. Maybe?"

Tess pursed her lips. "You know you want to. Admit it, what you did tonight made you feel more alive than anything you've ever done."

"Okay. True." Sadie let out a long breath, weighing the decision in her head. "I do *want* to do it again. But I don't know if I *can.*"

"Why not?"

"Eventually someone's bound to figure me out. I mean, I'm getting a little too public. If I start doing more shows, then more offers for recording contracts will come in and I won't be able to explain the reason why I have to turn them down."

"You know how many musicians would *kill* for a recording contract?" Tess asked, shaking her head. "I get your point, but I think you're being a bit of a Virgo right now."

"I know." Sadie sighed. "I worry too much."

"You need to chill out and go with the flow. This makes you happy, so do it."

Sadie looked in the mirror after Tess finished removing the makeup, pleased to see her own face staring back at her. Though a part of her missed the mysterious woman she'd become for the last few hours.

"I'll commit to one more show, but nothing more than that." She attempted a smile for Tess. "Can we go home now? I need wine."

"If by wine you mean more champagne, then you're in luck. I stocked up." Tess patted her shoulder and turned to start packing up their things. "Why don't you get changed and go out to the car, I'll just be a second. I need to talk to Leon about booking you that show."

Sadie grabbed her purse and shoved the makeup bag inside. "Okay."

She changed into jeans and a white T-shirt, then looked at herself one more time in the mirror, debating whether or not to remove the wig. Deciding it was best to maintain the disguise until she was safely at home, she left the room and headed for the exit that led to the discreet parking lot for performers and security.

When she opened the door, a small crowd of people greeted her.

"Oh." A wave of panic hit her as she took in the smiling, excited faces of some fans who'd found their way to the backstage door.

One girl about her age walked up, nervously holding up her cell phone. "I love your music so much. Can I take a picture with you?"

Sadie bit her lower lip, unsure what to do. She shot a nervous glance to Tess's car, which was parked several yards away. She wondered if she took off at a run if the crowd would follow her.

Don't be stupid. Of course they would, and then everyone would talk about what a lunatic you are.

"Sure." Sadie tried to smile and posed with the girl, hoping she had just enough makeup on to where no one would notice her real identity. Not that anyone gave a crap about Sadie McRae anymore, she reminded herself. Though she had to admit, they seemed to love Piper Gray.

As the others in the crowd approached her to take pictures and get autographs, she spotted a man dressed in black leaning against a nearby light pole smoking a cigarette. The light above him cast dark shadows over his face, giving him a dangerous look. Her stomach did a nervous flip and she had to look away.

"Thank you so much. You're amazing," another young girl said, all but gushing at the sight of Sadie. "Please do an album. We'd all buy it in a heartbeat."

"I...might." Sadie attempted another smile as the last few fans trailed off, waving goodbye to her. She started toward the parking lot, then realized the stranger was still watching her. Her hand tightened instinctively around her purse strap as she thought of the pepper spray she kept inside. Could she get to it in time if she needed to?

Realizing she had no choice but to walk past him, she kept her eyes focused on the ground and began to walk. In her peripherals, she saw the man blow out a puff of smoke and toss his cigarette to the ground, putting it out with his Converse sneaker.

Just keep walking. Please don't talk to me. Please.

She made it past him, her breath stalled in her lungs. After a few paces, she released it.

Then he spoke.

"Sadie McRae."

She stopped dead in her tracks, whirling around to face him. It took her a second to realize he'd used her real name. Not her stage name, not the name everyone at the venue knew her by. He knew her *real* name.

Oh God.

She turned around again and practically ran for the car. It wasn't until the stranger followed her and grabbed her arm that she stopped. She flung her elbow upward, nearly clocking him in the nose.

"Leave me alone!"

"Christ, McRae, calm down." He took a step back and held both hands up in apology, an edgy smile crossing his face. "I'm not here to hurt you."

"What do you want?" What she really wanted to know was how he knew her real name, but that question would only validate his claim.

"You don't remember me? I mean, it's been eleven years, but who could forget this face?"

He smiled again, this time with a kind of cocky, carefree swagger that lit up his roguish features. She stared into his eyes, dark and filled with charm. Her heart leapt into her throat as recognition hit her.

"Brody?" Without hesitating, she launched herself into his arms, a disbelieving laugh escaping her lips. "What are you doing here?"

"I should be asking you that question." He held her, startled by her easy affection and oddly grateful for it.

"I...I'm singing." She pulled away from him, feeling awkward. "Did you..."

"See? Yeah, I saw." He tapped under her chin to bring her eyes back to his. "I never thought I'd see you on a stage."

"I know, right?" She laughed and adjusted her wig, making sure it was still in place. "Shy little Sadie, scared of her own shadow..."

"No, shy little Sadie who swore she'd never be like her parents."

She felt a lump form in her throat and tried to swallow it. "I'm not *like* them. I just sing for fun."

"You killed it out there. I'd say you're more like them than you realize."

The observation bothered her, but she tried not to show it. "Thanks...so how have you been?"

Brody tucked his hands into the pockets of his slacks. "Not as good as you. You look great."

"Thanks...again." She crossed her arms for lack of something better to do and tried to act cool. Why was she so awkward? He was just an old friend. Though everything was different now, wasn't it? She wasn't even that same person anymore. And he...well, he looked like life had dealt some heavy blows that sharpened every last edge of him. "Anyway, I should probably—"

"Excuse me." Tess stormed over, stepping between Brody and Sadie. She eyed Brody with intense dislike. "You need to go now."

A cynical smile twisted his lips. "Hey, Tess. Long time no see."

"This was a cute little reunion but it's over." Tess turned to Sadie, reaching for her arm. "C'mon, let's go."

"Oh." Sadie blinked in confusion, staring back and forth between the two of them. "Okay. Why?"

"He's bad news, honey. Just trust me."

Sadie locked eyes with Brody. "You won't tell anyone about me singing, right?"

Tess scoffed. "If he does, he can expect a big fat lawsuit coming his way."

Brody ignored Tess, his irritation softening at the fear he saw on Sadie's face. She was clearly terrified of everyone knowing who she really was. "My lips are sealed."

"They better be." Tess led Sadie toward the car, leaving Brody behind.

He rocked back on his heels, sad to see her go. Again. "You never said goodbye to me, Sadie. Not then or now."

Sadie shot a look over her shoulder and managed a smile, amused by him despite Tess's warning. "Goodbye, Brody."

Seconds later they were climbing into the car. When Sadie turned to look back, he was already gone.

Chapter *nine*

"WHAT DO you know that you're not telling me?"

Tess shrugged. "Nothing."

"Liar." Sadie pouted, turning to stare out the passenger window as Tess drove her home. The beautiful city lights did little to distract her from the burning questions in her mind. "Why did you act that way to Brody?"

When Tess said nothing, Sadie glanced over at her. She saw her friend looking, surprisingly, at a loss for words.

"I guess I'm surprised you don't already know," Tess finally admitted, keeping her eyes on the road. Lights flashed over her face, casting odd shadows that darkened her eyes. "Then again, you've been living in the boondocks for the last decade. You probably don't keep up with the news."

An icy ball of dread dropped into Sadie's stomach. "What are you talking about?"

Anger tightened Tess's face and chased away her apprehension. "About two years ago he was one of the top photojournalists in the country. He had a gift. He could get the most incredible photographs you'd ever seen. Uprisings, protests, war—if there was something happening across the Atlantic you could bet he was there with his camera, ready to record history. *National Geographic* was even interested in him which is rare, especially for someone so young. Anyway, he went to the Middle East to cover our military's advances in Afghanistan. Apparently while he was there he botched an operation that resulted in the deaths of two Marines. His reckless actions led to their deaths at the hands of Taliban insurgents who'd been hiding in a marketplace. He was forced to resign, give up his career, and was essentially blacklisted by the industry. And rightfully so."

Sadie's mouth fell open, her heart panging. "He lost everything?"

A dark smile crossed Tess's face. "Yep. The fancy house in Malibu, the job, the accolades, many of his friends...I remember hearing people gossip about how he was a loose cannon just waiting to explode and no one wanted to be there when it happened. We all expected him to fight back, but instead he kind of just disappeared for awhile. Then when he resurfaced again, he was a paparazzi getting shots of celebrities for the tabloids. Talk about a fall from grace."

Sadie's hands clenched tightly in her lap, images of the hungry press after that horrific night eleven years before flashing through her mind. "Paparazzi?"

Tess shot her a sympathetic look. "Now you know why I freaked out. I'm sorry if I embarrassed you, but it had to be done. You *cannot* talk to him, Sadie. As it is, he's probably already counting dollar signs over what your exposure will net him."

Sadie felt lightheaded. "Oh."

They pulled into the driveway of Sadie's house and Tess shut off the engine. She reached over and held Sadie's hand in hers. "Don't worry, okay? I want this to be a happy night for you."

"It was..." Sadie trailed off, numbness taking over her body. She stared blankly out the windshield. "I was so happy to see him that I didn't even think twice about what he was doing there."

"There's no way he could have found out before the show. Nobody knew but you and me."

"Then that only leaves one explanation," Sadie realized dully, turning to face her friend. "He was in the crowd by happenchance, and he recognized me."

"I don't—"

"I knew this would happen," Sadie interrupted with a cynical half laugh. She shook her head and turned away. "I'm so stupid for thinking I could get away with this."

"Honey, we'll figure it out." Tess tried to comfort her, but Sadie slid from the car with her purse.

She leaned back in and tried to smile. "Thanks for everything, Tess. Really. I had fun tonight."

Tess started to reply, only to be cut off by the door closing. Sadie walked toward the house, keys in hand. Moments later, she was shut inside and safe.

Unable to do more, she leaned against the front door and closed her eyes. A tear fell down her cheek, silent and unwanted.

Her entire future hinged on Brody keeping his word.

ON THE drive back to Venice Beach, all Brody could think about was her.

He was sure that at that very moment, Sadie's opinion of him was being drastically changed. Clearly she had no idea what he had done or who he'd become. If she had, then her reaction would have mirrored Tess's to the letter. Hell, a paparazzi at her debut concert under an alias? That was a recipe for disaster and Tess had been right to put a stop to it. Though the fact that Sadie didn't know the truth meant she'd been more sheltered than he had assumed.

Not that he wasn't confident he could change her mind. He'd charmed his way into her life once, he could do it again. And this time there wasn't just a friendship in store for him. Now there was a mystery to solve and possibly a big cash payout if he played his cards right.

Though, he had to admit that the idea of exposing her made him feel downright slimy. And not just slimy, but a lower-than-dirt-and-grimier-than-scum kind of slimy. All he could picture was that fear in her eyes when she asked him if he would talk to the press. It had given such a haunting beauty to her features that made him want to gather her up and protect her from all the evil of the world. Why the hell he felt that way, he had no idea. He'd never felt that about anyone before.

Shaking off the thought, he pulled into a spot on the street and climbed out of his car. He whistled to himself as he walked, kicking his thoughts into more serious matters. He needed to find out everything he could about Sadie McRae post-2002. And maybe with a little help from her, he could even solve the mystery of who shot Lee Walker. That would sure get his father's attention and maybe even restore an ounce of his reputation within the journalism circles. All he needed was to find a way to contact her.

He unlocked his apartment, immediately going to the fridge for a beer. With a Corona in hand he sat down on the couch and opened his laptop.

He Googled her name first, curious to see when she'd last been mentioned in the news. He took a sip of his beer as he watched the results filter in, the first one a Wikipedia article. Clicking on it, he read through her biography and the well known details of what transpired the night Lee Walker tried to rape her. Most of it was stuff he already knew, things he remembered from the months following the incident.

She'd been cornered in her bedroom, slapped around, and almost raped. Then when she'd been on the verge of passing out, someone had come into the room, grabbed Lee Walker's gun from the dresser, and shot him. He'd died on the spot, right in front of Sadie. By all accounts she'd watched him die, but had blacked out before seeing the shooter. He'd always wondered if she *had* seen the person's face, but was covering up the person's identity. Why she would do that when it was clearly an act of defense, he wasn't sure. Unless, in some strange twist of circumstance, it wasn't. Was the killing of Lee Walker really as black and white as the police made it out to be?

He clicked back to the search results and found a scattering of websites about the scandal. *Time Magazine* called it one of the "Top Ten Unsolved Crimes in Los Angeles History" and a few websites spelled out every little detail of the investigation that was made public. He skimmed through them, absorbing it all like a sponge.

There were a few articles from a couple years back that mentioned the scandal, but nothing substantial. As he scrolled down, he caught websites that talked about Sadie's parents and their careers, with only brief mentions of the daughter they shared.

In the end, no one had talked about Sadie McRae or bothered to find her for several years. She'd practically disappeared from the public eye. Poof. Gone. No more.

So then why was she suddenly in Hollywood, performing under an alias? He realized he'd missed the opportunity to ask her. He'd been so caught up in the nostalgia of seeing her again that it had slipped his mind.

Next time he wouldn't let himself forget. Once he found her there was no stopping him from getting the truth.

On impulse, he clicked into the search result images. Pictures of her at fifteen years old popped up, one a school picture from Harvard-Westlake. It was the one that was spread around the most in the wake of what had happened. Other images were of her parents, some outside the courtroom or candid street shots from the tabloids. His eyes caught one image in particular showing Ben McRae leading Sadie out of the hospital, likely taken the day after it happened.

His brows furrowed as he stared at the image, sorrow washing over him. She looked terrified. Wounded, broken, and lost. The camera captured the wide, haunted look of her eyes and the pale, pasty tone of her skin. He also noticed that her father clutched her arm in a way that suggested he felt more inconvenienced than grateful his daughter wasn't hurt. Anger built within him at the thought. She'd deserved so much better than what she got. It was a shame that so nice a person could suffer at the hands of monsters.

Heart heavy with emotion, he clicked into another picture, this time of her on a college campus at about twenty years old. She read quietly beneath a tree, and clearly had no idea someone was taking photographs of her. Her waves of blonde hair fell down her lower back, and round sunglasses hid her eyes. She was beautiful, even then.

Even now, he realized. Not that he wanted to dwell on it, but she'd blossomed into quite a woman. A woman who, if she had any brain in her head, would stay as far away from him as possible.

He grunted and shut his laptop, too tired to look at her picture anymore. As bad as he felt for her, he still wanted to know the truth. The hunger for it would eat him alive before long.

Somehow, some way, he was going to find her and get answers.

Chapter *ten*

A TEXT MESSAGE jolted Sadie awake. She blindly reached for her cell phone on the nightstand, wincing against the morning sun that filtered through the windows. Her eyes struggled to focus on the screen as she read the message from Tess.

They LOVED you. Congrats, girl!

A smile spread over Sadie's lips, excitement chasing away the last dredges of sleep. Without hesitating she jumped out of bed, raced into the dining room, and opened her laptop. Within minutes she was poring over news articles about her performance.

After basking in the glow of praise from fans and critics alike, she realized she should do a quick search and make sure no one had figured out her secret. Other than Brody, of course. But from the looks of it he'd kept his word. So far, anyway.

She went back to reading an article about her show, biting her thumbnail as she absorbed every last word. At the bottom was a link to her most popular YouTube video, her performance of her song "All These Flames." When she clicked on it, her eyes went straight to the number of views and widened.

Her mouth fell open stupidly as she stared at the number, now edging close to one million. Within hours, it would likely surpass that. Giddiness swept over her at the thought.

The idea of her music reaching so many people brought a lump of gratitude to her throat. If it hadn't been for Tess pushing her, she would have never done the show. Time would tell if it was a good idea, but the doubt and anguish she felt the night before melted away. Confidence replaced it and filled her with hope.

She closed the laptop and went into the kitchen to make coffee, her steps lighter and a smile on her face. Humming to herself, she arranged the coffee filter and filled the pot with water. Her eyes flitted outside the kitchen window to the view of Los Angeles, and her heart swelled.

Maybe everything would be okay, after all.

Her thoughts drifted to Brody and had her biting back a grin. God, it had been good to see him again. She'd always wondered what happened to him, filled with regret that she'd never said goodbye. There just hadn't been an opportunity. After her father had picked her up from the hospital the day after *it* happened, she'd been sent straight to Lake Tahoe. She never even got to start the new semester at school. What would've been her last few months of tenth grade at Harvard-Westlake were robbed from her, and all of her friends along with it.

The only person she'd been allowed to contact was Tess, and that was only because Tess's father was the band's private physician. He'd been friends with Ben McRae for years and had personally seen to her that night at the hospital.

She wondered if Brody had been worried about her when she disappeared. They hadn't been best friends the way she was with Tess, but they certainly shared something she'd considered very special. Whether he felt the same, she didn't know.

As the coffee brewed, Sadie leaned her hip against the counter and closed her eyes. She pictured his face in her mind and smiled. He hadn't changed. He still had those dark waves of hair, carelessly combed, leaving strands to fall over his forehead. Those same sharp, angular features, more defined than the last time she'd seen him. She wondered if the events in the Middle East damaged him, darkened his spirit in a way that couldn't be repaired. Perhaps it had. Though she didn't know the full story, from what Tess had told her he must be riddled with guilt. How could he not be?

Then again, she didn't really know him. Not anymore. The fun-loving, adventurous boy she'd known had become a man with a notorious reputation. Though he had always been a rebel, seeking attention and danger and not giving a damn about the what-ifs of any situation. Back then she'd been drawn to him for those qualities. They were everything she wasn't. Everything she couldn't be.

When they'd met, she was nothing more than a shy, naïve girl overshadowed by her legendary parents, and he was just a lawyer's son prone to questioning any and all authority. They shouldn't have been friends, not by the natural order of things. Yet he'd stumbled across her on the one day she'd ever sat in front of the Principal's office. She'd been sent there by her English teacher who worried about her well-being, prompted by her lagging interest in school and her rapid drop in weight. It'd been a particularly stressful year dealing with the fresh wound of divorce, and she was suffering emotionally and physically. Brody had taken a seat next to her and launched into conversation as if they'd known each other all their lives. Talking to people came so naturally to him in a way it never had for her. He'd managed to cheer her up that day, and nearly every day that followed.

Sadie sighed, her eyes opening. The memory was bittersweet to her, both a reminder of the pain she'd suffered under her parents and of the hope Brody had given her. She'd even developed a little crush on him sometime during their friendship, but never had the courage to act on it. Just thinking about it brought a mysterious little flutter to her stomach that was not as unwelcome as it should have been.

She turned to the coffee maker and poured herself a cup, sipping it as she forced thoughts of Brody from her mind. She had to mentally prepare herself for the task of the day—taking her mother to her first chemotherapy appointment.

AFTER TAKING a shower and getting dressed, Sadie made the quick drive to her mother's house. When she pulled into the driveway, Valerie opened the front door with a sunny smile on her face. She lifted her hand in a regal wave, looking like a queen emerging from her castle.

"How do I look?" she asked as Sadie rose from the car, doing a quick twirl to show off the cerulean blue dress she wore. It was layered with beads and embroidered flowers with a long skirt that danced as she moved. Her long waves of blonde hair shimmered in the sunlight.

"Lovely." Sadie managed a smile, wondering why her mother felt the need to dress up for a doctor's appointment. Then again, if she *hadn't* dressed up, Sadie would think something was wrong with her. "Ready to go?"

"Of course, darling." Valerie glided down the steps and approached the passenger door of Sadie's Crosstrek, not looking at all like a woman dying of cancer.

Once they were both seated, Sadie pulled out of the driveway and onto the street. She flipped on the radio just to have something playing in the background. Sheryl Crow's peppy hit "All I Wanna Do" poured out of the speakers but did little to soothe Sadie's nerves.

She noticed her mother staring at her strangely from behind dark, oversized sunglasses. "Did something happen last night?"

Sadie's heart leapt into her throat. She stumbled over different responses before settling on ignorance. "No. Why?"

"I tried to call you but your phone was turned off, and you have that glow to your cheeks that girls only get when there's a guy involved. Are you seeing someone?"

"My phone died, and no, there's no guy." Unless she counted Brody.

"Liar." Valerie seemed amused as she looked away. "That's okay. I'll fish it out of you sooner or later. I can be very persuasive."

Sadie winced, choosing not to say anything else until they reached Cedars-Sinai Hospital. Her mother led the way into the cancer center building where they checked in and were sent upstairs to see the doctor. Sadie tapped her foot all the way up the elevator, nervous as a cat. By contrast, her mother seemed oddly calm and cheerful.

"I think we should go get our nails done after this," she suggested, shooting a playful glance at her daughter. "And our toes, too. A little pampering will do us both some good. Then you can look pretty for your boyfriend."

Sadie snorted, wondering what her mother would say if she knew her daughter hadn't been on a date, but instead performed for a crowd at one of the hottest venues in L.A.

When the elevator chimed and the doors slid open, she saw her mother tense and her smile fade. She didn't think Valerie would have the energy for a visit to the salon after the treatment, but decided not to mention it. She could respect her mother's need to maintain normalcy, as unrealistic as it was.

After the meeting with the doctor—a kind, gray-haired man with a German accent and cold hands—Sadie sat in a chair beside her mother as the nurses hooked Valerie up to a machine that would pump cancer-killing drugs into her system. They inserted an IV into her arm and began the treatment before exiting the room. Valerie closed her eyes and grew quiet, leaving Sadie to wonder what was going through her mind.

They sat in silence for awhile, Sadie unsure what to say and Valerie either too tired or troubled to speak. It left Sadie with nothing to do but stare around the small room with its tea green walls and faux wood flooring, lost in her own thoughts.

Eventually she chanced a look at her mother, gazing at the woman with a deep sense of regret. In this moment of complete and utter vulnerability, she appeared so different from the woman Sadie thought she knew. The woman who for years had commanded an audience with her heavenly voice and powerful presence. Who rode up and down the rollercoaster of life without a second thought to risk or consequence. She'd taken control of her life and really *lived*, and doing so cost her only daughter everything. And now, perhaps in a twist of fate, karma was back to collect its due.

Sadie's eyes became heavy with tears at the thought. She fought back the flow of emotion, not wanting her mother to see. Not wanting to think of this as retribution for what her mother had done, even though part of her couldn't help but feel that way. Lee Walker would have never been around had it not been for Valerie. She'd brought that monster into their home and practically delivered him to Sadie's bedroom. And for that she was paying the price.

"I hope you don't feel like you have to keep secrets from me," Valerie said suddenly, her voice serious.

Sadie glanced up from the floor, catching her mother staring at her. "What?"

"Despite what Ben has told you all these years, I'm not your enemy," she replied with a haughty frown. "I know I haven't always made the best decisions. For one, I shouldn't have let them take you away from me."

"You didn't have a choice," Sadie reminded her, irritated that her mother still seemed to think she'd done nothing wrong. "They were going to throw you in prison."

Valerie's lips spread in a coy smile. "But they didn't. If I'd fought a bit harder I could have retained custody. But *c'est la vie*."

Maybe I didn't want to stay. Sadie thought the words but couldn't say them, knowing they were true and knowing they would hurt. She didn't have the heart to cause her mother any more pain than what she was already going through.

After a few minutes of awkward silence, Sadie changed the subject. "How are you feeling?"

Valerie shrugged, glancing down at the IV. "I'm just praying my hair doesn't fall out. Can you imagine *me* bald?" She laughed brightly.

Emotion swam through Sadie as she attempted a smile. "I have a wig you can borrow."

"What do you need a wig for, darling? You inherited my beautiful hair." Valerie reached out and ran her hand through Sadie's long blonde strands, marveling at it.

Sadie realized she'd almost slipped and fumbled for an excuse. "It's just something I got for Halloween one year."

"And you brought it with you?"

Though her mother's voice was light, Sadie could tell her attention had sharpened. She tried to shrug the question off. "Tess had mentioned a costume party so I brought it just in case."

The nurse returned to check on Valerie, providing a much needed distraction. Sadie slipped from the room, needing air and a moment alone. Outside, she leaned against the wall and closed her eyes.

That had been much too close.

THE SECOND Brody stepped through his front door and dumped his gym bag on the floor, his cell phone rang. He lifted it out of his pocket, wiping sweat from his forehead as he checked the caller-ID. A scowl hardened his face as he answered.

"Well, shucks, Dad. I can't remember the last time you called me. I'm honored."

"*Don't be. This isn't a personal call, it's a business one.*"

"Business, huh?" Brody kicked the door shut and tossed his keys on the kitchen counter. He made his way over to the sofa and collapsed into it. "If you're offering me a job, I regretfully have to decline."

Max scoffed audibly, causing Brody to roll his eyes. "*I've spoken with Mr. Lovett and informed him that it was you who took those pictures. He's understandably outraged that someone connected to the firm would do such a thing and is demanding I fix this. Unfortunately, the damage has already been done.*"

"If it hadn't been me, it would've been some other lucky schmuck who got the picture. Maybe your client should think twice before fooling around with Miss Gold in public."

"*Maybe you should have had some sense and come to me before going to the tabloids. We could have worked out payment—*"

"Why Dad, that would be *illegal*," Brody said with mock horror. "You wouldn't want me going to jail, would you? Oh wait, who am I kidding? Of course you would."

He heard his father sigh on the other line and felt a stab of bitterness. He knew he was right. "*If you wish to continue being an Odell, you need to stop compromising the family business.*"

"You mean I haven't already been disowned?" Brody laughed. "And here I thought that ship sailed years ago."

"If it were up to me all contact with you would have ceased after that spectacle overseas. Do you know how many months of damage control I had to do to disassociate the firm from your reckless mistakes?"

"Gee, thanks for the support," Brody snapped sarcastically. He ran a hand through his hair, disgust in his voice as he continued. "I know you wish I'd just go die in a gutter somewhere, but I won't do it. I may be a fuck up but I never asked for your help or your charity so you can just leave me the hell alone from now on. Mind your own goddamn business, and if you're such a great lawyer then you should be able to save Lovett from the pile of shit he's fallen into."

He hung up without waiting for a response and tossed the phone aside. His hands were shaking with anger as he covered his face, wishing he could get the old man's voice out of his head. Over the years he thought he'd gotten used to it, but it still managed to get under his skin. It probably always would. Even after the old man was dead, his disapproval would live on.

His hands fell to his lap as he opened his eyes, taking in the clutter from last night's research. Printouts detailing the death of Lee Walker and the police findings from that night lay scattered on his coffee table, mixed with photographs of the scene. He sifted through them in an attempt to distract himself.

He'd spent the better part of the night gathering as much information as he could on what happened to Sadie. But no matter how many articles he read or details from the scene he uncovered, none of them would provide the truth. Hell, the cops hadn't come up with an answer, so how could he? What he needed was to talk to Sadie. And to talk to Sadie, he needed to find her.

He wasn't positive, but he had a hunch she'd be staying with her mother. And if he was a betting man, which he occasionally was, he'd bet she still lived in that same house up Laurel Canyon.

Feeling a boost of energy at the prospect, he jumped to his feet and grabbed his phone. Next stop, Valerie McRae's mansion. And hopefully a chance run-in with her talented daughter.

Chapter *eleven*

LIKE SADIE predicted, her mother had no energy for the salon after her treatment. She let Sadie lead her upstairs to her bedroom, her mood drastically different than before. All her sunny optimism was replaced by a dark despair that put tears in her eyes and a snap to her words. She doubled over in pain as she rolled herself into bed, sobs wracking her body.

Sadie held back and watched her, feeling distraught and helpless. Carla fluttered into the room, bearing a tray of hot tea and soup. As she took care of Valerie, Sadie retreated from her mother's bedroom in silence.

She wandered down the hallway, lost in her own thoughts. Before she realized where she was, she had stopped before her old bedroom. Her eyes took their fill of that haunted place, alarmed to find it looked so different than she remembered.

Her old bed was gone, replaced by a queen bed covered with violet-colored linens. All her furniture—the desk with all her school books, the dresser where Lee had laid his gun, the wicker armchair her grandmother had given her—were missing. In their place was a modern-looking white dresser and a matching padded bench at the end of the bed. She drifted into the room and lowered herself onto it, her heart a heavy stone within her chest.

She closed her eyes and breathed in the unfamiliar scent of the room. There was no evidence of her left anywhere. It had been scrubbed clean, leaving no trace of the fifteen years she'd lived there or of the nightmare that drove her away. For that, at least, she was grateful.

In all the years since, she had never once set foot in the room. Until now. Now that her mother was dying and likely wouldn't see Christmas or maybe even fall. Tears fell down her cheeks as she wondered what the hell the point had been in coming here. Why put herself through so much pain by reliving the past and witnessing the death of her own mother? What difference was it going to make in the end?

Her eyes squeezed tight and she wrapped her arms around herself, starving for comfort and finding none. She was foolish to think she was strong enough to handle this. Ridiculously self-righteous to think she could make a difference or somehow atone for years of neglecting the only mother she'd ever have. All those years of hate seemed so petty in the face of what her mother was going through.

She hadn't been strong enough then and she felt no stronger now. Deep down she still harbored that hate and despised herself for it. Wiping away the tears, she glanced up at the doorway to the room and for the briefest of moments pictured Lee Walker standing there, menacing and cruel. His dark eyes were locked on her hungrily, lustfully. That old fear rose within her like a crushing wave and sent her mind spinning.

She remembered the feel of his hands grabbing her, the burning slap to the face that stunned her senseless. The morbid twist of his mouth as he took pleasure in hurting her, as though her useless acts of defense amused him.

The rest was vague, like the name of an old acquaintance that lingers on the tip of your tongue. She knew he'd pinned her to the bed. Somehow she remembered the oppressive weight of his body and how much his hands hurt her wrists as he held her down. What he'd said to her or what she'd pleaded for were lost, but the sensation of being crushed by a mountain remained. Then he'd struck her again—at least, that's what she assumed happened. All she remembered was the hot, horrendous flash of pain and the dizzying darkness that saved her from experiencing his assault on her body.

At least, if he'd been able to follow through on his plans.

She stared at the doorway again, visualizing her dresser where it used to stand beside the door and wishing she had seen the person who'd come in to save her. Why hadn't she? She remembered the explosion, could recall the crash of his body and the emptiness of his eyes. What else was there? Surely the answer lay somewhere in her memories...

Disappointment filled her, knowing it was gone. If she hadn't remembered in the days following the assault, how could she remember now, eleven years later? It was simply a mystery she would never solve.

With one last look around the room, she felt an odd sense of closure. Maybe she would never learn the truth of who killed Lee Walker, but at least she could put the past to rest. And if—or rather, when—her mother passed on, maybe all those old demons would die right along with her.

BRODY WAITED in his car a short distance from Valerie's driveway, tapping his fingers against the steering wheel. Over thirty minutes had passed since he'd watched Sadie pull up the driveway with her mother and disappear behind the security gate. Thirty long minutes of wondering if he'd missed his chance for the day and should take a hike and go home.

Then he spotted Sadie's car slowly creeping down the driveway. Anticipation filled him when he realized she was alone. It was now or never.

He slipped from the car and leaned casually against the driver's side door, folding his arms over his black T-shirt. He grinned at her and waved as she drove by, pleased when she came to an abrupt stop. The look of stunned surprise on her face was quickly replaced with suspicion, then by a hint of fear as he motioned for her to roll down her passenger window.

She rolled it down a few inches, regarding him with a cool stare as he approached. "You know, I don't make a habit of talking to paparazzi."

"Glad you made an exception." Brody continued to smile as he tucked his hands into the pockets of his jeans. He eyed her through the slim crack in the window, his eyes hidden behind aviator sunglasses. "I take it Tess filled you in, then."

"She told me some things. She'd kill me if she knew I was talking to you. Apparently you're bad news."

He laughed. "Not much has changed, has it?"

Sadie's lips curved, bringing out that dimple he missed so much. "No, not really. So what are you doing here?"

"I wanted to see you again and since you forgot to give me your number, I figured I'd find you here."

"I just dropped by. I've been staying at my dad's old house." She bit down on her lip, unsure if she could trust him. "Look, I don't want anyone knowing I'm in town."

"I get that." He leaned in closer to the cracked open window, then rested his arms on the door frame when she rolled the glass down all the way. The scent of her perfume, all warm vanilla and feminine honeysuckle, assaulted his senses and he lost himself in it for a moment. When she only stared at him expectantly, he smiled again. "If I promise not to tell a soul about seeing you, will you have lunch with me?"

She considered his offer, weighing the pros and cons in her head. It *would* be nice to catch up, and she couldn't ignore the nervous excitement that coursed through her just by seeing him. Then again, she still didn't trust him. He needed to prove himself, but first she needed to give him the chance. "Okay. But only on my terms."

"Hit me."

"We go to the restaurant of my choice, sit in the back and you leave your camera and any voice recording equipment in the car."

"You drive a hard bargain, McRae. But we have a deal." He slapped the door frame and grinned. "Lead the way."

He walked back to his car and hopped inside. He followed her down Laurel Canyon and onto Sunset Boulevard, where she detoured down a few side streets before turning into a small lot behind a quaint, hole-in-the-wall café. He understood her preference when he walked inside and found it cozy and private, with small booths tucked safely behind beautiful plants and ornamental screens. They took a seat at one of the booths and he got his first real good look at her.

Without the black wig and makeup she looked just like he remembered, only refined. He drank in the old, familiar lines of her face, curious to know how much the girl inside had changed.

She glanced up from the menu and caught him staring. She blushed, then tried to hide her face behind her hair. Seeing her embarrassment delighted him in ways he couldn't explain.

"You know, you don't look any different," he mused, not even bothering with the menu. He was too fascinated by the subtle curve of her smile and the nervous, fluttery way she moved. All her calm composure seemed to crack now that they were in such close proximity.

"I certainly feel different," she replied, unable to look him in the eye. Her stomach was a riot of nerves only made worse by his intense stare. Had he always looked at her that way?

Sympathy darkened his mood, knowing full well what changed her. "I'm sure you do."

A waiter came by and took their drink order. When he left, Sadie chanced a look up at Brody and attempted a smile. "You don't look much different, either."

"And here I thought you barely remembered me."

"Of course I remember you." She tilted her head and eyed him curiously. "I can tell life hasn't been easy on you."

"I haven't been easy on life," Brody joked, trying to hide the unease he felt at her words. He shrugged it off, keeping the mood lighthearted. "You know what I did. I live with that guilt every day. But hey, we all have our demons."

Sorrow creased her brow, emotion clouding her eyes. "Funny how much those demons change us."

"They only do if we let them." He held her gaze, wishing to God he could erase all those years and go back to the place where they'd once been friends. Without the ignorance of childhood, everything seemed so radically complicated. "So will you stab me with your fork if I ask why you're in town?"

She laughed, releasing the tension in her shoulders. "I can't make any promises."

His teeth flashed in a devious grin. "I'm willing to take the chance."

"I'm sure you are…" she trailed off, wondering what she should tell him and how much he deserved to know. She had a basic story prepared just in case she ran into someone she knew, but this was Brody. He was one step below Tess on her list of trusted friends. At least, he had been eleven years ago. There was a time when she'd confided in him on everything—her parents' divorce, her feelings of being trapped between them, her anger over being used as a weapon in their war against each other. Other than time, what had changed from then to now?

A lot, and yet not very much.

"If you don't want to tell me, I can respect that," Brody said, interrupting her thoughts. She heard the disappointment in his voice and felt sorry for it.

"No, it's okay. I want to tell you." She lifted her eyes to his, a sad smile softening her face. "My mother has cancer. She doesn't have much time left."

"Valerie Ryan is dying?" Stunned surprise hit him like a wave and left him speechless. The legendary singer of Albatross was on her death bed, and no one had any idea. The urge to break the news exploded in his veins and the opportunist in him nearly snatched it, but he held back. He couldn't betray Sadie's confidence, not now. Not if he was going to use her to get to the bottom of what happened to Lee Walker.

Sadie nodded. "I came down to help her. I don't know how long I'll be in town…as long as it takes, I suppose."

"I didn't realize you two had become so close."

"We aren't, really." Sadie sighed, regret filling her at the thought. "But she doesn't have anyone else."

He could hear the sense of duty she felt and admired her for it. God knows he wouldn't do what she was doing if it was his father on his death bed. He'd laugh all the way to the funeral, then make a spectacle and laugh some more just to spite the old man who never gave him the time of day. "That's pretty damn noble of you, McRae."

She rolled her eyes and fought back a smile. "Not really."

The waiter arrived with their drinks and took their food order. Sadie welcomed the distraction as she tried to gather her thoughts. One look at Brody and she knew he was hungry for information. Hopefully it was just innocent curiosity and not copy for a headlining story.

Brody waited impatiently for the waiter to leave, then turned back to her. "So then how did you wind up onstage at The L.A. Rock Lounge?"

"Tess talked me into it," Sadie admitted, twirling a piece of hair around her finger. "I sort of have a YouTube channel under my alias…"

"Seriously? I gotta look this up." He reached for his phone but she stopped him, her hand grabbing his arm.

"No recording devices, remember?"

His eyebrows shot up, amused by her. "All right. Later, then. So tell me more about this alias. Pepper-something?"

"Piper Gray," she corrected, pulling back her hand. She took a deep breath and attempted to relax. "It was just something I did for fun one day. My grandpa helped me record and edit the video so that my face isn't really visible and I wear the wig and makeup. You'd never know it was me."

"Except I did," Brody reminded her. "But not everyone knows you the way I know you. We were best friends."

"It doesn't really matter now. I probably won't perform again." She sipped her iced tea, avoiding his eyes. "If I'm that easily recognizable, then it's only going to be trouble."

"Why have the alias at all? If anything, your name will only help you."

She grew quiet. "Of all the people out there, I thought you would be the first to understand."

He was caught off guard by the coldness of her tone. He reassessed his words, wondering how he'd upset her. When she lifted her face and he saw her hopeful expression, it clicked.

"Because the world only looks at you as the daughter of Ben McRae and Valerie Ryan."

She nodded. "And the world only looks at you as the son of Max Odell."

He absorbed her words, relishing the connection they shared. Suddenly it felt like he really was sitting across from the old Sadie, and they were sharing those feelings only the two of them could understand. The effect it had on him was troubling. "I'm surprised you remember all that."

"I told you I remember you." She smiled warmly. "Remember that one time we snuck off campus to get ice cream and your mom happened to be shopping next door and caught us?"

He laughed. "Oh, yeah. She wasn't going to tell my dad but Chase ran his big mouth and got me in trouble anyway."

Her expression softened. "Chase, wow. How's he doing?"

"Living the good life. He works at the family firm, has a wife and a baby on the way. He got all the virtue and I got all the defiance."

"I'm happy for him." She took a moment to collect her thoughts when their food arrived. Curiosity got the better of her as she poured dressing over her salad. "So if I ask you to tell me about what happened overseas, will you stab me with your fork?"

"No, I suppose it's only fair after the grilling I just gave you." He winked and took a bite of his bleu-cheese burger, then groaned. "God, that's good."

"Isn't it? I love this place." She swirled her tea around in her glass and continued to stare at him. "So you were a photojournalist?"

He nodded. "It was the perfect gig. I got to see the world, meet new people, get knee deep in trouble and danger. Back home I had the fancy house, the nice cars. I even had an entourage."

One of her eyebrows lifted. "Really?"

"Yep. People flock to money. They latch on and feed off it until it's all gone, which was eventually what happened."

"You lost everything?"

"Everything but my life." He looked her in the eye, haunted by the memories. "My mistake got two soldiers killed. Every day I breathe is one more they're missing. I'll have to live with that for the rest of my life."

"But it was only a mistake—"

"I know." He pushed his half-eaten burger aside, not feeling hungry anymore. "Trust me, I've heard all the rationalizations."

"I'm sorry," she stuttered, wishing she knew what to say. Her hands tightened over the napkin in her lap. They sat in silence until she garnered the courage to speak. "Brody?"

"Yeah?"

The little flutters in her stomach went into overdrive mode, but she didn't care. "I've missed you."

Surprise flashed over his face the instant before he grinned. "I know you're just trying to make me feel better, but that's okay, I'll take it."

"No, I mean it." She averted her eyes, then grabbed a scrap piece of paper and a pen from her purse. She jotted down her cell phone number, then pushed it across the table to him.

He eyed the paper then looked back at her, brows raised. "I guess this means we get to do this again?"

She nodded. "Now you can call me instead of waiting around like a creeper outside my mom's house."

"I'm a reporter. Creeping is what I do."

"I'd rather you be my friend."

He pocketed the piece of paper. "I would, too."

"Good." Her face flushed again and she picked at her salad, exhilarated at her own courage. Then again, before *it* happened, she'd always felt so at ease around him. It was nice to slip into that mode again, where she could be herself and not be so afraid of the outside world.

"So how come you never said goodbye to me?"

She glanced up from her food, her lips parting in surprise. It took her a second to realize he meant eleven years earlier before she'd left for Lake Tahoe. "I wasn't allowed to contact anyone."

"But you stayed in touch with Tess."

"Her dad was my doctor. They're part of the family."

Brody nodded. "I get that, I guess. And if Tess had liked me at all she probably would have kept me updated. I may have just been a hormonal seventeen-year-old kid, but I was worried about you."

"I'm sorry." Regret filled her when she saw the honesty in his eyes. "I really am. If I'd been able to—"

"Whatever. It doesn't matter, right?" he interrupted with an easy grin. "You're here now, and I intend to make up for lost time."

"You do?" She blinked, a jolt of excitement shooting through her.

"Why don't we head on over to the Pier? I bet it's been forever since you've been there."

"It has," she replied, her head spinning. "But I really can't. I told you before, I don't want to give the press something to gossip about. My being here needs to be a secret."

"So throw on the wig."

She laughed, wishing she was brave enough to try it. "Apparently the wig wasn't a good enough disguise. You found me out."

"What are you afraid of, Sadie?" he asked bluntly.

"Everything," she admitted with a nervous laugh. "I'm scared of the fact that I'm actually sitting here with you in L.A. of all places. I can't believe I performed last night for a real audience that loves my music. I'm scared I'm going to wake up and this will all be a dream and—"

"It's real," he cut in, a spark in his eyes. "And the clock's only ticking faster each day that goes by. Don't you want to seize every opportunity? Don't you want to live?"

The impassioned tone in his voice caught her off guard. She stared into his eyes, moved by the confidence she saw there. He believed every word of it.

"I guess."

"Look, I can't guarantee the press won't have a field day when they find out about your mom, but I can guarantee that it won't ruin you. It'll pass just like every other headline out there. You'll be okay."

She nodded, wanting to believe him. Needing to. "Okay."

"So you'll come with me?"

"Not today. But maybe soon." She smiled and hoped it was enough. "I have to go."

He sat back in his seat and watched her slip from the table. "Don't disappear on me again, McRae. This time I won't let you go so easily."

"I promise I'll at least say goodbye before I do." On impulse, she leaned in to kiss his cheek. Before he could reply, she'd slipped out the back of the restaurant.

He rubbed the spot her lips had touched, grinning like a fool.

Chapter *twelve*

AFTER SADIE left, Brody hopped back in his car and headed up into Laurel Canyon again. His business there wasn't finished. He needed to talk to Valerie. It was a long shot, but he was accustomed to lying in wait. She had to come out sometime, and he planned to catch her the second she did. And now that he knew Sadie wasn't staying there, he'd be able to catch her mother alone.

The time hadn't been right for him to pester Sadie about Lee Walker. If he'd broached the subject too soon, she'd be even more suspicious than she already was. And it wasn't like he didn't enjoy her company. In fact, he had a better time than he'd expected to. Seeing her again reminded him why he'd been drawn to her in the first place. She made him feel like he wasn't a bad person. She'd always looked for the good in people, even when everyone else thought they were worthless. He'd forgotten how much he enjoyed that about her.

He parked a ways up the street from Valerie's house and exited the car. The sun hovered directly overhead, so he sought relief in the shade of a nearby eucalyptus tree. He leaned against the trunk and fixed his eyes across the street on Valerie's driveway.

He didn't have to wait long. After about an hour, he spotted the gate sliding open. A blonde woman wearing a long, coral-colored dress walked out onto the sidewalk, preceded by a fluffy white Pomeranian on a matching pink leash. Sunglasses and a wide-brimmed straw hat shielded the woman's face from the sun and curious onlookers. But up here on her quiet street in Laurel Canyon, she clearly felt at ease.

Valerie smiled and cooed at her dog, who tried to rush ahead of her in ecstatic glee. Brody noticed her wince with pain as she moved, though she held her head high in defiance of what ailed her. It was obvious she had no intention of letting the world know she was dying. He had to admire her for that.

He saw his opportunity and retreated a ways up the driveway of a nearby house. When she was about to pass by, he walked down the driveway and pretended to head for a shiny new Mercedes Benz parked on the street. They met eyes and he smiled, then faked a look of polite surprise.

"Hey, aren't you Valerie Ryan?"

Valerie shook back her hair and eyed him up and down, a smile curving her lips. "The one and only, darling."

"Wow, I didn't know you lived on this street. I'm a big fan."

"Thank you." She scooped her dog up into her arms and beamed. "I'm not touring this year but I may do some shows next year. I'll be sure to get you a front row ticket."

Brody's brows rose. "That'd be awesome! Hey, speaking of shows, I saw your daughter perform last night at The L.A. Rock Lounge. She was great."

Valerie's smile fell. "Excuse me?"

"Your daughter. Well, she was using her alias but we all know it's her." He gauged the confused expression on her face and realized she had no clue what he was talking about. He didn't have time to dwell on why Sadie hadn't told her mother about Piper Gray and instead changed tactics. "I take it you didn't make it to the show?"

"No," Valerie replied, anger tightening her brow. Her voice noticeably hardened. "My daughter and I aren't exactly close. What is this alias she's using?"

"Piper Gray. You can look it up. She's very good. Really takes after you."

"You're sure we're talking about my Sadie?" Valerie asked, setting her dog down when he began to growl. He sensed her mood shift and cowered behind her legs, teeth bared at Brody.

He tucked his hands into his pockets, wondering if tiny Pomeranian teeth could pierce skin. "Positive."

"I can't believe this." Her hands began to shake as she turned to leave, distracted by this new information.

Brody wasn't letting her get away that easily. "Hey, Valerie?"

She turned to look at him, her dog circling her legs in a hyper little dance. "Yes?"

"Who shot Lee Walker?"

Her eyes widened, then turned to slits. She sneered and launched herself at him, jabbing a finger into his chest. "Who the hell are you? A reporter? Who do you work for?"

"Nobody." He held his hands up in a show of peace, laughing. "Just thought I'd ask. It's a valid question, don't you think? You were a witness that night."

"I didn't see anything. Now leave me alone." Angry tears fell down her cheeks as she turned and stalked away, yanking on her dog's leash. Within seconds she was gone, and Brody was left with a lot less than he'd hoped for.

"Well, shit." He ran a hand through his hair and walked to his car, running through the conversation in his head. Why the hell hadn't Sadie told her mother about her alias? He'd just assumed she had. It wasn't really something that was easy to hide from family and friends. Then again, she wasn't really close with her parents. It made sense that she would keep this from them if the reason she'd created Piper Gray in the first place was to erase her connection to them.

Great. Why hadn't he thought of that before? He climbed into his car and let his head fall back against the seat, pissed at himself. He'd hoped to use Sadie's performance as a way to segue into the Lee Walker mystery, but all he'd done was piss off Valerie and probably make trouble for Sadie. Who knew what Valerie would do now. Knowing her, it'd be something drastic and full of drama.

And as far as his investigation into what happened to Lee Walker, Valerie was now officially a dead end. If he tried to confront her again she'd probably tear his face off. If he hadn't screwed up so royally, he might have been able to butter her up enough to enlighten him as to what she knew. She was a notorious gossip and he knew how to play on that. But now the opportunity was long gone. He'd have to find another way to get to the bottom of what happened.

Which meant he definitely needed to talk to Sadie again. She was the key, he was sure of it.

His cell phone rang. When he saw it was Chase, he considered ignoring it but gave in.

"What's up, buddy?"

"*It's Abby. I had to take her to the hospital. Something's wrong.*" Chase's voice was clipped and distraught. "*She's in surgery. I don't know what to do. They won't tell me anything.*"

A bolt of fear shot through Brody. He shoved it aside and started his car. "I'm on my way."

HE SAT beside his brother in the waiting room at the hospital. He felt numb, like the world around him was some surreal plotline in a movie. This couldn't be happening, could it? The last time he'd felt this way was the day his life should have ended in Afghanistan.

Chase rested his elbows on his knees, his face buried in his hands. Brody glanced down at him, seeing his brother helpless for the first time in his life. Despite being younger, Chase had always been the stronger of the two. He'd always known the solution to every problem and the upside to every catastrophe. Now he just seemed broken. The fear had taken over and rendered him useless.

Brody patted his brother on the back, his heart heavy with emotion. It was up to him to be strong now for Chase, he realized. Chase had always supported him and been there for him even when he'd been a total asshole in return. The least he could do was try and help now.

The clock on the wall told him it'd been over an hour since he arrived. He stared around the neutral toned waiting room with its comfortable chairs and big screen televisions mounted to the walls, wishing for some scrap of news. Some sign that his brother's wife was going to be okay. That the baby would survive. If he didn't find out soon, he'd hunt down the doctors and demand answers.

Unable to sit still any longer, he jumped to his feet and began to pace. His brother looked up at him, a weary smile on his face.

"Thanks for being here. I know it's boring—"

"I wouldn't be anywhere else," Brody interrupted, facing his brother. They met eyes and he damned himself to hell for all the times he'd taken Chase for granted. He was the only brother he'd ever have. "You married a fighter, Chase. She'll pull through this. And no blood of ours is gonna go out without a fight."

"Fighting Irish, right?" Chase chuckled, easing back in his chair. He rubbed his face and let out a sigh. "I just hate waiting and not knowing."

"Want me to go bust down some doors?" Brody offered, already primed to go. He was itching to have some choice words with the nurses anyway for the lack of fresh coffee.

"No. Abby's in good hands."

Brody bit back a snide reply, knowing it wouldn't help. He didn't trust hospitals or doctors. Never had, never would. "Yeah. She'll be fine."

Chase nodded, staring down at his tightly fisted hands. Brody figured he was trying his best to keep them from shaking with anxiety. Seeing it had anger bubbling over in his system.

"All right. That's it. I'm going out there." Brody spun on his heel and started for the door, only to be stopped by the appearance of the doctor.

She smiled politely, then looked past him to Chase. "Mr. Odell? Can I have a moment?"

Chase leapt to his feet and was at Brody's side in seconds. "How is she?"

"The c-section went well, both mom and baby are fine and healthy."

"Thank God." Chase went weak in the knees and had to support himself against Brody. Brody simply wrapped his arm over his brother's shoulders and grinned.

"Good work, Doc. When can he see them?"

"Follow me." She motioned for the door and led the way out into the hall. Brody let Chase go ahead, prepared to wait until his brother had his turn.

Chase whirled around when Brody didn't follow. "Aren't you coming?"

"Go have your time with Abby and the kid. I don't want to get in the way."

"You're my brother. You never get in the way," Chase argued, grabbing Brody's arm and pulling him down the hall.

"All right. But your wife's going to kick me out."

Chase ignored his words as they neared Abby's room. The doctor opened the door slowly, then looked back at Chase. "She's still a little out of it. But visit with her and then you can see baby Charlotte in the nursery."

"Okay." Chase stepped into the room and went immediately to his wife. Brody watched from the doorway as his brother sat in a chair beside the bed and held her hand. She stirred, a smile lighting her face when she saw him.

"She's so beautiful," Abby murmured, tears in her eyes.

Chase caressed her forehead. "I haven't seen her yet. I wanted to see how you're doing."

"Fine." Her eyes drifted over his shoulder and fell on Brody. "Hey. I can't believe you came."

Brody shifted his weight and leaned against the doorframe, arms crossed. "There's no place I'd rather be."

She snorted, though her expression was kind. "I'm glad you're here. You're an uncle now."

Brody's eyebrows rose. "Well, damn. I guess I am, huh?"

Chase kissed his wife then got to his feet. "I'll be back. It's time to meet my daughter."

He grabbed Brody and the two of them left for the nursery, which was down the hall and on the right. There were wide windows flanking the doors, showcasing a dozen tiny bassinets with infants sleeping in them. Brody felt more than a little out of his element as Chase entered the room, approaching the doctor who stood by one of the bassinets.

"Here she is," the doctor said, motioning to the tiny, pink-skinned baby currently staring wide-eyed at Chase and shaking her fists.

Brody watched his brother interact with his daughter for the first time, stunned by the rush of envy he felt. It was only natural, he supposed, to be drawn to the idea of being a father. Certainly nothing he was ready to embrace just yet, though.

Before he could step in and see the baby, he heard footsteps behind him. He turned and saw his parents enter the nursery, their concerned looks turning to surprise at the sight of him.

"Brody?" His mother asked, looking dazed and unaffected by the drama they'd been enduring the last few hours. She reached for his hands, focusing her eyes on him. "What are you doing here?"

Brody sighed. "Why is everyone so surprised by that?"

"Because it is surprising," his father answered, pushing past Brody so he could see Chase. Brody ignored the comment, not willing to let his father ruin his good mood.

"You boys were both born here," his mother said wistfully, staring around the room. "Feels just like yesterday."

"I'm sure it does, Mom." Brody wrapped his arm over her shoulders protectively, pressing a kiss to the top of her head. He shot a look at his father, who was busy inspecting his first grandchild like she was one of his depositions.

Chase glanced over and smiled at him. Brody nodded, pleased that everything had turned out okay. He was grateful he could be there for his brother at least this once. Maybe it didn't make up for everything, but it was a start.

An hour later, his parents left. Brody returned to Abby's room with a cup of coffee for Chase. Abby was fast asleep, still recuperating from the surgery.

Chase accepted the drink and quietly thanked him.

Brody nodded. "If you don't need me for anything else, I can take off. You probably want to get some rest or something."

Chase sipped his coffee, exhaling in relief at the dose of caffeine. "Actually, I'd rather not be alone. Can you stay for a little while longer? Until Abby's awake?"

Brody couldn't ignore the hopeful tone in his brother's voice. He took a seat on a nearby chair. "Like I said before. There's no place else I'd rather be."

Chapter *thirteen*

SUMMER AIR breezed in from the open window, bringing the scent of freshly cut grass and jasmine. Sadie breathed it in as her fingers trailed over the keys of her father's piano, enchanted by the sunny view outside of Los Angeles.

Her father's old music room was more spacious and well-lit than her own back home in Lake Tahoe. And much like she'd felt while playing her mother's piano, she sensed so much of his emotions here. His music had always run deep, such a contrast to the cool persona he reflected on the outside. Also like her mother, he was such a mystery to her. Who was the man behind the mask he wore, the man who poured his soul into music that made him a legend? She wondered if she would ever truly know.

She practiced a new song she was working on, even though she had no idea if she'd perform again or not. Even if she didn't, she still had her YouTube channel. This would make a nice, light-hearted addition to her collection of music, something bright and summery just in time for the season.

She smiled to herself as her thoughts shifted to Brody. It'd been less than a day since their lunch date and she couldn't stop thinking about him. Not for lack of trying, though. She'd done all she could

to distract herself. Grocery shopping, a long jog around the neighborhood, a pathetic attempt at baking brownies that turned out
burnt and crispy. All of it failed miserably so she'd done the only
thing she knew she wouldn't suck at—she sat down at the piano
and wrote music.

And oh, how the music flowed. Despite everything with her
mother, she felt so alive. So *inspired*. For the first time in so long, the
music within her came from a place that wasn't dark and damaged. It
came from a place of joy.

She was back in L.A., bright and shiny and scary as it was. She'd
performed for an audience that adored her. She reunited with an old
friend who made her laugh and brought back memories of what life
was like before *it* happened.

Her mother was still dying, but that was completely out of her
control. Everything else brought a tiny glimmer of hope to her heart
that did wonders for her mood.

She heard the front door slam shut and smiled. "I'm in here, Tess!"

Moments later her friend came into the room, out of breath and
harried. Sadie looked at her, confused. "Is everything okay?"

Tess's mouth fell open, no words following. She shook her head
and leaned against the door frame, as if struggling to get her bearings.
"Honey, don't panic, but I have some bad news."

"My mom?" Sadie asked, rising to her feet in alarm. She was
already halfway to the door before Tess stopped her.

"No, it's not that," Tess replied. Her hands dove into her hair, then
fell to her sides. "Not really, anyway."

"So what, then?"

Tess sighed. "Someone told the press that you're Piper Gray."

Sadie paled, her knees giving out. She sat back down on the piano
bench and fought to control her breathing. "Oh, God."

Tess rushed to sit by her side and rubbed her back. "I know. I'm
so sorry. It gets worse."

"How could it get worse?" Sadie asked, meeting her friend's eyes
in desperation.

"Everyone knows Valerie's dying."

Sadie sucked in a breath, stunned. No, it couldn't be. Did he?

Tears formed in her eyes as she buried her face in her hands, unable to stop the anger from rushing through her. There was only one person who knew about Valerie other than Tess and the band. One person who she'd just told the day before...

"This is all my fault," she whispered, mortified. Betrayed.

Tess held her close. "It's going to be okay, honey. We'll figure it out."

"No." Sadie rose to her feet and began to pace the room, unable to face her friend. Her hands began to shake. "No, it won't be. It's all over. I can't perform anymore. I have to take down my videos, stop singing. My parents will find out. God, they're going to kill me. I shouldn't have told—"

She froze, the name on the tip of her tongue. Guilt and shame prevented her from uttering it, even though the truth tore her to pieces inside. How could he? Damnit, she'd trusted him...

Tess stood and grabbed her shoulders, forcing their eyes to meet. "Sadie, what did you do?"

"I had lunch with Brody yesterday. I told him everything."

Tess closed her eyes, her hands falling back to her sides. She turned away and sat down on the piano bench. "Well, that explains it, then."

"He said he wouldn't say anything. I believed him," Sadie stammered.

"Yeah, well, I told you he was trouble, didn't I?" Tess snapped.

When Sadie only turned away, Tess let out a huff of breath and went to her. "I'm sorry, honey. I'm just so angry for you. But hey, lesson learned, right? Now you know and we can move past this. Everything's going to be okay."

Sadie nodded. "Yeah. You're right."

"I know I am." Tess pulled her in for a tight hug, then released her. "Why don't I go get us some man-bashing wine and we can drink to his early death?"

Sadie managed a weak smile. "Okay. I'll just go lie down..."

"You do that. I'll be right back."

Sadie watched Tess leave, all her earlier optimism shattered. She went to the window and shut it, drawing the blinds closed and closeting the room in darkness. There was no place left for light now. She couldn't stand it.

"I'M SORRY I didn't tell you," Sadie said with a sigh. She lay curled up in bed, her cell phone to her ear and the man who might as well have been her father on the other line.

"*I'm just shocked, kiddo. I mean, this is a big deal,*" Tommy told her, kindness in his voice. "*I watched all your videos. They're incredible.*"

Sadie smiled sadly, wiping a tear from her cheek. "Thanks. God, I feel so stupid."

"*Why? You have real talent. You should be proud.*"

"I'm stupid for thinking I could remain Piper Gray forever. Eventually it was going to fall apart. Maybe if I'd stayed in Tahoe—"

"*You know I'm not a fan of the what-ifs, Sadie-bug. You did what you did and that's the end of it. Make this work for you. If you haven't been watching the news, this story is huge. People are really excited.*"

"I'm sure he got a nice big paycheck, then," Sadie blurted out bitterly, only to wince at her own carelessness. Tommy grew quiet for a second.

"*He? I thought you didn't know who leaked it.*"

"I have a pretty good idea." She sighed again, hating herself. "Brody Odell."

"*Oh. Well, that makes sense. What'd he hide in the bushes and catch you talking about it or something?*"

"No, I knew him in school. You wouldn't remember that…" Sadie explained. She rolled onto her back and closed her eyes. "When I performed the other night at The L.A. Rock Lounge, he was there. He recognized me. So we had lunch and I kind of spilled the beans. It's my fault."

"*It'll be okay. Everyone in the family knows and we're all rooting for you, kid.*"

"Everyone?" Sadie asked, thinking of her parents.

"*I haven't heard from Val, but Ben's excited about it.*"

Sadie chuckled. "Liar."

"*What?*"

"Stop trying to protect me from him. He probably just shrugged it off like everything else that involves me."

"*Maybe he did. But I caught a hint of excitement on his face, I promise.*"

"Sure. Whatever, what does it matter now, anyway? The secret's out. I'm exposed. Piper Gray is no more."

"*But Sadie McRae has one hell of a future,*" Tommy said proudly. "*I mean it.*"

"Thanks, Tommy." Sadie smiled, feeling a little better. "I'm gonna go drown in a bottle of wine. I'll talk to you later."

"*Okay. Love you, kid.*"

"Love you too." She hung up and climbed out of bed, wandering into the living room. She spotted Tess pacing the kitchen, arguing with someone on the phone. Before she had a chance to listen in, Tess hung up and tossed the phone aside.

"Bastards," Tess muttered. When she spotted Sadie, she sighed.

"What now?" Sadie asked.

"I got a hold of the original tabloid who published the story. I tried to tell them it wasn't true and that they need to rescind it, but they say their source is very reliable. They won't pull it."

"They trust Brody." Sadie shrugged, feeling bitter. "They have no reason to doubt what he tells them."

"I guess. But for them to ignore our denial flat-out seems fishy to me." Tess shook her head and reached for a bottle of Cabernet sitting on the counter. "Anyway, it's done. I did get a call from Leon, though. He said he'll give you his first born son if you perform your first Sadie McRae show at his place."

Sadie managed a weak laugh and rolled her eyes. "Yeah, right. There won't be any more shows."

Tess busied herself uncorking the wine. "You sure? Don't lie to me and say you didn't get a kick out of performing the other night."

"I did…" Sadie began, resting her hip against the kitchen counter. She crossed her arms and chewed on her lower lip. "I don't want the fame, Tess. The very thought of it terrifies me. I just want to make music and still have my private life."

"I know, honey. But you can't have everything. There's got to be some give and take," Tess reasoned, grabbing two glasses and pouring the wine. She handed one to Sadie with a smile. "Look, I know this all still new and scary for you. Just take it one day at a time, okay? No one's forcing you to decide your whole future right now."

Sadie stared at her glass of wine, swirling the red liquid around in the glass. "The future I wanted is no longer possible. Thanks to Brody."

"He's a man. Men are assholes." Tess clicked her glass against Sadie's and took a long drink. She then set it down and poured more wine into it. "He's only looking out for himself. That's what assholes do."

Anger swelled inside of Sadie. "I should have known better, but I let my old feelings for him get in the way."

"He's not the same person he was."

Sadie nodded, then took a sip of her wine. "I see that now. He doesn't care about me. Everything we once had is gone."

"I'm sorry, honey." Tess tried to touch her, but Sadie pulled away.

"I need some time alone. Give me an hour?"

"Sure. Why don't you go take a nice hot bath and I'll make dinner?" Tess suggested. "Then we'll put on *Kill Bill* and watch men get their asses kicked."

"Stupid men. I hate them." Sadie poured more wine into her glass and met her friend's eyes. "Next time I start to fall for one, punch me in the face, okay?"

Tess smiled and raised her glass in a toast. "Will do."

Chapter *fourteen*

BRODY SQUINTED at the screen of his laptop, reading through one of the witness testimonies from the night Sadie was attacked. It read like a murder mystery novel. The witness, one-time singer and occasional porn star Shelly Harlow, had the imagination of a ten-year-old. Either that, or she was high as a kite at the time of the interview.

She claimed she remembered Tommy talking to Sadie at the foot of the stairs, right before Tommy walked past Shelly and gave her ass an affectionate squeeze. She didn't mind, of course. He was rock royalty. She then saw Lee Walker come out of the chaos of the party like a big black bat, covered head to toe in his trademark color and as brooding as ever. According to Shelly, no one understood why Georgina wasted her time on him. He was a creep. Then he flew up the stairs and disappeared, but no one thought anything of it. Except for, according to Shelly, Tommy Barnes. She claimed she saw Tommy eyeing Lee with disgust, and that he said something to someone else nearby that to Shelly sounded like, "That fucker's up to no good."

The valuable part of Shelly's testimony ended there. The rest was less useful than the babbling of a toddler. But he'd gathered one curious bit of information from her, something he was sure the police must have looked into. Had Tommy Barnes seen Walker follow Sadie? And if so, had he gone after him?

It was widely known that Tommy was the one who found Sadie *after* the gunshot was fired, but was it possible he fired the gun himself? The police reports claimed there was no evidence of gunshot residue on either Tommy or Valerie, but cops could be bribed and these *were* rock stars, after all. Was he looking at a possible cover-up?

Brody let out a rush of breath, feeling a headache coming on. God, this was more convoluted than he ever could have imagined. What the hell would be the reason for a cover-up, if there even was one? He found it hard to believe that Tommy Barnes wasn't involved in some way. Either he saw something—or did something—that he planned to take to the grave.

Well, he wasn't going to let that happen. Sadie deserved the truth, and he wanted to get it for her.

Thinking of her, his eyes fell from the screen to a printout of her school picture. Beside it lay a couple of photographs he'd found in storage, taken one time when they were goofing off at school. In one, his arm rested casually over her shoulders, his eyebrow cocked in a devious grin with sunglasses hiding his eyes. She held the camera pointed down at them, angled so the sunlight glowed over their hair like halos. Her smile was big and delighted, her green eyes bright with humor. She looked happier than he'd ever seen her. In the next photograph, she was overcome with laughter at something he'd said, and he was acting cool as though nothing in the world could touch him. He stared at his old self, missing the days when school was a sanctuary away from his parents, if only because Sadie was there.

He graduated that year, but not before facing six months of not knowing where she'd gone or if she'd be coming back. Six months of nothing but reporters gossiping over what happened to her, when he had no way of knowing if any of it was true. She was swept away and protected, which he knew now was what saved her. But back then all he'd wondered was if he would ever see her again.

Eventually it hadn't mattered, he realized sadly. He moved on to college, then dove into the high life sponsored by his career as a photojournalist and never looked back. She became a distant memory, one he'd occasionally think of if an Albatross song came on the radio, only to fade away once again.

Things were different now. She was back, and whether it was fate or luck or just coincidence, he was ready to seize the opportunity to help her.

On impulse, he reached for his phone and the little scrap of paper she'd given him at lunch the day before. He dialed the number, then sat back and waited impatiently.

It rang five times and before he could decide if he should leave a voicemail, she answered.

"*Hello?*"

"Glad to see you didn't give me a fake number," he joked.

She was quiet for a moment, long enough that he checked his phone screen to see if she'd hung up. "*Who is this?*"

His brows knit together. "It's Brody. What, did you give your number to another guy besides me yesterday?" He heard her breath quicken and concern hit him square in the chest. "You okay?"

"*Why are you calling me?*" she snapped.

Honestly taken aback, he laughed. "Traditionally, when a phone number is given it's expected that the receiver will call."

"*Didn't you pump enough information out of me yesterday? What the hell else do you want?*"

The first hot flare of anger spiked in his system. "Okay, hold up. What exactly did I do to piss you off? I thought we left on good terms."

"*Do you think I'm an idiot? I saw the headlines, Brody. Did you think I wouldn't find out that you sold my story?*"

"What headlines?" He braced the phone against his shoulder and quickly dove into his laptop, bringing up Google. It only took three seconds for him to see what she was referring to. "Oh, shit."

"*Yeah, shit. Don't ever call me again.*"

She hung up before he could respond, and though he tried to call her again he knew she wouldn't answer. Why the hell would she? She had every right to be pissed off.

And so did he. He hated being falsely accused of something he didn't do, especially something like this. After catching up on the story the press had leaked, he realized why Sadie had come to the conclusion that he was guilty. It was exactly what she'd told him at lunch; that her mother was dying of cancer and that she was Piper Gray. Combine that coincidence with his unsavory reputation as a soulless paparazzi, and he knew he couldn't blame her for being upset. But, damnit, he was innocent.

Now he just needed to prove it to her. It wasn't going to be easy, especially if she continued to ignore his phone calls. Somehow he needed to find a way to get her the truth that her own mother was enough of a publicity whore to expose her.

Valerie Ryan was scorned, and this was undoubtedly her disgusting attempt at retribution.

SADIE TOSSED her phone aside and slipped beneath the frothy water of her bath, wanting nothing more than to drown out her own anger. She failed miserably.

How dare he call her after what he did? And to act as if he'd done nothing wrong on top of it. Did he really think she was that stupid? That she wouldn't realize it was him who went to the press? It was all so predictable, after all. He was a paparazzi, of course he would want to exploit her secrets. Clearly the friendship they once had meant less to him than the money he'd get for her story.

Realizing that, understanding it, broke her heart. She came up for air, the tears in her eyes blending with the water that spilled down her face. Her lungs filled gratefully with air and it took all she had to combat the sob that hovered there, ready to unleash the pain. Anger was an easier emotion to deal with, she knew. Crying sucked and she refused to let herself shed any tears for him. He wasn't worth it.

But when the image of his face flew into her mind, she lost some of her resolve. The truth was, the betrayal stung worse than the act itself. She didn't even really care that the press knew about her mother, or about her alias. It bothered her more that Brody could do this to her. That he would forfeit everything between them for money.

He'd put on quite the act, though. Pretending he had no idea what she was talking about. She might have believed him if she wasn't so pissed off. Then again, she wouldn't be played for a fool. Not by him, and not by anyone. The press could have their field day with the information they already knew, but she would not be giving them anything more.

With the water going cold, she rose from the tub, toweled off, and slipped into a sapphire blue robe. The silky material was cool over her skin and smelled comfortingly like pine needles and wood smoke. Like home. Lake Tahoe seemed a million miles away—some far off place that might as well be a dream. Every day that passed it grew dimmer in her memory as the city hardened her heart to stone.

She wandered out of the bathroom and into the music room. She needed to vent, to release her frustrations until she was too exhausted to move. Music was the only answer, the only cure for the misery she felt.

Sitting down on the piano bench, she placed her fingers over the keys and took a deep, soothing breath.

Now. She launched into a fast, furious song that took all of her skill to play, losing herself in the sound it made. Her fingers were rough over the keys, slamming them into place and inciting sharp, crisp notes. She tossed her head back and let it take over, let it drive her to a place where nothing existed and nothing mattered. There was no tomorrow, no yesterday. Nothing for her to face in the morning when the sun came up. There was only the sound of the music and the feel of her hands as she made it come alive.

She played until her fingers were raw, until she could barely move her hands. Her eyes closed as she fought to catch her breath, thrilled the way an athlete is after a good run. She fed off the feeling until she could hold back those dark thoughts no more. They filtered in, slowly but surely, only this time she saw them with clarity. She'd beaten out the worst of the anger and sorrow, and in its place was nothing but reality.

Damage had been done by coming back to L.A. She knew that now. In the morning she would need to face her mother and somehow explain how she'd kept such a terrible secret from her. A secret that should have been shared with delight and a shared passion for music.

Instead, she'd assumed her mother would disapprove. She still believed that. Valerie Ryan, being the vivacious celebrity that she was, would never understand the need for an alias. She thrived under the limelight. How could she fathom the idea that Sadie wanted no part of it?

And who knew what her reaction would be to the news that her own secret was now out. The world knew she was dying. Their beloved Valerie, the Goddess of Albatross, would likely never grace the stage again. Could she accept their pity at the realization that she was no longer young and radiant? That cancer was killing her beauty and ripping the life from her body with each day that passed?

No. Sadie knew the answer without even finishing the thought. Her mother would likely enjoy the attention from the press for awhile before retreating into depression over her situation. Some days she'd be joyful, other days it would be like the world was falling apart. That was just how Valerie was.

There was a soft knock on the door before Tess entered. She eyed Sadie hesitantly. "Hey. You hungry?"

Sadie nodded, massaging her hands as she got to her feet. "Hungry for more wine, if that's what you mean."

"Did you get a call earlier? I thought I heard you yelling."

"Brody called," Sadie replied, gritting her teeth. "He acted like nothing happened. I, in so many words, told him to fuck off."

"Good girl." Tess wrapped an arm over her shoulders and led the way out to the kitchen. "Let's get you that wine and my mom's famous spaghetti. Then for dessert we have chocolate cheesecake."

"Did I mention I love you?" Sadie smiled, hugging Tess's waist.

"Once or twice." Tess poured wine into two glasses and nudged one to Sadie. "You know, if you want to go home no one will blame you. Just throwing it out there."

Sadie stopped mid-sip, blinking in surprise. "What do you mean?"

"I mean if you don't want to deal with this shit—Brody and your mother and the press and all that—no one will blame you for going back home to Tahoe. I'll miss you, of course, but I don't want you to put yourself through hell just because you feel like you have to help the woman who calls herself your mother but never really stepped into the shoes."

Sadie considered her friend's words, taking a thoughtful sip of her wine. "You know, my first instinct is to run. Which is exactly why I won't be leaving."

"Okay…why not?"

"Because it's occurred to me that I didn't just come here for my mother," Sadie began, shaking her head. "I want to help her, but what I really want is to face this demon I've lived with for eleven years. I need to prove to myself that I can live without the fear. Does that make sense?"

Tess smiled and lifted her wine glass in a toast. "All the sense in the world, honey."

Sadie raised her glass as well, releasing a nervous breath. "Okay, good. Because I think I might be a little out of it right now and I'll probably feel like running away in the morning, so you need to promise you won't let me escape."

"I'll tie you to the bed if I have to," Tess promised with a laugh. Her expression softened as she regarded Sadie with pride. "I think I'm starting to rub off on you."

Sadie's brows rose as she knocked back the rest of her wine. She held out the glass for another pour. "Lucky me."

Chapter *fifteen*

BRODY FOUND himself parked across the street from Valerie's house again, this time fuming with anger. A sleepless night and four cups of coffee meant his mood was cagey and mean, and he looked forward to going head-to-head with the woman who used him as a patsy. Maybe she hadn't done it intentionally, but he wasn't happy about taking the fall for her.

Just like before, Valerie walked down her driveway and out the security gate, her white marshmallow of a dog skipping ahead of her. He didn't try for a diversion this time, he just threw open his car door and went straight for her.

She froze in place the instant she saw him. He watched her mouth open and close in a soundless attempt at words.

"Do you realize what you've done?" Brody spat, getting within mere inches of Valerie's face. Her dog growled and yapped, cowering behind his mistress's legs.

Valerie regained her composure. "I'm calling the police."

"Go ahead. I'll be gone by the time they get here. I just have to say my peace and then I'll go."

Valerie pulled out her cell phone but didn't dial, eyeing him warily. "All right."

"You went to the press with what I told you, about Sadie being Piper Gray."

A coy smile tightened Valerie's face. "So?"

"Wow. You really don't give a shit, do you?" His hands dove into his hair as he let out a bitter laugh. "You're ruining Sadie's life and you don't even care."

Valerie tilted her chin up. "She shouldn't be hiding behind a stage name. She's my daughter."

"The same daughter you let almost get brutally raped under your watch?" Brody shot back, getting in her face again. "The same daughter you lost custody of after they found drugs in your system? Don't think I didn't read all the police reports. I know you were using heavy that night, and probably for awhile beforehand. It's no secret you would rather get drunk and high than be a mother."

Valerie snarled and slapped him across the face. "How dare you?"

Brody winced at the blow but didn't falter. His teeth clenched in a sneer. "Tell me what part of what I said isn't true."

"I care about my daughter. She was stolen from me. I should have never let them take her," Valerie rambled, her hands shaking as emotions boiled over. "She should have been raised here, with me. Then I could have helped her with her music and she wouldn't be hiding in the shadows."

"You forgot one thing here, Val. You let Lee Walker into your house and into Sadie's bedroom. It's your fault she got hurt. Don't for one minute try and pretend that never happened, because it did. And when I find out who shot him, all of this is going to come out again and everyone's going to remember what a rotten bitch you are."

Valerie blanched, clutching her chest. Her lips trembled as she tried to form a response. "Excuse me?"

"You heard me. I'm breaking out the ol' reporter skills and digging into what happened that night. And you can bet I'll get to the bottom of it, because I don't give up when I want something. And right now, I want nothing more than to watch you burn for what you did to Sadie."

Valerie gaped at him, unable to speak. When Brody spotted Sadie's car approaching, a hard grin crossed his face.

"Good. Now we can tell her together." He turned back to Valerie, who was struggling to breathe. She doubled over in pain, and shock raced through him at the alarming thought that he'd given her a heart attack. "Hey. Hey now, you're okay."

He grabbed her arms to keep her from collapsing just as Sadie squealed to a stop and raced from the car.

"What's going on here?" she cried out, glaring at Brody for an instant before gathering her mother into her arms. "Are you okay? What's wrong?"

Valerie wheezed, tears spilling down her cheeks. The leash fell from her hand and her dog skittered back up the driveway and out of sight. She managed to meet Sadie's eyes and looked ready to faint. "I need to lie down."

"Okay. Let's go inside." Sadie supported her with one arm and shot a furious look at Brody. "Stay the hell away from my mother."

"Sadie, wait—"

Carla ran down the driveway, assessing the situation. Sadie pointed at Brody. "Call the police. He's harassing us."

Brody lifted both hands in a show of peace, resigned that he'd ruined his chance. "All right. I'll go. But we need to talk, Sadie. Please call me."

Sadie looked back at him once more, her face contorted with anger and misery. He couldn't get the image of it out of his mind as he sulked back to his car and drove away.

THE INSTANT Sadie lowered Valerie onto the sofa in her lushly decorated living room, she was bombarded with questions.

"When were you going to tell me about Piper Gray?" Valerie asked breathily, her voice thin but clipped with anger. She struggled to meet Sadie's eyes. "The whole family had *no* idea."

Sadie's lips formed a tight line as she rearranged pillows and helped her mother lay back with her feet up. Busying herself with the task at hand helped keep the emotions at bay.

Carla rushed in with a cold compress, which Sadie applied to Valerie's forehead. "Just calm down and rest."

"I can't." Valerie's chest heaved as she sucked in air, shaking her head. "I'm too distraught. That horrible man—"

"What did he say to you?" Sadie almost didn't want to know, but curiosity got the better of her.

Valerie sniffed. "He came here the other day asking questions about you. I refused to humor him, so he came back to harass me."

Sadie sighed. "He won't be coming around anymore. I promise."

Carla returned to the room with a tall glass of ice water, which she held up to Valerie's lips. "Drink this, Ms. Ryan."

Valerie did as she was told, then shoved the glass away disdainfully. "I'm fine. Don't fuss over me."

"Well, don't push yourself too hard just yet," Sadie advised, earning a cold laugh from her mother.

"I suppose you expect me to act like I'm dying now just because everybody knows the truth."

Sympathy washed over Sadie. "I'm sorry."

Valerie sat up and tossed aside the cold compress, regaining her wits. "Do you know how much it hurt to realize you kept that secret from me? I feel like such a fool talking to you about singing when you're already out there performing in my city, right under my nose."

Sadie sat down on the coffee table, unable to look at her mother. She was reduced to a child, unable to speak up and too afraid to fight back. "I didn't think—"

"No. You didn't think, you selfish creature," Valerie snapped, tossing back her hair. "You felt the need to go out and do this all on your own, behind my back, instead of utilizing my experience. I don't know if this is a late-blossoming teenage rebellion, but it ends now. I will be managing your music from now on, and that's that."

Anger flushed Sadie's face. Her eyes rose from her hands. "No."

Valerie waved away Sadie's refusal. "You need me, especially now that your gig is up. You can't be Piper Gray anymore."

"I don't need you," Sadie shot back. "Even if I do decide to continue singing, it'll be on my own terms."

She watched the emotions pass over her mother's features. "Well. I can tell you enjoy the thought of ripping my dream away from me. Here I am just trying to help you…"

Sadie tried not to let her mother's manipulation have an effect on her. "I'm not trying to hurt you—"

"But you did anyway." Valerie sniffled, tears brimming in her eyes. "And who knows how long you would've kept your little secret from me if it wasn't for that asshole reporter."

Sadie stared down at her hands again, unsure what to say. Until something her mother said set off warning signals in her brain. How could she know it was Brody who leaked the information? She looked up, her eyes searching Valerie's. "What are you talking about?"

Valerie bristled. "That man outside. How come he knew about your alias and I didn't?"

"Because I told him…" Sadie began, only to pause as everything clicked into place. "Wait, you went to the press, didn't you? Brody told you about me and you got upset and this was your revenge."

Valerie's chin lifted. "I wouldn't call it revenge. It was my way of helping you out of the closet, so to speak."

"God, I'm so stupid," Sadie breathed, mortified. She shot to her feet, her hands clenched into fists at her sides. "How could you do this to me?"

Surprise flashed over Valerie's face. "Do what? Give you the *exact* publicity you need to propel your career?"

Sadie's heart raced with a dozen different emotions. Most prevalent of which was the horror of knowing she'd blamed Brody for something he hadn't even done. "I can't do this right now. I have to go."

She fled from the room before her mother could respond, digging into her purse for her cell phone. As she hopped into her car, she hit redial on Brody's number and felt her heart tighten with anxiety.

"Answer. Please," she begged, starting the car and wrenching it into drive. She headed down her mother's driveway when Brody answered.

"*Sadie. It wasn't me. I swear to you, I—*"

"I know," she managed, her voice shaking with both anger and relief. "It didn't take long for me to get the truth out of her. I'm so sorry."

He sighed. "*It's okay. I would've blamed me, too.*"

She let out a half laugh as she took the road toward her father's home. "I know this sounds weird, but I really don't want to be alone right now. Can you come over?"

For a moment he didn't say anything and she wondered if she'd lost the call.

"*Sure. Just tell me where to go and I'll be there.*"

She gave him the address, then hung up and continued driving. A few minutes later she pulled into the driveway and parked, her heart still a wild mess within her chest.

Brody would make it better. He had to.

Climbing from the car with her purse, she raced inside and prepared herself for the big apology she owed her old friend.

Chapter *sixteen*

IT WASN'T often he found himself in the Hollywood Hills, but now he was about to make his fourth trek up the mountain that week. This time, he detoured down a different street that took him up to Ben McRae's Spanish-style rancher with million dollar views of the city.

Brody parked beside Sadie's car in the driveway, his eyes on that view. There was just a glimpse of it beyond the trees that flanked the house, but there it was. Hot and glittering like a jewel in the sun.

He trotted up to the front door and knocked, making sure to wipe the sweat from his hands on his jeans. The fact that he was nervous bothered him to no end. What did he have to be afraid of? This was Sadie. His Sadie. And she knew he wasn't at fault for outing her secret, so all was good. Now he just had to work at keeping their relationship on solid ground so he could get what he needed out of her—the truth that would set them both free.

When the door opened and she appeared before him, he blinked. If he'd expected hysterics from her, he was dead wrong. There was a hint of anger behind her eyes, but other than that she only looked tired.

"Hey," she greeted. She smiled awkwardly and pushed a strand of hair behind her ear, then stepped back to invite him in.

"Hi." He entered and took a quick look around, admiring her father's home. It lacked the personal touches of photographs and knick-knacks, but then again Ben spent most of his time in Boston with the family he chose over Sadie. Brody wondered how it felt for her to live in the home her father had abandoned, just like he had abandoned her. Maybe she didn't make that correlation at all.

"Would you like something to drink? I have water, juice…"

"Do you have beer?" Brody asked, turning to her with a grin. When she blushed, he felt his confidence come roaring back. She was just as nervous as he was and for some reason he enjoyed the hell out of it.

"Um, I might. Let me see if Tess bought any." She wandered into the kitchen, prompting him to follow. Instead he went past the kitchen and straight for the sliding glass doors, his eyes on the view outside.

He could hear her rummaging around in the fridge and glass clicking together. The snap and hiss of the bottles opening preceded the sound of her footsteps. She came up beside him and offered a bottle of Stella Artois. "Thanks. You have one hell of a view, McRae."

She let out a nervous laugh, her fingers clenched tightly around her own bottle. "Yeah. I like it."

He took a long swig of beer and faced her. "You doing okay?"

A rush of breath left her lungs as she shook her head. "I'm really sorry, Brody. I feel awful."

"There's nothing to be sorry about." He tapped his bottle to hers in an attempt to make her smile. "Like I said before, I would've blamed me too. I think it's the face. Everyone always thinks I'm up to no good. Of course, nine times out of ten, they're right."

Humor softened her features. "You're what we call a bad boy. It comes with the title."

"I suppose it does." He glanced around the room again, spotting the sofa and flat screen television. Soft, folksy music emitted from the speakers, reminiscent of quaint coffee houses in the city. "Nice place you got here."

She shrugged. "I couldn't bring myself to stay at my mother's. Too much history. And now, too much drama."

Now it was his turn to apologize. "You know, I didn't go to the press with your secret, Sadie, but I did tell Valerie. So this is still pretty much my fault."

Sadie nodded, toying with the wrapper on her beer bottle. "Yeah, she told me. There was no way you could've known that I hadn't told her yet, though."

"No, but I still talked to her behind your back. I'm sorry for that."

"Why did you go see her?" Sadie asked, realizing she hadn't thought about that. Her eyebrows furrowed as she looked up at him.

"I wanted to see if she'd tell me the truth about who shot Lee Walker."

Sadie flinched, panic a sharp jolt to her system. It was an instinctual reaction to hearing that name. "What? Why?"

Brody sipped more of his beer and continued calmly, figuring blunt honesty was more effective than lying to her. She wasn't stupid; she'd figure him out eventually. "When I saw you again, it reminded me of what happened to you and how it was never really figured out. I want to find the truth for you."

"And for yourself," she added, inching away from him. Distrust hardened her eyes. "So this *is* all just for a story."

"Yes and no." He ran a hand through his hair, hating to see her doubt him. "It's fifty percent me wanting to spend time with you, and fifty percent me wanting to find the truth so I can stick it to all the bastards who said I'd never be a journalist again. That's fair, right?"

She frowned, considering his explanation. She was too practical to not see his side of it, *if* he was telling the truth this time. And *if* he was being honest with her, then she'd be stupid to deny she wanted the truth about Lee Walker's death even more than he did. "I guess so."

"Look at me," he requested, resisting the urge to touch her. He didn't know what flames he might spark if he did. When she met his eyes, he smiled with as much sincerity as he could muster. "Lying sucks and I hate to do it. I don't want to lie to you. I want to keep seeing you because it makes me happy, and because I think we have a mutual interest. You can help me figure this out. Together we can get the truth, then you'll know and then maybe I can weasel my way back into respectable society. It's a win-win."

She pouted. "I hate it when you make sense. I should be pissed off at you."

He chuckled and set his beer aside on the counter, stuffing his hands into his pockets instead. In a move that was as casual as it was suggestive, he shifted closer to her until they were barely a foot apart. "You always had trouble staying mad at me."

Her head tilted back as she looked up at him, realizing in that instant just how close he was. The fresh scent of his soap and that grin of his sent her pulse skipping. "I still don't trust you."

"Fair enough. I'm willing to earn it." He nodded, pleased she wasn't angry. "So we cool?"

"For now." She pulled away from him, needing space. She knocked back the last of her drink and set aside the bottle. "More beer?"

"I don't turn down a free beer."

She grabbed two more from the fridge, then gestured for the sofa in the living room. "Want to watch a movie or something?"

"Sure." He followed her to the sofa, where she sat down and curled her legs beneath her. He settled in beside her. "So what's the plan now that Piper Gray is no more?"

"I don't know," Sadie admitted. "I guess I haven't really accepted it yet."

"You want my personal-and-only-slightly-biased opinion?"

Her lips curved. "Okay."

"I think this is the best thing that ever happened to you. Now you have no choice but to be yourself."

"You sound like Tommy and my brother," Sadie realized, laughing. "Always my beacons of positivity."

"I'm plenty cynical on most things," Brody replied. "But since you brought up Tommy Barnes, mind if I ask you an investigation-related question?"

Sadie's smile faded, but she nodded. "Just one for now."

"Did Tommy ever say he saw Walker follow you upstairs that night?"

Sadie's brow creased as she gave it some thought. "I don't think so...he told the police he went upstairs after he heard the gunshot."

"So nothing ever slipped out in conversation that would suggest otherwise?"

Sadie shook her head. "No. If you're thinking Tommy did it, I can tell you that's not true. The first thing I remember is him asking me if *I* had shot Walker. Why would he ask that if he had done it himself?"

"Really?" Brody's interest was piqued. "There was nothing about that in the reports I read."

"I never told anyone that." She sipped her beer, losing herself in the bad memories. "I wish I *had* been able to shoot him, though. Instead I was helpless."

"You were a kid."

She shot him a dark look. "I could've fought back more than I did. I let myself become a victim."

"No, the asshole that tried to rape you made you a victim," Brody affirmed, anger coursing through him. Not at her, but at the fact that even dead, Lee Walker was causing her grief. "You don't really blame yourself, do you?"

She sighed. "No, I don't. I just wish I had done more. Then maybe I could've gotten help and no one would have shot him and this whole thing could've been avoided."

"I'm sorry, but it didn't play out that way." He reached for her hand, knowing exactly how she felt. "You think I don't relive what happened in Afghanistan in my head every single day, wishing I had made a different choice?"

Tears filled her eyes but didn't fall. She nodded.

He continued. "We can't control what happens to us, Sadie. But we can control how we deal with it."

"You're right." She turned her palm up so she could lock her fingers with his. Their eyes met and she attempted a smile. "Thank you."

He realized she was a hell of a lot tougher than he'd given her credit for. She had moments of fear that made her feel weak, but at the core of it, she was the strongest person he knew. "Not to quote Tommy again, but stay positive. You deserve a happy life."

She squeezed his hand. "So do you."

"Me? I gave up Heaven for Hell a long time ago." His teeth flashed in a wicked grin that made her chuckle.

"I don't believe that."

"Ask my poor brother," he mused. "He's gotten nothing but a hard time from me."

"I'm sure Chase still loves you."

"For some reason, I think he still does." He stared down at their joined hands, wondering why he hadn't thought to let go yet. "He made me an uncle the other day."

One of Sadie's brows lifted. "Uncle Brody. That makes me feel old."

"Tell me about it."

She smiled before grabbing the television remote from the coffee table. "So, what do you want to watch?"

"Surprise me." He sipped his beer with his free hand, enjoying the flash of humor that brightened her face.

"Cheesy girlie rom-com it is."

AT SOME point during the movie, his arm had made its way around her and her head had come to rest comfortably on his shoulder. As the credits rolled, he could feel her breathing softly against him, fast asleep. A slow grin spread over his face as he looked down at her, taking in the view. One of her hands rested on his knee, like it belonged there.

It amazed him how quickly they'd fallen back into the old way of things. She'd accepted him back into her life with more faith than he deserved, but there he was. Cuddling with her on the couch in her father's home, acting like the last eleven years had never happened. They'd only been friends before, but sitting there with her now made him hunger for something else. Something considerably more risky.

The thought should have alarmed him, but somehow it didn't. It felt more natural than anything in the world. That alone was enough to have him wondering if he was getting in too deep, and too quickly. Falling for her wasn't part of the plan. She deserved so much better than a disgraced journalist turned paparazzi who spent the majority of his time making celebrities like her into nothing more than trashy headlines. He'd never been ashamed of his job before, but diving back into Sadie's life and seeing the view from her side troubled him.

He couldn't deny he had this insane urge to protect her. She brought that out in people. Tess, Tommy, her brother. Everyone treated her like some fragile doll on the verge of shattering into a million pieces, and as a result she viewed herself in that same light. But underneath that porcelain was rock harder than should have been possible. She wouldn't break. She might fracture in places when she fell, but there was glue keeping her together. Glue that she'd established up north, away from the bloodlust of the city.

Away from greedy reporters and parents who used her more than loved her.

He trailed his hand down the side of her arm, rousing her. Her eyes blinked sleepily awake, angling up to meet his own. The sweet smile that spread over her face had him itching to kiss her, instantly desperate for a taste of all that honeyed warmth.

"Did I fall asleep?" she asked, her words barely more than a husky whisper. She sat up and stretched her arms, not seeming to mind the fact that she'd fallen asleep in his.

"Out like a light," he mused. "You missed the ending. The fluffy white dog turned everyone into zombies and then they all did a flash mob of 'Thriller.'"

Her face contorted with confusion. "Ryan Reynolds became a zombie?"

"Yep. He chewed off Sandra Bullock's face."

"Shut up." She smacked his leg and laughed. "You're messing with me."

"Hey, I'm the one who watched the movie. You passed out after two beers. Lightweight." He winked at her and got to his feet. He gathered up their beer bottles, taking them into the kitchen. When he came back into the room, she was still seated on the sofa, eyeing him strangely.

"Brody?"

He stuffed his hands into his pockets. "Sadie?"

"I was going to offer you another drink, but you look like you're ready to go."

"Yeah, I should head out."

She nodded, rising from the sofa to meet him at the front door. Her hand fell on the knob and she turned her face up to his. "If you call me again, I promise not to yell at you like last time."

"Good to know." He stared into her eyes, wondering what she was thinking. Did she feel, as he did, that somehow simultaneously so much and yet so little between them had changed?

"Well, goodnight." She opened the door, standing back so he could leave.

He smiled. "I'll see ya around, McRae."

"Okay."

He felt her eyes on him as he left and climbed into his car. When he turned on the engine and looked back to her door, she had disappeared inside.

"Great," he grumbled, backing down the driveway and onto the street. He flipped on the radio and rolled down his windows, needing fresh air to cool the fire in his blood. He didn't like complications any more than he liked refusing what felt natural. Unfortunately, Sadie was turning out to be an ironic mix of both.

Chapter *seventeen*

TWO DAYS had passed since Sadie last spoke to her mother. Two days of avoiding the news, the radio, the internet. She didn't want to hear what everyone was saying about her. Instead, she shut herself in her father's home and did nothing but work on her music.

Isaac and Tommy had both checked in on her, but she'd kept the conversations brief and impassive. The last thing she needed was to be reminded that things outside were no longer the same for her. Everything would be different from now on.

She took a break from practicing a new song, realizing she hadn't eaten all day. It was past noon and her stomach was ready to revolt. Caffeine in the form of coffee and the occasional soda were all she'd been running on for nearly twenty-four hours, making her a jittery mess. If she didn't eat soon, she wouldn't have the strength to continue working. And right now, the music was all that was keeping her sane.

She threw together a turkey sandwich and brought it out to the patio to eat. The weather was a favorable seventy-five degrees, with a light breeze coming in from the sea. Settling into one of the patio chairs, she bit into her sandwich and sighed.

Brody hadn't called her. She didn't know why she cared. It wasn't like she didn't have enough to occupy her mind without him hound-ing her with questions about Lee Walker. But she'd gotten that oh-so-typical female fear of rejection that came when a guy didn't bother to call after a date.

Not that what they'd had was a date, she reminded herself. They were barely even friends again much less dating. It would take time for her to fully trust him, and even more time for her to figure out these insane feelings stirring within her just at the thought of him.

She frowned as she chewed, hating herself for feeling so much so fast. Thinking of that night and how it felt to curl up beside him, completely at ease, sent her mind reeling with thoughts she knew she shouldn't have. They were old friends, so that connection would always be there. But she couldn't let it become anything more. She wasn't in L.A. to start a relationship that would only fizzle up when she went back to Lake Tahoe. She was here to help her mother. End of story.

Though helping her mother was turning out to be one big, fat mistake. Now that the world knew of Valerie Ryan's illness, everything had changed. Her mother was off basking in the publicity and the sympathy of the public, putting on a strong face and promising a full recovery. She was acting as if the cancer was her ticket back to chart-topping stardom.

Maybe it was. And maybe now that the truth was out, she didn't need her daughter for emotional support. Maybe Sadie could just go home, leave this mess behind and wipe her hands clean of it.

The thought troubled her. Excited her. Then scared her. Like Tess had suggested, she could leave. She'd done what she came to do. She'd also blown her alias and reignited an old crush, but that could be dealt with. In fact, if she left L.A., she could escape all those things and try and reclaim her old life. There may be the occasional paparazzi sniffing around her grandparents' house, but if they weren't bothering her at her father's then surely they wouldn't make the trek up north.

She could do it. She could go home.

Or maybe not.

Sadie felt a knot form in her stomach. Her breath caught in her throat as she realized there was some part of her, undoubtedly a big part, that couldn't bear to go. Leaving meant ending this adventure. It meant leaving Tess and her mother behind. And though she didn't want him to matter, it also meant leaving Brody.

Brody. Her mind spun as she closed her eyes, recalling the sound of his laughter and the charming curve of his mouth. She didn't know what was going to happen there, but she didn't have the strength to end it just yet. Besides, he needed her help. They were going to solve her mystery together. If she left now, she'd be letting him down.

The thought pained her. She couldn't leave. Eventually, her mother might realize she still needed her. And Brody definitely needed her. So leaving would be incredibly selfish and she just couldn't do that to them.

A smile lifted her spirits at the thought. Yes, she'd stay. She'd stay and do all the things she still had left to do. One of them being her music.

If the world really wanted Sadie McRae, then damn it, she'd give it to them.

BUMPER TO bumper traffic cluttered all five lanes of the 405 South, just below the legendary Getty Museum. Brody stared out the windshield, his eyes on the looming appearance of the West L.A. skyline. It was shrouded in the usual late-afternoon haze, the buildings nothing more than silhouettes against a burnt blue sky.

Without working air conditioning his car was a sweltering hot mess, but he was used to it by now. Just as he was used to the petroleum aroma of heated steel and exhaust fumes from the sea of cars that surrounded him. He'd grown so accustomed to the entire ritual of things that the traffic and the smells barely fazed him anymore. He just relaxed back in his seat with one arm hanging out the window holding a cigarette, and let the radio blare loud enough to tune out his thoughts.

When there was a break for commercials, he took a drag on his cigarette and hastily flipped through the stations. Bouncy pop and Mexican polka flooded his ears before he landed on a station playing the latest Coldplay song. He grinned and began to sing along, tapping his free hand against the steering wheel.

Moments later the song wrapped up and the DJs cut in, their voices gossipy and arrogant. He was about to change stations again but froze when he heard them mention Sadie. His hand hovered over the dial, irritation flooding his veins.

"I still can't get over it. Piper Gray was already a big deal, but now that we know she's actually Ben and Valerie's daughter? I just can't believe she fooled everyone. And why? Why not bank on mommy and daddy's reps and make millions?"

"Maybe she's got something to hide," another host suggested, earning snickers from the others. *"What? You never know. I remember when the whole thing went down eleven years ago. She practically disappeared. I bet money she knows something that the family wants to keep under wraps."*

"So what, she knows she can't perform as Sadie McRae so she makes up a fake identity and gets her kicks performing that way?"

"Exactly. She didn't want to attract attention to herself or to what happened to her. A lot of good that did."

The hosts erupted in gleeful laughter at the irony of it, sending Brody's blood boiling. He flipped off the radio and sucked in a deep breath, unable to listen any longer. The hyenas were out in full force, and had been for the last few days since the news broke. It was all anyone could talk about—Sadie McRae and her mysterious reappearance in L.A. as the popular YouTube artist Piper Gray. Speculation and rumors were running rampant, made only worse by the resurgence of articles about Lee Walker. The media was having its heyday all over again, which meant the conspiracy theories were front and center.

Hoping they were done, he chanced turning the radio back on. It annoyed him to find they weren't—in fact, they'd only ramped up their gossip by entertaining calls from listeners. He listened to one such caller claim he always thought Valerie Ryan bought off the cops, and that what they *said* happened that night wasn't at all what really went down. He claimed Georgina likely caught Lee drunkenly making out with some other woman in Sadie's bedroom—since witnesses claimed they saw Sadie downstairs—and that she shot him for cheating on her. The whole business with Sadie was merely a cover-up of the real crime, and they'd sent her away to keep the press from questioning her.

Another caller suggested that Sadie was actually the one to shoot Walker, but the family and the police covered it up. It would explain why no other shooter ever emerged, even after the police located most of the party guests and interviewed them. Valerie Ryan likely spun it that way to protect her daughter, even though it notoriously backfired on her.

Disgusted, Brody turned off the radio for good. Traffic was beginning to lighten up, so he veered into another lane and cruised up to thirty miles per hour, wishing none of this was happening to her. Exposing her alias in the long run would be a good thing, he was sure of it, but the embarrassment she must be facing now destroyed him inside. Even though she'd forgiven him, it was still his fault. He needed to make it right.

The best way would be to figure out what really happened to Walker and stop the wagging tongues once and for all. If he didn't get on it, someone else might get to it first and then this would all be for nothing. Maybe it was selfish, but damn it, it was important to him. He needed to know the truth, and so did she.

Feeling determined, he cut in and out of lanes to expedite his trip south, making his way to the Hollywood Hills. He'd drop in on Sadie and convince her she remembered more than she thought.

"YOU'VE BEEN avoiding me."

"For the last time, I have not," Sadie defended, looking up from the game of Scrabble to eye her best friend. They sat together on the floor of her living room, passing time in the only way that didn't involve cable or the internet. "I've just been…out of it."

Tess sighed, completing the word "foxy" on the board. "Look, I know the last few days have been hard to swallow, but it is what it is. You can't hole up inside this house and wallow forever."

"Sure I can," Sadie replied. "As an artist, I think holing up inside is a perfectly respectable life choice."

"There's an entire world out there, honey. A world that desperately wants more of you. And not just the scandalous parts, either. They want your music."

Sadie toyed with her selection of wooden letters, knowing her friend was right. "I know. And I'm trying, I promise. I just need some breathing room."

"But you let Brody in before you even called me," Tess pointed out, her voice flavored with frustration. "I know you said Valerie was the one who leaked the story to the press, but I still don't trust him. And this bullshit about him helping you find out who shot the asshole that tried to rape you…I just don't buy it."

Sadie felt her face redden at the mention of Brody. "I want to know the truth, Tess."

"Yes, but—"

The doorbell interrupted her thought, causing both of them to turn around and face the front door. Sadie started to rise but Tess motioned for her to stay put. "I'll get it."

She went to the door and looked through the peep hole, only to let out an annoyed sigh. Throwing open the door, she glared at the visitor. "Speak of the Devil. What the hell do you want?"

"A million dollars and a private island in the Caribbean, since you're asking."

When Sadie heard Brody's voice, she leapt to her feet and stumbled toward the front door. She came up beside her best friend, not so gently shoving her out of the way. Her eyes met his with a flustered smile. "Hey."

Brody's teeth flashed in that cocky grin, sending her insides twisting. "Hey, McRae. Your bulldog almost scared me away."

"Ha. Ha." Tess crossed her arms as she stood behind Sadie, eyeing Brody with intense dislike. "You still didn't answer my question, buddy."

Brody's gaze didn't leave Sadie as he responded. "I desired to speak with Miss McRae."

A shiver ran through Sadie that had nothing to do with the temperature of the room. "Come in."

Tess frowned but said nothing as Sadie gave Brody an awkward hug, somehow needing to solidify her trust in him. Maybe it wasn't perfect, but she needed to show Tess that he was welcome.

"Would you like something to drink?" she offered, all but pulling Brody into the room. He chuckled and shot a look at Tess.

"If you're offering. You know what I like."

"Beer." Sadie grinned, breathless and dizzy. "One sec."

She disappeared into the kitchen, leaving Brody standing beside Tess. Tess glared at him distrustfully, as though fighting back every urge she had to tear him to pieces.

In the kitchen, Sadie's hands shook as she opened the refrigerator and grabbed a bottle of Stella. She set it on the counter and twisted off the top, biting her lower lip to keep from panicking. This was the first time Tess and Brody were in the same room since that first night at The L.A. Rock Lounge. Already she could feel the sparks igniting in the air and prayed they could be civil long enough to not kill each other.

As she re-entered the living room, she watched them carefully. They both stood in silence, arms crossed and eyes averted. That was better than going for each other's throats, she supposed.

She extended the beer to Brody. "Here you go."

"Thanks."

Tess gritted her teeth and grabbed Sadie's arm. "Can we talk for a second. Alone?"

Sadie nodded, shooting Brody an apologetic look as Tess dragged her back into the guest bedroom. She shut the door and turned to Sadie.

"I don't have a good feeling about this, honey. I just don't."

Sadie wrapped her arms over her torso, hating that Tess didn't understand. "Well, I do. He's my friend."

"He *was* your friend, and even back then I never understood what you saw in him. He's trouble, good and dangerous. And he has only ever looked out for himself. What makes you think he's changed?"

"He promised he wouldn't go to the press, and he didn't," Sadie defended.

"But he did tell Valerie, didn't he? He went to her looking for a story and look what happened. Big shock." Tess threw up her hands in exasperation, even as sympathy softened her face. "Look, I'm just trying to protect you."

Sadie frowned. "I know. And I love you for it. But please, trust my judgment on this. He's not going to hurt me."

"Are you sure?"

Doubt sunk in and wallowed in Sadie's gut, sending an unwelcome frost over her skin. She shook her head and forced it away. "Maybe not a hundred percent, but close."

Tess nodded. "All right. Let's grill him on those last few percentage points and make sure he's legit."

Sadie managed a small smile. "Okay."

As they headed back into the living room, Sadie spotted Brody admiring the sunset view of the city out the patio doors. He turned when he heard them approaching, his eyes catching hers. She inhaled deeply at the slow way he smiled at her, like she was the only person in the room. How did he manage to do that?

She motioned for the dining table. "Do you want to sit down?"

"Sure." He took a seat, prompting her to sit across from him. Tess went and grabbed their wine glasses and the bottle, bringing both to the table. She slipped into the chair beside Sadie and refilled their glasses.

"Don't expect another beer unless you behave like a good little dog," Tess remarked to Brody with a sly grin, enjoying the comparison far too much.

Brody laughed. "Calm down, Tess. I'm not here to shake things up. I just wanted to see Sadie."

Sadie blushed and passed her wine glass back and forth between her hands. She chanced a look at him. "Did you have more questions for me?"

He took a sip of his beer, wishing Tess wasn't staring daggers at him. It made it harder to think clearly. "Well, we can talk about it if you want to. But if you don't, no pressure."

"No, it's okay. Please. I want to help." Sadie's fingers tightened over the glass as she fought back the sick feeling that swept over her. "I haven't looked but I can only imagine the press has been reliving the scandal all over again."

"You're all anyone can talk about," Brody told her, as if it was obvious. When he saw her face pale and that panic come into her eyes again, he cursed himself for being careless. "Not that most of it hasn't been positive, of course."

"That's what I keep trying to tell her," Tess added, looking to Sadie. "The public wants your music, and they want it bad."

"They want the scandal," Sadie corrected, though she only half-believed it. Her heart began to race as worry set in. "They'll probably be disappointed by whatever music I put out from now on. I'll be relentlessly compared to my parents and to the stuff I was doing under Piper Gray and it'll all fizzle out in less than a year and then I'll have nothing. No money, no fans, no music, *nothing.*"

Both Tess and Brody blinked at her, clearly taken aback by her neurotic fears. Because that's exactly what they were, and she knew it. She was being stupid. So, so stupid.

"Okay, so maybe it won't be that bad…" she added feebly, sipping her wine.

"You have a long career ahead of you, McRae. Just trust me." Brody held his beer up in a toast, sincerity in his voice. When her eyes leveled with his, she felt some of his confidence fill her with hope.

"If you say so."

Tess rose to her feet. "Why don't I get dinner started?" She faced Brody, resting her hands on her hips. "I'm guessing you're hungry."

A hopeful grin crossed his face. "I don't turn down food. Or another beer. I'm behaving."

She rolled her eyes. "I suppose you are."

As Tess wandered into the kitchen for a beer and to prepare dinner, Sadie looked to Brody with a shrug. "She's coming around to you. Otherwise, she wouldn't offer to cook you dinner. I'd say that's progress."

"What about you? Are you coming around to me?" Brody asked, enjoying the way she squirmed at the question.

"I guess. You're nice enough. And you make a good pillow for watching movies."

He snorted out a laugh. "Good to know."

She smiled, feeling the worst of her nerves fade away. "Remember when we snuck in to see *Titanic*, and you let me cry like a baby on your shoulder when the boat sank and all those poor people died?"

He did, and realized he had always associated that film with her. Not just for the similarities between her and the compassionate Rose, but because of how she'd sobbed during those horrific scenes. It was the first time he'd ever taken care of someone other than himself. "It's a depressing movie."

"You made it better," she told him, her hands tangled tightly in her lap. "Maybe I never said it then, but you made a lot of things better."

"Likewise." He finished off his beer and looked at her, determination in his eyes. "I want to keep doing that. Making things better."

Her heart did a little flip. "I'd like that."

Chapter *eighteen*

F OR SOME reason, the opportunity to ask Sadie more about the night she was attacked never seemed to come. Instead they laughed, talked, reminisced—lost in those long forgotten days he wished had never ended. Even Tess lightened up, joyfully bickering with him while Sadie looked on with nervous amusement, unsure if they were seconds away from starting a fight or hugging it out like old friends.

He enjoyed watching her. The way she twirled a strand of her hair around her index finger when she was anxious or thoughtful. How her sea-green eyes lit up with joy at the mention of music or of the mountains she called home. That little dimple she got in her cheek when she smiled, something so wonderfully girl-next-door that he was astonished no guy had swept her off her feet yet. She was bright and quick-witted when she wasn't a nervous mess, and genuinely considerate of other people. It took all his focus to try and stay on task, to get down to the much-needed facts of what she had witnessed that night. His priority was to get to the bottom of things, but somehow everything else was getting in the way. *She* was distracting the hell out of him.

And now, she was fast asleep. She rested her head on her arms at the table, her eyes closed and her lips parted slightly as she breathed. Tess smiled at her affectionately, patting her on the back.

"Poor thing. I always forget she's such a lightweight."

Brody continued to stare at Sadie, amused. "We can't all guzzle five glasses of wine a night like you."

Tess's gaze shot to his. "Don't insult me. I can drink seven on a good night."

He chuckled and finished off the last of his third beer. "I'm sure you can."

She exhaled softly and toyed with her wine glass, as though trying to find the right words to say. "You were always more Sadie's friend than mine, Brody. But that doesn't mean I don't know you."

"You might've known me a little back then, but you don't know anything about me now."

Her brown eyes met his and held. "I know you've convinced Sadie that you want to help her. But at the heart of it, you're a paparazzi. You make money off celebrities, and that's what she is. Not to mention this is one hell of a big story. I just don't believe your motivations are sincere or in any way noble. In fact, I'd bet they're leaning toward the sleazy snake variety."

Brody's eyebrows rose. "First I'm a dog, now I'm a snake? Make up your mind, Tess."

She pursed her lips in annoyance. "The point is, Sadie trusts you, which means I *want* to trust you. I'm just having a hard time getting over the whole slimeball reporter thing."

"Fair enough." He leaned forward, resting his arms on the table as he leveled his gaze with hers. "The truth is, I *am* doing this for a story. A damn good one, too. But it's only one reason why I'm here. The other is that I care about Sadie and I've missed her. Maybe you don't believe that, but it's true. She matters to me, just like she matters to you. So the best thing we can do is join forces and both do our best to keep her happy."

Tess's eyes narrowed. "The story being 'Who Shot Lee Walker'?"

He nodded, a side grin brightening his face. "Tell me you're not a little curious about it. Besides, Sadie deserves the truth."

"What she deserves is to know that the people she trusts are actually trustworthy," Tess countered, tilting her chin up defensively. "She probably doesn't realize that this story you want to publish—if you end up learning the truth, anyway—will only reopen old wounds for her, worse than the ones split open by Valerie's betrayal. The press could run on this for weeks, and it might overshadow any attempt she makes to enter the industry. Have you even *thought* about that?"

He grimaced, hating that she was, in part, correct. It still didn't change anything. "Once the truth is out, the scandal dies for good. She can finally move on."

"Or you can leave well enough alone and stop digging," Tess pointed out, shaking her head. "I don't know why, but she has this stupid crush on you. Don't use it just to get what you want out of her. She deserves better than that."

Heat flushed over his skin at her words. "I'm not using her. I care about her."

"If you cared, then you'd want what's best for her. We both know that feeding this scandal is not the answer."

"But feeding her denial is?" he fired back, trying to keep his voice down despite his anger. "She needs to face what happened to her head-on. Surely you understand that—you encouraged her to come back here, to perform onstage under her alias. That was a big risk, and look, she did great. She's stronger than you think she is, Tess. Stronger than everyone thinks she is."

Tess frowned. "I know. But I also know what she's been through these last eleven years. I've seen her struggle with her confidence and self-esteem. She went through a lot of shit you don't know about, a lot of pain. The only thing that fixed any of it was the music and Piper Gray. That alias gave her hope, and now she's back at square one. So excuse me if I'm not sympathetic to your mission to expose her even further."

Brody hesitated, unable to think of a good response. Silence fell over the room as they stared at each other, both still heated with anger but emotionally drained. Surprisingly, Sadie was still asleep, unaware that her friends were waging a war over her.

He let his head fall as he exhaled, realizing he couldn't win with Tess. She made sense, even though he knew he couldn't give up. Though maybe it was in everyone's best interest if he backed off for a little while and gave Sadie a chance to breathe.

"I should probably go," he said as he got to his feet. He looked at Sadie then to Tess, who nodded silently at him. Nothing more was said as he left the house, shutting the door behind him. He hopped into his car and drove off into the night, knowing he wouldn't sleep. Not with Tess's words ringing in his mind, or with the image of Sadie asleep on his shoulder. She was, other than Chase, the only person who'd ever trusted him with so much easy faith.

In truth, he knew he didn't deserve it.

WHEN SADIE awoke the next morning, she realized she'd put off seeing her mother long enough. She couldn't stay away forever, despite how pleasant that idea sounded half the time. Sooner or later she had to face Valerie, and today was as good a day as any.

She knocked lightly on her mother's front door, half hoping no one would be home and she could just leave a note. Her illusion was shattered as the door opened, and her mother stood on the other side.

Valerie's face brightened. "Darling Sadie! How nice of you to stop by." She gestured for Sadie to come in.

Sadie stared at her, taken aback by her mother's enthusiasm. "How are you feeling?"

Valerie hugged her, eyes dancing with glee. "Fabulous. Did you know I received a phone call this morning from none other than Sir Elton John? He's written a duet for he and I to sing together. All proceeds will sponsor some cancer charity he has lined up."

Sadie blinked in surprise. "Wow, really? That's great."

"I know," Valerie preened, guiding Sadie into the kitchen where Carla was busy making fresh iced tea. "Tell her, Carla. Tell her about Elton."

Carla whirled around to smile at Sadie. "Such a nice man."

"I bet." Sadie took a seat at one of the barstools flanking the marble kitchen island, flustered by her mother's energy. "So I take it you're doing better? How was your doctor's visit the other day?"

"We brought the cameras in and they filmed the entire thing for my upcoming interview with Oprah. Imagine that? I'm now the face of cancer-fighting women all over the world." Valerie clapped her hands excitedly, accepting the glass of tea Carla shoved at her. A pill case was also pushed over the marble countertop, which Valerie ignored.

"Take your medication, Ms. Ryan," Carla instructed, casting a knowing look at Sadie.

"I will later. It always makes me drowsy and right now I'm just too happy to take a nap," Valerie contested. She reached for Sadie's hand and smiled. "I know I was angry with you before, darling. But let's just put all that behind us. I was playing around on the piano earlier and have some wonderful song ideas for you."

One of Sadie's eyebrows rose. She wanted to roll her eyes and scream at her mother for not listening to her before, but didn't have the heart to do so. "That's nice."

"Has that mean reporter stayed away from you?" Valerie asked. "Maybe you should get a bodyguard. These paparazzi types just don't know when to stop. Trust me, I should know."

Sadie fought back a smile. "He's behaving."

"Good. Why don't we go for a walk? It's so beautiful out today."

They went outside, taking the stone pathway that wove through the gardens. It led them past a pond filled with vivid orange koi fish and Valerie's vast array of colorful flowers. Butterflies floated on the breeze, joined by the zipping sound of a hummingbird's wings and the soft rustling of wind caressing the eucalyptus trees. Sadie let her mother ramble on, only half listening as she tilted her face back and let the sun warm her skin.

She'd always loved her mother's garden. It was like a tiny slice of paradise amidst the hustle and bustle of the city. Large enough for a child to get to lost in, yet contained by the comforting walls and security cameras that kept the evil outside from breaking in.

Well, most of the evil.

The thought of Lee Walker soured her mood. It threw her out of her memories and back to the present, where her mother was excitedly chatting about Oprah, oblivious to her daughter's distress. Sadie's arms came around her body as she fought back a wave of uneasiness, wishing it would all just go away. Wishing it didn't have such a hold over her anymore.

"Mom?" she interrupted, turning to Valerie with uncertainty.

Valerie paused, irritation flashing over her features. "Yes?"

Sadie looked away, unable to hold her mother's gaze. "Why did you *really* go to the press with my secret? Was it all just to get yourself back in the news again?"

Valerie gasped at the accusation. "Of course not."

"Then why?" Sadie stopped walking, wanting nothing more than to sit down. She settled for a nearby boulder and lowered herself onto it. "Because you're sure enjoying all the publicity."

"No daughter of mine should be ashamed of where she comes from and who she is," Valerie declared, straightening her back in defiance.

Sadie lifted her gaze to her mother's, her heart aching. "But I *am* ashamed."

Valerie stared back at her in stunned surprise, clearly at a loss for words.

Sadie continued, letting the bitterness take over. "What happened here ruined me, don't you see that? It's this blemish I can't get rid of, this mark I wear like a big red 'X' on my chest. I hate that the first thing people think of when they hear my name is that I was attacked and nearly raped by your drummer and that you did nothing to help prevent it. You let him into our lives and he hurt me, and what he did continues to hurt me to this day. Piper Gray was the only way I could put myself out there and know people would only associate me with my music, not my past. And now you've taken all that away from me."

"You don't need to feel that way—"

"God, shut up. I do feel this way, okay?" Sadie shot to her feet, feeling irrational and recklessly mad. Tears blurred her vision and only made her more upset. "I'm not looking for a rationalization of my feelings. I just want you to understand what you did and how it's hurt me. Though I doubt you even care."

Valerie reached out to try and touch her, but Sadie flinched back. "No. Enjoy your publicity, but I hope you realize that when you're hurting and afraid and really need someone, those people won't be there for you. I'm the only person who will ever be there, in spite of everything you've done to me."

She left before her mother could speak, not wanting to hear it. She'd said her peace, and though her body shook with emotion and she feared she might faint from the adrenaline rush, she was proud of herself. She'd stood up to the woman who essentially ruined her life. Never again would she let something Valerie said or did take a toll on her the way Lee Walker and the exposure of Piper Gray had.

From now on, she'd stand on her own two feet.

SHE LET her anger give her a sort of reckless courage that carried her all the way down the hill and into the parking lot of a local coffee shop. She'd parked before she realized where she was, which led to that first white-hot lick of panic.

Oh, God. What am I doing?

Getting a nice cup of coffee like any other normal person, Sadie told herself. She checked her face in the rearview mirror, wondering how stupid she'd look if she wore her sunglasses inside. Did anyone fall for that anymore? Or would they all know she was hiding something?

Who cares, the reckless side of her declared. The rest of her cowered in submission and fell silent, giving her just enough time to gather her purse, slip on her round, silver-rimmed sunglasses, and exit her car. She headed for the entrance of the coffee shop, faltering as a kind, middle-aged man held open the door for her. She gave him an awkward smile and went inside, toying with her purse strap as she stared around the room. It was busy, as the lunch crowd was taking advantage of a coffee break. Hopefully she'd blend in.

With her face all over the headlines lately, she knew hiding in the crowd could be tricky. But as long as she acted casual surely no one would care.

She got in line to order, her eyes straining against the darkness of her sunglasses to read the chalkboard menu on the wall. Folksy rock music played in the background, masked by the sounds of voices and laughter that echoed off the exposed ceiling and brick walls. The short brunette standing in front of her wore perfume that smelled like strawberry heaven. She focused on the scent and let it calm her.

When it was her turn at the counter, she ordered a small cinnamon vanilla latte. It was lame and not very creative, but she wanted the ordering process to be as quick and painless as possible. The clerk smiled cheerfully at her and took her cash.

"What's your name?"

Sadie froze, her entire body vibrating with mortification. "Um."

"So we can call you when your drink's ready," the clerk supplied, patient despite the confusion.

"Oh, right. Um, Piper."

"Piper." The clerk jotted down her name on a cup and set it aside. "It'll be ready shortly."

"Thanks." Sadie slipped away on shaky legs and tried not to feel embarrassed. Of course that's why they needed her name. It's not like this was her first time ordering coffee.

Resigned that she was being beyond stupid, she found a secluded spot near the back counter and waited beside a rack of coffee packages for her drink order. She avoided all contact with the others in the room, not wanting to give anyone a reason to talk to her.

When her drink was finally ready, she grabbed it and retreated to a tiny table in the front corner of the coffee shop near the window. It was close enough to the door for her to feel like she could escape if she needed to, but tucked back far enough that no one should bother her.

She sat down and grabbed a book from her purse, *An Introvert's Guide to Being Extroverted*. She sipped her coffee while she read, her sunglasses still perched on her nose. Slowly but surely, all thoughts of her mother faded from her mind.

She felt more than saw someone take a seat at the table beside her, in a chair that was only a few feet from her own. The light scent of cologne flooded her senses, prompting her to cast a curious glance at the stranger. It was a man, roughly her age, with shoulder length waves of russet hair. He wore all black—tight jeans and a button up shirt that strained against attractive arms decorated with tattoos. When he tilted his head to catch her eye, she was startled by his poetic beauty and the stunning blue of his eyes. Day old stubble graced his jaw line and cheeks, enhancing the rawboned look of his face.

A shy smile crept over his features, only intensifying his beauty. "Hi."

Sadie flushed and looked back at her book, pretending to be too busy for conversation. "Hey."

For a moment she thought maybe the beautiful stranger had gotten the hint that she wanted to be left alone. But when he spoke again, she realized she'd made a huge mistake by going there.

"I love your music," he said, his voice soft and deep and filled with admiration. She bit back an awkward smile and nodded in his direction.

"Thank you."

"Are you saving that seat for someone? Do you mind if I sit with you?"

She looked up at him, startled by his question, but he was already shifting to her table. He sat down across from her with his own cup of coffee and grinned.

"You're even more beautiful in person."

Sadie felt her mind successfully drain of all thought. "Um, thanks."

He sipped his coffee and eyed the book she was reading with great interest. "I suppose living up in Lake Tahoe all these years has made you quite the introvert, huh?"

"I guess." She slipped her bookmark back in place and set aside the book, realizing she wasn't going to get to read. She knew she needed to come up with an excuse to leave without being rude, but couldn't process anything beyond the extremely good looking man sitting in front of her. Something about him was oddly familiar, like she'd seen his face in a magazine or something.

"I'm Drew, by the way." He extended his hand, warmth flashing in his eyes.

She accepted it numbly, unsure what she was even doing there. "Sadie. Oh, duh. You know that." She tried to laugh but only felt pathetic. God, she was going to have to get better with this public relations thing if she wanted to be in the industry.

He laughed and released her hand. "I'd know you anywhere, Sadie McRae."

"That's great…just great," she murmured, twirling a piece of hair around her fingertip. She avoided his eyes and drank her coffee, wishing she felt more protected by her sunglasses. "Listen, you're not a reporter, are you? Because I already have one of those."

Amusement softened his features. "No, I'm just a fan."

"Okay, cool." She blushed, feeling horrendously out of place. "Well, it's nice to meet you."

"Likewise. Will you be doing more shows? I was sad to find out I'd missed the first one."

She shook her head. "I don't know yet."

"I hope you'll make a big announcement when you do," he said, brushing back his length of hair. He seemed just as nervous as she was, which helped put her at ease.

"We'll see." She lifted her cup to her lips for lack of something better to do, still trying to come up with a reason to leave. "So what do you do?"

"I paint," Drew replied, flashing that brilliant smile at her. "It helps relieve the tension, you know?"

"I do." She started to remove her sunglasses, only to second guess herself and leave them on. "What kinds of things do you like to paint?"

"Mostly abstract stuff. It's a bit dark, actually," he admitted, seeming embarrassed by it. "I had a pretty messed up childhood."

His words clicked with her and she smiled sweetly. "I understand that."

He nodded, thankfully not pursuing the topic of her childhood the way most would have. Instead, he launched into a discussion of favorite bands and styles of music. He confessed to never really liking Albatross, in spite of their popularity. Something about his honesty charmed her. It took guts to tell the daughter of rock stars that he didn't like her parents' music. But then again, it was exactly what she needed to hear.

"So you grew up here in L.A.?" she asked, resting her chin on her palm with her elbow on the table. She leaned in, captivated by him, so much so that everyone else in the room seemed to melt away.

"No, Seattle." Drew pushed his coffee cup back and forth between his hands. "I just recently moved here."

"So did I. But you already knew that, too," she replied with a laugh.

He only smiled. "If it's not too presumptuous, can I give you my number?"

Her lips parted in surprise. "Sure. I guess."

He reached into his pants pocket for a pen, then awkwardly grabbed her hand. He jotted his number down on her palm.

"I'd like to see you again. I know that's probably not possible, but—"

"Maybe we can." Sadie gathered her book and purse, rising to her feet. He stood up as well, and she realized then just how tall he was. She rocked back on her heels, her skin still tingling from where his hand had touched hers.

"Great," he replied.

She bit back a smile and waved goodbye to him, closing her palm tightly to hide the number he'd scribbled onto her skin. It took her back to being a teenager, and how it felt to like a boy at school.

This wasn't anything like that, though, she reminded herself. He was a nice guy and a fan, but still so much a stranger. Who knew what his motives really were?

Paranoid, much? Sadie grimaced, climbing into her car. She stared down at her palm and sighed, wondering what she was going to do with this newfound fame.

Chapter *nineteen*

ACROSS TOWN Brody was busy taking out his frustrations on a defenseless boxing bag. He'd worked up a sweat throwing punches and vicious upper-cuts, his mind focused on the contact and not on the burning in his shoulders and biceps. The pain took a backseat to everything else, because as much as he wanted to clear his mind he was finding it impossible.

Sadie was still there. Hell, she was always there these days. He couldn't get rid of her, couldn't find a moment's peace from the nagging thoughts of how to help her or just what it meant now that she was back.

What did it mean, anyway? So she was back in town for awhile, what did that really matter to him? Why did he care so much about seeing her, about helping her? Sure, there was the hopeful possibility of a hard-hitting story that he could sell to the right people and get an ounce of his reputation back, but other than that why was she constantly on his mind?

She mattered to him. Somehow, by coming back into his life she'd reminded him of what it felt like to care for someone other than himself. He'd gone so long being selfish and carefree, and now it all seemed so recklessly pointless. He needed a mission, a purpose. He needed someone to look out for.

And that was exactly the problem.

"Shit," he cursed under his breath as he threw one final blow to the bag, collapsing against it in a heap of exhaustion. His chest heaved as he drew in air, closing his eyes so he could salvage some manner of clarity. There was no way in hell any of this was good for him. Needing Sadie, *wanting* her...he couldn't do it. The very thought terrified him.

He lowered himself onto a nearby metal bench, grabbing his towel. He wiped his face and neck with it, still sucking in air and working to settle his racing heart. The black sleeveless shirt he wore clung to his skin, hot and slick with sweat. It, and the thoughts racing through his mind, made him feel horribly suffocated.

All around him the gym bustled with muscular men and over-tanned women, all vying for an impossible perfection. In L.A., nothing was prized more than vanity. Sadie didn't belong here, he knew. She was better than any of the Barbies and Kens with their cruel gossip and petty vices. She had more class in her little finger than the whole of them combined.

She really should just go back home, he realized. Find a way to make music back in Tahoe, maybe do a couple shows a year, but get the hell out of Los Angeles before it corrupted her. Before it sucked out every last ounce of loveliness she possessed and left her as empty as the rest of them. As empty as he was. Cynical and battered and lost in an unforgiving sea of sins and arrogance.

He lifted a bottle of water to his lips and drank, disgusted with the entire state of things. Even then, he caught a glimpse of a television displaying the news out of the corner of his eye. Video of Valerie leaving a local restaurant with her entourage in tow filled the screen, and he despised knowing she'd exposed her daughter for her own publicity.

Then again, what was he was doing, exactly? Just like Tess said, he was using Sadie for his own selfish gains. No matter how much he tried to sugar coat it and shield himself from the truth, the reality was he *was* in it for the story. He was always in it for the story. He was a goddamn reporter, willing to sell his soul to expose whatever truths people didn't want exposed. How was it any different with Sadie? Her story was huge and he knew it, and he had a direct link to the source. That put him in a position to reap rewards most journalists would kill for.

That feeling of slimy disgust rolled over him again, reminding him of his weakness for her. He'd always had a weakness for her, even eleven years ago. It made doing his job without feeling guilty nearly impossible. She claimed she wanted to learn the truth about Walker's death too, but like Tess pointed out, had she really considered the damage it could cause? The additional press that might hinder her attempts at doing what she loved, singing?

The truth was important, there was no doubting that. But maybe, just maybe, he was in over his head in thinking that he should be the one to find it. For thinking he *could* find it without hurting Sadie in some way.

Then again, she was going to suffer regardless. There was no way out of her situation now that she was in it and she seemed to under-stand that. So why was he having such a hard time coming to terms with it? Why did just the thought of hurting her tear him up inside?

Because she mattered, he thought again. She mattered so much more than he wanted her to.

He looked back to the wall-mounted television above the punch-ing bag, reading the subtitled words the reporter was saying. What he read had his brows creasing as he rose to attention, forgetting every-thing else.

"*The police may have a new lead on the Walker investigation and are exhausting their efforts to at last solve the mystery of what happened to Sadie McRae, daughter of rock band Albatross's lead singers Ben McRae and Valerie Ryan. Drummer Lee Walker's violent attack on Sadie McRae happened over eleven years ago in Valerie Ryan's Hollywood Hills home, and has remained the subject of controversy ever since. Now it appears investigators are looking deeper into members of the band itself, and soon we may have some much-needed answers.*"

Members of the band. Did that mean they considered a member of the band to be the shooter? With Sadie's insistence that it wasn't Tommy, and with Valerie reportedly being too tossed that night to walk a straight line, that left only one other band member who was present.

Georgina Harris. Girlfriend of Lee Walker and back-up singer slash keyboard player that had never made a secret of her jealousy of Valerie Ryan. Why hadn't he considered her before? It made sense—too much sense. If Georgina had walked in on Lee attempting to rape Sadie, in her disgust and anger she very likely could have pulled the trigger. And to save her own skin and cause Valerie as much harm as possible, she'd wiped the gun and fled the scene, washing away any evidence before the police had the chance to catch up with her.

He sat back down, his mind spinning with this new revelation. Undoubtedly, things were about to get a whole lot more interesting, and fast.

WITH TESS working late, Sadie was once again keeping herself company. She had no desire to leave the house, anyway. The incident at the coffee shop had been enough to frighten her away from going out in public for awhile, even if only one person had bothered to notice her. And though he'd been easy on the eyes, there was just something weird about Drew she couldn't put her finger on.

She stood in front of the kitchen sink and stared at the palm of her hand, debating if she should just wash away his number and forget she'd ever met him. Then again, he *did* seem like a nice person and he'd been genuinely interested in her music. And, though it was hard to acknowledge it, he'd seemed genuinely interested in her, as well.

Her whole life she'd been the awkward wallflower too shy to dance and too nervous to talk to guys. She'd dated a couple times, but nothing ever really stuck because she was too afraid to expose herself that way to someone else. Too nervous to trust. It came with the territory, she knew. Coming from the spotlight meant you never took obscurity for granted. In fact, it was such a welcome contrast to the anxiety of public life.

But that was all in the past now. She was out, and even running back to Tahoe wouldn't change that. Now that she'd had a taste of what it felt like to perform for a crowd that loved her music, she knew she couldn't stop. The urgent desire to feel that thrill again keep her moving forward, no matter how much anxiety she felt in public. And incidents like what happened with Drew were bound to happen again, so she might as well get used to it.

She flipped on the faucet, her hand pausing only an inch from the rush of water. Her gaze hovered over the phone number as she chewed on her tongue.

God, like I'd ever have the guts to call him anyway. She doused her hands in the water, scrubbing off the ink he'd put there. In the end she knew it would never become anything. She'd never been allowed to make friends the way most people did. There was no place for that in her life, not if she wanted to be a star.

Besides, there was Brody to think of.

She let out a frustrated sigh, hating herself for even thinking it. Scrubbing harder to get every last trace of Drew's number from her hand, she tried desperately to convince herself she wasn't doing it for Brody. There was no future there, how could there be? She'd alluded herself to having feelings for him, and that was it. There was no evidence he felt the same and she sure as hell wasn't going to pursue him only to have him laugh in her face. He'd only ever treated her as a friend, and that was all she would ever be to him.

Tess had been suspiciously vague over what kind of conversation they'd had while she slept the night before. All she'd said was that he admitted he was in it for the story about Walker, which wasn't a surprise, he'd told her as much before. But what if she wanted something more than that?

She shut off the water and dried her hands, pouting at the thought. In the end, she supposed she wanted the impossible. The music career without the celebrity status, the parents without all the drama and scandal, and the man without the complication of his job choice making him her untrustworthy enemy. Was it so much to ask?

Her cell phone rang on the countertop beside her. When she saw it was Tommy, her spirits lifted.

"Hey, you."

"How're you holding up, Sadie-bug?"

"Fine, I guess," she sighed, resting her hip against the counter. A quick glance at the clock showed it was already nine o'clock, meaning it was midnight for Tommy. "You're up late."

"Yeah, I am…listen, I have a favor to ask of you."

"Of course. What is it?"

"I don't know if I mentioned it before, but we've got a show in L.A. tomorrow night at The Forum. We're actually leaving in an hour so we can be there first thing in the morning."

Sadie perked up. "That's great! I can't wait to see you."

Tommy chuckled. *"Likewise, sweetie. Anyway, the band got to talking and we thought it would be fun if you got up and performed 'Dying In The City' with us, singing Val's parts. Just the one song. We were thinking of making it a big surprise for the fans. They'll love it."*

Her mouth went dry. "Sing? Tomorrow?"

"Yeah. We'll come pick you up for rehearsal in the afternoon, so you don't need to worry about driving or anything."

"Have you told my dad about this? Surely he thinks it's a bad idea. I mean, I haven't even spoken to him since my secret got out. I can only imagine how irritated he is with me—"

"Actually, it was his idea."

Surprise washed over her. "Seriously?"

"Seriously. It'll be so great having you up there and the crowd's gonna go wild for you. Plus, you know the song by heart. I've been watching you sing it since practically before you could talk."

A sad smile came over her face. "It's one of my favorites. I remember watching Mom and Dad sing it together before the divorce and thinking how lucky I was to have such beautiful, talented people for parents." Her breath caught in her throat, her eyes wet with sudden tears. She covered her mouth with her hand to fight it back, despising the emotions the memory gave her.

Tommy grew quiet. *"If it's too tough for you kid, we'll all understand. You've been through so much lately…"*

"No," she cut in, shaking her head even though he couldn't see it. "I'll do it."

"Great. Get some sleep and don't freak out. I know how you like to panic."

She laughed, a stray tear falling down her cheek. She wiped it away and grinned, wishing she didn't have to wait a handful of hours to see him. "I love you, Tommy."

"Love you too, kid. Have a good night."

She hung up and pressed the phone to her lips, closing her eyes on a long sigh. Waves of emotion rolled over her, ranging from excitement to dread to outright panic. Focusing on the positives, she let her head fall back and her heart rate come down. Once it settled, she knew what she had to do.

Bringing up Brody's number on her phone, she hit call and held it to her ear. He picked up on the third ring, sounding surprised to hear from her.

"Hey, McRae. What's up?"

"Hi." She brushed a strand of hair behind her ear, nerves fluttering wildly in her stomach. "I'm going to leave a ticket for tomorrow's Albatross show at the ticket counter for you. Show up and bring your camera—there's going to be a big surprise during the show. If you want a good story you'll want to be there."

When he said nothing, she frowned. "Brody?"

"A good story, huh?"

"Yeah. I'm going to sing 'Dying In The City' with my dad."

"Good for you. I'll show up to watch you make music history, but I'm not bringing my camera."

"Why not?"

"Because believe it or not I'm not just after a story when it comes to you."

She pursed her lips, wishing she could believe him. "Yes, you are. I'll see you tomorrow night."

She hung up before he could respond, part of her wishing she'd been nicer to him. The other part of her was proud she'd gotten the last word in. She'd set up the test, and now it was his turn to prove himself.

Once he did that, she could decide what step to take next.

Chapter *twenty*

S HE AWOKE after a restless night's sleep at half past five, her entire
body humming with nerves. Unable to soothe herself back to sleep,
she got up to make coffee and practice her father's song. Spending
quality time with the piano and caffeine put her in better spirits,
though those little flutters in her belly remained. Part of her wanted
nothing more than for it to be over, while the rest of her eagerly antic-
ipated the rush of being onstage and doing something she'd never
imagined she could do—sing with her father.

She worried about disappointing him. It was only natural to feel
that way, she supposed, but Ben McRae was notorious for not accepting anything less than perfection. If she failed him by slipping up on
the lyrics or tripping onstage or God knows what else, he may never
forgive her. Then again, they barely spoke as it was. So what difference
would it really make?

She sighed and reminded herself that this wasn't about him.
This was about cementing a place for herself in the industry as Sadie
McRae, and part of that was opening up to the idea of performing
with her parents.

Just this once, anyway.

She rested her face in her hands, her eyes aching from staring at the print out of lyrics she'd gotten online. She knew them all, of course. But it was always prudent to practice.

A sudden knocking on the front door had her eyes shooting to the clock. It was already after one o'clock, which could only mean one thing. She jumped to her feet and raced out of the room, a wide smile on her face. As she swung open the front door she faced two of her favorite people in the entire world.

With an excited laugh she threw herself into Tommy's arms. He caught her and joined her laughter, his tall, slender frame shaking with it.

"Hey, kid." He kissed her forehead, then stepped back to get a better look at her. "Christ, if I didn't know better I'd swear you were Val."

Sadie's smile faltered, but she knew he didn't mean to insult her. She took in his carefree waves of graying chestnut hair, weathered, laughter-lined face and sparkling blue eyes and couldn't believe how much she'd missed him.

She turned to face her younger step-brother, tears misting her eyes. "I didn't know you were coming, too."

Isaac grinned and wrapped her in a tight hug. "I'm on break from Med school and Dad couldn't keep me away."

Her gaze lifted to his, the worst of her worries fading. "Not like you ever listen to him, anyway."

"Doesn't stop him from trying," Isaac joked, earning a knowing smile from her.

He rose to a lanky six feet tall, with dark curls of hair and wide, poetic hazel eyes. She'd known him since they'd been kids and her father married his mother. Though there had always been thousands of miles between them, Isaac was there for her in ways her own parents never knew how to be.

"Come in." Sadie backed into the house and invited them in, her hands twisting together in front of her. "I just need to grab my stuff and then I'm ready to go."

"You nervous?" Isaac asked, rubbing the back of his neck as he looked around. "Not that you should be, you'll do great."

Sadie managed a weak laugh. "We'll see about that. Just so you know, I invited someone who's going to be sitting in the front row. I'm telling you now so you don't freak out later."

Tommy turned to her with a questioning look. "Who?"

"Brody Odell."

Isaac's mouth fell open. "You're joking, right? Isn't that the paparazzi guy that Dad hates?"

"He's hated by a lot of people," she mused. "But he's an old friend and we've gotten back in touch and—"

"Sadie, did you tell him that you'll be performing tonight?" Tommy asked, concern clouding his eyes.

Sadie caught his meaning and shook her head. "Oh, no. I mean, I did, but he won't say anything, I promise. I just gave him the heads up so he could get a few shots of us onstage. He won't tell anyone."

"All right. If you say so."

Guilt coursed through her as she walked over and reached for his hands. They met eyes and she tried to smile. "He's a nice guy. Maybe you can meet him after the show."

"I don't think that's how it works, Sadie. You're not supposed to befriend these guys. You file restraining orders to keep them away from you." Isaac chuckled, patting her on the back.

Sadie felt her face flush as she looked away. "Like I said, he's an old friend. The fact that he's a reporter has nothing to do with this. I'll go grab my stuff."

She left the room, wishing she'd just kept her mouth shut.

WHEN THEY arrived at rehearsal, she felt her anxiety come roaring back. Being there made it all suddenly very real.

She considered calling Tess for emotional support, but hated to bother her. Her friend had already done so much, but she had her own life to live. She couldn't be Sadie's crutch forever. Sooner or later Sadie knew she had to rise to the occasion and take what she wanted on her own.

And what she wanted right now was to throw up.

Pushing back the feeling, she followed Tommy and Isaac through the empty halls of The Forum. They led the way up a flight of stairs that opened to the entire arena, filled with thousands of empty seats surrounding a stage that looked so very far away from where she stood. It took her a moment to comprehend that she'd be standing on that very stage in just a matter of hours, singing alongside the band her parents helped build. The feeling was impossibly surreal.

When Tommy and Isaac headed off to greet Glenn Turner, the band's drummer, she turned her gaze back to the stage. Her father was standing there, busy testing notes on his trademark black and white electric guitar. A lump formed in her throat as she walked down the long aisle, her eyes never leaving him.

She was just a few yards away when he finally noticed her. The quick flash of surprise that crossed his face shifted into a strained half smile.

He was still as handsome as ever, refined in age and dressed in designer jeans and a black button down shirt with the sleeves rolled up to his elbows. Silver rings cluttered long and nimble fingers, the tips well-worn after years of stubbornly playing guitar without a pick.

He knelt down and extended his hand to her when she reached the stage. "Come on up."

Sadie accepted his hand and stepped onto the platform. They came face-to-face and those sea-green eyes that matched her own quietly assessed her, as though looking for flaws in a piece of artwork. His russet curls of hair were cut short and feathered with hints of gray. Combined with the soft age lines beginning to take shape on his honed and meticulously tanned face, she saw only a glimpse of the rock star he'd once been. Life had been easier on him than on her mother, but the years still made their mark.

"How are you?" she asked, wondering if he expected her to hug him. Physical affection had always been awkward ground between them. He patted her on the shoulder instead.

"Good. Isaac had me watch a couple of your videos. Not bad." His mouth tightened in an odd little smile, as if he were trying to hold something back. She hoped it was pride, but knew better than to believe it. "Clearly you inherited something from me, after all."

Sadie felt her face grow hot and avoided his gaze. "Thanks, I guess."

When he only continued to stare at her, she chanced another look at him. He was eyeing her clothes, looking thoughtful.

"You're a bit taller than her, but I think it'll still fit."

"What will?" Sadie asked.

His eyes rose to hers. "I have the dress your mother wore when we first performed 'Dying In The City' back in '85. I want you to wear it tonight."

"Really?" She couldn't believe what he was saying. He wanted her to look *more* like Valerie than she already did? "Are you sure that it won't be…weird for you?"

"No," he replied, stiffening his spine. "My goal is to make tonight something our fans will never forget. They'll be talking about this for a long time, Sadie. A very, very long time."

She nodded, her knees weakening a bit at the thought. "I don't know if I can be as exciting as she used to be onstage, but I promise to try."

"You're not her." He adjusted the guitar strap on his shoulder and reached for a nearby mic, handing it to her. When she accepted it, he gave a quick little nod. "You're my daughter. Be yourself."

Emotions swam over her at his odd words of encouragement. It'd been so long since he'd said anything even remotely personal to her. "Okay, I will."

He strummed a few notes on the guitar, keeping his eyes on her. When he nodded again, she understood he wanted to launch into a practice run of the song.

The instant he began to play the sultry, bluesy opening to 'Dying In The City,' she felt her entire world zero in on this one crucial, life-changing moment. Nothing else existed except for him and the song, and once he started to sing her lips spread in a knowing smile.

"Father tells his son, he says, go back now, just run away. This place isn't safe no more. This city, she's become a whore."

From the corner of her eye she spotted Tommy, Isaac, and Glenn sit down in the front row, settling in for the practice performance. She knew she should feel nervous, but instead she was exhilarated. This was her chance to prove herself.

The cue for her mother's lines arrived, and Sadie hit the notes without missing a beat. She sang into the mic, losing herself in lyrics she knew better than even her own.

"City begs, boy please stay. Honey, don't let your doubts get in the way. I love you, I need you. And like hell you need me too."

Her eyes shot to her father and caught him grinning at her. The feeling was like a shot of electricity coursing through her body, sharp and invigorating. Why had she always dreaded this moment when it was so incredibly empowering?

He gave a quick nod the second the chorus began, prompting her to join him as he sang. Together, their voices rang out in a haunting harmony that seemed so natural, as though it were never meant to be any other way.

"This boy can't leave. His blood runs in these streets. Those chains they bind too tight. He'll never win this fight. He'll just die in this damn city. Dying in the city, dying in the city…"

After they'd finished the rest of the song, Sadie noticed her father staring at her with a kind of stupefied wonder. It made her curious if he was reliving those good old days of being onstage with Valerie after all.

Isaac and Tommy burst into loud cheers, clapping wildly. Beside them, Glenn grinned like a fool and rose to his feet.

"You sure it isn't 1985 all over again? I swear I've been shot back in time."

Sadie laughed, meeting Glenn at the edge of the stage when he approached. She knelt down and reached for his hands with a smile.

"Last time I checked, we're in the twenty-first century," she reminded him, admiring his trademark length of blond hair tied back in a low ponytail, matching blond beard, and those calm blue eyes that never seemed to take anything too seriously. Glenn had and always would be a California surfer boy, even though he was nearing sixty. He'd spent the better part of his youth running wild with Dennis Wilson of the Beach Boys, back before he first met Valerie Ryan and stole away with her to Boston. The rest, after that, was the stuff of music legend.

"Long time no see, kiddo. How've you been?" Glenn asked, releasing her hands.

"Good, I guess. I'm back in L.A. for awhile."

"So I hear. How's Val?"

Sadie hesitated, not wanting to ruin her father's good mood with talk of her mother. She glanced over at him but noticed he was busy making adjustments to his guitar. "She's doing better."

"Good to hear." He winked at her and turned back to Tommy and Isaac. "If this was really 1985, I'd have a beer in my hand and some weed to smoke right now."

Tommy chuckled, lazing back in the seat with his arms spread over the backrest. "If this was 1985, you'd be a lot less ugly, too."

Glenn burst out laughing, prompting Sadie to smile fondly at Tommy. She realized then just how much she missed being around the family. Her real family—the band. As much as she loved her grandparents, they'd never been able to replace the bonds that came from something as tight-knit as Albatross. Even with Valerie and Georgina splitting from the group, the basic core remained in her father, Tommy, and Glenn. Being part of it now brought a strange sort of rightness to her heart.

"Let's get everyone together and start the song from the top," Ben said suddenly, motioning for Glenn and Tommy to get onstage. He looked at Sadie, settling back into business mode. "This time, I want you to move around more. See if you can keep your voice steady."

She nodded, swallowing back a second wave of nerves that hit her. How hard could it be?

Chapter *twenty-one*

NOT THAT it should have surprised him, but The Forum was packed to the brim. Albatross fans flooded the walkways leading up to the entrance, eagerly awaiting a concert he knew they'd never forget. They may not know what was coming, but Brody did. And he carried that knowledge with him like the blazing torch it was.

Pride filled him as he realized Sadie was really going for it. She wasn't letting the media get to her, despite the scandal resurfacing in full force. He had to admire her resilience. When the press had turned their ugly heads on him after the incident in Afghanistan, he'd run from it. Guilt had driven him underground and away from the life he'd once lived.

But not Sadie. They weren't scaring her away. Which meant that maybe, just maybe, she wouldn't be leaving L.A. after all.

A spark of hope lit within him as he walked up to the ticket counter and gave them his name. The clerk handed him the ticket with a polite smile, which he would have returned if he hadn't been so shocked by the seat location.

Front and center, arguably the best seat in the entire house.

He shuffled toward the entrance doors, a mix of gratitude and humility churning inside his gut. She wanted him there for her big night, close enough that he could almost touch her. It couldn't just be for the photographs she'd asked him to take. It had to be because she needed a familiar face in the crowd, someone to ground her when the nerves took over and she wanted to run. The fact that she'd chosen him had all the feelings he'd been fighting for her rushing to the surface. He tried to reason with himself as he walked through the crowded halls of The Forum, but a brazen excitement jumped in to blind him. She wanted him. This was proof, it had to be. And he'd be damned if he'd let her slip by without knowing he wanted her too.

With a determined grin he took the stairs two at a time, then emerged into the expansive stadium already buzzing with voices and laughter. He made his way down to the very front and located his seat. It was mere feet from the stage, which was set up with the band's equipment and an illuminated sign of Albatross's trademark flying seabird logo.

Glancing back at the crowd had him smiling again. Even years after their glory days, Albatross could pack in the fans. And although Valerie and Georgina no longer performed with the band, Brody had a feeling that tonight their presence would not be missed.

The instant he sat down, someone fell into the seat beside him. He glanced over and eyed the stranger with curiosity.

The young man held out his hand with a bright grin. "Hey. I'm Isaac."

Brody's eyebrows rose as he accepted the handshake. "Brody."

"Odell. Right. I know who you are."

Brody felt his body tense. "I see my reputation precedes me. You really into Albatross, Isaac?"

Isaac shrugged. "I guess I have to be. My step-dad's the lead singer."

A half laugh escaped Brody's throat, understanding hitting him. "I see. That makes you Sadie's step-brother."

"Yep. She told me she invited you here tonight so I just wanted to come over and introduce myself. Let you know that I'm watching you."

Amused, Brody patted Isaac on the shoulder. "That's very brotherly of you, but she can handle herself."

"It's not her I'm worried about," Isaac replied easily. "It's you. No matter what she says I don't believe you're not just using her to get a hot story."

Anger rumbled within him, but Brody didn't let it show. "Join the club."

Before Isaac could respond, the lights in the stadium dimmed to black, signaling the start of the show. The crowd exploded with noise as all eyes went to the stage. Several people surrounding him shot to their feet, clapping and cheering in anticipation. Brody shrugged and rose as well, noticing that Isaac had turned away and was busy chatting excitedly with the woman beside him.

Brody watched as silhouetted figures emerged onto the stage, shielded by the darkness. One settled in behind a large drum set, another took stage left and lifted what looked like a bass guitar, and a third came front and center and reached for a guitar. When he secured the instrument over his chest, he hit a few tell tale notes from one of Albatross's most famous songs, and the crowd screamed with hysteria.

Lights flashed on and illuminated the stage, showing the remaining three members of Albatross. All eyes went to Ben McRae as he polished off a long, haunting note, and hit the mic with his infamously deep and husky voice.

It was a song Brody knew well, one he frequently heard on the radio despite it being thirty years old. Around him, adoring fans sang along with Ben and danced to the beat of Tommy's bass and Glenn's quick and clever drumming. The combination was electrifying, and as much as Brody tried not to give Ben credit he had to admit the guy was an incredible performer.

He could see where Sadie's love of music came from. It was there in her father, and watching the man perform up close was like watching parts of Sadie. Ben lacked his daughter's quiet softness, but the passion and frank emotion shone with clarity from his eyes just as they did in hers. When the music filled the air, it was impossible to ignore his magnetic pull. The same was true with her. How else could she have built such a fan base with nothing more than a YouTube channel and the mystery of an alias? People were drawn to her, just as they'd always been drawn to her parents.

Clearly all her years of trying not to be them had failed. She was their daughter, through and through.

After they wrapped up the song, Ben called out a greeting to the crowd. They roared with approval and elation, quieting down only when he continued to speak.

"We have a real surprise for you this evening. I know there's a certain element to Albatross that many of you have been missing…well, tonight we bring it back, but with a twist." Ben stepped back from the mic and motioned toward the side of the stage, where Sadie emerged. The second the light hit her free-flowing golden hair and face, Brody thought the ceiling might come down from all the noise.

She smiled and waved at the crowd as she approached her father. They exchanged a brief hug, much to the crowd's delight, before heading for their own microphones.

Brody felt a jolt run through him when Sadie's eyes fell to his and a pretty smile lit up her face. She sent him a nervous wave just before the band launched into the song.

His heart was racing as he watched her, stunned by the transformation. They'd dressed her up just like her mother, yet her smile and movements were so very Sadie. The sparkling gypsy gown she wore flowed around her legs in layers of silk and lace the color of peacock feathers. Intricate beadwork covered the bodice and thick shoulder straps, leaving her arms bare. She held a wooden tambourine which she tapped in time with the beat, looking like she truly belonged there. Like there was no place else she was meant to be.

When she sang, her voice stole the breath out of him. He'd heard her before, but not like this. Not singing a song he'd grown up listening to, one he'd enjoyed all his life. Her mother may have been a goddess of a woman in her day, but he had to admit the daughter was even more captivating. And from the emotional cheers erupting all around him, he had a feeling the fans couldn't agree more.

Sadie and her father began the chorus, their voices blending in perfect harmony. Brody lost himself in the image of the two of them together, just as he knew everyone in the audience did. Ben had succeeded in making tonight something for the world to remember. He'd made music history. And Sadie—whether she was ready for it or not—was going to be a star.

The song came to a close and Sadie gave her father another hug, this time tighter and more meaningful. Brody was close enough to see her wipe away a couple tears before waving cheerfully at the crowd. When she stepped offstage, he reached for his cell phone and shot off a text to her. He couldn't wait until after the show to see her. It had to be now.

A few minutes later she wrote back, asking him to meet her by a door off to the far right of the stage, used primarily for sound and lighting equipment. He took off without saying a word to Isaac and found his way to the door, which opened before he could reach it. Sadie tugged him inside a dimly lit storage area that led back stage and firmly shut the door.

"Hi," she greeted, facing him with a bright smile on her face. "Well, what'd you think?"

Brody shook his head, drinking in the sight of her. The combination of that dress, the smokiness the makeup gave her eyes, and the delighted flush of her cheeks made her completely irresistible. "For once in my life I have no words, McRae."

She giggled, unable to help herself. "I can't believe that just happened. I'm not dreaming, am I? Maybe you should pinch me."

He shifted closer to her, reaching up to touch her face. His fingertips grazed her cheek and drew back into her waves of hair, his eyes lowering to her mouth. "If it is a dream then it's a damn good one. You were amazing."

Sadie's lips parted, stunned by the heat radiating off him. She had to remember to breathe as she fought to keep her knees steady. "I'm really not. It's the song, it's so great. I just sang."

"It blew me away." He brought her face within inches of his own, breathing in the scent of her honeysuckle perfume. His other hand found her waist, pulling her in until their bodies were touching. He could feel her shivering against him, and from the desire that softened those bright eyes of hers he knew he was a doomed man.

Those eyes fluttered closed as she leaned in. "Brody, we should—"

The door beside them opened, revealing Isaac. Behind him, the crowd continued to sing along and enjoy the show.

"Sadie, I was looking for you," he interrupted, eyebrows creased with confusion as he slipped through the door. He assessed the scene, concern tightening his features. "Everything okay?"

Sadie drew back from Brody, embarrassed. Her arms came around her torso as she looked at her younger brother. "Yeah, I'm fine. We were just talking."

Isaac didn't seem to believe her. His gaze shot to Brody distrustfully. "Are you sure?"

Sadie sighed. "Yes. Everything's okay. I promise."

He frowned. "Okay. I'll leave you alone to continue...*talking*. If you wanna come watch the rest of the show, you can sit next to me."

"Thanks, Isaac." Sadie nodded as her step-brother left. Once the door shut behind him, she let out a rush of breath and faced Brody sheepishly. "Sorry about that."

Brody rolled his shoulders, wishing it didn't bother him so much that no one seemed to trust him with her. He'd never cared about what other people thought before, so why start now?

Because it involved Sadie. And Sadie meant something to him.

"He's just looking out for you," he replied. "I guess I can't blame him. I'm more evil-villain-plotting-to-take-over-the-world than Prince Charming."

Sadie's face softened with humor. "You're not all bad. Besides, Prince Charming is boring."

"Very true." Brody chuckled, running a hand through his hair. "Look, what you said on the phone last night about me only wanting a story—"

"I'm sorry, I was being unfair to you," Sadie interrupted, avoiding his gaze. "You deserve better than that."

"Not really, but I did want to make something clear to you." He grabbed her gently by the shoulders, urging her to meet his eyes. "I want to keep seeing you. Not because I want a story, but because being around you makes me remember what it was like when things were simpler and I was happy. I don't want to lose that."

Her brows drew together. "What about Walker?"

"I honestly don't give a damn about anything right now except for you."

"Me…" The word trailed off as the sound of her father's voice and loud cheers echoed from the stadium. She stared into Brody's eyes, lost in all that dark intensity. Lost in memories of the past blending with the face of the present. "When did everything change? We were friends, and then we weren't. And now I don't know what we are. I need to know that I can trust you."

He framed her face with his hands, drawing closer to her. A slow grin spread over his features. "Admit it. You like living a little dangerously. And as for being your friend…I don't see why that has to stop me from doing this."

She started to reply only to be cut off by his mouth taking hers. Her hands rose to grip the front of his black T-shirt, pulling him in even though her brain told her to push him away. The feel of his hands and the heat of his mouth as it raged over her own fired off sparks of hope and uncertainty within her heart. But soon it and everything else fell away. The sound of Albatross in the background, the fears of what her brother, Tommy, and Tess would say, the ache of wondering what place she had in this strange new world of fame. None of it seemed to matter, not when she could give in to this crazy blend of past and present and savor the awareness of being genuinely wanted by a man like him. By a man who embodied a reckless sort of freedom she craved with every breath she took.

It was madness. But then again, so was he.

When he broke the kiss, he rested his forehead against hers and fought for air. The blood in his veins ran hot and fast with a fire he hadn't felt in years. From the delirious way she trembled against him, he had a feeling she felt it too.

Her hands weakened their grip on his shirt as her head fell languidly back, inviting him in. He pressed his lips to the soft curve of her neck, consumed by the scent of her.

"God, you're beautiful," he murmured.

She stepped back, fighting for some semblance of control. If she didn't she knew she'd never be able to come up for air. A weak smile curved her lips. "You're just saying that because tonight I look like the Goddess of Albatross."

He grinned, though that intensity remained. "Yeah, you're probably right."

She smacked him playfully on the arm. "Shut up."

"What? She's a beautiful woman." He slowly backed her up against the nearest wall, a predatory look in his eyes. "You know you knock her out of the park, right?"

Her back hit the wall the second before he kissed her again. On instinct, her hands dove into his hair. He gripped her waist, holding her there as his mouth found her neck once more and sent shockwaves of heat through her body. It was like being devoured whole, and her hunger for it alarmed her. Needing to stop, to reclaim her sanity, she pushed him away.

"I really should go," she said breathlessly, dizzy from the dark emotions he'd stirred within her. "Isaac's probably wondering where I am."

Brody nodded, stuffing his hands in his pockets. "Right. Wouldn't want to worry little brother."

Sadie frowned, taken aback by the irritation in his voice. "He cares about me."

"Yeah, you've got quite the group of bodyguards ready to protect you from me," he joked halfheartedly, unsure why he let it bother him so much. "Am I going to have to go through them every time I want to see you? A man can only take so much interrogation before he just gives the hell up."

She adjusted her dress, unable to look at him. "I don't know what to say to that."

"Just tell me you'll let me in, Sadie. Tell me you don't give a shit about what anyone else thinks and that I can be a part of your life again."

Guilt coursed through her as she crossed her arms. "This is a lot for me to handle right now. I just did two things I thought I'd never do and the potential consequences of both are scaring the hell out of me."

"What are you talking about?"

She looked up at him, eyes bright with unshed tears. "What's my mother going to say when she finds out I performed with Albatross tonight? And what am I going to do if I let these insane feelings I have for you keep me in L.A. when it comes time for me to leave?"

He struggled for something to say back to her, but came up empty.

"Right. I should go." She turned and disappeared down the hallway that led backstage, leaving him standing alone to stew in his guilt.

Chapter *twenty-two*

S O, HOW'D it go?" Tess asked, a giddy smile on her face. She sat at the dining table across from Sadie and handed her the newspaper. "Don't be modest. I already read every word the paper had to say on the topic. 'A brilliant, almost bittersweet addition that brought fresh light and splendor to an already killer rock band.' They loved you, not that it surprises me. You're a natural."

Sadie stirred her coffee absently, her mind elsewhere. "It was fun."

"Fun? Honey, this was your first show being yourself. Don't you think it deserves a better adjective than 'fun'?" Tess laughed, retrieving the paper so she could look at the picture released by the venue from the night's performance. It showed Ben and Sadie standing side-by-side looking at each other and singing. She sighed. "I wish I could've seen it. If stupid Richard hadn't kept me working late—"

"I kissed Brody," Sadie blurted out, covering her mouth the instant she said it. She eyed Tess warily, gauging her best friend's reaction.

Tess's eyes widened. "Oh. Well, then…how was it?"

"Amazing." Sadie bit back a smile, knowing she was blushing. "But then we kind of argued or something and I left…I don't really know where we stand."

"What'd you fight about?" Tess asked, concern creasing her brow. "Do I need to go kick his ass?"

"No," Sadie replied, winding a strand of hair around her finger anxiously. "In fact, that's exactly why he was upset. None of you trust him around me."

Tess scoffed. "Well, duh. He's—" Sadie's hurt look had her pausing. She rolled her eyes as she continued. "Okay, fine. I'll play nice and back off a bit if that's what you want. He hasn't given me any real reason to distrust him so far, so maybe he's okay."

"I care about him, Tess. A lot," Sadie admitted, realizing it even as the words poured out of her. "He and I shared something I never had with anyone else. He understands me and doesn't treat me like I'm going to fall apart all the time. Instead he makes me feel like I did before Walker hurt me. Things weren't perfect back then, but at least I wasn't broken."

"You're not broken now, Sadie," Tess cut in, reaching for her hand. "And if I treat you like you are then I'm sorry. I'm just trying to look out for you."

Sadie attempted a smile. "I know. And you push me to do things outside my comfort zone, so thank you. I would have never performed onstage last night if you hadn't pushed me to break out the first time."

"Well, you're welcome." Tess squeezed her hand and released it, looking down at the paper once again. "You really should read this whole thing. I think it'll give you a good boost in confidence."

"Maybe." Sadie tilted her head to look at the image of her with her father as her cell phone began to ring. She saw her mother's phone number and a jolt of dread shot through her. "Give me a minute, Tess."

She rose to her feet and retreated into the guest bedroom before answering the call.

"*How could you?*" Valerie cried, sounding miserable and furious. "*Did you think I wouldn't find out that you were onstage with Albatross? I don't even know what to say I'm so upset.*"

Sadie lowered herself onto the edge of the bed, closing her eyes as guilt swam over her. "I'm sorry, Mom. It was all very sudden. Tommy

188 ~ KATIE JENNINGS

called me the night before the show and asked me to join them onstage. It was just for one song."

"My *song*," Valerie shot back. "*Ben had no right having you sing my parts like that.*"

"I'm sorry. It was a one-time thing."

"*So you'll perform with your father but you won't do a duet with me? Do you even understand how that makes me feel? I offered to make you a star and instead you go behind my back and betray me like this.*"

"Betray you?" Sadie repeated, stunned. "All I did was sing one song as a favor to the band. That's a far cry from letting you write music for me."

For a moment Valerie said nothing. When she spoke again, there was added venom in her voice. "*Fine. But don't come crying to me when Ben throws you out like garbage the way he did to me.*"

She hung up, leaving Sadie holding the phone and cursing under her breath. She fell back against the bed, wishing things weren't so complicated.

FIGURING SHE could win over her mother if she brought something more than just apologies, Sadie stopped in at the quaint coffee shop she'd visited a few days earlier. This time she didn't bother covering her eyes with sunglasses, knowing she couldn't hide forever. If someone recognized her, so be it. She had more important things to worry about.

She walked from her car up to the entrance of the shop, coming to an abrupt stop when someone opened the door for her. Her lips curved in a thankful smile, only to falter when she recognized the man before her.

"Drew. Hi," she greeted, flustered and uncomfortable. "T-thanks."

"Welcome." Drew smiled and followed her inside. "I was hoping I'd run into you again."

She gripped her purse strap tightly with one hand, the other immediately snaking through strands of her hair. He came up behind her when she got into line and she had no choice but to address him. "I'm just grabbing something to go."

"Me too. Hey, I heard you performed last night with Albatross. I bet that was amazing."

Her eyes met his as she struggled not to feel so horribly awkward. "Yep, it was cool," she replied lamely.

"Wish I could've seen it. You should've called me, given me a heads up."

She flushed as she realized she couldn't admit to losing his number on purpose. "It was a surprise, anyway. I wasn't allowed to tell anyone."

Drew nodded, looking sheepish. "I get that. So, what do you usually get to drink here?"

Relieved he wasn't going to press her on the issue, she smiled. "They make a good cinnamon vanilla latte."

"Yeah? I'm partial to the mocha myself." He flashed those perfectly white teeth at her, sending her mind into a frenzy of cluttered thoughts. She watched him brush back his length of brown hair and couldn't help but once again catch a hint of the cologne he wore. "I'd like to pay for your drink, if you don't mind."

Sadie blinked, taken aback by his offer. "Oh. No, that's okay. I need to get something for my mom, too."

"For Valerie Ryan?" Drew's mouth spread in a wide grin, his voice loud enough to catch the attention of a few other customers.

Sadie bit her tongue, wishing she'd thought up some kind of excuse instead of blurting out the truth. "Um, yeah. Anyway, I can get it."

"It's no trouble, Sadie," Drew replied, coming up beside her as she approached the barista. She didn't know how else to say no, so she placed the order and stood by uncomfortably as he paid for her.

"You really didn't have to do that," she told him as he got the receipt and led her to a nearby table. She lowered into the seat but remained perched on the edge, ready to go the second the drinks were ready.

Drew sat across from her, his eyes never leaving hers. "You're worth it. Besides, consider it repayment for all the hours of pleasure I got from listening to your music on YouTube."

A strange feeling licked at Sadie's insides, somewhere between discomfort and delight. "Hours, huh? You must be my number one fan."

"I probably am." He grinned again, an odd sort of arrogance in his eyes that hadn't been there before. "Which is why I'd hoped you'd call me."

"I've been busy." She turned away, wanting nothing more than to leave. He seemed nice enough, but there was something about him that bothered her. Maybe she just needed to get used to being fawned over by fans, she realized. Her mother didn't seem to mind it when fans approached her. In fact, she seemed to thrive on it.

"Looks like the drinks are ready. Let me grab them for you," Drew offered, rising to his feet. She watched him wander over to the counter and thank the barista, returning seconds later with a trio of tall paper cups.

She stood, not wanting to get suckered into another long chat. She accepted two of the drinks from him. "Thank you, again. You really didn't have to do this."

"It was my pleasure." Drew stared down at her intently, as though admiring her. "Take care, Sadie."

"You too." She clutched the coffee cups tightly in her hands as she retreated away from him, catching the curious stares of a few customers as she passed. Thankfully, none of them stopped her from leaving the coffee shop and getting into her car.

She turned on the engine and pulled onto the road, breathing a heavy sigh of relief. "Well, that was weird," she mumbled to herself, shaking off the strange feelings she felt. She wanted to chock it up to just social awkwardness over being recognized in public, but somehow she had a feeling there was more to Drew than met the eye.

Shrugging off the thought, she drove up Laurel Canyon on her way to her mother's home. She sipped her coffee as she hit the buzzer and pulled into the driveway, parking behind her mother's Corvette. Grabbing the hot tea for her mother, she made her way to the front door and knocked.

Carla opened the door, looking distracted. "Miss Sadie. Come in."

"How's she doing?" Sadie asked.

"She's in her room, resting. I can let her know you're—"

"I'll just run up and bring her this," Sadie cut in, lifting the cup of tea. "I won't be long."

She climbed the long stairway, wishing her heart would stop trying to beat its way out of her chest. Nerves at facing one of her mother's notorious moods brought back all sorts of childhood memories she'd long ago tried to forget.

When she came upon her mother's bedroom door, she knocked lightly. Hearing no response, she opened the door and peered inside.

The drapes were drawn, cloaking the room in near darkness. She spotted her mother sitting in her four-poster bed, knees pulled up to her chest with her face buried in her arms. Pity washed over Sadie as she entered the room.

"I brought you some tea," she said, approaching the side of the bed and sitting down.

Valerie lifted her face, her eyes bloodshot and mean. "I don't want your apology. I won't accept it."

Sadie pursed her lips. "Then at least drink the tea I brought you."

Valerie turned away. "I saw a picture of you from last night. You wore my dress."

"Dad had it." Sadie shrugged. "He asked me to wear it."

"Oh he did, did he?" Valerie fired back, looking at Sadie again. "I guess you'll be my official replacement now."

"It's not like that," Sadie reasoned, hating to be—yet again—caught between her parents. "What can I do to convince you?"

Valerie pouted, not seeming to know the answer. She grabbed the tea from Sadie's hands and took a long, thoughtful sip. "You hurt my feelings. It's like you don't care about me at all."

Sadie's hackles rose, the question she'd been wanting to voice for days finally erupting from within her. "If I don't care about you, then why am I here? God knows I'd rather be back in Tahoe than dealing with any of this."

The instant the words were out she regretted them. Valerie shot her a hurt look as a tear fell down her cheek. "I'm dying, Sadie. For once I wish you could get over your hate for me and make me feel loved."

Sadie winced, her temper fizzling. "I'm here, aren't I?"

"It seems like you came here to start your career, not to see me."

"I didn't. All that just sort of…happened." Sadie sighed, knowing it wasn't good enough. It still didn't explain why she never told her mother about her alias. "Look, I want to put that behind us. I want to help you."

"No you don't," Valerie retorted, her eyes dry now. "You made it perfectly clear that you still blame me for what happened and that I ruined your life. So much so that you're *ashamed* of who you are and where you come from. If only I'd done something differently that night, maybe you wouldn't hate me the way you do."

It was the first time Sadie had heard her mother willingly take the blame for anything. Emotion swelled inside of her as she patted her mother's arm. "I don't hate you."

Valerie exhaled tiredly and lay down in the bed, curling up beneath the covers as she turned away from her only daughter. Her voice was hollow with dark amusement as she spoke. "You shouldn't tell a lie, darling."

Sadie rose to her feet, feeling her heart tear apart at the seams. Damn the woman for her mind games. One second she was riding on fury, the next she could turn on the guilt and reduce even the most pious man into a withering puddle of shame. Sadie knew better than to let it get to her.

Without another word, she left the room. She closed the door behind her, not knowing when she'd return.

THE SECOND she started her car she blasted the radio, needing to drown out the noise of her mother's voice. It pounded in her head incessantly, spreading remorse and anger until both clashed inside her in a great war of conflicting emotion. Focusing on the music helped shift her thoughts onto other things as she pulled onto the road and began the short drive home.

She wouldn't have noticed the black sedan following her if she hadn't looked in the rearview mirror to check her makeup. When she did, a dozen irrational fears about crazed on-the-loose murderers and fanatical stalkers leapt into her mind.

The sedan was close enough that she could just see the front bumper, yet tinted windows shielded the driver from view. It occurred to her that maybe the person was irritated at her slow speed, but when she checked the speedometer she noticed she was inching toward forty-five miles per hour in what was a solidly twenty-five zone. Any faster and she'd careen down the winding hill and slam into another car or a tree that lined the road.

Biting her lip, she came to the street that led to her father's home and slowed, making the sweeping left turn. She watched the sedan in her mirror, realizing with panic that they also turned. Knowing she couldn't lead them straight to where she lived, she reached for her cell phone and with a trembling hand managed to bring up Brody's number and hit send.

While it rang she jumped up her speed and took a detouring route through the hills that would lead back to Laurel Canyon and out to safety. The car revved up to join her, seemingly enjoying the chase. The thought only frightened her more.

When Brody answered, her hand was shaking so badly she nearly dropped the phone.

"*I was hoping you'd call.*"

"I need help. Please," she breathed, her heart galloping inside her chest.

Brody's voice darkened with concern. "*What's wrong?*"

"Someone's following me. I'm driving through Laurel Canyon right now and they won't go away. I can't go home."

"*Okay. Stay on the phone, I'm going to give you directions to my place. It's a good thirty minute drive—if he doesn't give up after the first ten then just keep going and I'll take care of it when you get here.*"

Sadie nodded, anxiety forming a lump in her throat. The steady calm of his voice lessened some her panic. She focused on it instead of the stranger in the black sedan as Brody guided her out of the Hills and onto La Cienega boulevard.

When the car continued to follow her through the city, this time keeping a couple of car lengths behind, she took her eyes off the mirror and simply drove.

Chapter *twenty-three*

H E WAS standing on the curb waiting for her when she pulled up. Only then did she glance back at her mirror and notice the sedan was gone. Shock and relief had the breath rushing from her lungs as she came to an abrupt stop directly in front of Brody, not even bothering to park properly. She opened the car door and stepped out, willing her knees not to collapse.

"He's gone," she told him, hugging herself tightly.

Brody only shook his head, his eyes on the entrance of the palm-tree-lined street. "Not yet."

Sadie whirled around and saw the black sedan come to a stop in the middle of the road less than a hundred yards away, silent and still. Without warning, Brody took off at a run, aiming to catch the stranger. Sadie watched helplessly from the sidewalk as the car whipped into gear and did a tight U-turn, squealing down the street and away from them. Clouds of white smoke fumed up from the burnt rubber left behind by the tires as the car disappeared from sight.

Brody stopped running, cursing himself for not being able to at least see the plate number. Out of breath and frustrated, he walked back to Sadie. "Did you get the license plate?"

She bit her lower lip and shook her head. "I-I couldn't really see it."

He nodded, knowing he couldn't blame her. She'd sounded terrified on the phone. "All right. Come here."

She let him pull her close and rested her head on his shoulder, still fighting to slow her heart rate. "I'm sorry to bother you. I didn't know what else to do."

Brody chuckled, easing her back so he could meet her eyes. "It's not like you were scared out of the house by a spider, McRae. Someone was following you. That's serious stuff."

"I know," she replied, rolling her shoulders to shake the nerves away. She glanced at her car with a sigh. "I should probably park somewhere. Unless you want me to leave?"

She faced him again and he was sorry to see how badly shaken up she still was. "Stay as long as you like. It's not as fancy as your place, but it's home."

A small smile chased some of the apprehension from her face. "Thanks. Give me a second to park."

She pulled into an open spot across the street before wandering back to him, her eyes instinctively going to where the black sedan had waited. The fact that the person was willing to follow her all the way to Venice from Hollywood just to see where she'd go troubled her.

Brody wrapped an arm over her shoulders and led her upstairs to his apartment, unwilling to speak more on the subject of the mysterious car until they were safely inside. He didn't trust the neighbors not to listen in and spread gossip, especially if they recognized Sadie. Nothing was private for celebrities in this town.

When they entered his apartment he closed the door behind him and locked it, then went to the fridge. "Beer?"

She paused inside his living room, taking in the cluttered space before nodding at him. "Sure."

When he came back into the room, she'd settled onto the sofa, a vague look in her eyes. Her brows were pinched together as she no doubt relived the panicked experience she'd just had.

"Hope you like Corona. It's all I have," he said as he handed her a bottle and sat down beside her, taking a sip from his own.

Sadie took a long pull from the beer, trying to chase away the last dredges of anxiety from her system. Though the bitter, skunky taste didn't agree with her, she swallowed it anyway, desperate for the relief it promised.

Brody watched her with amusement. "Slow down there, cowgirl. Unless you're planning to stay the night I may have to cut you off."

Sadie laughed, unable to help it. She eyed him with a sardonic grin. "You can't ply me with alcohol just to get me to sleep over."

"Who said anything about sleeping?" One of his brows lifted in good humor as he tapped his bottle against hers.

She snorted and took another sip of the golden beer. She lost herself in her thoughts, more questions than answers swirling around in her head.

"Did the car look familiar to you at all?" he asked, breaking the silence.

"No," she replied, fingers tightening over the bottle. "I've never been followed like that before."

He patted her knee. "It was probably just some paparazzi asshole. We've done worse things than tail a celebrity in her car for ten miles."

Sadie looked down at the beer in her hands, turning over the thought in her mind. Even though she still had doubts, the notion of it being a reporter comforted her a little. As annoying as paparazzi could be, at least they weren't out to physically harm anyone. "Maybe."

To distract herself, she gazed around his apartment, taking in his hodgepodge of used furniture, movie posters, and take-out containers. "Nice place."

Brody snorted. "You don't have to be polite. I don't bruise easily."

"Well, in that case…" she joked, shooting him a playful look.

With a hard grin he stared around the room, taking it all in. "I'm right where I belong, McRae. It'd be nice to get my life back, but I'm not holding my breath."

She hesitated, concerned by his sudden change in mood. "You can't keep doing this to yourself, Brody. You deserve to be happy."

"I deserve a lot of things. Happiness isn't one of them," he countered, setting aside his nearly empty beer. He reached for his laptop and opened it. "Anyway, I heard something the other day that might interest you. It's fine if you want me to drop it, but I figured you deserve to know."

Sadie frowned, leaning in to stare at his computer screen. "What is it?"

He tapped at the keys and brought up a news article online. Without a word, he sat back to let her read the headline.

Sadie's lips parted in surprise. "Wait, *what?*"

"That's what I said." Brody chuckled darkly. "But I think this could be a big deal."

"They have a new lead on the shooter? Possibly a member of the band?" Sadie stammered, still in disbelief. "Who, though?"

"The only person I can figure is Georgina," Brody supplied.

Silence fell as Sadie absorbed his theory. She stared unseeing at the news article, thinking back to the night that Walker attacked her. Had Georgina stumbled in on them and consequently shot her own lover? If so, then why did she drop the gun and run?

"I don't understand," she murmured, sitting back to face Brody. "If she shot him, why leave the room and lie to the police? She was only preventing him from…from raping me."

"I don't get it either." Brody scratched his chin, his dark eyes meeting hers. "But you swear it wasn't Tommy, and by all accounts your mom was high as a kite. And since neither Glenn nor your dad were in California that night, that leaves Georgina."

"But she never even really liked me. And Walker was her boyfriend…" Sadie trailed off, frowning.

"Maybe that's the point. She saw him follow you upstairs, knew what he was up to, then had her suspicions confirmed when she walked into the room. Then in the heat of rage, she grabs his gun and shoots him. She probably didn't even think twice about what was happening to you. She was just pissed that he was capable of something so disgusting."

"Then why lie about it?"

Brody shrugged. "To avoid a scandal. Or maybe she lied on instinct and then got buried too deep to dig herself out. I always felt the cops didn't do a thorough enough investigation…it's possible she paid a hefty sum to keep the truth buried."

"Or my mother did," Sadie theorized, feeling a heavy weight drop in her gut. "To keep the media attention focused on her. It wouldn't surprise me."

"Well that backfired, didn't it?" he reminded her. "She lost custody because of this. I don't even think *Valerie* is that much of a media whore to sacrifice motherhood for attention."

Sadie grimaced. "You don't know her as well as I do, then. You wouldn't believe how furious she was at me for stealing her limelight at the show last night."

"She'll get over it."

"I'm not so sure this time," Sadie predicted, sadness washing over her. "I should've never come back here. I just keep hurting her without even trying."

"She hurts herself, Sadie. There's nothing you can do about that," Brody told her. "She's the one who blabbed about your alias, which led to you performing with Albatross. And she told the world about her cancer, not you. Anything she reaps from this point on is solely from what *she* sowed. It has nothing to do with you."

"I guess." Sadie set her beer on the coffee table and rose to her feet. "I should probably go."

"You sure?" he asked, standing as well. "I can follow you home, make sure that creep doesn't show up again."

She smiled tiredly. "No, that's okay. I appreciate the offer, though."

"Hey, what're friends for?" he joked, following her to his front door.

She paused before it, turning her face up to his. She wondered if he would kiss her again, if it was even a good idea. "Is that what we are? Friends?"

"Of course."

Her heart skipped at the way the brown of his eyes seemed to darken, to intensify. Biting back a smile, she reached up to run her fingertips over his cheekbone and along his jaw line, her eyes tracing the movement. "All of this is such a bad idea."

"Is it?" he asked as he closed in, backing her up against the door. His hands found her hips as her back hit the cheaply painted wood and brought a flash of awareness to her eyes. The corner of his mouth lifted in a devious grin. "Is this you damning the consequences and letting me in?"

She gave a weak nod the second before he kissed her, the movement fast and desperate and out of control. Her arms encircled his neck as she hung on, her heart stampeding with both joy and fear. Joy at getting what she wanted, and fear of how it could inevitably burst into flames and destroy them both.

The intensity simmered as he savored the taste of her, his mouth trailing to her cheek and then her forehead. Just having her there, feeling those hands of hers on his body was enough to send all kinds of wild thoughts into his brain. She had that effect on him—that enchanting, mind-numbing effect that made everything else seem radically insignificant.

And now he was a doomed man. A seriously, undeniably doomed man.

"I'll walk you out," he murmured, nudging her aside so he could open the front door. He lightly grabbed her arm and led her outside, knowing if he kept her there any longer it would lead to something he knew they both weren't ready for.

Sadie walked with him down the hallway and stairs, unsure what was happening. Unsure what she was letting happen. He said nothing to her until they reached her car.

"Call me when you get home, okay?"

She reached into her purse for her keys, avoiding his eyes. "Okay."

When she clicked the unlock button on her key ring, he reached over and opened the door for her. "I don't mean to nag, but are you sure you don't want me to follow you?"

Sadie climbed into the driver's seat and faced him with a reassuring smile. "I'm good."

Brody nodded, then leaned in to give her one last, lingering kiss. He backed away and shut the door, waving to her as he walked backwards across the street.

As he watched her drive away, he mentally kicked himself for letting her get to him the way she did. Then again, from the delirious way she kissed back, it was clear he was getting to her, too.

THOUGH SHE kept an eye on her rearview mirror the entire time, she saw no sign of the black sedan. She took a roundabout route to get back to her father's home, not using the same street she normally did. By the time she pulled into the driveway and turned off the car, the sun had set and she felt relieved to be home.

She grabbed her cell phone as she locked the front door and did a quick sweep of the house. Satisfied everything was as she left it, she dialed Brody's number.

"*Everything good?*" he asked, not even waiting for her to speak.

"Yeah. No sign of the black car. It probably was just paparazzi."

"*Probably. Get some rest, McRae.*"

"I will. Goodnight."

She hung up the phone and went into the kitchen to pour herself a big glass of wine. Settling onto the sofa, she turned on the television, needing to distract herself before bed. The only thing on was *Family Guy*, so she let the mindless humor drag her out of reality.

Hours later, she'd polished off nearly two-thirds of the bottle of wine and was feeling dizzy and humorous. She giggled as she almost tripped over her own two feet on the way to the bedroom, where she slipped into cotton shorts and a T-shirt. Her eyes drooped as she crawled into bed and turned off the bedside lamp, plunging herself in near darkness. It was enough to send her catapulting into a deep sleep, finally losing the last of her anxiety.

She didn't know what woke her. It could have been the nightmare of Walker chasing her through the streets of Los Angeles in the black sedan, or perhaps the dull ache of an oncoming headache spawned by too much red wine. Either way, she tossed and turned until she realized she wouldn't fall back asleep until she got a drink of water and some aspirin.

With a groan, she hauled herself upright and rubbed her eyes. When she opened them, she let her vision adjust to the dark room. Silvery moonlight came in through the window, reminding her that she'd forgotten to close the drapes. She slipped out of bed, only to freeze as a shadow walked across the lawn outside, momentarily blocking the light.

Fear constricted her throat and froze her in place. Her eyes were wide with terror as she stared into the darkness, straining to verify what she saw. Hoping to prove she was just imagining things.

When the silhouette of a man passed right in front of her window and paused, as if staring inside at her, she stumbled backward in panic and fled from the room.

Racing for the kitchen, she snatched her cell phone and frantically dialed 9-1-1. Her body shook with violent tremors as she collapsed onto the kitchen floor, shielding herself from view behind the cabinets.

"*Nine-one-one, what's your emergency?*"

Her mouth moved but words couldn't seem to form. She smacked herself in the forehead and struggled to breathe. "T-there's someone walking around outside my house."

"*What is your location?*"

Sadie gave the address of her father's home, trying to keep her voice steady.

"*Okay, help is on the way right now. Have they attempted to break in?*"

"I don't think so," she replied, pulling her knees up tight against her chest. "Please tell them to hurry. I'm alone."

"*I need you to stay calm. Are you somewhere safe?*"

"The kitchen, on the floor. I'm too scared to move, they could be right outside. It might be the same person who followed me in my car earlier."

"*Stay put and be quiet. Tell me if you hear anything. Help should be there any minute.*"

Sadie bit down hard on her lip and hovered in silence, listening for any sound. Within minutes there was a loud knocking on the door, causing her to jump.

The police announced their arrival, so she climbed shakily to her feet, thanked the operator and ended the call. She opened the front door and faced two police officers with their flashlights shining in her face.

"Hi, ma'am. We got a call of a disturbance?" One of the officers said while the other one began to walk around the perimeter of the home, checking for signs of an intruder.

Sadie nodded, her entire body still shaking. "Yes. Come in."

She showed him the guest bedroom where she saw the shadow and explained how she was followed earlier that day by a black sedan. He took down notes as he listened, then eyed her thoughtfully.

"Ms. McRae, do you think it's possible you could have a stalker?"

Sadie lowered herself onto the edge of the bed, her head beginning to pound. She rubbed her temple wearily. "I don't know. Maybe."

Sympathy crossed his face as he knelt down before her, patting her knee. "Do you have someplace you can stay for the night just in case?"

She thought it over, realizing if she bothered Brody or Tess that they would just freak out. The only other option she had was to go to her mother's and hope Carla could let her in without bothering Valerie. Though she felt sick at the thought, she nodded.

The other officer walked into the room and said he spotted some footprints outside in the planter, but nothing more. He suggested that she install security lights and possibly even a full alarm system.

"Okay, thank you." She walked them out, then quickly gathered up an overnight bag and left for her mother's. The drive felt surreal, as though she were living someone else's life. This never happened to her. In fact, before tonight, she'd never even called 9-1-1 before. Never needed to. But this was L.A., and it was a world away from the peaceful life she'd led in Tahoe.

When she arrived at her mother's, she hit the buzzer at the gate and prayed Carla was still around. Instead, Valerie answered and after a moment's hesitation, let her in. As Sadie parked, her mother came out of the house dressed in a lavender robe with curlers in her hair. Her lips parted in surprise at the sight of her daughter.

"What are you doing here?" she asked, eyes flicking to Sadie's overnight bag.

Sadie sighed, wishing she was a better liar. "Someone was walking around outside the house. I got spooked so I was hoping I could stay with you for tonight."

"Oh my God." Valerie gaped, her hands clutching her chest. "Come in, darling. I knew it was a bad idea for you to stay over there. You belong right here, in your home."

Sadie kept quiet and let herself be ushered upstairs to her old bedroom, too tired to care. Her mother fluttered about the room to make her comfortable, then at last left her alone to sleep, promising they'd discuss the whole thing in the morning.

Wanting nothing more than to forget it ever happened, Sadie collapsed onto the bed and fell into a troubled, restless sleep.

Chapter *twenty-four*

THEY MET at an upscale French restaurant tucked away on Sunset Boulevard. It was one of Tess's favorite spots, one frequented by celebrities who appreciated the private booths, low-lighting, and award-winning list of fine wine.

"I don't know, just pick something for me," Sadie said, closing the menu and shoving it aside. Her lips pursed in a playful pout at her friend's raised eyebrows. "What?"

"Last time I suggested something for you, you nearly bit my head off," Tess reminded her.

"That's because you wanted me to eat some sort of mushroom thing that cost over a hundred dollars. I just can't do that, Tess. It's a freaking mushroom. For a hundred dollars."

Tess snorted. "They're called golden chanterelle mushrooms and if you knew how rare and delicious they are then you'd understand the high price."

"Whatever. I'll just pick something easy." Sadie flipped the menu back open and quickly selected some sort of chicken dish, figuring it was safe enough.

"Suit yourself." Tess closed her own menu and eyed Sadie. "I will say though that the *Loup de Mer* is spectacular. You would love it."

Sadie shook her head. "Nope. No thanks. I don't even want to know."

Tess laughed. "You know, for someone who's never had to worry about money, you sure don't like to partake in the finer things in life."

"Maybe we just define 'the finer things' differently," Sadie countered, a smile softening her features. "You can keep your fancy food, cars, and limousines, Tess. I just want the fresh air and the mountains."

"That's not all you want, honey." Tess sipped her glass of golden Pinot Gris, amusement brightening her eyes.

Sadie flushed, grateful for the interruption of the waiter. After they placed their orders, she twirled a strand of hair around her finger and sighed. "About that…"

"Oh my God, did you kiss him again?" Tess asked, nearly dropping her glass. A stupidly big smile filled her face. "Do tell. Please. Throw a bone to the sex-starved lunatic over here."

Sadie hesitated as she tried to think of where to begin. The whole point of meeting Tess for dinner was to get a recommendation on a good security company and quietly break the news that she may or may not have a stalker. So far, she'd been unable to bring up the topic. It swam in the back of her mind, an icy reality she still refused to face.

"Promise you won't disapprove?" Sadie met her friend's eyes with a teasing look.

Tess waved off the question. "I'm over it. Now tell me what happened."

"Well…I was sort of followed yesterday after I left my mom's house, and—"

Tess held up her hand. "Stop. Rewind. You were *what?*"

Sadie swallowed back a prickly ball of nerves, her throat closing in on her. "Followed, I guess. It was probably just a paparazzi. A black car tailed me from my mom's house almost to my dad's, which is when I realized it was following me. So I called Brody, and—"

Tess's mouth fell open. "You called Brody before you called me?"

Sadie rolled her shoulders in an attempt to relieve some of the tension she felt. "I could barely think clearly, Tess. And to be honest, he's a guy. What were you going to do if it was some crazy stalker with a knife?"

"Shoot his ass," Tess replied with a confident snort. "You think I don't keep a nice little .22 tucked away for situations like that?"

Sadie sighed. "Okay, well, I didn't know that before. Can I just finish, please?"

"Go ahead." Tess drank more of her wine and sat back, crossing her arms.

"So I drove to Brody's place in Venice, and the car followed me all the way there. Brody tried to chase it down, but the car drove away before he could get the plate number. We went upstairs to his apartment, had a beer and talked about Lee Walker—"

"He's still bothering you about that?"

Sadie wrung her hands together in her lap. "Well, he had something pretty interesting to tell me. So I'm glad he did."

"What?"

"The police have some kind of a new lead on who may have shot him. Someone in the band. Brody thinks it was Georgina."

Tess blinked in surprise and leaned forward, lowering her voice. "That's really serious. Are you sure?"

Sadie nodded. "It makes sense. But anyway, we won't know for sure until the police look into it."

"Is Mr. Paparazzi going to take a chill pill now or is he only more eager for the story?"

A small smile danced over Sadie's lips. "He said he doesn't care, but I know he wants the story. A thing like this could be his ticket back into the industry."

"What do *you* want?" Tess asked, concern creasing her brow.

"The truth," Sadie admitted, feeling a weight lift off her shoulders. She straightened with a smile. "And I want him to be happy. I care about him."

"Oh, God." Tess chuckled, brown eyes glittering with humor. "You're head over heels for him, aren't you? Let me guess, he kissed you on the way to his front door and you let him because you're a hopeless sap and can't resist that moronic grin of his."

Sadie started laughing, unable to help herself. She let it brighten her spirits in spite of her lingering fears of being stalked by an unknown stranger. "He has the best smile. I love it."

Tess eyed her friend knowingly. "You love more than just the smile."

"Let's not go there, okay?" Sadie pleaded, taking a sip of her Chardonnay.

"Look at you, all flustered and in love," Tess mused. "And here I am, singing 'One Is The Loneliest Number' and drowning my sorrows in wine."

Sadie snorted. "Well, I met this other guy recently at a coffee shop. You'd probably like him; he looks like a freaking model."

"Really?" Tess's interest piqued. "I want details."

"Tall, well-built but lean, shoulder length brown hair, blue eyes…" Sadie began, trailing off as she remembered her last run in with Drew and that odd vibe she'd gotten from him. "He was kind of weird though. Persistent, I guess."

"A fan of yours?"

"Yeah. He was just trying to be nice and I made the whole thing awkward. But if I run into him again I'll mention how hot and single you are."

"Sounds like a plan." Tess winked. "So tell me what happened after this kiss. Sex?"

A shocked laugh bubbled from Sadie's throat. "What? No. Of course not."

"Damn."

"We just…stopped, and he walked me to my car like a gentleman, kissed me once more, and then I went home."

"Aw, shucks, honey. What a swell guy," Tess replied with a hokey southern accent, laughing at herself. "I'm glad he's behaving himself."

Sadie let out a slow release of breath, realizing now was as good a time as any to breach the subject of the security system. "He is. Anyway, so I wanted to ask if you knew of a good security company that could install some lights and a system at my dad's house. The one he has hasn't worked since the mid-nineties."

"Totally. I can get you Marc Green's number. He'll hook you up." Tess grabbed her cell phone and began looking up the number, only to pause. "Wait. Is this because you were followed? Or did something else happen?"

Sadie started to reply, only to be cut off as the waiter dropped off their food. She stared down at the sautéed chicken breast smothered in brie sitting on her plate and tried to formulate a proper response.

"Well?"

Sadie took a deep breath. "There was someone outside the house last night. I had to call the police."

Tess nearly fell out of her chair. "*What?* You waited until now to tell me this?"

"I didn't want to worry you," Sadie admitted, trying to wave off the seriousness of the situation. "It was probably just a teenager wandering around the neighborhood."

"Or maybe the same guy who followed you," Tess pointed out, not even bothering to eat her food. "Tell me you aren't staying there tonight?"

"I'm at my mom's for now, until I can get a good security system put in." Sadie poked around at the chicken, not really hungry.

"Okay, well I'll give Marc a call and get him over there ASAP." Tess returned to her phone, hunting down the number. "And you're more than welcome at my place if you don't want to shack up with Valerie."

Sadie smiled, grateful for her friend. "I'm fine. But thank you."

"Of course," Tess replied, reaching for Sadie's hand. She squeezed it as she held the phone to her ear.

Sadie watched Tess come to her rescue yet again, and breathed a quiet sigh of relief.

AWHILE LATER, they left the restaurant and said their goodbyes. Tess went east down Sunset, while Sadie went west to where she'd parked her car a couple blocks down the street. She didn't mind the walk, or the cool breeze that kicked up the night air. It gave her a chance to gather her thoughts and mentally prepare herself for another night in the house she'd avoided for more than half her life.

It wasn't as bad as she'd feared. As long as she didn't focus on the past, the house was nothing more than wood, drywall, carpet, and furniture. That made it no different than her father's home or her grandparents' place back in Tahoe, which meant she could stay there and not give in to the nightmares.

People walked all around her and cars rumbled past, the city alive with lights and energy. She enjoyed blending in with this world of concrete and indulgence, even though she remained an outsider. She'd never fit in here, never really belong. Before, she'd embraced that fact; now she realized she wanted nothing more than to carve a notch for herself and prove she could handle the city that the angels had long ago forsaken.

The town had ceased to be a happy place the day Lee Walker tried to hurt her. But now, in spite of everything, she felt those old wounds closing and the fear subsiding.

She could be happy here, maybe. If she really tried to make it home, then it would be.

A smile crossed her face at the thought as she passed through a small group of female twenty-somethings, their skinny jeans and loose fitted tops hanging over their lanky frames. One of them caught her eye and stared, surprise bringing a bright grin to her face.

"Oh my God, aren't you Sadie McRae?" the girl blurted out, trailing after her.

Sadie turned with a weak smile, brushing a strand of hair behind her ear. "Yeah."

"I love you so much. Can I get a picture with you?" the girl gushed, prompting the rest of the group to crowd around in excitement. A few were already taking pictures, the flashes like lightning in the dark.

"Um. I really have to go, but…" Sadie trailed off, realizing it was useless as the girl was already at her side posing for a picture.

Sadie let the girl hug her and wander, star struck and breathless, back to her friends. As they left, Sadie noticed a black sedan come to a stop at the curb just ten feet away. Through the tinted windows, she could see a ghostly figure sitting in the driver's seat, watching her.

Panic raced down her spine in an icy shiver, paralyzing her. Knowing she had to move, to run away, she unstuck her feet from the sidewalk and urged herself to turn around. After five stiff, shaky steps, she regained her momentum and raced past a clothing boutique, hair salon, and organic café, wondering if she could seek refuge inside any of them.

Most were closed, leaving her few options. She shot a look over her shoulder and saw the car following her, driving slowly. Terror gripped her as she kept going, until a hand reached out and dragged her into a crowded Irish pub.

"What's the hurry, McRae?" Brody asked, his happy grin faltering when he saw the terror on her face. "Okay, for real. What's wrong?"

Sadie shoved him back into the bar until they were both safely inside, her hands shaking. "That black car. It's out there."

He didn't bother asking more questions before launching himself out of the pub and onto the sidewalk, his eyes careening up and down the street looking for the car. Seeing nothing and realizing the creep had fled, he headed back inside and found her seated at the bar, badly shaken up.

He plopped down beside her and ordered them both a beer. When she only stared at the old oak bar top like a catatonic mental patient, he nudged her with his elbow. "He's gone. You're okay."

"No, I'm not." She let out a rush of breath, shaking her head. "Whoever it is, they were at my house last night, walking around in the backyard. If it's just some paparazzi then I'm going to *kill* him for scaring me this way. It's just not right."

Brody's eyes widened as he tensed with rage. "Someone was at your fucking house?"

She winced, wishing she hadn't said anything. He didn't need to know. "I called the cops, they told me to put in a security system. Tess knows a guy who can do it…"

"You're not staying there until it's put in," he ordered as the bartender dropped off their frothy glasses of Guinness.

Sadie tilted her head to look at him, feeling her patience wearing thin. "Do you think I'm stupid? I'm staying at my mother's."

"Oh, yeah, because that's better," he retorted, grabbing his beer and downing a few big gulps. He set it down and tried to control his temper, feeling helpless at the thought of her cowered in panic on the phone with 9-1-1 while some creep lurked outside.

She was wrong. If it was just some paparazzi, *he'd* kill him.

Sadie exhaled and took a tentative sip of her own beer, willing the panic out of her system. When she began to feel better, she reached over to hold Brody's hand. Their eyes met and she managed a smile. "I'm glad you saw me. If you hadn't been there, he might not have left."

He squeezed her hand, then on impulse pulled her face toward his for a quick, tender kiss. He rested his forehead against hers, sorry to feel the distress vibrating off of her. Sorry to know some obsessive freak caused it. "I'll get to the bottom of this, okay?"

She pulled away, her eyes on his. "How?"

"I'll do some digging. If it *is* paparazzi, it's probably one of three or four guys that are notorious for pulling crap like this. Let me put some feelers out and see what I can find."

She nodded, feeling a weight lifting off her chest. "Thank you. Really. You don't have to go to the trouble…"

"Shut up." He nudged her shoulder with his, enjoying the warmth of humor that filled her eyes. "I would do anything for you. Except wear a dress. A man's gotta have his limits."

She let out a bright laugh, lifting her beer for another sip. After a moment's consideration, she tilted her face toward his. "What about a muumuu?"

Brody grinned, not missing a beat. "Do I get to wear boxers underneath?"

"Hmm…no," she decided.

"Ah, I see what this is. You just want to see me naked," he fired back, raising his glass in a toast as she sputtered and choked on her beer. "Muumuu provides easy access. You know, this might not be a bad idea…"

"Oh, God, stop," she managed, laughing uncontrollably. "So inappropriate."

He glanced around the bar, then back at her. "What? No one's listening."

She rolled her eyes and elbowed him in the side. "You're such a guy."

"I hope that doesn't surprise you…otherwise this muumuu conversation is gonna make a lot more sense."

She started laughing again, only to sigh as she realized her beer was nearly empty. She downed the last of it, feeling much better than when she'd arrived. In fact, she nearly forgot why she was in the bar in the first place. It came back to her in fluttering waves of negativity that dampened her cheerful mood.

He noticed her smile falter and lifted her chin, urging her to look at him. "Hey. It's going to be okay, all right?"

She gave a quick nod. "Okay."

He finished his beer and threw some cash upon the bar, then rose to his feet. "Why don't I walk you to your car? You can drop me off at mine, then I'll follow you home and make sure you get in safe."

"I'm staying at my mother's," she reminded him, gathering her purse as she stood up.

He cursed under his breath. "Right. Forgot. Well, I'll still follow you there. Hopefully Valerie doesn't call out the hounds when she sees me."

Sadie chuckled. "If by hounds you mean that hyper snowball then I think you'll survive."

He wrapped his arm over her shoulders and led the way outside, walking with her to her car. She liked the way he was affectionate with her, not seeming to care if anyone saw them or what they'd say if they did. Tonight she felt like any normal girl walking with a funny, charming guy that wanted the world to know she was his. The feeling was so surreal she wondered if she'd wake up and this would all be some kind of crazy dream.

"Better hope your meter didn't run out," Brody said when they reached her car. "Looks like you might've gotten a ticket."

Sadie groaned, spotting the slip of white paper tucked under the driver's side windshield wiper. "I know I put in enough money…"

She pulled the paper from the windshield and turned it over, expecting a parking ticket and finding something else entirely. It was a nearly blank page with nothing but the word "WHORE" in big black letters written upon it.

When she only stared at it in shock, Brody grabbed it from her and grunted out a violent curse. He started to tear the letter to shreds to save her from having to look at it again, but reason took over. Instead, he set it down on the hood of the car and turned to her.

"Do you have a book or a notepad or something in your purse?"

She jolted at his words, startled back into reality. With a nod, she reached into her purse and pulled out *An Introvert's Guide to Being Extroverted*, handing it to him.

Under other circumstances he would have teased her about her book choice, but he couldn't muster up enough humor for it. He tucked the mysterious letter inside the pages and shut the book.

"You're going to give this letter to the police so they can dust it for fingerprints, okay? And make note of this exact location. They'll want to check surveillance cameras of nearby stores to see if they can find out who did this."

Sadie's brows furrowed. "Why would they go to that much trouble?"

"Because it's you, Sadie. And like it or not you're a celebrity, which means they don't take these things lightly."

She frowned, digging for her keys. "Whatever. I just want to get home."

Brody ran a hand through his hair, frustrated by her. "All right. My car's another block down. Give me a sec and I'll follow you."

He walked away before she could argue, so she slid into her car, locked the doors, and waited for him to pull up beside her. When he did a few minutes later, she pulled out onto Sunset Boulevard and headed for the Hollywood Hills, watching his headlights in her rear-view mirror.

WHEN SHE rolled up to her mother's place, Sadie entered the security code Valerie had given her to open the gate. They both drove in and parked in front of the house.

Brody stepped out first, eyes sweeping the front yard and driveway. He noticed Valerie had plenty of security lights and even cameras, keeping watch of even the farthest reaches of the grounds. Unlike Ben, who couldn't be bothered to update his security system, Valerie had a top-notch one in place for her protection.

Sadie would be safe here, he knew. But she wouldn't be happy.

He went to her when she surfaced from her own vehicle, clutching her purse to her chest. She faced him, uncertainty in her eyes. "Do you want to come inside?"

Brody started to say no, to make the case that everything looked good and that he should go, but Valerie stepped out of the front door and interrupted him.

"What is *he* doing here?" Valerie demanded, racing down the steps. She came to a stop beside Sadie, clutching the folds of her silk robe around her body. Her bronzed eyes looked at him with disdain. "How did you get in?"

Brody folded his arms, matching Valerie's derision. "The gate just magically opened and I drove right on through."

Sadie rolled her eyes, pulling her mother away from Brody. "I invited him. He's my friend, Mom, in case you forgot. He's worried about that person who's been following me."

Valerie faced her. "Did something else happen? I knew you shouldn't have gone out tonight. I just knew it."

"I saw that same black car, but it's okay. Nothing happened," Sadie reassured her, deciding not to mention the creepy note on her car. She looked to Brody. "Brody followed me home to make sure I was safe."

He held her gaze, taken aback by the warmth of gratitude he saw there. It was a similar look to the one Chase had given him that night at the hospital. Seeing it brought an odd fullness to his heart. "Just doing what I can."

"Thank you." Sadie smiled, then awkwardly stepped forward to hug him. "We'll talk tomorrow. Okay?"

He nodded, eyeing Valerie over Sadie's shoulder. The woman looked positively flabbergasted. It brought a snide grin to his face. "Sounds good."

He brushed his lips against Sadie's forehead as he pulled away, wishing they were alone so he could do more. As it was, even that small gesture of affection was giving Valerie an aneurism.

Amused, he hopped back into his car and left, imagining the argument Sadie was about to have with her mother. It couldn't be prevented; the woman didn't trust him.

He supposed he couldn't blame her. He'd done very little, until now, to earn her trust.

But that was going to change.

Chapter *twenty-five*

HE COULDN'T remember the last time he'd set foot in the family law firm, though not much had changed. It sat atop the prestigious Aon Center, the second tallest building downtown, with sweeping views of the city all the way to the Pacific. Odell & Son occupied the entire top floor, decked out in frosted glass, scarlet mahogany, and brushed nickel accents. It was an oddly modern design for a stuffy, traditionalist firm, but Brody figured if they used grandfather clocks and cigars it might turn away most of the L.A. crowd.

As it was, he spotted a few celebrities among the clients scattered about the lobby awaiting their appointments. No one famous enough to warrant his father's immediate attention, but the aging B-list actress, veteran cable news anchor, and anxious supermodel kept their heads low and their eyes to themselves as if nervous they might be recognized.

A law firm was rarely a happy place, a fact Brody understood all too well. He hated coming here almost more than he hated the reason for his visit.

Without a word to the doe-eyed receptionist, he wandered down the hallway that led to his brother's office. Though he vaguely remembered its location, his eyes trailed over each stainless steel name placard as he walked past all the opaque glass doors. When he found his destination, he gave a quick knock and poked his head in.

Chase was at his desk, phone pressed between his shoulder and ear. He glanced up at Brody and gave a tired smile, waving for him to enter.

"Right. I understand Ms. Hale, but you still have to provide us with those bank records. The court's demanding them, there's nothing I can do," Chase said into the phone, rubbing his temple.

Brody took a seat in the plush armchair across from his brother, crossing his right leg so his ankle rested on his left knee. He tapped his hands on his thighs as he waited, taking in the stunning view outside the windows. Even with the smog, it brought a twinge of affection to his heart. He loved that damn city, chaos and all.

When Chase finally hung up the phone, he took a moment to collect his thoughts and make some notes before turning to Brody. A cheerful grin lit up his face. "What's up, buddy?"

"Nothing good," Brody replied. "How's the baby?"

"Great. God, she's cute. Abby's got her hands full, though. She won't sleep much at night just yet." Chase grabbed a silver picture frame from his desk and handed it to Brody. It showed baby Charlotte, smiling up at the camera from her pink bassinet.

Brody grinned. "She's got your stupid smile. Good job."

"Right? I love that kid." Chase laughed as he replaced the picture on his desk. He eyed it fondly before facing his brother again. "So what's the not-so-good stuff? You in some legal trouble?"

"Nope. Look, I don't even know if you can help me, but I need to talk to someone rational who can look at this from an outside point of view." Brody brushed strands of hair from his forehead, debating where to even begin. "My friend is being stalked by some creep. First he followed her in his car, then he showed up at night to walk around her backyard, and last night he tailed her on Sunset when she had dinner with her friend. I've checked around with my contacts and if it's paparazzi, he's not fessing up to it. So I'm thinking it's a bonafide stalker."

"Geez," Chase murmured. "I'm assuming this friend of yours is some kind of celebrity?"

"It's Sadie, Chase," Brody said, all that anger and pain rising up within him just at the mention of her name.

Chase blinked, taken aback. "Wait, Sadie McRae?"

Brody nodded.

"You're seeing her?"

"What? No," Brody countered, scratching his chin and shifting his right leg to the floor. He leaned forward, resting his elbows on his knees and focusing on his hands. "Okay, I don't really know what we're doing, but I *am* trying to help her out. She needs protection."

A slow grin lifted Chase's features. "You guys were really close. I didn't know you were still talking to her."

"I ran into her when she came back to L.A. a few weeks ago," Brody admitted. "Anyway, it doesn't matter. What does matter is that she's in danger."

Chase swiped a hand through his hair with a sigh. "She's also being sued."

"Wait, *what*?" Brody's brow creased as his eyes lifted. "By who?"

"Her mother." Chase shuffled through some papers on his desk, locating the one he needed. His eyes perused the page quickly, then met Brody's again. "She claims Sadie infringed on her stage persona without permission."

"You've got to be fucking kidding me," Brody muttered. He sat back against the chair, rubbing his face in his hands. "That psycho bit—"

"I'm actually supposed to send out a subpoena to her today," Chase interrupted, earning a disgusted look from Brody.

"She hired Dad," Brody stated flatly, a cynical laugh escaping his throat. "Why does that not surprise me?"

Chase shifted in his chair uncomfortably. "She really doesn't have much of a case. I'm sure it won't go very far."

"That's not the point, Chase," Brody shot back, rising to his feet to pace the room. "She's suing her own *daughter* out of spite. What kind of sick, twisted person does that?"

"Some people take these things very seriously." Chase shrugged. "If I remember right, Sadie and her mother never really got along, anyway."

"Sadie came back to L.A. to take care of her, and this is the thanks she gets? And worst of all, our greedy bastard of a father is the one who's going to help her."

"Valerie's been a client of ours for some time—"

"I don't care. This is bullshit," Brody growled. He stormed from the room, not waiting for Chase to respond. He went straight for his father's large, corner office. Not bothering to knock, he threw open the door uninvited instead.

When his father saw him, the subtlest hint of anger flashed in his cool, composed eyes.

"Brody," Max Odell greeted, sitting back in his oversized black leather armchair to face his oldest son.

Brody grunted as he slammed the office door shut and approached his father's mahogany desk. He planted his hands down upon its surface and leveled his gaze with the old man's. "Tell Valerie Ryan to call off her stupid fucking lawsuit."

One of Max's sculpted white eyebrows slid up. "Why?"

"Because it's wrong, that's why." Brody pushed off the desk and crossed his arms instead, shaking with raw energy and rage. "Sadie doesn't deserve this, especially not from that woman."

For a long moment, Max said nothing. He eyed his son with a kind of curious disdain, one that only made Brody more irritated by the second. When he did speak, his deep voice held a hint of snide humor. "How is it that you are always somehow involved in the cases of this firm? What goes on here is none of your business."

"Sadie is my business," Brody snapped. "You know this lawsuit won't go anywhere. So tell Valerie to drop it."

"Until I've examined all the angles of a case, I won't tell a long-standing client to 'back off' on anything," Max replied, immune to Brody's anger.

Brody shook his head. "I guess that's exactly what I expected you to say. Points for consistency, Dad, but a big fat penalty for lack of humanity."

He stalked out of the office, leaving the door wide open just because it was rude. He called Sadie on his way out of the building, hating that he had to bring her even more bad news.

When she answered, he was crossing Wilshire Boulevard on the way to his car. "Hey, we need to talk. Where are you?"

"At Le Petit Four getting lunch with Mom. Mind if I call you when we're done?"

"It can't wait. Trust me, you'll want to hear this. I'll be there in twenty minutes."

SADIE TUCKED her phone away, an anxious chill creeping down her spine. Brody sounded pretty upset. With a deep breath, she willed the thoughts away and focused back on her mother.

"How are the treatments going?"

Valerie let out a long exhale as she perused the menu, her eyes shielded by bug-eyed, tortoiseshell sunglasses. They were seated on the outdoor patio, within arm's reach of Sunset Boulevard and protected by a large yellow canopy. The wind caught pieces of her thinning hair, which she brushed back impatiently. "Just awful. They poke me with needles and run all these tests…I can hardly eat anything anymore. It's making me sicker, I'm convinced. Those bastards are trying to kill me."

Sadie pursed her lips, wishing she knew what to say. "I know it's not easy…"

"You don't know," Valerie simpered, folding up the menu and taking a long sip from her glass of Perrier. "But at least you're home now. I can rest easy knowing you're back where you belong."

Sadie closed her own menu and sat back in her chair, ignoring her mother's statement. She didn't know what to say to that, anyway. The instant the new security system was in, she'd be going back to her father's house. Nothing could change that, not even one of her mother's manipulative guilt trips.

A couple of Albatross fans shyly came by the table to wish Valerie a speedy recovery, bringing a bold and brilliant smile to her mother's face. Sadie only felt embarrassed, wishing her mother didn't insist on eating out so often. Valerie loved the attention. Even the cancer hadn't changed that.

But when she spotted a familiar face coming toward her from the restaurant, Sadie panicked.

Oh, great. Not again.

"Sadie! How great to run into you again," Drew greeted, stopping beside their table. His blue eyes went from Sadie to Valerie and widened. "Valerie Ryan. Wow. It's an honor."

Valerie beamed up at him, removing her sunglasses to get a better look. She eyed him up and down curiously. "Thank you."

When both of them turned to her expectantly, Sadie realized she should probably do introductions. "Mom, this is Drew. I met him at a coffee shop last week."

"How interesting!" Valerie preened, eyeing Drew again with fascination. "Why don't you sit with us? If you're not too busy, that is."

"Thank you." Drew pulled out the chair beside Sadie and sat down. "I was supposed to meet someone here but they never showed."

"That's too bad," Valerie replied with a sympathetic pout. "Such a handsome young man, how could anybody stand you up?"

Drew looked embarrassed and ran a hand through his length of brown hair, turning to Sadie. "I've been waiting on a phone call that never came, too."

Sadie winced, mortified he'd bring that up. She opened her menu and pretended to be busy so she wouldn't have to look at him.

Valerie must have read the signals, bringing a delighted grin to her face. "So, tell me all about yourself, Drew."

He chuckled, glancing at Sadie who refused to give him any attention. "Well, I'm something of an artist. And I love Sadie's music. Isn't she the best?"

Sadie flushed, feeling his eyes burning a hole right through her. When she felt his hand touch her knee under the table, she jumped and shifted away from him.

"She learned all she knows from me," Valerie proclaimed, false pride in her voice.

Sadie looked up then, one eyebrow cocked. She wanted to say something, but Drew cut her off.

"You two look so much alike, wow." He smiled at both of them, intending it to be a compliment.

Instead, both women fumed.

"Well, she's still young. She has a lot to learn about the big bad world," Valerie simpered, casting a knowing look at Sadie. She then launched into a detailed discussion with Drew about life in the music business, giving Sadie a much needed break from the conversation. The waiter came by to take their orders, then left them alone.

Sadie rested her chin in her palm, gazing out at the busy street full of cars and people. She would've given anything to be one of them, anonymous and carefree.

Her heart jumped when she spotted Brody walking down the sidewalk, making a beeline for the restaurant. She waved, catching his attention.

He came up to her, his gaze falling on Drew. Suspicion hardened his face. "Who's this?"

Sadie rolled her eyes as she rose to her feet. "It's not important."

Valerie sniffed, prepared to say something. Sadie cut her off with a warning look before leaving the outdoor patio and meeting Brody off to the side where they could have some privacy. She could feel the fury vibrating off of him. "What is it?"

Brody glared at the back of Valerie's head, then faced Sadie. "She's filed a lawsuit against you."

"What?" Sadie's brow furrowed as she shook her head. "I don't understand."

"She hired my dad to make the case that you stole her stage persona when you performed with Albatross," he explained, shoving his hands into his pockets. A dark, morbid thought occurred to him. "I wonder if he's been having you followed by a P.I. That could explain the black car."

Sadie paled. "Do you think...*really?*"

His jaw clenched as he gave it some thought. "Then again, the 'whore' note doesn't play into that theory."

Wrapping her arms over her torso, Sadie tried to come to terms with this new information. Through all her inner reasoning, all she could find was anger. "I can't believe this."

She took off before Brody could stop her, approaching her mother with fire in her eyes. "How *could* you?" she snapped, not even bothering to keep her voice low.

Valerie glanced up at her in shock. "Excuse me?"

Drew watched Sadie intently, eyebrows raised.

Sadie ignored the looks they were getting, letting her anger fuel her. "You're *suing* me?"

Valerie bristled, sitting up taller in her chair in an attempt to regain some dignity. Her lips spread in a placating smile. "I'm just protecting my interests, darling. You understand."

"Um, no, I don't," Sadie retorted, shaking with disbelief. "I can't believe you could be this…this *petty*."

Valerie started to reply, but Sadie cut her off. "No. Don't. Find your own way home, I'm done."

She turned on her heel and left the restaurant, not even caring who saw or where she was going. Brody caught up with her, his hand finding her elbow.

"You did the right thing," he told her, glancing back at the restaurant. Valerie hadn't bothered to follow them.

Sadie felt tears brimming in her eyes and sniffed. "She really doesn't care about anybody but herself."

"That surprises you?" He laughed, though it fell short. He urged her to stop walking and pulled her into his arms, giving her a moment to breathe. "I'm sorry, Sadie."

She closed her eyes, letting him comfort her. Her arms came around him and held on as the tears threatened to fall again. "I'm going back to my dad's house. I can't stand to stay with that woman anymore."

Brody tensed. "Is the security system in yet?"

"Not for a couple more days, but I don't care. I'll manage."

"I'll stay with you," he decided as he pulled away. "You don't mind, do you?"

She shook her head, both grateful and nervous at the idea. "I'd like that."

"Just until the system is in, I promise." He grinned, holding up his hand in a scout's salute. "Unless at that point you don't want me to leave. But we'll cross that bridge when we get to it."

Sadie's face broke into a sly smile. "No rent-free living for you, buddy."

He winked and wrapped his arm over her shoulders. "Damn, and here I thought you were my ticket out of the slums of Venice."

"You don't live in a slum."

"Maybe not. But it sure ain't Beverly Hills."

Chapter *twenty-six*

AFTER A tense and emotional phone call to Tommy, Sadie lay back against the pillows of her bed and closed her eyes. She tried to breathe away the tension that bunched in her shoulders, but nothing seemed to help. That nagging, sick feeling was still there, polluting her body and weighing down her mood. It was just another brick added to the already heavy load of stress she'd been carrying since her return to L.A., and it was by far the most infuriating brick of all.

As much as she resented her mother for pulling a stunt like this, Sadie couldn't help but feel sorry for making a scene at the restaurant and leaving her to fend for herself. It wasn't like her to do something so irrational, but she'd been beyond reason at that point. All those heavy bricks had dragged her to her knees, and her mother's petty lawsuit was enough to break her back at last.

Needing to distract herself, she rose from the bed and went to the second guest bedroom across the hall, where Brody was busy unpacking his duffle bag. He turned when she entered, his eyebrows raised.

"How'd it go?"

Sadie crossed her arms and leaned against the doorframe. "My dad's pissed. They all are."

"Has he contacted his lawyer?"

Sadie nodded. "They're handling it."

"Did you tell him about you being followed?"

She let out a sigh and stared at the floor. "No. I couldn't do it. Tommy would freak out."

"And rightfully so," Brody replied as he walked toward her. He gripped her shoulders, urging her to look up at him. "They're going to find out eventually. Your dad's going to ask why you added extra security to his house without telling him."

She pouted, knowing he was right. "I know. I'll tell them soon."

He let his hands fall as a grin brightened his face. "Good. Now, why don't we grab a bottle of wine and relax?"

She perked up at the thought. "You read my mind."

He followed her into the kitchen, where she poured them each a glass of Chardonnay. She handed it to him, watching him sniff it before taking a sip.

"It's Tess's favorite. I don't know much about wine," Sadie admitted as she glanced at the golden bottle with a shrug. "The label says it's from Santa Barbara."

Brody chuckled. "Fancy."

Sadie tasted it herself, delighted by the fragrant scent of honeysuckle and cool, crisp hints of apricot. "Not bad."

"So other than drinking wine, what do you do to relax these days?" Brody asked, resting his hip against the counter. "If you say you watch baseball I might just have to kiss you again."

One of her eyebrows lifted as she smiled. "I've been known to watch a game now and then. My grandpa is a big fan. He drives my grandma crazy with all his baseball references."

"Don't break my heart and tell me he's a Giants fan."

Sadie laughed. "Nope. Good ol' Dodger blue, all the way."

"Thank God." Brody grinned, setting his glass on the counter. "Okay, so baseball is a sorta yes. What else?"

"Music," Sadie said without hesitation, a wistful look coming over her face as she took another drink of wine. "When I have those piano keys under my fingertips, the rest of the world just melts away. It's the only time I can really let go and…" She caught Brody staring at her in amusement and felt her face redden. "What?"

"Why don't you play me something?"

"Oh." She twisted her wine glass around in her hands, nerves getting the better of her at the thought of an audience. It was only Brody, but for some reason she felt the need to impress him. To show off. "Okay, I guess I could."

She set her wine glass aside and led the way down the hall to the music room, where she settled onto the piano bench. It surprised her when he sat down next to her, urging her to scoot over to make room.

Feeling him so close to her sent nervous shivers down her arms, but she avoided looking at him as she placed her fingers on the keys. She closed her eyes and inhaled once, slow and deep, to center her focus.

Then she began to play.

Perhaps instinctually, she'd chosen a song that told of the long-lost, rosy days of youth. Of running through an endless sea of freshly cut grass, soaring from a swing until it felt like flying, and that first taste of summer in the form of strawberry ice cream. The song absorbed every part of her until she nearly forgot he was there. When she finished the last, bittersweet note, the feel of his hand on her knee brought her back to reality.

Her face turned to his as her eyes fluttered open, almost afraid to see what he might be feeling. But the warmth in his expression soothed her fears and brought a shy smile to her face.

"Well? What'd you think?" she asked.

Brody squeezed her knee, then nudged her out of the way and placed his own hands over the keys. "I think it's my turn now."

A surprised laugh escaped her lips as he began to play the first notes of Billy Joel's "Only The Good Die Young." It took him a few tries to remember the notes, but once he got going his skill surprised her. She couldn't stop smiling as he jumped into the song, singing about letting go of tradition and having fun for once. He smiled at her and winked as he launched into the chorus, charming her to pieces. And when he was done, he leaned in to press a hot and fast kiss to her mouth that sent her heart fluttering.

"Wow," she said, bemused. "I didn't know you could do that."

"Don't you remember my mom used to make me take lessons after school? I'm not about to sing to a packed house at The Hollywood Bowl, but I do all right," he joked, nudging her with his elbow. "I would say that last song was dedicated to you, but I think this one is more fitting."

His fingers danced over the keys, re-creating the timeless sound of Paul McCartney's "Maybe I'm Amazed." She watched him play, feeling the muscles of her body loosen and relax, her heart lighten. When he wasn't concentrating on the keys, he was staring at her with those dark eyes of his that combined reckless charm and warm intensity all at once. She couldn't look away as she inched closer to him.

He noticed the light come into her eyes and brighten there, casting that sea foam green an impossibly bluer shade. She smiled before resting her head against his shoulder, her hand trailing along his leg as he finished the song.

"That was beautiful," she mused, pleased when his arm came around her and pulled her close. She tilted back her face to look at him, more at ease than she'd been in weeks. "Just when I think I've got you figured out, you turn everything upside down again."

"No one's ever accused me of being predictable." He pressed his lips to the top of her head, then voiced a concern he'd been holding back since earlier that day. "So who was that guy having lunch with you and the big bad witch today?"

Sadie rolled her eyes and slipped from his grasp. "Just some guy—a fan—I met at a coffee shop that I keep running into by accident. I think he's got a crush on me or something."

His eyebrows rose. "A crush, huh?"

She noticed more than just curiosity on his face and started to laugh. "Are you jealous or something?"

He grinned. "Not really. You're here with me, not that guy. So I'd say I'm winning."

"It's not a competition." She toyed with strands of her hair, unsure why the thought of him competing for her affections thrilled her so much. "And to be fair, you're only here because I might have a stalker."

"Fair enough, but I'd probably be here even if you didn't."

She bit back a smile and averted her eyes. "Either way, I'm glad you are."

"You sure you wouldn't prefer Mr. Abercrombie & Fitch over me?" Brody teased, brushing aside a strand of her hair to reveal her face. "You know, *he* could be your stalker. Crazed fan wanting you all to himself. Haven't you seen *The Bodyguard?*"

"Yes, I have. And no, I don't think Drew is the same creep that's been following me," Sadie replied. "He might be annoyingly persistent, but he's a nice guy."

"Don't you know it's the nice ones you have to worry about?" he reminded her, running his hand down her back. When she tilted her face up to his, he grinned. "At least assholes like me are honest about what we are."

"I don't think you're an asshole."

He watched her lips curve, forming that dimple he had such a weakness for. Combined with the soft, warm way she was looking at him, he felt his humor fade behind a rising need. His hand rose to the back of her neck, bringing her face closer to his. "Clearly you haven't been paying attention, Sadie."

He closed the distance between them, his mouth finding hers. He heard a small, helpless whimper escape her throat when he changed the angle of the kiss, his tongue sliding along hers. His hand tightened in her hair as he dove deeper, somehow needing to prove to her that he meant what he said. He wasn't a good person and didn't deserve to be treated like one. Not by anyone, and most definitely not by her.

He knew he could easily take advantage of the situation. Everything from the way her body leaned into his to the way her breath caught in her throat indicated she'd let him in. All he had to do was ask. Instigate. Take.

The devil on his shoulder cheered him on. It would be easy. But the side of him that was more gentleman than asshole reminded him that she deserved better.

He eased back from her, fighting to keep a nonchalant smile on his face. Her eyes opened slowly, as though waking from a dream. She blinked, seeming surprised by the swift change of mood.

"Is everything okay?" she asked.

"I'm gonna grab us some more wine." He rose to his feet and didn't look back as he left the room, needing to cool his blood and distance himself before he changed his mind.

Back at the piano, Sadie let out a soft sigh. She turned to the keys, striking a few notes absently as her pulse settled and her heart ached. She wanted him, more than she knew was probably healthy. So why did he keep pulling away? What was he so afraid of?

SLEEP EVADED him. He lay awake staring at the ceiling of the guest bedroom, restless knowing she was just a room away.

Before she'd gone to bed, he'd walked of the outside perimeter of the house and inspected the darkest corners of the backyard. Then he'd checked all the locks, twice, before shutting off the lights and closing her inside her bedroom. She'd be safe. For tonight, anyway. It was all he could offer her for now.

Though she hadn't said anything, he'd noticed the shift in her mood after he'd returned with more wine. She continued to play songs for him, but her smile was a little sad around the edges. She'd sensed his hesitation, but he doubted she really understood it.

How could she? She allowed herself to be happy in a way he never could. He didn't deserve happiness. What he deserved was exactly what he had—a lonely, miserable existence at the bottom of the society's barrel.

She may know some of the details of what he'd done overseas, but she'd never be able to grasp the full extent of his guilt. She'd never caused the death of another person. Never had to live with the shame of being ostracized by those who had once been called friends.

Then again, she *did* know what it was like to wage wars with family. It was something they both understood. And how ironic was it that just as they were growing closer, his father and her mother were busy trying to tear everything apart? The cynical side of him couldn't help but laugh at the situation, despite how frustrating it was. Valerie was the same old attention whore she'd always been, and his father was in it for the money she shoved into his pockets. And while they both satisfied their baser desires, he and Sadie were left to pick up the pieces of the devastation left behind.

He let out a heavy sigh, rubbing his face with his hands. At least he'd given up on his father loving him a long time ago. It without a doubt saved his sanity. Sadie, on the other hand, still held out hope that Valerie would change and start treating her less like a prized pet and more like a daughter. But he knew it was a long shot. Even dying, the woman was a selfish creature. There would be no getting through to her.

And as for him, being around Sadie, being close to her, was getting harder to resist. Even though he told himself time and time again that it wouldn't be good for either of them, it just didn't seem to matter now. Not after what they'd been through. What *she'd* been through.

She was in this mess because of him, which meant he owed it to her to help her through it. But it was getting more difficult by the day to hold back his need for her, not when it was so close to the surface. She made him look at the world in an entirely different light—in her light. Her positivity and gentleness, her soft humor and compassion. They were things he'd lost years ago when she'd left the first time. Now he didn't think he could stand it if she ran away again. What would become of him when she left?

Not liking the answer to that question, he shut his eyes and rolled over, hoping to lull himself back to sleep.

Chapter *twenty-seven*

BRODY WOKE abruptly, shaking off some kind of dream involving his mother and the hot sands of the Middle East. It lingered for a second then dissipated, leaving him groggy and irritated. With a grunt, he rolled upright into a sitting position and ran his hands through his hair. The vague smell of bacon perked him up and had him inhaling deeply.

At that moment he remembered where he was, and who he was with.

Sadie.

A tired smile teased his lips as he got to his feet and wandered out into the kitchen, seeing her bustling around cooking breakfast. She sang quietly to herself as she whisked pancake batter and turned the bacon crackling on the stove.

When he approached, she tilted her head and grinned at him. "Hey. Happy Independence Day!"

Brody chuckled and stretched his arms over his head. "It's July fourth already?"

"Yep, best day of the year." Sadie beamed, pouring globs of pancake batter dotted with blueberries onto a molten hot skillet. They fanned out into imperfect circles and bubbled up in the center. "Are you hungry?"

Brody checked the pulse on his neck, then nodded. "Well, I'm still alive. So yes, I'm hungry."

She giggled and began chopping up bright red strawberries. "Good. It's tradition in my family to serve red, white, and blue pancakes with bacon on the Fourth of July."

"Lucky me," he mused as he came up behind her, his arms wrapping around her waist. He placed a kiss on the curve of her neck, enjoying the fresh scent of soap on her skin.

She leaned into him, her arms folding over his own. "How'd you sleep?"

"Decent. How about you?"

"Much better knowing you were here." She sighed, then turned around to face him. The glow of sunlight through the kitchen window brightened her eyes, as did her happy smile. "Back home my grandparents and I always watch the fireworks over Lake Tahoe." She looked outside, her smile widening. "I think from the view up here we should be able to see the ones over Grand Park."

Brody followed her gaze. "Probably. But that's not till tonight. What do you want to do today?"

She pressed her lips together as she considered. "Maybe the beach?"

He grinned, then shifted away from her to flip the pancakes. "You read my mind."

Once the pancakes were ready, Sadie decorated them with strawberries, more blueberries, and a dollop of fresh Cool Whip. When she was finished, he couldn't help but laugh at the proud look on her face.

"Looks good. I didn't know you could cook."

She waved off the comment. "I can't. But a sacred family pancake tradition doesn't count as cooking. It's a rite of passage."

She winked at him and carried their plates into the dining room. He followed her, pleased to see she wasn't letting her mother or fears of being stalked get to her. She deserved a day to not think about those things.

And he wanted nothing more than to make it the most special, perfect day of her life.

AFTER BREAKFAST and a shower, Brody was ready to take her out on the town. While he'd brushed his teeth and dressed, he thought of all the things he wanted to show her, all the things he knew she'd missed out on all these years. The Pier with its thrill rides and colorful populace, the white sandy beach with views of nothing but the luminous sapphire water of the Pacific, the hip taco joint with its to-die-for carnitas.

He wanted to show her the best of L.A., maybe in a subconscious attempt to convince her to stay. It was selfish, maybe, but he knew part of her didn't want to leave. Ever since performing with her father's band, she'd been different. Less afraid of crowds, more open to the idea of city life. It was important that she continue in that direction and not let anything else get in the way.

And it was important to him that she trust him enough to show her the life she could have. The life she truly deserved.

When he came into the living room, he found her standing beside the front door, colorful tote bag in hand. She'd slipped into a cerulean blue sarong that showed glimpses of a white bikini and the soft, lightly tanned skin underneath. Her long waves of hair were tied back in a loose bun that sat atop her head, leaving strands to frame her face.

With a hesitant smile, she lifted her tote. "I packed sunscreen, granola bars, four bottles of water, two towels, my iPod and a couple of books for us to read. Is there anything else you'd like to bring?"

As he walked toward her, he couldn't help but laugh. He got such a kick out of her neurotic tendencies. "You know, I might need a fifth bottle of water. I could dehydrate out there."

Her smile faltered. "Oh. You're right. I'll go grab one."

"Sadie." He grabbed her elbow to stop her and pulled her in for a quick kiss, amused by the worried look on her face. "I was joking with you."

"Oh. Right. I forgot you like to do that." She slipped from his grasp with one eyebrow raised in good humor. "You know, if I was more like you we'd just take off without being prepared and then where would we be?"

"Sunburned and thirsty," he replied, grinning again as he threw his arm over her shoulders and led her out of the house. "Now let's go before the beach fills up. I want a good spot."

She nodded. "Okay. Oh! Maybe we should get an umbrella?"

"Too late. We're leaving." He ushered her outside and grabbed her keys to lock the door for her. As he clicked the deadbolt closed, he heard her let out a startled gasp. He whirled around, seeing her standing with her hands clasped over her mouth and her eyes on the front end of the curved driveway. "What? What is it?"

Instead of responding she only hovered in stunned silence. His eyes followed her gaze and caught sight of it. Rage filled him, followed quickly by remorse that he hadn't seen it first. Maybe then he could have shielded her from it.

Spray painted in large, black letters over the concrete of her driveway right by the street was the word 'WHORE.' He walked over and glared down at it, shaking his head. His vision hazed with red as he stared around the street, seeing nothing out of the ordinary. Whoever had done it had come in the night while they'd been sleeping. Which meant that being there for her had done nothing to help. The creep had still returned.

He bit back a frustrated growl and turned to Sadie, who looked ready to faint. He gathered her into his arms and ran his hand over her hair, soothing her. "It's all right. Let's just go, okay? We'll deal with this later."

She nodded, swallowing back the bile that had risen in her throat. "Okay."

He led her to his car and opened the door for her. After she'd slipped inside, he leaned in. "Give me a quick second. I just need to check on something."

He shut the door and wandered over to the side of the house, where he reached for his cell phone and called Chase. His brother answered on the second ring.

"I need a big favor."

After he explained the situation, his brother was quiet for a moment before replying. "*You really like this girl, don't you?*"

Brody sighed, ready to rip out his own hair. "Just do it, please."

He hung up the phone and returned to Sadie. Now that the shock had worn off, she seemed only quietly sad. He reached for her hand and tried to smile against the anger he still felt. "Ready to go?"

"Yeah. Can you turn on the radio?" she asked.

"Of course." He shoved the key in the ignition and started the car, flipping through the stations until he found good old classic rock. Joe Cocker's throaty voice sang about getting by with help from friends as Brody pulled out of the driveway and gunned it down the street.

SADIE LIFTED her face to the sun, closing her eyes and welcoming that red-orange glow. Even with the layers of sunscreen she'd applied and the sunglasses she wore, she could still feel the hot rays cooking her skin. She didn't care, though. She couldn't even remember the last time she'd been to the beach and wanted to enjoy every aspect of it, even if she did get a sunburn.

To her left, she could feel Brody beside her. She opened her eyes and looked at him, embracing the quiet thrill that raced through her. He'd stripped off his white T-shirt and kept only the navy blue board shorts, and though she felt mildly embarrassed about looking, she couldn't help it.

He rested back on his hands, his tanned legs spread out in front of him and a boyish grin on his face as he watched the people all around them. She loved the way he looked at the world, as though there was no detail worth ignoring. Everything from the gangly teenagers playing a rowdy game of volleyball to the exhausted parents passed out under an umbrella while their twin eight-year-old boys ran amuck in the surf was worth watching. For all his cynicism, she knew he loved life. He loved people and places and getting into the thick of things where all the action was happening. If he'd brought his camera, she was sure he'd be scoping around for everyday moments to capture on film.

She nudged him with her shoulder, smiling when he looked at her. She stared at her reflection in his mirrored aviator sunglasses, her pulse skipping at his quick grin.

"Having fun?" he asked.

She nodded, turning to watch the white waves crest and then crash into the sand. Squeals of laughter from children dancing out of the water's reach blended with the roar of the ocean and the pealing squall of seagulls. "Thank you for this. I forgot how fun it could be."

"The beach is always fun."

"No, that's not what I meant…" She bit her lower lip and wondered how to explain it. "I just feel so…free, I guess. I mean, we're *exposed* out here. Anybody could recognize me, and yet I don't care. Let them come. I'm just happy living my life and being here with you."

He chuckled. "It *is* national celebrate freedom day."

"True." She rested her head on his shoulder. "I don't want it to end."

He glanced at his phone to check the time. "Well, it's not over yet. In fact, I'd say it's time for some tacos."

"Tacos?" She met his eyes as he got to his feet and helped her up.

"Yep. We can come back here after if you'd like, but we gotta beat the lunch crowd if we want a seat on the outdoor patio."

"Where are we going?" She gathered up her tote bag and her belongings, then shook out her towel to rid it of sand.

He took her hand, his teeth flashing in a charming grin. "To the Pier, McRae. It's time you saw what you've been missing all this time."

They got a prime seat on the outdoor patio of the Pier's one and only Mexican food joint, which sat at the far west tip and offered panoramic views of the sea. Sadie stared out at the calm blue waves while Brody ordered them each a Corona with lime. Chips and salsa were dropped off, along with menus which Brody refused. Sadie eyed him curiously as the waiter walked away to get their drinks.

"What? I don't get to choose?" she asked, eyebrows raised.

"Nope." He reached for a chip and scooped up a big bite of salsa. "You'll just have to trust me on this one. If you're gonna enjoy authentic Mexican food, you need an expert."

Sadie bit into a tortilla chip, fighting back a smile. "I see. How silly of me."

The waiter brought them their beers and Brody placed the order—a big plate of carnitas tacos al carbón with rice and pinto beans on the side. When it arrived, Sadie watched Brody scarf down one of the tacos without taking a breath. Amused and a little daunted, she tasted one herself and was delighted by the flavor of roasted pork coupled with crisp cilantro and juicy white onions.

After lunch, they walked hand-in-hand down the Pier, Brody pointing out fun and interesting things for her to look at. There was Pacific Park with its colorful Ferris Wheel and roller coasters that she dare not try, hoards of visitors of all shapes, colors, and sizes, touristy bicyclists zipping in and out of the crowds, and an overwhelming sense of joy that could only be had under the sweet Santa Monica sun. She basked in it and the feel of her friend beside her, who kept his hand tucked firmly in hers.

For the first time, she felt content in her own skin. She didn't worry about being recognized, about her mother's stupid lawsuit or about the lunatic who'd defaced her father's property just hours before. She'd even managed to forget about the police investigation into Walker's death. In the end, what difference did it make? She was alive, and she was free.

Free at last.

Brody bought her ice cream which they enjoyed at the edge of the Pier, overlooking the ocean. She lapped up vanilla with rainbow sprinkles, unable to keep the smile from her face. And when he leaned over to steal a kiss from her, she wondered how she'd ever lived without him.

When they drove back to her father's home, they sang along with Katy Perry on the radio, laughing at each other. Her cheerful mood continued until they pulled onto her street and made the ascent to the top, and the memory of that morning came flooding back. She fought the dread she felt at seeing the word again, only to inhale sharply with surprise when they pulled up and the word was gone.

Beside her, Brody let out a relieved sigh.

Sadie turned to him as he pulled into the driveway, brows creased. "Where did it go?"

He parked the car and shut off the engine. "I called in a favor. Not that he owes me anything, but he was willing to help you out."

"Chase," she murmured, tears springing into her eyes. Gratitude flooded her as she slipped from the car and walked over to where the word had been, finding Chase had painted over it. She couldn't even see a trace of black.

Brody came up behind her, taking her hand in his. "C'mon. Let's go inside and clean up. It'll be dark soon and you don't want to break tradition and miss the fireworks."

She wiped at a tear that fell down her cheek. "Please tell him I said thank you."

He nodded and led her inside, not wanting her to dwell on the situation anymore.

WHEN DARKNESS rolled in, they lounged outside on the patio with a box of pizza and a six pack of Corona. It wasn't fancy, but it was quickly becoming the best night of her life.

Sadie laughed, sipping her beer and staring at Brody fondly. "Remember that time we took Hendrix out for a walk and we ended up all the way down Hollywood Boulevard and that creepy homeless guy tried to barter with us using an old pair of socks?"

Brody snorted, shaking his head. "Oh, yeah. We were both like, dude, we don't want your socks."

"But he wouldn't leave us alone. I think you even offered him a five dollar bill and he still kept shoving those smelly socks in your face."

"I can't believe you remember that," Brody replied, amused by her. "And Hendrix, wow. I haven't thought about him in years."

"He was the only dog I ever loved," she told him, honesty softening her expression.

"He loved you, too." Brody tipped back his beer and finished it, then set it aside and reached for another. "He *hated* my dad. But who doesn't?"

Sadie smiled. "At least you got to have pets. I was always too nervous to ask for one and my parents were too clueless to see I needed it."

"Parents can be that way." He tapped his beer to hers with a wink. "Assholes."

"Yep." She drank, then let out a quiet sigh. "At least we turned out okay."

"We did?" he mused.

She turned the beer bottle around in her hands. "Well, yeah. I mean, we're not *that* bad."

"You're afraid of your own shadow and I'm a greedy sell out. I'd say we *are* that bad," he joked, dodging out of the way when she tried to punch his shoulder.

"What I mean is we're doing okay. And now we have each other, so it's even better," she decided, only to feel embarrassed by her own words and turn away.

When he reached for her hand, she met his gaze. Even in the dim light, she could see his dark eyes warm for her. "Yeah, it is."

He wrapped his arm over her shoulders and brought her closer. She curled into him, closing her eyes and reveling in the feeling of comfort he gave her.

"Hey, look. It's starting."

Sadie lifted her head and looked at the Los Angeles skyline, seeing a burst of fiery lights above the cityscape. Her heart lifted and a big smile came over her face. "It's so beautiful."

"They put on a good show." He held her close and sipped his beer, enjoying her enthusiasm. He'd never really cared about fireworks, but seeing them through her eyes made them special. It reminded him that no matter what happened from here on out, at least she'd have this day of relaxation and fun.

Sparks of blue and pink and purple flooded the night sky, joined by showers of gold and big, beautiful globes of white. Sadie loved them all, up until the grand finale that quite simply took her breath away.

When the last of the sparks faded from the sky, she tilted her head back to press a soft kiss to Brody's cheek, just because it was there. He caught her mouth instead, teasing her with a tender kiss. Her heart began to race as he pulled her in, one hand drawing back into her hair.

Maybe it was the beer or her impossibly good mood, but she realized she couldn't wait any longer. She needed to tell him—to show him—how she felt before the moment was gone and her bravery extinguished.

"Can I play something for you?" she asked, hoping her voice didn't betray her nerves.

"Sure."

"Give me a quick second." She jumped to her feet and raced inside to get her guitar. When she returned, she sat down in the patio chair across from him and cradled the guitar in her lap, a pick held between the fingers of her right hand with her other held tight over the strings. Her gaze lifted to his as she bit back a nervous smile. "This is something I've been working on since I came back to L.A. I hope you like it."

He nodded as she strummed her guitar in a warm, breezy tone that seemed best suited for summer nights and bonfires. She began to sing, her voice sweet and soothing like quiet drops of rain. Her eyes rose to his, a boldness flashing in them he wasn't used to seeing.

When she launched into the chorus, he realized why. She wasn't just singing to him. She was singing *about* him.

"I remember your face, like it was yesterday. You followed me home, and I stopped feeling so alone. To see you now, all our innocence gone. It breaks my heart, I have to say. I always knew you were the one. Even then, with hopeful colors in all that gray..."

Floored and impossibly moved, he set aside his beer and leaned forward, his elbows resting on his knees. He watched every move she made; every subtle smile, every quirk of an eyebrow, every flicker of that dimple he loved. She opened herself up in complete vulnerability before him, and he couldn't find words to describe what it meant. He just knew it was the most incredible thing anyone had ever done for him.

"This damaged heart is shy, I know. The past has turned it to stone. But darling you, only you, show me where to go. When all else fails me, you're the only one, you know…"

As she polished off the final notes, she took a deep breath and released it. She dared to look at him, gauging his reaction. He only appeared disquieted and a little confused, which sent a jolt of panic ripping through her.

Had he not understood her meaning? Or was it just not what he wanted to hear?

She tried to find something to say, but could only stare at her hands that still clutched her guitar like a protective shield. When he rose to his feet and stood beside her, she chanced a look up at him.

A slow smile spread over his face. "You know they say that once there's a song written about you, you live forever."

She let out an anxious laugh. "Guess I just immortalized you, then."

"Lucky me." He reached for her guitar and lifted it out of her arms, setting it aside. She stared at him, eyes bright and her heart laying in her palms, ready for him to take. He didn't have it in him to refuse her, not anymore.

"Did you like it?" she asked.

He smiled again, then pretended to give it thought. "As far as love songs go, it wasn't bad. You could've talked up my manliness a bit more, but I guess I can forgive you."

Her face broke into a smile as she kicked him playfully in the shin. "Shut up."

In response he swept her up out of the chair, his arms encircling her waist. His eyes held hers as his humor faded and something darker, deeper, replaced it. "What was that last line again?"

"When all else fails me, you're the only one," she murmured, unable to help the smile that curved her lips. It was true, after all. Every last word of it.

"God, that's good." He crushed her mouth with his, overtaken by the feel of her body pressed tight against his own. She molded into him, as lost in the heat as he was. As driven by it.

He broke the kiss and scooped her into his arms, his pulse hammering beneath his skin. She laughed brightly as he carried her into the house and to her bedroom. When he reached the bed he laid her down upon it and crawled over her, his mouth finding hers again.

She tore at his shirt, pulling it over his head so she could run her hands along the smooth skin of his chest and shoulders. All her senses were heightened, the world around her surreal. Every touch sparked an intense reaction that shimmered over her skin. Every glimpse of his face, those dark eyes, brought her back to the moment and sent her heart soaring with ecstasy.

Soon her dress and everything else was on the floor and nothing mattered except that he not stop, that he kiss her again on the tender spot by her collar bone that promised heat and dark delight. As he did, her arms came around him, welcoming him in. Her breath caught in her throat as he hovered over her, his eyes intense on hers. For the briefest of moments, she saw the beast he held at bay and thrilled in it.

She cried out when he drove himself into her, losing all reserve. All sanity. She held on to him in desperation as he took her, her hands in his hair and her mouth roaming eagerly over his. When the shockwave hit and stunned her breathless, all she could do was whisper his name and hope he knew, hope he could understand, just how much she cared for him.

How much he mattered. And just how desperately in love with him she was.

Chapter *twenty-eight*

SADIE WATCHED the installer test the new security lights, grateful the system was finally in. To her right, Brody sat at the dining table with his laptop, knee-deep in emails and the gossip column.

When she glanced over at him he met her eyes, his mouth twisting in a charming grin that had her insides fluttering. She had to turn away before she blushed, wishing she knew better how to play it cool after what they'd shared the night before.

A swift knock on the front door followed by Tess breezing in brought her back to reality. Her friend went straight for her, ignoring Brody completely.

"Hey. Is everything almost ready?" Tess asked, pulling Sadie in for a hug.

Sadie nodded, motioning out the window. "They're just testing the lights now. The alarm system is done."

"Great. I'll have a look before they leave, but if I know Marc he's pulled out all the stops for you. Almost all his clientele are celebrities."

"I'm still not used to that word…celebrity."

"Well, get used to it because I booked you a show for next week." Tess threw her hands out to her sides and smiled brightly. "Surprise!"

Sadie's mouth fell open. "Oh, God. I'm not ready."

"Shut up, yes you are." Tess turned to Brody, as if just noticing he was there. "Back me up on this. She's ready, isn't she?"

One of Brody's eyebrows lifted, his gaze shifting to Sadie. "She was born ready."

Sadie snorted out a laugh and fell into the dining chair across from him, shaking her head. "You guys are going to be the end of me."

"No, we're the ones making sure you actually *live*, honey," Tess defended, taking the seat beside her. She rested her chin in her hand and eyed Sadie seriously. "So, anything new with this stalker creep?"

Sadie shrugged, wondering if she should mention the message painted on the driveway that Chase had covered up. She decided against it, not even wanting to think of it herself. "Not really. The police didn't find any fingerprints on the letter left on my car and the security cameras nearby didn't catch anything. So basically we've found out nothing."

"Well, the offer's still open for you to come stay at my place," Tess reminded her, glancing over at Brody with a sly smile. "Though from the looks of it, you're shacking up with the enemy these days."

Brody's eyes narrowed as Sadie shot her friend a warning look. "Tess."

Tess held up her hands in an offering of peace. "All right, all right. I'm sorry, I take it back. At least you're out of Valerie's house, though. I can't believe that woman had the audacity to file a lawsuit against you."

Sadie softened, leaning back in her chair. "I know. I should probably go try and reason with her. I haven't talked to her since I found out."

"I don't think that's a good idea," Tess began, reaching for Sadie's hand. "It's only going to upset you more than you already are."

"She's right, Sadie," Brody cut in, brows creased with concern. "You need to let the lawyers duke it out first. Anything more you say to her is just going to fuel the fire."

Sadie pursed her lips. "I know better than anyone how to deal with her. Besides, it's not like I'm some fragile little lamb. I can handle getting upset once in awhile." She rose to her feet, frustrated. "I'll just run over there real fast and check on her. It won't take long."

"I'll come with you," Brody offered, standing up.

Sadie shook her head. "Please, don't. I need to do this on my own."

"You sure?" Tess asked, worry in her eyes.

"Yeah," Sadie replied, grabbing her purse and keys from the kitchen counter. "This is my burden to bear, not yours. I can handle it."

Without another word, she left.

AS IF by fate, on the short drive to her mother's house Albatross's "Dying In The City" came on the radio. Sadie smiled, remembering the thrill of performing with her father and the band. It was by far one of the greatest nights of her life. And soon, she'd get to perform again. This time without the mask of Piper Gray or the prestige of her father's band. She'd perform, at last, as Sadie McRae.

The thought put her in a better mood as she pulled into the driveway and parked, then ascended the short steps and knocked on the front door.

When it opened to reveal someone completely unexpected, Sadie thought she was hallucinating. Or at the wrong house.

"Drew?"

"Hey, Sadie. Long time no see." Drew grinned, reaching out to take her hand and tug her inside. "Come in. Your mom's been hoping you'd stop by."

She let him lead her through the parlor, struggling to find words to say. "What are you doing here?"

He chuckled. "After lunch the other day, I offered to drive Valerie home. Since you'd left, she didn't have a ride. I didn't mind, of course. In fact, I was honored to help. I've been keeping her company ever since."

Sadie flushed, annoyed that he'd taken advantage of the situation like that. Then again, she *had* left her mother in a bind. "Well, thank you. I guess."

"No problem." He flashed that bright smile at her again before bringing her into the music room with its wide windows and piano. Valerie was seated on one of the ornate sofas, a glass of iced tea in her hand and Coco in her lap. Her smile fell the instant she saw her daughter.

"I was wondering when you'd be back," Valerie said, stroking her dog's white fur.

Sadie crossed her arms, inching away from Drew. "I needed some time to cool off. I'm sure you can understand that."

"I suppose." Valerie's chin lifted in a haughty gesture. "That's how I felt after finding out about that little performance of yours."

Sadie's jaw clenched as she fought back the words she so desperately wanted to say in favor of civility. When Drew left her side and went to sit with Valerie, Sadie watched in horror as her mother caressed his hand with hers.

Valerie spotted the shock on Sadie's face and smiled indulgently. "While you've been off making a fool of yourself in public with that reporter, I've been in the presence of a true gentleman." She tilted her head to look at Drew, adoration softening her features.

Disgust filled Sadie, only to be followed by confusion. "What do you mean, making a fool of myself?"

Valerie giggled. "Didn't you see the tabloids this morning? They're all abuzz about it." She leaned over and snatched a magazine from the coffee table in front of her, holding it out for Sadie to take. "Really, darling, I thought you'd have better sense than to put yourself out there like that. Gossip like this isn't good for the reputation."

Sadie stepped forward and took the magazine from her mother's hands, filled with dread. There on the cover were three shots of her with Brody at the Pier and the beach—snuggled close, exchanging a heated kiss, laughing. The headline read: *Sadie McRae's Disturbing Love Affair With Shameless Paparazzi.*

Dizziness swept over her as she tossed the magazine back onto the table, not wanting to look at it any longer. She knew better than to be surprised, but part of her regretted being so careless. And now Brody had been dragged into the spotlight, making everything more complicated.

"Look, I came here to talk to you about the lawsuit," Sadie began, trying to keep a level head. "My personal life is none of your business."

"Your life is everybody's business now," Valerie reminded her. "You wanted fame and fortune. This is the price we pay."

Sadie grimaced. "No I didn't. You forced me into the spotlight against my will when you exposed my alias. I never wanted any of this."

"But now that it's here you're sure taking advantage of it, aren't you?" Valerie argued. "The first chance you got you stole my song, my look. You paraded around with the band *I* made legendary and made a mockery of me. Did you know some people *dared* to say that you're better than me?"

Her mother tried to laugh off the thought, but Sadie could see she was really hurt by it. Instead of dwelling on the guilt that sliced through her, she turned back to anger. "I'm sorry, okay? It's done. Now what can I do to get you to drop this lawsuit?"

Valerie's brows lifted as she considered. "Promise you'll never wear my outfits or copy my style without permission again, and I'll drop it."

"Done." Sadie exhaled, feeling the weight lift off her shoulders. "I'll contact the lawyer so he can draft up some kind of agreement for you and Brody's dad to look over."

"Max Odell is the reporter's father?"

Sadie frowned. "You didn't know that? Brody and I were friends in school. I can't believe you don't remember."

Disapproval flashed in Valerie's eyes. "And now you're dating him? Is it serious?"

"Again, it's none of your business."

Valerie waved away the comment. "All right, darling. I get it." She turned to Drew, leaning into him and running her hand over his thigh. "I do think you've missed out on a much better man, though. Drew has a real appreciation for music."

Drew smiled, those startling blue eyes of his shifting to Sadie. "Valerie's going to teach me to play the piano."

"It's the least I can do." Valerie beamed. She patted his knee and shot Sadie an amused look. "Poor thing had such a troubled home life. No one ever gave him the time of day."

"Until you," Drew replied, turning to Valerie. There was so much affection in his eyes it made Sadie sick to her stomach.

"Okay, I'm sorry, but you just met him two days ago. What the hell is going on?" she asked her mother, shaking her head.

Valerie only smiled. "We've bonded. I guess you could say we both know what it feels like to lose what we love at the hands of someone else."

Confused, Sadie looked back and forth at the two of them. "I don't understand."

"I don't expect you to." Valerie set her dog down on the wood floor, then rose to her feet as it scampered away. She winced with pain as she stood, but tossed her hair back and ignored it. "Now, why don't you go get your things so you can come back home?"

Sadie's eyes narrowed. "Why would I do that?"

Valerie frowned, as though it were obvious. "You aren't safe, Sadie. You belong here with me."

"I don't want to come back," Sadie replied, crossing her arms. "I'm perfectly safe at Dad's house."

"Because that reporter is staying there, isn't he?" Valerie scoffed, dark humor and pity flavoring her voice. "You still have so much to learn about men, darling. They're never as reliable as we want them to be."

Sadie rolled her eyes, decidedly done with the conversation. "Right. I'll see you later."

She turned and left the room, only to be stopped by Drew at the front door. She faced him with irritation in her eyes. "What?"

Drew managed an awkward smile. "Look, I know this all seems strange to you, but your mom is just being nice to me. You really don't have to leave."

"Whatever the two of you want to do is none of my business," Sadie told him, reaching for the door knob. He grasped her elbow and pulled her back, the firm touch of his hand sending an icy chill through her body.

"Stay," he said, his other hand trailing up her arm in an affectionate gesture.

She was so taken aback by it that she could barely form words. When he only eased closer to her, a dark, lustful look coming over his eyes, she wrestled free and shoved him back. "Don't. Leave me alone."

He sucked in a sharp breath and closed his eyes as if to reign in a sudden flash of temper. When he looked at her again, any sign of anger was gone.

An odd smile spread over his lips. "See you soon, Sadie."

She threw open the front door and fled to her car, her hands trembling. She managed to get the car door open and start the engine, relieved he didn't follow her as she drove down the driveway and onto the street.

Once she was safely on the road, a stunned laugh that was more horrified than amused caught in her throat. Had she done something to encourage his behavior? Given him any indication she was interested in him that way? She didn't think so, which made the entire thing that much more mortifying and awkward. What would she say to him the next time they ran into each other? Moreover, what would he say to *her*?

With her pulse still hammering, she drove on autopilot, lost in her own thoughts. The entire thing was just *weird*. Her mother inviting Drew into her home and treating him like some adorable lost puppy. Drew's odd looks of affection toward Valerie and his insistence that Sadie stay despite the obvious tension in the room. Her mother's assumption that she should return to live with her.

What the hell was happening? Sadie wondered, shaking her head. Why did it feel like all these things were done with purpose and not randomly, as it appeared on the surface?

A thought occurred to her then that stunned the air out of her lungs. She gripped the steering wheel as she realized it not only made sense, it made *perfect* sense.

Drew had to be the one who'd been stalking her. He'd come into her life around the same time, showed an interest in her that was more disturbing than it was flattering.

And her mother was in on it. It was obvious by the way they acted that she'd known him longer than just two days, despite pretending otherwise. She was using Drew, likely paying him, to scare Sadie away from Ben's home and back into her own, where she'd be "safe."

Her mind reeled at this revelation, certain it was the truth. She now regretted going over there alone. She should have brought Brody or Tess. Someone else who could connect the dots and convince her she wasn't crazy. Convince her that her own mother would really stoop so low just to get her back.

Now that she knew, she realized what a fool she'd been for ever believing she could be a part of her mother's life. Her father had been right to keep her away from the woman. He'd known all along what a selfish monster she was.

She'd been blind to it before, but now she saw it all with a damning clarity that made her sick to her stomach.

Chapter *twenty-nine*

BRODY SKIMMED through the gossip columns, reading the latest news being reported about Sadie. It'd been nearly two weeks since the story first broke about her alias and her mother's cancer, so most of the initial gossip had died down. There were the occasional blips about Lee Walker and the new lead the police seemed to have, but nothing substantial.

That is, until he came across pictures he recognized all too well.

"Oh, shit."

Across the table, Tess perked up. She set aside her cell phone and eyed him curiously. "What is it?"

Brody bit back another curse as he met her eyes, debating if he should show her or not. "You might die from the irony on this one."

"Oh, goodie. Let me see." She turned his laptop so she could see the screen, eyes narrowed as she reviewed the images from the beach and the accompanying tabloid article. Brody watched her features harden to stone as she shook her head. "Oh yes, very ironic, Mr. Paparazzi. Did you put her up to this?"

Brody grunted. "Hey, it's not like she can stay inside forever. She deserved a day to have a little fun."

Tess scrolled through the images, her scowl deepening. "This is just great. Don't you know better than to P.D.A. in public?"

He sighed, running a hand through his hair. "Honestly, I didn't think about it."

She pushed his laptop away and faced him angrily. "What, you were so caught up in being lovey-dovey with Sadie that it didn't occur to you that someone could be watching?"

"Pretty much," he replied, closing his laptop so he wouldn't have to look at the images anymore. He threw up his hands and fell back against the chair. "Whatever. It's done now."

Tess pressed her lips together, her eyes searching his. "You're really serious about her, aren't you? I can see how beat up you are about this. It's kind of weird, actually. I would expect you not to care."

One of his eyebrows rose. "Why shouldn't I care? Because I'm just some asshole who fucked up his career and now has to chase celebrities around for money?"

Amusement softened Tess's face. "No. Because you're a man and in my experience, men are selfish pricks."

Brody snorted. "We're only selfish pricks until we meet the right woman."

"Is Sadie the right woman?" Tess asked bluntly.

He shook his head with a tired laugh. "Like you'd believe me even if I said yes."

"Try me." Tess leaned over the table, folding her hands together. "I mean it. If you love her, say it out loud. Get it off your chest. Then maybe I'll finally be able to accept this weird little relationship you guys have."

He knew she was serious, and though he wanted nothing more than to blurt the words out then and there, something inside of him refused to budge. Did he really love Sadie? Was that what it was? How could it happen so quickly, so unexpectedly?

And what would he do now that everyone knew?

The front door opened, distracting them both. Sadie walked in, looking tired and miserable.

"Honey, what is it?" Tess asked. "Are you okay?"

"I'm fine," Sadie brushed off her friend's concerns, shaking her head. "I just need some time alone. I'm sorry."

She walked off before either of them could ask her more questions, disappearing inside her bedroom. Brody turned back to Tess, irritated with himself.

"I should've gone with her," he murmured, his hands balling into fists on the table.

Tess shrugged. "You offered. She refused. Not much you can do about that."

"If Valerie won't drop that lawsuit, I'll—"

"You'll what? Go break down her door and make her?" Tess sniffed, rolling her eyes. "There's something called the law, Rambo. Being a lawyer's son, I'd think you'd understand that."

Brody's lips quirked in a dark grin. "Being a lawyer's son also means I know what constitutes as trespassing and harassment and what doesn't."

Tess chuckled, settling back in her chair and toying with her phone. "Well, either way, there's nothing we can do right now."

He sighed, feeling restless. "I could go reason with Valerie."

"You and I both know that's not a possibility."

Hating that she was right, he got to his feet and went to the fridge. He grabbed a beer, then nodded at her. "Want one?"

Tess shrugged. "Why not? What the hell."

He uncapped two Coronas and set one down in front of her before taking his seat again. His gaze drifted out the window, where the setting sun was illuminating the city in rich golden light.

Across from him, Tess sipped her beer and watched him closely. After a few quiet moments, she set down her drink and spoke again. "I'm still waiting on an answer to my question."

Brody kept his face carefully blank. "You want me to say that I love her."

"I want to know that you mean it," Tess corrected. "She's my best friend. If she's going to get all tied up in you to the point where it changes her plans, I need to know you're not going to drop her the second something younger, hotter, or more interesting comes along."

256 ~ KATIE JENNINGS

He shifted his eyes to hers, irritation flashing in them. "What makes you think she won't be the one to drop me?"

"She cares too much," Tess told him. Sympathy softened her voice. "She's cool as a cucumber on the surface most of the time, but there's depth there that most people don't see."

He nodded, seeing her point. "I can tell just by listening to her music." He sat back and stared around the room, his mouth twisting in a sneer. "Ben and Valerie really screwed with her head."

"And the incident with Walker didn't help," Tess reminded him. "It only made the divide between the three of them even bigger."

They sat in thoughtful silence, weighed down by the demons of the past that refused to let Sadie go.

"I want her to stay," Brody admitted, realizing then just how badly he meant it.

Tess nodded. "Me too. You know what just might do it?"

"What?"

Her lips curved as she lifted her beer in a toast. "Tell her you love her, and mean it."

His eyebrows rose. "I thought you didn't want her to change her plans for me?"

She took a long sip and continued to smile. "I don't. But I do want to see her happy. And despite all my warnings and worries, you seem to make her that way."

"So, I'm not the big bad wolf, after all," he mused, drinking his beer.

"You're not perfect, either. But I will say you're not as bad as I thought you'd be."

He nodded, losing himself in his own thoughts. He supposed he couldn't blame her. With his reputation, he was used to people being wary of him.

When he didn't say anything for a few moments, she spoke again. "What really happened in Afghanistan, Brody?"

He downed the last of his beer, then set it roughly back on the table. "I got two Marines killed."

"They said you incited a riot on the streets of Sangin for the sake of a story."

He grimaced. "I'd hardly call it a riot, and I didn't want anyone to get hurt. I saw what I thought was a suicide bomber and tried to warn the troops. Being the arrogant son of a bitch that I am, I yelled 'bomb' before realizing the guy was only hiding stolen fruit under his shawl. That gave the real threat a chance to draw their weapons from within the crowd and fire."

Tess's brows drew together with pity. "The families blamed you, but it sounds like a simple mistake to me."

"It's a mistake that should've never happened. I was hungry for action and saw things that weren't really there. Whether intentional or not, it's still my fault those men died."

Tess sighed. "I'm sorry that happened to you. And I'm even more sorry everyone turned on you. I can't imagine how lonely you must have felt."

He managed a dry laugh before looking at her. "Everything was shit, Tess. *I* was shit. Then Sadie came back, and suddenly life makes sense again."

Emotions swam over her face. She reached for his hand, squeezing it in her own. "I feel the same exact way."

AN HOUR later, Sadie slipped from the bathtub and into a silk robe the color of smooth ivory. She brushed her hair and stared at her reflection, soothed from the bath and calmer than when she'd arrived home. Though the startling revelation she'd had earlier still hung over her shoulders, she'd accepted its presence. It was the only thing that made sense, after all.

Belting the robe tighter around her waist, she ventured out of the bathroom and found Brody alone in the music room, tinkering with the piano. A smile came over her face as she watched him from the doorway, her heart swelling with gratitude and relief. He'd make everything better. He always did.

She went to him and ran her hands over his shoulders and down his chest, resting her chin on top of his head. "Hey," she greeted, exhaling softly.

"Hi." He tilted his head back, inviting her to kiss him. She did, letting her lips trail over his, soft and warm. He turned to face her, pulling her down into his lap.

Their eyes met and she smiled. "I'm sorry I took so long. Did Tess leave already?"

"Yeah." He brushed strands of hair away from her face, leaving his hand cupped over her cheek. "Is everything all right?"

She nodded, leaning her face into his hand. "Remember that guy from the restaurant the other day? The one I said I kept running into?"

"What about him?"

"He was at my mom's house this afternoon. They were...*affectionate*." She felt that sick feeling wash over her again, but tried to ignore it. "I think he's the one who's been following me."

Brody's eyebrows lifted. "Really?"

She pouted and rose to her feet to pace the room. "I think my mom hired him in an attempt to scare me away from this house and back to hers. It makes perfect sense."

"Does it?" Brody questioned, shaking his head. "You really think she'd do something that crazy?" He caught himself and let out a bitter laugh. "Okay, this *is* Valerie we're talking about, so maybe she could."

"Exactly," Sadie replied, twirling a piece of hair around her fingertip absently. "Something about the way they acted with each other told me they hadn't just met the other day. She's known him for awhile. And then he got all touchy-feely with me, and—"

"He did *what?*" Brody demanded, heat flashing in his eyes.

Sadie waved off his concern. "Nothing, really. Just flirting. He did it at the restaurant too. But it made me realize that this all seems *way* too orchestrated to be a coincidence."

Brody rubbed his chin in thought. "So in this conclusion of yours, have you figured out how your mother met this guy? I doubt she took out a Craigslist ad saying, 'Calling all Sadie McRae fans, come stalk my daughter. Must be good looking and have abs.'"

Sadie snorted out a laugh, but continued to pace as she gave his question some thought. "She might have met him through a friend or at a show. I'm not really sure, but the point here is that she definitely knows him."

"Well, I can go talk to him. Beat it out of him if I have to." He winked at her with a sly grin.

She bit back a smile. "As much as I'd enjoy watching you interrogate him, I think it's best if we just leave them alone for now. She said she'd drop the lawsuit as long as I don't copy her anymore, and I agreed."

He nodded. "Good. If that's what you want, then that's what we'll do."

He reached for her hand and pulled her back into his lap, his mouth finding hers. Holding her close, he could feel the smooth curves of her body beneath the silk robe and felt his own body awakening in response.

"Sadie?" he murmured, pulling out of the kiss to meet her eyes.

Her lips curved in a warm smile. "Brody?"

"Do you want me to stay again tonight?"

Surprise flashed in her eyes, realizing she hadn't even thought about it. "I guess now that the security system is in...do you want to stay?"

Though his emotions were a tangled mess inside his gut, he threw on a carefree smile and ignored them. "How much booze, sex, and rock 'n' roll can one guy handle? Oh wait."

She giggled and kissed him again. "I think you can hang. Besides, we should really give the press more to gossip about. Did you see we made headlines today?"

"You saw that, huh?" he asked, surprised by her good-humored reaction. "Did it bother you?"

"What, to be accused of having a steamy love affair with a paparazzi?" She grinned, realizing the whole thing was actually very freeing. "Honestly, I want the world to know. I'm not ashamed. Are you?"

His eyebrows rose in amusement. "I don't know, you do come with some pretty heavy baggage, McRae. Being seen with you could damage my impeccable reputation."

"We wouldn't want that," she teased, slipping from his grasp and rising to her feet. She grabbed his hand and pulled him with her out of the room. "Why don't I show you just how little I care about our reputations?"

His teeth flashed in devious grin. "Once it's gone, you know you can't get it back."

"Good. I don't want it, anyway."

Chapter *thirty*

A WEEK PASSED with no word from Valerie. The stalker was also MIA, which led Brody to think that maybe Sadie was right. Drew *was* the one who'd been following her around, possibly provoked or supported by Valerie herself. As much as he wanted to march up to Valerie's door and demand answers, Sadie refused to let him. Let it go, she'd said. No more fighting.

It went against his very nature, but he respected her wishes. So instead of fixing the problem, they'd gone the entire week pretending it didn't exist.

Sadie had spent nearly every waking hour practicing for the show Tess had booked, while he jumped back into research on Walker's death. The fact that the police were keeping a tight lid on the whole thing frustrated him. It meant they were hiding something, or a deal was being worked out behind closed doors. If that was the case, then they knew who shot Walker and were busy trying to settle matters without public interference. The only reason they'd do something like that would be to protect the identity of the shooter. And the only person who'd need protecting would be someone famous with a lot to lose if word got out.

Did that mean Georgina really was the one? Or was there more to this, as he suspected, than met the eye?

Deciding to look into it a bit more after the show, Brody turned his car onto Wilshire Boulevard and glanced at Sadie. "You know, no one would judge you if you had a drink or two before the show. I guarantee your dad does it. And Tommy *definitely* does. No one's that cheerful all the time."

Sadie managed a weak laugh, fidgeting in the passenger seat of his car and staring out the window. Night was setting in, which meant her first official show as Sadie McRae was only hours away. "Back in the day they did bumps of cocaine before a show. I remember seeing the trays of bottle caps filled with white powder being passed around. Of course, at the time I had no idea what it did. Or how addicting it could be."

Brody shrugged. "It's tough dealing with all that pressure."

"They were younger than I am when they got started," Sadie mused, letting nostalgia roll over her. "Kids, really. Not even legal to drink but desperate to get onstage and make music. They became famous so quickly I don't think they ever really had time to grow up. They just got swept up in the money and the fame and never looked back. I made a point not to let that happen to me."

He reached for her hand and held it tightly. "Which is why you'll never be like them. You have the talent but none of their egotism and greed. You should be proud, McRae. Really proud."

She smiled, squeezing his hand. "Thank you." The butterflies rioted in her stomach again, bringing back her anxiety. "God, I'm nervous. This is a bigger venue than The L.A. Rock Lounge."

"But not nearly the size of The Forum," Brody pointed out. "You'll be fine."

"If you say so."

They pulled into the private parking area of the venue off Wilshire Boulevard. Brody turned to Sadie as he shut off the car. "Ready?"

She bit her lip and nodded, then got shakily out of the car. He helped her with her things and walked with her toward the back entrance of the building, where a beefy security guard nodded and let them inside. Brody held Sadie's hand in his, keeping her close as they navigated through the hallways backstage to the dressing room.

When they found it, he made sure she was settled and left to scope out the venue. He toured the backstage area, found it crowded and busy as most were, then watched them set up Sadie's piano onstage. It was a gleaming black Steinway, her favorite brand.

He walked along the towering black curtains that divided the stage from the equipment area beyond, admiring the white, oval sign Tess had commissioned displaying Sadie's name in curvy, feminine lettering. He nodded to a few of the stage hands and turned to look out at the rows of empty seats. Soon the entire place would be unrecognizable, filled with adoring fans and excited chatter. Sadie would be in the spotlight, a bundle of tightly wound nerves and eager anticipation. And he would be waiting just offstage, impatient to have her all to himself again.

Because onstage, she belonged to the world. Off of it, she was simply his Sadie.

He let out a rush of breath, disquieted by his own thoughts. Before he had time to dwell on them, the manager announced that they were opening the doors.

Showtime was in less than an hour.

BRODY WAITED in the wings with Tess and watched the venue fill to capacity, leaving only a row of empty seats in the front. He eyed them suspiciously, wondering who could have booked those seats. His question was answered when Tess let out a strained groan and elbowed him in the ribs, pointing at the entrance.

Valerie and her entourage descended the aisle, heading straight for the front row. Star struck fans twisted in their seats and craned their necks to get a glimpse of her, though her bodyguard hovered close behind and kept anyone from getting too close.

The Goddess of Albatross settled into the center seat in the front row and straightened her scarlet-red dress, beaming wistfully at the stage and exchanging laughs with her friends. Brody noticed Georgina seated beside Valerie, dressed all in black with her trademark flame-colored hair curled over her shoulders. The two whispered to each other and grinned like old friends, but he knew the game they played. It was less out of friendship and more out of duty that they'd stuck together all these years. After all, they'd left Albatross as a unit.

"Can you believe she had the nerve to show up?" Tess muttered, shaking her head. "I hope Sadie doesn't notice her."

"Oh, she'll see her," Brody replied, gritting his teeth. "Which is exactly what Valerie wants."

Before Tess could stop him, he stormed down the steps and across the theater toward Valerie, fighting against all hope to keep his temper in check. Valerie's brows rose when she spotted him approaching, and her bodyguard stepped between them and put his hand on Brody's chest.

Brody scowled, ignoring the bodyguard and focusing his attention on Valerie. "What the hell are you doing here?"

Valerie fixed a hurt look on her face. "I just came to watch my baby perform."

"You and I both know that's bullshit," Brody growled, earning a few curious stares from nearby fans.

Beside Valerie, Georgina angled her head and eyed Brody with disdain. "Are you the paparazzi who's been sniffing around our Sadie?" She turned her gaze to Valerie and pursed her lips. "Looks like a gold-digger to me."

Brody's jaw clenched.

Valerie laughed brightly. "Oh, don't you remember who he is? He's that reporter that got those poor soldiers killed a couple years ago."

Georgina's lips parted in surprise as her eyes swept over Brody once again. "How awful. What is Sadie thinking?"

"I have no idea," Valerie replied, shooting Brody a wry look. "If you're done bothering us, darling, we'd really like to watch the show."

Brody's hands curled into fists at his side, prompting the bodyguard to give him a light shove in warning. With the anxious looks he was getting from those around them, he knew it was best to give it up.

"You won't ruin this for her, you know," he told Valerie, shaking his head. "But the simple fact that you're trying to should make you ashamed of yourself."

Without waiting for her response, he stalked back to where Tess was waiting behind the curtains to the side of the stage. His body was humming with anger, made worse by the laughter he heard coming from Valerie and her entourage.

Tess met his eyes worriedly the second he returned, but any chance to ask him what happened was squashed by the lights in the theater dimming.

The show was about to begin.

SADIE CHECKED her hair and makeup one last time in the mirror, pleased by the more natural look she'd donned for this performance. She wasn't the mysterious Piper Gray this time. She was simply Sadie McRae, blonde and softly feminine and a little bit shy. Hopefully the world adored her true persona as much as they loved her alias.

The dress she wore was knee-length and made of white linen and lace, cinched at the waist with a brown leather belt and strapless, leaving her shoulders bare. She'd slipped into matching white, open-toed heels that she hoped she didn't trip over on her way to the piano.

When her cue arrived, she hobbled out of the dressing room and was led to the side of the stage, where Brody and Tess were waiting. She exchanged hugs and a brief kiss for luck with Brody before venturing out onto the stage. With the darkness of the theater, she had to follow tiny glowing markers that led to her piano, where she sat down.

Taking a deep, soothing breath, she rested her fingers over the keys and waited for the lights to return. When a single stream of golden light illuminated her, she felt a smile come over her face as she began to play her biggest hit 'All These Flames.'

The crowd roared to life, drowning out the beginning of her song. She didn't mind, though. She was getting used to the sound of praise. It gave her a boost of confidence that chased away the worst of her nerves. As the applause and cheers quieted down, she leaned into the microphone and told the story of her life.

"I thought a heart made of two hearts, was created to be loved. I thought flesh made of two parts, had to be loved. Now I see I lost this game, when all that binds us are these flames. They burn to black every last thing that I wanted…"

She chanced a look out at the crowd, only to spot her mother sitting in the front row. Valerie stood out like a shocking red bird amid a sea of sparrows, and the raw emotions that swam over her face startled Sadie. Was she really listening? Did she hear the words of the song and realize they were about her? That it was *all* about her?

"These tears burn my eyes till they're gone. They harden the very soul you walked upon. How dare you think I could forgive? All I want now is to live.

"So forget you, forget me. Just leave me be. I ask you, don't you see I'm suffering? How could I ever think you'd love me? These flames destroyed us. These flames made us. These flames are all that remain. When the ashes fall, will you remember my name?"

Fueled by a desire to prove something to her mother, she sang with as much heartache and passion as she could, pouring her soul into the song. She could tell it worked when she saw people in the front rows wiping away tears and staring at her in wonder, as though they'd never heard something so beautiful.

It made her feel powerful. Untouchable. And for the first time in her life, she felt liberated.

Then the lights cut out.

Sadie stopped playing, blinking into the darkness as the crowd began to murmur in confusion. The hum of voices rose to a staggering level as uncertainty and nervous laughter filled the air. She wondered if it was just a power outage or the result of faulty wiring, but decided it was best to stay seated just in case it came back on. Surely someone backstage was attempting to fix the problem.

It was then that she spotted the shadowy figure slip through the curtains onto the stage. Her first thought was that it was someone coming to let her know it may be awhile before the power was fixed. But when the person got closer and she squinted in the darkness to try and get a better look at him, she realized he had no face. It was hidden behind some kind of mask, and his hands were covered in black gloves.

Before she could even think to scream, the stranger cupped his hand over her mouth and dragged her from the piano bench, roughly carting her from the stage. She kicked and knocked over a small speaker and mic stand, but through the din of the crowd no one seemed to notice what was happening to her. Panic set in and survival instincts had her clawing at the man's clothes in an attempt to break free, only to find herself grasped tighter against his chest as he hauled her backstage. She couldn't see anything but black as he shoved her into some dark, isolated corner behind the stage, pinning her against the wall. His hand fell from her mouth and latched onto her throat instead, sending a bolt of terror down her spine.

He was going to kill her.

She tried to twist and claw her way free, but he only shoved her back against the wall so hard her head hit the concrete and sent a dizzying wave of white hot pain through her body. A startled gasp escaped her throat only to be cut off by his hands pressing hard against her trachea, pinching off her air. Tears spilled from her eyes as she felt her body going limp, losing oxygen. A deafening hum filled her ears as the world slipped away, and she welcomed it compared to the horror of what was happening. Images of Lee Walker flashed in her mind, and she let herself believe he'd come back to finish the job he'd started.

Just let it end. The pain is too much. It's always been too much.

Before she slid out of consciousness, the hands released her and the stranger fled, leaving her alone in the darkness. Her legs crumbled as she gasped wildly for air, her hands fluttering over her throat. She heard Brody's panicked voice getting closer. She sobbed, terrified and relieved all at once.

A flashlight fell over her face, blinding her. She cringed and inched away, only to be gathered up into Brody's arms a second later.

"Christ, Sadie," he breathed, letting her sob against him. He fought to settle his own raging heart, thankful he'd found her. "What the hell happened?"

Before she could respond, the lights came back on and in an instant, three armed security guards were at their side, hands poised tentatively over their weapons.

"Put your hands up and back away," one of them ordered.

Brody did as he was told, only then noticing the red marks wrapped around Sadie's throat. She continued to fight for air and the ability to speak, but the guards saw all they needed to see.

"Put him in handcuffs," the first guard said, nodding to the others. They approached Brody, cuffs out and ready.

Brody stared at them in shock. "I didn't do this!"

"We need to secure the area. I'll call the ambulance," the guard told the others before turning to Sadie and inspecting the marks on her skin. "Get him out of here."

Sadie watched them handcuff Brody, mortified by what she was seeing. She tried to cry out, to tell them he was innocent, but only a hoarse rasp came out. Instead she was forced to watch them drag him away, kicking and raging. He called out to her, letting her know it'd be okay. That he'd be with her soon.

Her mind spun as she suddenly felt Tess beside her, pulling her close. Unable to do more, she broke down and cried in her friend's arms.

Chapter *thirty-one*

BRODY SAT at the curb on Wilshire, surrounded by cop cars and flashing lights. Though they'd removed the handcuffs, he still wasn't allowed to see Sadie. She was being treated in an ambulance some twenty yards away, shielded from the cameras of the hungry press and the mortified stares of her fans. Until the fat-excuse-of-a-cop in charge gave him the go ahead, he was glued to the curb like a disobedient child.

From what he'd gathered by overhearing the police, Sadie had been dragged off the stage and strangled. His hands balled into fists at the thought, fury setting his blood on fire. The ease of how it happened scared the hell out of him. The breaker being shut off, dousing the entire building in darkness. The masked attacker slipping onto the stage and grabbing Sadie while the crowd stirred in confusion just feet away. All while he'd been mere feet away, himself.

He knew he'd always regret not having the forethought to go out to her, to take her with him offstage. At the time, he'd assumed the power would kick back on in a matter of seconds and he didn't want to embarrass her. Little did he know her life was in danger and he could have prevented it.

That anger surged again, hazing his vision with red even as he shut his eyes tight against it. Remembering the moment he realized something was wrong pained him. He'd stolen a flashlight from a nearby stage hand and taken off backstage, frantically calling out for her. It must have been his voice that scared off the attacker, because he was nowhere to be found when he stumbled upon Sadie.

She'd been so terrified. Dazed and struggling for breath with her neck marred by evil hands.

Once again, he realized. For the second time in her life, she bore the marks of a madman. That thought alone was enough to have him thirsting for retribution.

"Mr. Odell?" A gangly rookie cop with sandy blond hair crouched down in front of him, notepad in hand.

Brody grimaced. "Can I go yet?"

"Almost. Miss McRae claims a man wearing a black mask attacked her. Did you see anyone backstage fitting that description?"

"No. By the time I got there he'd left," Brody explained, eyes hardening as he stared pointedly at the cop. "Look, I think I know who did this. A guy named Drew. I don't know his last name, but he's been shacking up with Valerie Ryan so you'll probably find him there."

Surprise flashed over the cop's face as he jotted the information down. "How do you know it was him?"

"I have a hunch he's the one who's been following Sadie, so it's a good place to start." Brody climbed to his feet, peering over the police cars at the ambulance. He saw the doors open and one of the paramedics help Sadie out onto the street. "I gotta go."

Ignoring the cop's cry of protest, he raced around the patrol cars and straight for the ambulance. When Sadie turned and saw him, relief chased away the anxiety on her face.

He said nothing as he scooped her into his arms and held her close, breathing in the familiar scent of her and letting it soothe him. Cameras flashed as the press swarmed in as close as the police would allow, but he couldn't care less. Let them get their photo op. Sadie needed him.

She was still shaking, but when he looked into her eyes he was relieved to see they were dry and focused. His gaze went to the side of her neck, where light bruises were beginning to form. He could only shake his head, the relief he felt squashed by rage. "That asshole better hope the cops find him before I do."

Sadie bit down on her lip, distressed by his anger. "I told them about Drew. I left my mom out of it, though. I don't think she had anything to do with this."

He sighed. "No, I have a feeling he went rogue on this one."

"Can we go home?" she asked, forehead creased as she glanced around at the press and curious onlookers vying for a glimpse of her. She winced at the camera flashes and intrusive questions being hurled her way, feeling like a tiger on display at the zoo. "It's just like it was before. I can't handle it. I need to go."

He nodded and took her hand. "They'll want to send a patrol car with us, but I think we should be able to slip away. Come on."

She went with him, eager to leave the entire nightmare behind.

WITH SADIE tucked safely in bed attempting to get some rest, Brody was left to stew in guilt, rage, and alcohol. It was a volatile combination that left him restless and irritable, but at least it was better than the grief he'd feel if she was dead.

As it was, there was so little he could do, so little he could say, to make things better. And although Sadie was putting on a strong face for his benefit, he could only imagine how she felt reliving the night-mare she'd run from nearly her entire life. How terrified she must be to know the person stalking her, whether it be Drew or not, didn't just want her attention—he wanted to kill her.

But why? Brody wondered, opening his laptop on her dining table. He absently searched the web for coverage of the incident, feeling the need to do something other than sit and brood. How did obsession turn into violence?

He mindlessly scanned breaking news articles mentioning Sadie's name, his temper sparking when he saw the images his fellow paparazzi had nabbed of her outside the venue. There were a few shots of him holding her, and more of her facing the crowd looking weak and terrified. He wished the camera could have captured more of her strength and less of her fear, if only to show the world she was tougher than they thought. But that didn't make a good story, he knew. You always chose moments of brokenness and tears over quiet strength—it carried a higher price tag.

The reports didn't carry many specifics on what happened, other than that Sadie had been assaulted while onstage during her performance. The spokesman for the venue claimed they were looking into the break in their security that allowed someone unauthorized to get backstage and access the electrical panel to shut down the power.

Brody knew it wouldn't be difficult to do. He'd walked the backstage area and seen just how little everyone was paying attention. It wasn't a venue accustomed to high profile performers in need of extensive security. They hadn't been prepared for this, plain and simple. And if he was being honest, never in his wildest dreams would he have imagined Sadie getting attacked onstage, either. Things like that just didn't happen. Which was exactly why Drew, or whoever it was, had been able to pull it off.

He exhaled slowly and ran his hands through his hair, mentally pushed to the limit. If he wasn't so afraid to leave Sadie alone he would go to Valerie's house himself to see if Drew was there. Instead he was stuck waiting on the police to find him, helpless to do more than sit in front of the computer and sulk.

His cell phone vibrated in his pocket, startling him back to reality. He pulled it out and saw it was Chase. "Hey."

"*How's Sadie doing?*" Chase asked, concern in his voice.

Brody closed his eyes and kneaded his left temple tiredly. "Sleeping, I hope."

"*I assume you're staying with her for the night.*"

"I'll stay as long as she wants me here," Brody confirmed, sitting back in his chair. "She wanted me to tell you thanks, by the way, for painting the driveway."

"*No problem, I was happy to do it. Hey, so I came across something today that I think you should know about.*"

Brody's eyebrows creased. "What is it?"

"*Well, Valerie called me this morning to discuss dropping the lawsuit, which is good news. But while she had me on the phone, she asked me to look for an old case file from 2002, a wrongful death lawsuit that was filed against her. She said she couldn't remember the name of the person who filed the claim, but that she was curious. I didn't ask why, of course.*"

"Why have I never heard about this lawsuit before?" Brody wondered aloud, already leaning forward to type into the computer and do a quick search on it.

"*Probably because it was dropped before it ever went anywhere,*" Chase replied. "*Anyway, it was filed by Lee Walker's ex-girlfriend after he died. Apparently the woman thought she could get some money by claiming his death caused her financial hardship.*"

"How so?"

"*Child support.*" Chase paused, letting the words sink in. "*When Walker died, the money he was sending her dried up.*"

A chill ran through Brody. "Walker has a kid?"

"*Yes. A son who was sixteen years old at the time of his father's death. Back then he lived with his mother in Seattle, but he could be anywhere now. I was thinking it's possible he could be your stalker, and maybe Valerie had a hunch about it.*"

Brody let out a long rush of breath, stunned by the revelation. "Let me guess, this kid's name is Drew."

"*Yeah, how'd you know that?*" Chase asked.

"Because he's been here in L.A., hanging out with Sadie and Valerie acting like he's a fan or something," Brody told him, shaking his head and mentally cursing himself for not making the connection sooner.

Chase sighed. "*I wish I'd known about this before. I hate thinking this could've been prevented.*"

"What I want to know is why it was never mentioned in the press that Walker had a son? You'd think that would make it in there somewhere."

"*It probably didn't help that he had his mother's last name. Really, the only connection between the two would be the child support paperwork, but no one ever thought to look. Walker had no interest in knowing his son. I doubt any of his friends even knew he had a child.*"

"What's the last name?" Brody asked.

"*His given name is Andrew Lee Hewitt. He has a pretty impressive rap sheet—possession of illegal substances including marijuana and metham-phetamine, domestic abuse, a couple D.U.I.s. From what I can tell, after the domestic abuse charge he was under a court order to see a psychiatrist, who determined he has Bipolar Disorder with frequent manic episodes.*"

"Christ," Brody managed, disgusted. "He probably came to L.A. when he heard Sadie was back. He couldn't resist fucking with her."

"*I suggest you call the police and give them a heads up, Brody. And don't make any rash decisions until you do,*" Chase warned.

Brody let out a dark laugh. "Even if I knew where he was, I couldn't kill him. I don't own a gun. Then again, I could choke the life out of him like he tried to do to Sadie."

"*I'm going to pretend I didn't hear that part.*" Chase sighed. "*Good luck and stay safe, okay?*"

"Thanks, Chase. I mean it." Brody hung up the phone, setting it aside as he absorbed everything he'd just learned. This was huge. Suddenly everything made a hell of a lot more sense, including the reason for the attack on Sadie. If Drew had gotten it into his twisted, psychotic head that Sadie was somehow responsible for his father's death, then that easily could have driven him to hurt her.

Without wasting another second, he jumped to his feet and went to the front door. He opened it, peering out into the night. The patrol car that had followed them earlier was parked on the street, the two cops inside mere silhouettes in the dark.

He turned on the porch light to catch their attention, then walked out to the car. They rolled down the passenger window and eyed him curiously.

"Everything okay?" One of the cops asked.

Brody tucked his hands into his pockets and nodded. "You get the guy?"

"No confirmation yet," the cop replied.

"Right." A hard grin played over Brody's features. "Well get on the radio and phone this in. I have his full name and I know exactly why he did it."

Chapter *thirty-two*

THOUGH SHE'D woken hours earlier, Sadie stayed in bed and pretended to sleep. She heard Brody get up, leaving her with nothing but the silence of her bedroom and her troubled thoughts.

Sleep had eluded her for most of the night, but she wasn't surprised. There were too many questions swirling around in her mind for her to rest. Questions and worries for what lay ahead of her now that the media surely must be having a heyday with this latest incident.

The attack itself frightened her, but unlike when she'd been a teenager, she wasn't going to let it break her. What happened, happened, and there was nothing she could do now except help the police find the person who did it and move on with her life.

Should she feel more afraid? she wondered, her eyes opening to stare at the white ceiling of the bedroom. Was she a fool for pushing back the emotions she thought she should be feeling in favor of a level head?

Maybe it was because everyone expected her to break down and recoil with horror from what happened. The fact that doing so seemed natural bothered her. She was better than that, stronger.

She'd been through this before, after all. And experience had shaped her reaction to it.

Taking a deep, cleansing breath, she climbed out of bed and slipped into her robe. Whatever the day had in store for her, she was ready to conquer it. There would be no shattering to pieces. That was exactly what the maniac wanted. He wanted her terrified, but she wouldn't give him the pleasure.

She was going to win this fight, come hell or high water.

When she walked out into the living room, she spotted Brody in the kitchen cooking bacon and eggs. A small smile crept over her lips as she approached him, winding a strand of hair around her finger.

"Smells good," she said, catching his attention.

He took a second to look her over, his gaze pausing on the bruises she knew must be on her neck. "Want some coffee?"

"Please." She watched him pour a cup and doctor it with plenty of sugar and creamer before handing it to her. Her eyes held his as she took a sip. "Thanks."

"How'd you sleep?"

She shrugged. "Fine, I guess."

"Good." He turned away to shut off the burners and plate their breakfast of cheese omelets and bacon. "I may not be much of a cook, but I make a killer omelet."

She followed him to the dining table, taking a seat and eyeing the plate he set down in front of her. "I'm impressed."

He sat across from her and smiled. "I'm not completely useless."

As she bit into a piece of crispy bacon, she noticed him watching her closely. He had a strange look on his face, like he wanted to say something but couldn't. Annoyance soured her mood.

"Is something wrong?" she asked, eyebrows raised.

He took a long sip of coffee. "Not wrong, per say. But I do have something to tell you. I wasn't sure if you'd want to talk about it just yet."

She frowned. "I'm fine, Brody. Just tell me what it is."

He nodded and set aside his cup, keeping his eyes on hers. "Drew is Lee Walker's son."

Surprise had her forgetting her annoyance in an instant. "He is? How do you know?"

"Chase found out Walker's ex-girlfriend had filed a wrongful death lawsuit against your mother, claiming financial hardship due to loss of child support."

Sadie sat back in her chair, stunned. "God, I never knew he had a son."

"Neither did I. The lawsuit was dropped early, so very few people caught wind of it. Valerie contacted Chase and asked him to look up the name of the ex-girlfriend. I think she suspected Drew was the same kid."

Sadie brushed back her hair with both hands, shaking her head. "So that's the reason, then. That's why he's been following me, why he attacked me. It's because of Walker."

"I gave the police his name last night so they should be able to track him down."

"He's not with my mom?" she asked, fear licking her insides at the thought. "She could be in danger, he might hurt her."

"I haven't heard word either way, so I don't think he's there," Brody explained. "You may want to call her, though."

She rose to her feet and snatched her cell phone from her purse on the counter. With shaking hands she brought up her mother's phone number and hit dial. When it went straight to voicemail, she bit back a curse.

"No answer?" Brody asked.

"Her phone's turned off." She faced him, worry in her eyes. "We need to go check on her."

"I'm sure the cops have—"

"Please," she begged, holding her phone tightly in her hands.

He let out a rush of breath, then nodded. "Okay. Let's go."

ON THE way to Valerie's, Brody filled her in on Drew's numerous drug offenses and mental illness. It only troubled her more, but she was glad he told her. At least now she knew what they were dealing with.

It bothered her how well Drew had concealed the truth. There had been those few moments where she'd noticed things about him that hinted at something suspicious, but it didn't compare to the true dark nature of his attentions. He'd slipped into her life under the guise of adoration and friendship, only to let something much more sinister take hold and drive him to hurt her. Whatever was going on in his mind was a mystery to her, one she was almost too afraid to learn.

Bolstering the courage she'd woken up with, she stared out the passenger window of Brody's car and tried not to feel anything but determination.

The second he parked in Valerie's driveway, Sadie leapt from the car and went straight to the front door. She knocked, tapping her foot impatiently as she waited.

Brody came up beside her, his eyes scanning all around the front yard looking for any sign of trouble. The officer stationed at the base of the driveway had told them Valerie had been home since the night before, but Brody knew Sadie needed proof that her mother was all right.

When Carla answered the door, Sadie nearly wept with relief. "Is my mom here?"

"Ms. Ryan's out in the garden. Come in." Carla's eyes honed in on Sadie's neck, but she said nothing.

They followed Carla into the house and out to the backyard, where Valerie was resting on one of the chaise lounges. Coco lay in her lap, perking up at the sound of Sadie and Brody approaching. Valerie's face angled toward them, sunglasses shielding her eyes.

"Oh, Sadie," she said breathlessly, rising to a sitting position. She clutched at her chest, looking at a loss for words.

Sadie swallowed the sob that tightened her throat, emotions shimmering just under the surface. "Hi."

Valerie removed her sunglasses and got shakily to her feet, her gaze shooting to Sadie's neck. She reached out to touch the bruises, her fingertips feather-light on Sadie's skin. "My baby. I don't even know what to say."

Tears filled Sadie's eyes as she felt her strength waning. She let her mother pull her into a hug, ignoring the awkwardness she felt and embracing the comfort being offered.

Beside her, Brody cleared his throat. "Where's Drew, Valerie?"

Valerie let out a long sigh as she released Sadie. She faced him, bronzed eyes filled with regret. "I don't know. I haven't seen him in days."

"He's Lee Walker's son," Sadie told her mother, carefully gauging her reaction.

Valerie's lips curved in a sad smile. "I know. I knew from the moment I saw him at *Le Petit Four*."

Sadie blinked, taken aback. "You did?"

She nodded, eyes brightening with emotion. "He looks just like his dad. Lee was one of most handsome men I'd ever seen."

Sadie met eyes with Brody, catching the odd hint of affection in her mother's voice. "Why didn't you say anything to me?"

"I knew if you found out you'd never give him a chance," Valerie admitted. "I'd hoped he was a better man than Lee turned out to be, but I was wrong. He's worse."

"You wanted to set me up with him?" Sadie managed, disgusted by the thought.

Valerie only smiled. "It's twisted, I know. But in my head I guess I thought you two could live the life Lee and I might have had together, had things worked out differently."

Dizziness swept over Sadie and had her sitting down on the chaise lounge, alarmed by what she was hearing. "You and Lee had an affair?"

Valerie sat beside her, lost in the nostalgia of the past. "It started just before I hired him; he'd only been with Georgina a few weeks. No one ever knew about it, not even her. He talked of leaving her to be with me, but we were having too much fun going behind everyone's backs." She glanced at her daughter, a guilty look crossing her face. "I know it was wrong. At the time I didn't care who got hurt or why. But in the end, Lee could never be Ben and he knew it. Ben was the love of my life, no one could ever compare. And Lee hated that. One time he got aggressive with me during an argument, so I ended the affair. That was the night before my birthday party. The night before he went after you because of what I'd done."

Sadie paled, unable to breathe. Her heart shuddered with pain. "Why did you never tell me any of this?"

Valerie looked away, her spine stiffening as she tried to recover some of her dignity. "There was no reason for you to know the horrible things I've done."

Sadie reached for her mother's hand, though her eyes rose to Brody. His face was unreadable, but she noticed the tension bunching his shoulders. He was holding back his anger as best as he could for her benefit. But despite how he felt, she couldn't muster any resentment for her mother. She only felt pity.

"Thank you for telling me the truth," she murmured, squeezing Valerie's hand.

Tears filled Valerie's eyes, but she brushed them away and tried to laugh it off. "Not that it makes up for anything."

"No, it doesn't," Sadie agreed, earning a hurt look from her mother. "But at least it helps me understand you a little bit better."

Valerie's lips pressed together as she nodded. Before she could speak, Carla emerged from the patio doors.

"Ready for your appointment, Ms. Ryan?"

Valerie sighed and patted Sadie's leg affectionately. "I don't know why I put myself through this torture."

So you can live, Sadie thought silently, a sob threatening her throat again.

"You two are welcome to stay if you'd like," Valerie said as she stood up. Her gaze swept over Brody, evaluating. "Your brother's a very nice man. I think you could learn a thing or two from him."

She winked at Sadie over her shoulder before wandering back into the house, leaving behind the lilac scent of her perfume and the weight of her words.

Sadie let out a long, unsteady breath, unsure what to make of it all. Brody frowned down at her, his arms crossed. "This has to be the biggest blow to my ego ever."

One of Sadie's eyebrows rose. "Why's that?"

He sniffed. "Not only did she say Chase is better than me, but what kind of reporter am I if I missed all these crucial details about Walker? The lawsuit, his son, the affair with Valerie? I might as well toss in the towel right now and quit."

Sadie broke down and laughed, unable to help it.

"I'm serious," he told her, though his teeth flashed in a grin. "Guess my dad was right. I am a loser."

"Shut up." She got to her feet and wrapped her arms around his neck, pressing her lips to his.

"So I'm not a loser?" he asked, deepening the kiss.

She broke free, a coy smile playing over her mouth. "You do have a *Cone Heads* movie poster hanging in your living room. That's pretty lame."

"Hey, that's a one of a kind collector's item. I wouldn't expect a square like you to understand." He brushed strands of hair off her forehead, his dark eyes on hers. "Then again, I seem to recall you really liking *Cone Heads*."

"Guess we're both losers, then."

"Loserville, population two," he joked, pulling her in for a tight hug. He released a long, burdened sigh. "Do you want to take off or stick around awhile?"

She pulled away and glanced around her mother's garden. "You know, I think I'd like to hang out for a bit. For the first time in forever, I actually want to be here."

"Okay. Why don't I go inside and grab us something to drink?"

"I'd like that, thank you." She watched him go, her heart filled to the brim with appreciation for him. She didn't want to imagine what it would have been like to face everything she had without him by her side.

She walked through the garden, enjoying the warm sun on her face and the cool breeze that teased her skin. Settling beneath her mother's beloved magnolia tree, she laid back on the grass and stared up through the leaves at the hints of blue sky. Birds danced in and out of the branches, the sound of their conversations soothing to her. Her eyes fluttered closed as she let the worst of her worries slip to the back of her mind, contented for now that things were going to be okay. Drew would be apprehended soon and life would go on.

A few moments later, she heard Brody approaching and opened her eyes. He smiled down at her, the filtered sunlight casting a halo around his face. Joy filled her in an instant, sending warmth straight to her heart.

"Brody?" She watched as he knelt beside her, holding two tall glasses of iced tea.

"Sadie?" he replied, handing her one of the glasses.

She accepted it, her pulse skipping as she sat up on an elbow and faced him. When he met her eyes, her lips curved. "I just wanted to thank you for being here for me."

"Thanks for letting me hang around," he teased, taking a long sip of tea.

"And I think you should know something…I'm in love with you."

When he choked on his tea she started laughing. He stared at her, an odd mix of surprise and humility on his face. He rubbed his right ear, shaking his head. "Hold on. I think I might have something in my ears. I swear you just said you love me."

"I do. I think I always have." She looked down at her tea glass with a sad smile. "I hate thinking that if things had been different, if I hadn't left L.A., I could've been here for you. We could've gotten through the hard times together and then maybe they wouldn't have hurt us so badly."

He tilted her chin so he could see her eyes, a dozen emotions crossing his face. "That's how it played out though, Sadie. Life handed us both shitty hands, but without them we wouldn't be where we are now."

She nodded, knowing he was right. "Even still, I hate thinking of all the years we missed out on."

"I know." He leaned in to kiss her, his hand cupped around her face. "Wanna know a secret?"

"Okay," she breathed, lost in the feel of his lips on hers.

"I realized something that day at the Pier." He met her eyes, humor flashing in his. "I watched you enjoy what I'd always taken for granted, and it made me see that I'd been going about this life thing all wrong. I was an asshole just for the sake of being one. I didn't care about anything but myself. But that day I did everything I could to prove to you that I was worth staying for, and instead you made me see that it didn't matter if you stayed. I'd follow you even if you went halfway around the world, because I'm in love with you, too."

Her eyes filled. "Even after everything that's happened, I know I'll never be able to go back to the life I had. I want this too badly to give up now."

He grinned, kissing her again. "Good, because you're right where you belong."

Chapter *thirty-three*

T HIS IS a really nice building," Sadie remarked as they stood in the elevator, heading up to the Odell & Son law firm.

Brody scowled. "It's where happiness goes to die."

She chuckled, squeezing his hand in hers. "Stop being so dramatic. Chase won't let that happen."

"Are you kidding? Chase is the guy wielding the sword." The elevator came to a smooth stop at the top floor and the doors opened soundlessly. "Come on. Let's just get this over with."

He directed her through the lobby, past the reception desk and back toward the private offices, not bothering to show her around. It wasn't like he was proud of the place, anyway. It wasn't his and never would be.

"So what do you think Chase wants?" Sadie asked, glancing around at all the frosted glass, stainless steel nameplates, and cherry wood doors.

"Probably to sign some paperwork or something," Brody replied, coming to a stop in front of Chase's office door. He knocked before stepping inside, finding Chase hard at work at his desk.

Chase looked up with a tired smile. "Hey, guys." He got to his feet, rounding his desk to shake hands with Brody. He turned to Sadie, his smile widening. "Long time no see, Sadie."

"Chase." She hugged him tightly, truly glad to see him. "I hear you're a dad now."

"Yep." He reached for the picture on his desk and handed it to her. "Her name's Charlotte."

"She's beautiful." Tears welled in her eyes as she gave back the picture. She looked him over, realizing she'd never noticed just how much he resembled his brother. Though he wore a trim, slate gray business suit and tie instead of Brody's favored jeans and T-shirt, the similarities were there in the shape of his blue eyes and the charm of his smile. That smile faltered as he looked between her and Brody.

"So the police still haven't found him?" he asked, tucking his hands into the pockets of his slacks.

Brody shook his head. "They located his apartment in North Hollywood and are keeping a close eye on it, but he hasn't been back there. Neighbors confirmed he drives a black Chevy Impala with tinted windows, just like the one that was following Sadie."

Chase attempted another smile. "He'll turn up. Don't worry."

"Easier said than done," Brody grumbled. He turned and walked to the windows of his brother's office, too restless to stand still.

Sadie stared after him, sorry to hear the stress in his voice. In truth, they were both on edge. They'd expected Drew to be in police custody by now. The fact that he was on the loose meant any control they thought they had over the situation was now gone.

He could be anywhere, preparing to do the unthinkable.

She turned back to Chase, trying to hide her worries. "So what's going on? Do I need to sign anything to close out the lawsuit?"

Chase chuckled and stared down at his watch. "Not exactly. Why don't you have a seat, Sadie? I can get you some coffee or tea if you'd like?"

"No, thanks." She sat in one of the chairs opposite his desk, crossing her legs.

Brody turned and eyed his brother curiously, only to stiffen when the door opened and his father entered the room.

Max looked to Brody first, his expression impossible to read. Then he glanced down at Sadie and something that passed as a polite smile crossed his face.

"Miss McRae."

Sadie gaped at Brody's father, unsure what to do. She shot Brody a questioning look before meeting the older man's eyes. "Mr. Odell."

Not forgetting his manners, Max extended his hand to shake hers, sympathy warming his ice blue eyes. "I'm very sorry to have heard of your recent troubles."

"T-thank you," Sadie replied, holding his cold hand for only a second before releasing it.

"All right, what do you want?" Brody demanded, coming up behind Sadie protectively.

Irritation hardened his father's face. "I need to speak to you."

Brody grunted. "By all means, speak away."

"Privately," Max insisted, losing his patience. He nodded to Chase before leaving the room, prompting Chase to grab Brody's arm and usher him out of the office.

"I'll keep an eye on Sadie," Chase murmured, patting his brother on the back. "Just hear him out, okay?"

Brody rolled his eyes. "What is this, an intervention?"

Chase grinned. "Something like that."

He pushed Brody out into the hallway and shut the door, leaving him standing alone with his father. Brody shoved his hands into his pockets, avoiding his father's eyes. "Let's just get this over with."

Max said nothing as he led the way to his own office, inviting Brody inside. He shut the door behind them and motioned for Brody to sit.

"I'll stand, thanks," Brody replied.

"You'll sit," Max ordered, settling into his desk chair. "If you want to protect Sadie."

Brody's eyebrows rose. "Excuse me?"

"Sit," Max repeated, nodding at the chairs in front of him.

Brody bit back a retort and did as he was told, resting his elbows on his knees as he leaned forward and leveled his gaze with his father. "What are you talking about, protect Sadie?"

Max sat back in his chair and steepled his fingers together, eyeing Brody thoughtfully. For a long moment he said nothing, he simply watched and considered. Brody was about to ask him again when he finally spoke. "Even as a child, you were rebellious and ungrateful. We gave you everything you could have ever wanted, yet you still spoke out of turn and raised hell every chance you got. I guess that's why it doesn't surprise me you turned out the way you did. There was no fixing you."

Brody's jaw clenched, his temper sparking. "You always were great at making me feel like shit, Dad. Thanks."

Max frowned, concern deepening the lines of his face. "There was a brief period of time when you were a teenager that I thought you might be turning a new leaf. Your grades improved, you stopped arguing with me just for the sake of fighting, and you got along better with your brother. At the time I didn't realize what it was that brought about this change, I just assumed you were growing up. But then in the summer of 2002 you fell back into your old ways, only worse. I had no choice but to give up on you. You were never going to be the son I'd always wanted. The son I felt I deserved."

That old pain shuddered through Brody, but he ignored it. "Yeah, well, you were never the father I deserved, either."

To his surprise, his father nodded. "Perhaps not. But that's not the point of this conversation."

"What is, then? Because I don't have all day," Brody countered, crossing his arms and sitting back in his chair.

Max let out a long, slow exhale, keeping his gaze focused on his son's. He pointed an index finger at the door, in the direction of Chase's office. "That girl out there is what did it. I know because I see the good in you now that she's back in your life. And I know that if you lose her again, I may never have my son back."

Emotion tightened Brody's throat as he shook his head. "I didn't realize you wanted me back at all. You've made that pretty clear."

"I didn't," Max admitted bluntly, the first flicker of regret passing over his face. "But that doesn't mean I lost hope I might one day change my mind."

Brody was at a loss for words. He turned over what his father said in his mind a dozen times, figuring the angles and the intention. What was the old man trying to say?

"So what's the goal here, exactly?" he asked finally, eyes narrowed.

His father's mouth was set in a firm, unwavering line, revealing nothing. He opened up his right hand desk drawer and pulled out a gleaming steel pistol, which he set on the desk in front of him.

Brody stared at it in shock, a million different scenarios playing out in his mind, most of which included his father shooting him in the chest.

He started to stand up, but Max only nudged the gun across the desk toward him.

"Take it," he instructed, his face still carefully blank and his voice edged with ice. "And protect that girl."

Brody's eyes went from the gun back to his father's face, unsure he'd heard him correctly. "Just...take it?"

Max nodded, watching closely as Brody lifted the gun and inspected it. "It's a 9mm Beretta. It's loaded, so don't take off the safety and for Heaven's sake don't point it anyone unless you intend to kill them."

Brody stared at the gun, admiring the stainless finish. He set it back down on the desk, his gaze meeting his father's. "Did Chase put you up to this?"

A cynical half smile twisted Max's features. "He actually tried to talk me out of it."

Brody laughed, certain this was some kind of sick, messed up dream. But when he held the gun in his hand again and felt the weight of it, and saw his father muster up a smile for him, he knew it was reality. A very strange, warped reality, but real all the same.

"Thank you," Brody said slowly, unused to those words being directed at his father. He cleared his throat and averted his eyes. "I don't know if you realize what this means to me, to be able to protect her."

Max tilted his head in consideration. "Ms. Ryan and I discussed you and her daughter at length the other day. She said she'd been proven wrong about you. I tried to convince her otherwise, but she was persistent. She claimed you were taking care of her daughter better than even she ever had. I can see now that she was right. For the first time in your life, you've stepped up to the plate."

Brody nodded, realizing it was the truth. "I love her more than I've ever loved anyone in my entire life. I'd die for her."

"Let's hope you don't have to." His father stood and reached into the cabinet behind him for a small black carrying case. He handed it to Brody. "Unload the pistol and put it in this. Keep it in the trunk of your car. If you get pulled over, any paperwork you need is inside. Just show it to the police and if they have any concerns, they can contact me."

Brody popped out the magazine and checked the chamber, then stored the pistol inside the case. When he looked up, he noticed his father had his hand held out for him.

He rose to his feet and accepted the handshake, impossibly moved. "Thanks again, Dad. Seriously."

Max's brows lifted. "When they catch the bastard, I expect to get my gun back."

Brody's face broke into a wide grin as he released his father's hand. "You always were such an Indian giver."

"Don't make a fool out of me, Brody," Max retorted, standing firm. "Don't mistake this small olive branch for a license to wreak havoc."

"I won't." Brody gave a quick, grateful nod. Carrying case in hand, he turned and left the office, shutting the door behind him. He went straight to Chase's office and collected Sadie, ushering her out to the lobby.

Once they were safely inside the elevator, Sadie turned to him. "So what happened?"

Brody frowned, still in disbelief. "He gave me a gun."

AFTER THEY arrived back home, Sadie busied herself with cooking an early dinner.

Brody disappeared into the bedroom with the gun, intending to store it in her nightstand in case they needed to use it. The very thought terrified her, but she tried to be reasonable about it. If Drew were to show up at the house, she would definitely feel much safer knowing she could protect herself.

Brody had shown her how to handle and load the Beretta, though she'd been to the range with her grandfather a few times. If it came to it, she could do what needed to be done. She just hoped that moment never came.

While she cut up russet potatoes, the doorbell rang. Her heart jumped into her throat, but she remembered that the police were still stationed outside and probably needed to speak to her. She walked to the front door and looked through the peep hole, then let out an excited yelp.

She opened the door and launched herself at Tommy, hugging him tightly. "Hey! What are you doing here?"

Tommy released her, looking her over carefully. "We were worried about you, kid."

Sadie glanced over his shoulder to both Isaac and, surprisingly, her father, who was staring at her with strained concern in his eyes. "You guys really didn't have to come all the way out here from Boston. I'm fine, I promise."

Isaac let out a bitter laugh, shaking his head. "You seriously thought we'd stay away after what happened to you? I thought we were a family?"

Her smile faltered as guilt set in. "We are. It's just..." Her eyes drifted back to her father, who seemed out of place and uncomfortable. But despite everything, he was still standing there on her doorstep, concerned for her. "I'm glad you're here."

Ben nodded, staring at the new security lights she'd installed. "Your mother thought it was best that I come see you."

Sadie's eyes widened. "You talked to her?"

"She called me," he admitted, running a hand over the back of his neck. "She said you needed me here."

Her heart broke at the hopeful tone in his voice, as if he didn't really believe it. Unsure what to say, she attempted a smile. "Thank you."

Brody emerged from inside the house, his teeth flashing in a grin. "Hey look, a family reunion."

Sadie looked at him, feeling awkward. "Dad, Tommy, this is Brody Odell."

"Nice to meet you," Brody greeted, extending his hand to Tommy first.

A knowing grin lit Tommy's face. "So you're the boy who's been watching over our Sadie-bug."

"Well, she's actually been babysitting me, but I can see how you could get that confused," Brody joked, shaking hands with Isaac before facing Ben. The two men sized each other up before Brody finally held out his hand, his grin sharp around the edges. "Nice to finally meet you, Ben."

Ben accepted the handshake with a curt nod, saying nothing. His gaze fell to his daughter. "Can we go inside?"

"Of course," Sadie stammered, motioning toward the house. "It's your home."

He and Tommy went inside, Brody close behind. Sadie followed with Isaac, who wrapped an arm around her shoulders and pulled her close.

"Still no word on the creeper, huh?" he asked.

She shook her head, glancing over her shoulder at the patrol car that was parked a ways down the street, keeping an eye on things. "I doubt we'll see him again. He's probably halfway to Mexico by now."

"So Dad said Valerie told him it's Lee Walker's son who's doing all this," Isaac said, stepping into the house and shutting the door. He turned her so she was facing him, his hands resting on her shoulders. Concern tightened his brow. "Is it true, Sadie?"

She swallowed the lump that formed in her throat and nodded.

"After all this time, he's just now trying to hurt you?"

She looked away, feeling uncomfortable. "He's disturbed. He has a history of drug abuse and violence, mental illness..."

"Maybe you should get out of town for awhile, come back to Boston with us," Isaac suggested.

"No." She stood firm, her eyes meeting his. "I won't run away."

Disbelief flashed over his face. "This isn't the time to stand on principle, Sadie. He tried to kill you."

She frowned, her courage dampened by the memory of those hands tightening around her neck. It sent a shiver down her spine. "I know what he tried to do."

"So then come with us."

She shook her head. "What makes you think he won't just find me there? The press reports every move I make. I can't escape, Isaac. All I can do is protect myself while he's still on the loose."

"And if they don't find him?" Isaac asked. "What then?"

"They will," she asserted, more for herself than for him. "I have to believe they will."

In the kitchen, Brody opened the fridge and pulled out beers for Ben and Tommy. He popped off the tops and handed over the bottles. "Hope you guys like Corona."

Tommy grinned and lifted the bottle in a toast. "I like anything that's free."

Brody snickered and opened a beer for himself as well, taking a long pull from it. His eyes fell to Ben and he gave a light nod. "Can I talk to you alone for a second?"

Ben's lips pressed together in a tight frown. "Sure."

While Tommy went to bug Sadie, Brody followed Ben out to the backyard. They sat down in the comfortable armchairs, facing the view of the city.

Brody took a few moments to collect his thoughts. When he spoke, he tried to leave any hostility he felt for the man out of his voice. "You probably remember my dad, Max Odell."

Ben let out a derisive sniff, taking a sip of his beer. "Val's lawyer."

Brody nodded. "So then you know what a coldhearted son of a bitch he can be. Being his son, I should know better than anybody. He's spent most of my life trying to fit me into a convenient little box, but if you know anything about me, which I think you do, you know I'm something of a rebel." He paused and drank his beer, his gaze shifting to Ben. "I know you may not realize this, but Sadie's a rebel, too. She probably gets it from you."

Ben's jaw tightened, though he said nothing. He continued to stare at the city, silently listening.

"The happiest I've ever seen her was when she was up onstage with you," Brody continued, sorrow and anger churning within him. "Not only was she able to be herself, she was able to be your daughter. That's all she's ever wanted. She inherited this voice from you, this love of music, yet you ignored her all these years."

When Ben still said nothing, Brody let out a frustrated sigh. "At least my dad had a reason to push me away; I was an ungrateful brat most of the time. But Sadie, she's never done anything to hurt anyone in her entire life. She's the best person I know, and she became that way in *spite* of you. It's the rebel in her that created an alias so she could still sing, because it's what she loves. She's never let your lack of love for her stand in the way of what makes her happy."

"Of course I love her," Ben retorted, his face still carefully devoid of emotion. He shot Brody a cold look. "After what happened to her, I made sure she was safe."

"You sent her away," Brody countered, temper sparking. "I'm sure your parents are great people, Ben, but they aren't you. And what she needed after nearly being raped was her father to hold her close and tell her it was going to be okay."

The first crack appeared in Ben's mask, regret softening his face. He looked away, hands clenched tight over his beer. He was silent for a few moments before clearing his throat and speaking again. "With my schedule, I'm hardly ever home. She was better off in Lake Tahoe, where—"

"Christ, Ben, stop making excuses." Brody threw up his free hand and let out a dark laugh. "Is it really so hard for you to admit you screwed up with her? That you were a shitty father?"

A dozen emotions contorted Ben's features, all of them painful. His eyes met Brody's, the blue in them darkening. "I didn't know how to help her. It was easier to ship her off to someone who would know what to do."

Brody's temper fizzled. He sat back in his chair, taking a long pull from his beer.

Ben continued, his voice solemn. "Val and I, we should've never been parents. We spent so much time at war with each other instead of paying attention to what really mattered. Sadie's the only good thing that ever came out of that mess."

Brody glanced over at him, pleased to see him admit the truth. "Well, there's a couple of good Albatross songs that came out of that freak show, too, but that's beside the point."

Ben cracked a smile, tilting his head to look at Brody. "Val said you were a funny guy."

One of Brody's eyebrows lifted. "Apparently she's been singing my praises all around town. Guess I should be flattered."

"I didn't want to believe her. You're still a paparazzi, after all." Ben chuckled, drinking his beer. He sighed, a pensive look crossing his face. "Then again, Val's usually a pretty good judge of character."

"Except for Lee Walker," Brody put in casually.

Ben nodded, his humor fading. "I don't know what she saw in him."

Brody shrugged. "The heart wants what the heart wants."

Ben tensed. "So you know they were having an affair?"

"She told us. How'd you find out?"

"Tommy." Ben rolled his shoulders, irritation in his voice. "She has no idea I know. But she does know I blamed her for what happened to Sadie. I still do."

Brody passed his beer between his hands thoughtfully. "If I asked you who shot him, would you tell me if you knew?"

Ben faced him, shaking his head. "Your guess is as good as mine."

Chapter *thirty-four*

ONCE PERSUADED that Sadie was safe, Ben, Tommy, and Isaac left for their hotel. The patrol car continued to wait down the street, the officer inside ever vigilant, allowing Sadie and Brody to settle in for the evening.

They curled up together on the sofa, mindlessly watching *Casablanca* as the sun went down. Sadie rested her head on Brody's chest, enjoying the quiet sound of his heartbeat and the feel of his arm around her. She breathed deeply, closing her eyes to savor this one moment of calm in the storm that had become her life.

A low, distant rumbling sound intruded on her thoughts. Her eyes flew open as she sat up, ears honed in on the sound, noticing that it seemed to vibrate through the walls as it got louder. Brody heard it too and muted the television.

"Is that…" Sadie began, that first flicker of anxiety washing over her.

"Helicopter," Brody finished, rising from the sofa to pull back the blinds on the living room window. When he glanced outside, his eyes went from the street up to the sky. "There's a fire."

"What?" Sadie jumped up to stand beside him. Above the sloping hills, trees, and houses of the neighborhood rose a massive tower of thick, dark smoke. "God, I wonder how close it is."

"Let's find out." Brody walked out the front door to stand in the driveway, his eyes on the smoke. Through the haze, the light of the sun cast the entire street in an ominous red-orange glow. He caught the scent of burning wood as the wind kicked up around him, swirling tiny flakes of ash in the air. It dotted Sadie's hair as she approached him, hugging her torso. Overhead, a low-flying, water-dropping helicopter swept past, disappearing beyond the trees.

Brody wandered over to the patrol car, leaning in when the officer rolled the passenger window down. "Where's the fire?"

"Just north of Mulholland," the cop replied. Brody recognized him as the same young rookie cop from the night Sadie was strangled. "I'll let you know if they start evacuating."

Sadie came up beside Brody, adrenaline pumping at the sound of distant sirens. "Do you think they will? Is it coming this way?"

Around them, the winds picked up again and sent her hair flying around her face. A few neighbors emerged from their homes, looking up at the sky apprehensively as they packed their cars or took snapshots of the smoke.

The cop shook his head. "Not sure. Car fire started it around 3 o'clock, winds carried it up the mountain. From the look of the smoke, it might've gotten a structure or two."

Sadie shivered at the thought of someone's home burning to the ground. She bit down hard on her tongue and glanced back at the house, wondering if they should gather their things and get out early.

"All right, keep us posted," Brody told the cop. He grabbed Sadie's hand and led her back to the house.

Her eyes went to the billowing clouds of smoke once more, seeing a vague haze of white within the roiling darkness. "I hope my mom's okay," she murmured, imagining the grand Victorian home engulfed in flames.

Brody closed the front door behind them and shut the blinds. "Don't worry so much, McRae. It's not the first fire to hit this area. Valerie's been through them before."

Sadie sat down on the sofa, feeling restless. She tried to smile when he joined her. "You're right. Worrying doesn't help anything."

"Nope." He kissed her nose with a playful grin. "If it'll help you relax, I can open a bottle of wine."

"Okay." She stared after him as he went into the kitchen, hearing another helicopter pass over the house. A chill swept over her that she tried to ignore.

Her cell phone rang, signaling a call from Tess. She answered it quickly, a shaky smile lifting her lips. "Hey, Tess. You hear about the fire?"

"*Sadie, listen to me very carefully,*" Tess began, the distinct sound of fear in her voice. "*I-I need you to come over to my place. Right away. Come alone.*"

Panic bubbled up within Sadie. "What? Wh—"

"*I don't have time to explain,*" Tess interrupted. She grew quiet, and Sadie could hear a low, murmured voice in the background.

"Who's with you?" Sadie asked as Brody came up beside her, concern hardening his features.

A frightened sob escaped Tess's throat as the sound of a man's voice, Drew's voice, grew louder. She screamed into the phone. "*Run, Sadie. Stay away from here!*"

The line went dead and Sadie shouted her friend's name into the phone, terror gripping her heart. Her eyes shot to Brody, filled with dread. "He's hurting her. Drew's hurting her."

Brody's hands dove into his hair as he inhaled sharply. He gritted his teeth, his mind made up in that instant. "It's a trap. He's trying to lure you over there."

"I don't care," Sadie snapped as she jumped to her feet and pushed past him. "She's at least twenty minutes away. We don't have much time."

"Stop," Brody ordered, grabbing her hand and urging her to face him. When she did, he saw the panicked tears in her eyes that contrasted with her determination to help her friend. "Think for a second, okay? Don't play into his hand like this. It's what he expects you to do."

Her breath came out in ragged gasps as she tried to focus, finding it useless. Her friend was in danger. She had to help. "So we'll have the cop drive us over there."

"You're not going." Brody stood firm. "I'll get the cop and go, but you're staying here. I'll have him call a backup patrol car to watch you, okay?"

She wiped away a tear that fell down her cheek, her composure breaking. "God, if he hurts her..."

"He won't. I promise." He dragged her against him, holding her close for the briefest of moments. When he pulled away, he met her eyes. "I won't be long. Lock the door."

He left without another word, slamming the door shut behind him. He ran down the driveway, startling the cop when he came to an abrupt stop right beside the passenger door.

"Let me in," he barked, tugging on the door handle.

"What's going on?" The cop unlocked the door, eyeing Brody uneasily as he slipped inside.

"Just got a call from Drew. He's got Sadie's friend Tess at her place off Wilshire near Highland. Call for another car to take your place and let's go."

The cop let out a rush of breath as he processed Brody's words, clearly debating what action to take. With a decisive nod, he turned on the car. He grabbed his radio as he pulled onto the street and relayed the situation. Flipping on the emergency lights, he gunned it and took them quickly through Laurel Canyon.

Brody braced himself in the passenger seat, catching a better glimpse of the fire as they rounded a curve. In the dying light of the sun, he saw the glow of flames licking at the sky.

They dodged fire trucks and panicked residents on the way down into the city, everything in a state of pandemonium. Road blocks were being set up at the base of Laurel Canyon to discourage non-residents from driving up to the flames and impeding the fire relief effort. Plumes of smoke spread over the Hollywood Hills, driven by unforgiving winds that carried snowflakes of ash.

As they weaved in and out of traffic on Sunset, Brody caught the rookie cop staring at him. "What?"

The cop turned his attention back to the road, a flush of red appearing on his neck. "Nothing. I guess I was just wondering how a lowlife paparazzi like you gets in with someone like Sadie McRae."

Brody gave a dark laugh as he glanced back out the window. "I'm just as surprised as you are, buddy."

With the help of the patrol car's emergency lights, the trip to Tess's condo took just under twenty minutes. Backup was on the way, but they didn't want to scare Drew into doing anything brash. They just needed to get to the front door and talk to the guy, and hopefully convince him to turn himself in.

The cop wanted Brody to wait in the car, but he wasn't having it. He stormed up the stairs to Tess's third floor unit, locating her front door. He waited for the cop to catch up, then knocked.

There was no answer. He knocked again, this time hearing a dull thud from inside. His brows furrowed as he met eyes with the cop, who reached for his handgun warily and grabbed the door knob. When he turned it and realized the door wasn't locked, they both froze for a brief, questioning moment.

A muffled shout came from inside, and the cop had no choice but to open the door. He stepped in first, gun drawn and ready. Brody followed close behind, spotting Tess tied to a chair in the middle of her living room. Black rope was wrapped around her torso and legs, a swatch of duct tape covering her mouth. Her tawny eyes were filled with panic as Brody swooped in to help her.

"Where is he?" Brody demanded as he removed the tape from her mouth.

"Gone," she gasped, a sob hitching in her throat. "Is Sadie with you?"

"She's back at the house." Brody began untying her bonds while the cop did a quick sweep of the house, declaring it clear.

"Call her, now," Tess growled through clenched teeth. "Tell her to run."

"He won't get in. They're not letting anyone but residents up Laurel Canyon because of the fire," Brody told her, trying not to let her panicked state affect him.

"He left hours ago."

Brody stared down at her, confused. "How's that possible? We got your phone call twenty minutes ago."

"It was a recording." A pained look crossed her face. "He tied me up, put a knife to my throat and handed me the recorder. He told me what to say, when to pause to make it sound real. I figured by warning her at the end that he might not use it, but he thought it was brilliant. Now I know why."

Brody cursed under his breath and whirled around to face the cop. "Did that patrol car get up to Sadie's place yet?"

The cop quickly called the station to find out, then shook his head moments later. "They got stuck assisting with a minor collision on the way up Laurel Canyon."

"You have to get back there." Tess rose on shaky legs and glared at Brody, pointing an index finger at the front door. "Stop wasting time and go!"

Brody nodded and dragged the cop outside, a new kind of horror exploding within his chest.

God, how could he have been so stupid?

SADIE PACED the living room, her gaze shifting to the window every few seconds. A reddish glow filled the darkening sky, the smoke as thick as ever. She spotted some of her neighbors fleeing, while others began to hose off their roofs as a precaution.

As of yet, another patrol car hadn't come. Part of her seriously considered getting into her own car to escape the danger that lurked just over the ridge, but she had nowhere else to go.

More sirens sounded off outside, only perpetuating her anxiety. With her arms crossed, she walked to the window and stared up at the smoke and the helicopter that dove in to drop water on the flames. It sent up plumes of white recovery, but soon they were swallowed by the dark.

She heard a sound behind her, coming from the patio doors across the room. When she turned, she spotted the silhouette of a man standing just outside the glass. Panic tore through her in an instant.

He's here.

For what seemed like several long, mortifying moments, she stared at Drew through the glass. Though she tried to tell her feet to move, fear froze her in place. It shivered through her in a violent tremor, disabling her.

She could just make out the coldness of his eyes. He stared at her intently, an odd, manic little smile contorting his lips. His right hand rose in a playful wave, and she nearly fainted from fear.

Her cell phone exploded to life in her back pocket, shocking her back to reality. Her hand trembled as she answered it.

Outside, Drew disappeared from view.

"Brody?" Sadie managed, angling her head to see where Drew went.

"Get in your car and leave the house, Sadie. Now. He's there."

Her breath rushed out of her lungs a second later as Drew reappeared, carrying one of the patio chairs. He held it up and threw it violently against the door, shattering the glass to pieces.

"It's too late," she whimpered, dropping her cell phone before bolting for the bedroom.

Drew barreled in after her, only a breath behind.

Chapter *thirty-five*

BRODY'S BLOOD went cold.

"Sadie?" he shouted, checking his phone to see if the line had gone dead. When he lifted it back to his ear, he could hear the sound of footsteps and screaming, and his fingers tightened over the phone. He screamed her name again, despite knowing it was useless.

The cop looked at him in panic. "What happened?"

Brody gritted his teeth, eyes ablaze. "I don't care what you have to do, you get me to that house."

With a nod, the cop kicked up the speed of the patrol car and swerved around the traffic cluttering Highland Avenue. He radioed in for more back up as a precaution, only to be told that all the patrol cars in the area were tied up due to the fire.

When Brody heard this, his hands dove into his hair. It took all he had to not fly into a rage and take the wheel. He was helpless to do more than sit back and try not to imagine how scared she must be.

Get the gun, Sadie. Get the gun and aim to kill.

THOUGH SHE knew it was pointless, Sadie slammed the bedroom door shut and fumbled for the flimsy lock on the handle. Seconds later she heard him ram against it, accompanied by the sound of his breathless laughter. Retreating further into the room, she eyed the door with terror as he attempted to kick it down.

A roaring sound filled her ears, a panicked sob stuck in her throat. Feeling like an animal trapped in a cage, she stared around frantically, searching for a way out.

Thoughts of breaking through the window died as the door blasted open, sending splinters of wood flying into the air. The door rebounded off the wall with a thud and Drew pushed past it, barely more than a silhouette in the darkness. He hovered in the doorway, his hands clenched into fists at his sides. The lines of his face were just visible in the glow of the fiery sky outside.

Overhead, another helicopter thundered past.

Before Sadie could do more than step backward in retreat, he lunged at her. She screamed and tried to fight back, only to find her arms pinned as he dragged her onto the bed. His strength surprised her, as did the manic gleam in his eyes. It was the same as last time. So much the same.

"Stop it, please!" she cried, writhing against him in an attempt to break free. He held her wrists and forced her legs down with his knees, shaking his head.

A dark laugh shuddered out of him as he stared into her eyes. "But the party just got started."

She winced with pain, her heart fluttering like a mad little bird inside her chest. "The police are on their way, they'll stop you."

"Why can't you just accept that it's too late for you, Sadie?" He released her right hand to slap her violently across the face. It sent a shocking jolt of pain into her system, dizzying her. "I can't figure out why my dad risked everything just to have a taste of you. You're nothing special."

He leaned in to run his tongue along the side of her face, then over her mouth. She fought weakly, disgusted and horrified all at once as he kissed her. It was sloppy and violent, his teeth biting down hard on her lower lip until she tasted blood. When she whimpered in pain, he pulled away with a grin.

"You kiss like a whore. But that doesn't surprise me."

Sadie struggled until she was out of breath and weak, strands of her hair splaying across her face. He made a move to brush them away, and she saw her chance.

This time around, she wasn't going to be a victim.

The hand he released went straight for his face and she dug her thumb into his eye socket. He howled in agony, shoving away from her and attempting to stand. He clutched the side of his face and stumbled into the corner of the room, shouting curses at her.

Sadie rolled over and reached into the bedside table for Brody's gun, finding it in the case. She fumbled for the latch and unleashed the weapon, wasting no time getting it into her hands. Shoving in the magazine, she released the safety and racked the slide. When she whirled around to face him, Drew began to laugh.

"Isn't this ironic?" His hand fell away from his face, showing his reddened eye. He blinked furiously, struggling to focus on her. "You going to shoot me like you did my old man?"

She clutched the gun in shaking hands, her finger poised over the trigger as she aimed it straight at his chest. Her voice trembled as she spoke. "I didn't shoot him. No one knows who did."

"Bullshit," Drew replied with another disturbing laugh. "You're a goddamn lying whore. Everyone knows that. He came on to you, so you grabbed his gun and shot him. He might not have been perfect, but he didn't deserve to die."

Sadie's upper lip curled as indignation shot through her. "Oh yes, he did."

In an instant Drew's expression changed. It went from alarmingly humorous to contorted with rage, and the snarl that emitted from his throat sent an ice cold shiver down her spine. "You Albatross whores tore my family apart. You took him from me."

Sweat slicked Sadie's hands and loosened her grip on the pistol. She gritted her teeth, feeling braver with the weapon. "I didn't kill him, Drew. But I *can* tell you the things he tried to do to me. I'm not sorry he's dead."

He slowly reached into his back pocket, revealing a switchblade. Pressing the button released the blade with a sharp click, the steel glinting in the reddish light.

That smile returned as he edged closer to her, blue eyes filled with violent hate. "You whores always blame the man when he's seduced by you. I'll never understand that. Valerie was notorious for it. After I'm done here I'll drop by her place again and see if she'll flirt her way right onto my knife."

A horrified breath shuddered from Sadie's lips, but she held firm. "Stay back."

"But we're having so much fun." Drew launched himself forward, knife flashing as he aimed it straight for her gut.

She pulled the trigger, the blast of the resulting bullet a bright light in the darkness.

THE TRAFFIC on Sunset Boulevard was unbearable.

Brody was losing his mind to impatience and the cold grip of fear, but he couldn't make the drive to Sadie's place go any faster. No matter what he did, he couldn't stop thinking about what he would find once he reached it. Once he reached her.

After the patrol car broke through the mad rush of evacuating residents and curious onlookers, they stormed up Laurel Canyon with emergency lights blazing. The smoke was thicker now that the fire was being extinguished, making the drive through the dark canyon nail-bitingly perilous. The car's high beams cut through the choking brown smoke, but the road was still hard to see. Brody imagined them careening off the side somewhere, and lamented that his life was in the hands of a rookie cop no older than he was.

At last they turned onto Sadie's street and barreled up to the house, squealing to a stop before it. Brody was halfway out the door before the car fully stopped, not sparing time for a plan of action. He only had one goal—get to Sadie.

Dragging his key out of his pocket, he unlocked the deadbolt and threw open the door. He froze and silently took in the sight before him.

Shards of glass littered the dining room from the broken patio door, a chair from outside slumped halfway through the opening. He spotted her cell phone lying on the carpet where she must have dropped it. The living room light was still on, but the rest of the house was dark. And much too quiet.

"Sadie?" he called out, coming back to his senses. He darted for the hallway that led to the bedrooms, unable to breathe. He approached her room, where he saw the wooden door kicked in and splinted to pieces. Dread filled him as he shoved inside, expecting to find her body lifeless on the floor.

Instead, he found her hovering by the nightstand, shaking uncontrollably. In her hands was his father's gun, pointed at Drew who sat upright on the floor by the bed. He was panting with pain and grasping at the bleeding wound on his chest.

"You bitch." Drew let out a manic, gasping laugh. A sheen of sweat covered his pale face as he attempted to crawl toward her, an eerie smile contorting his lips. He gave up and collapsed, blood spilling through his fingers and onto the carpet. His body shuddered as he struggled for breath, a stream of curses leaving his mouth.

Sadie's eyes were glassy and huge as she looked at Brody. "He came after me with a knife," she told him, her voice oddly steady despite the tremors that raced over her body. "It was so loud. The gun."

"I know, baby." Brody exhaled with relief and went to her. He slowly released the gun from her hands as the cop came into the room behind him.

They met eyes and Brody nodded in Drew's direction. "Careful. He's got a knife."

The cop held up his weapon and approached Drew, seeing the switchblade on the carpet. He kicked it aside, then knelt beside Drew to examine his wound and call for an ambulance.

Brody gently set his father's gun down on the nightstand, making sure the cop saw him leave it there. Then he wrapped an arm around Sadie and urged her from the room.

She glanced back at Drew and caught him staring at her with that horrifying grin, blood dribbling from between his lips.

THEY SAT together on the living room sofa while the police swarmed over the house. Red and blue lights flashed outside, accompanied by the occasional helicopter and wailing siren.

Sadie couldn't look when they wheeled Drew out on a stretcher. The image of his bloodied grin was still burned into her brain and the last thing she wanted was another glimpse of it. Brody simply held her closer, her shield against the ugliness of what had happened.

He calmly explained to the police that the Beretta had come from his father, borrowed for protection in light of the threats Sadie was facing. In retrospect, Sadie knew she owed Max Odell her life.

As the crime scene investigators came in to document the scene, Brody led Sadie to sit on the front porch steps. She stared out at the cluster of patrol cars and officers and noticed that the glow of flames had receded into darkness. The fire was being contained.

"At least the fire kept the press out," Brody mused, pressing a kiss to the top of her head.

Sadie nodded. "They'll be here the moment they get a chance, though."

"We can arrange for somewhere else for you to stay."

"No. I won't be chased away again." She sat up a bit taller, proud of herself for fighting back. Even if she hadn't been very brave, at least she'd managed to get the upper hand in the end.

The memory of it was something of a blur to her now. It merged with her distorted memories of the night Lee Walker attacked her, his face blending with that of his son. Both men became one, nothing more than a monster in disguise. Likeable and charming on the surface, but infested with cruelty inside. How she'd missed the hatred in Drew's eyes, she'd never understand. But the fact that she had made her realize how naïve she was. How foolish.

And how incredibly lucky.

"I should call Tess." Sadie reached into her jeans pocket for her cell phone, only to have Brody stop her.

"I already did, while you were talking with the cops. I called your parents, too."

"Both of them?" She winced, imagining what a firestorm of panic her mother must have been in. "What'd they say?"

He shrugged. "They're glad you're okay. I told them you needed some time to rest before they could bother you."

She let out a breath, grateful. "Thanks."

Brody nodded, a thoughtful look coming over his face. "Did Drew tell you why he did all of this?"

"He said I killed his dad, even though that's impossible. Walker was shot from the doorway while he had me pinned to the bed. I couldn't have physically done it." Sadie frowned. "Maybe he figured everyone lied about it. Though I don't know why."

"Whoever actually shot him did lie," Brody pointed out. "And I find it suspicious that the investigation was just sort of…dropped. Either the new lead they got was a dead end, or it solved the mystery once and for all and they're protecting the person responsible. I've seen it happen before. They're not required to make everything in an investigation public record. They can get a court order."

Sadie lost herself in thought over his words, troubled by them. In the end, she supposed it didn't matter. She'd given up hope on ever learning the identity of her rescuer. But what if the police *did* know the truth? Would they tell her?

The bigger question, she realized, was why the shooter would need their identity protected in the first place.

Chapter *thirty-six*

A T DAWN, the smoky haze gave the light an eerily orange tint. Sadie watched the sun rise over the mountains to the east, seated with her legs folded up against her chest on the patio. Tess sat beside her, smoking one of Brody's cigarettes.

"Did you get any sleep?" Tess asked, blowing out a stream of smoke. Her eyes were tired, reflecting her mood.

"An hour or two, maybe." Sadie shrugged, resting her chin on her knees. "I didn't want to go back into that room so I slept on the couch."

"We'll get someone here to clean all this up for you." Tess patted her on the back, mustering up a smile. "You know the offer's always open for you to come stay with me. I'll even let you bring Brody."

Though she felt a hitch of emotion in her throat, Sadie's eyes remained dry. She shook her head. "I'm sorry Drew hurt you, Tess."

Tess pressed her lips together as though fighting back a wave of anger. "It's not your fault, honey. None of this is."

"And since he's alive, what happens if he comes after us again?" Sadie asked, dread settling over her.

"You shoot to kill next time," Tess replied bluntly with a dark laugh. She pulled Sadie close and hugged her. "Don't worry about it. For now he's in custody, so he can't hurt you. And they should have enough evidence to keep him behind bars for awhile."

"I know." Sadie chewed on her thumbnail, wishing she could stop fretting over the what-ifs and instead embrace the what-nows.

She heard voices and footsteps and glanced over her shoulder, seeing Tommy, Isaac, and her father. They hovered in the doorway, clearly unsure if she wanted to see them. She let out a sigh and rose to her feet.

"Hi," she greeted, welcoming Isaac into her arms when he stepped forward.

He squeezed her tightly, then released her. "I knew you should've taken me up on the Boston idea."

"Hindsight's twenty-twenty, right?" Sadie said with a weary smile. She turned to Tommy, disquieted by the tears in his eyes. He pulled her close and held on until she could barely breathe. "Tommy, I'm okay. I promise."

"I know, kid," he managed, stepping back to cup her cheek with his hand. He flashed her one of his trademark grins. "I just needed to see it for myself."

She nodded and faced her father. His brows were furrowed with concern, so different from his usual cool façade. He said nothing as he wrapped her in his arms, holding her tighter than even Tommy had. She embraced the sensation, waves of relief settling over her.

When he broke the hug, she met his eyes. He had a strained look on his face, like there was something he desperately wanted to say and yet he had no idea how to say it.

To be fair, she didn't know what to say to him, either.

They began to ask her questions about the night before, ones she was already so tired of answering. Brody drifted outside, filling in the parts that were still hard for her to think about. Soon, she grew weary with the conversation, wanting nothing more than to hide away in a room for some peace and quiet. But seeing as her bedroom was still a crime scene and there was no way she would be left alone, she had only one other option.

Escape.

"I have to use the restroom," she told them, edging her way past Brody and into the house. She checked to see if any of them were watching her, then picked up her purse and snuck out the front door. Within moments she was in her car and on the road, heading for the one place she had never thought she'd seek comfort. But today, it called to her like a safe haven.

The streets were littered with ash and fragments of burnt leaves, but the menacing smoke from the night before was gone. All that was left was the rusty haze and the lingering scent of scorched wood.

She pulled into the driveway of her mother's home and parked behind her blue corvette, sad to see it covered in murky gray ash. She walked up to the front door and knocked, offering a shaky smile when Carla answered.

"Is my mom here?"

Carla nodded. "Come in."

Sadie followed her inside. She could hear the bright, poignant sound of her mother's piano, and her heart clenched. Coming to a stop just outside the music room, she peered in and silently watched her mother play.

Valerie was radiant. Early morning sunlight brought out the gold in her hair, shimmering with every movement she made. Her fingers danced over the keys, well accustomed to the notes. They were ones she'd made famous thirty years earlier, the song that brought Albatross out of the shadows and into the limelight.

Her voice rang out, the soothing beauty of it still so very much the same. Though it had taken on a more tired, haunting tone these days, Sadie still marveled at the emotions it evoked inside of her. All she'd wanted her entire life was to sound half as good as her mother. Even now, she knew she could never compete. The woman was truly a legend.

Tears welled in her eyes when her mother brought the song to a close. She watched as Valerie hung her head and closed her eyes, emotionally moved and exhausted by it.

Sadie stepped into the room and clapped, unable to help the smile that brightened her face. Her mother looked up at her, only to freeze as though she'd seen a ghost. Her face went slack as she stared intently at Sadie, her bronzed eyes darkened with regret.

When Valerie stood and approached her, Sadie held her gaze, unable to speak. She could feel the tears spill down her cheeks as her mother enfolded her in a warm embrace, one she hadn't even realized she craved so badly.

Sadie gave in and let go, her earlier reserve shattering to pieces. She cried, becoming that child once again, the one who needed her mother in times of crisis. The one who hungered for what so many others took for granted. She let the deep wounds that had always been within her be filled, her heart patching itself together, piece by tattered piece.

"It's okay darling, I'm here," Valerie crooned, petting her head softly. "You just get it all out."

Sadie sniffled, wiping her eyes as she pulled away. A shaky laugh bubbled from her throat. "I'm sorry. I'm such a mess right now."

"Come sit, I'll have Carla make us some tea." She led Sadie to one of the elegant sofas, then disappeared briefly to request the tea. When she came back, she sat down beside Sadie, her hands bundled in her lap. "That reporter of yours called me last night. Woke me up in the middle of the strangest dream. You were just a child and I was chasing after you in the garden. You kept slipping through the flowers and hiding from me. I wondered afterward if it was something of a premonition. A warning that you were going to run away from me again." Her voice caught, but she smiled. "But now you're here. You came back to me."

Sadie nodded, meeting her mother's eyes. "I'm so tired, Mom. I don't want us to fight anymore. I just...I just want us to be together, in case there's not much time left."

Valerie let out a light laugh. "Don't worry about me. I'm going to be just fine."

"Are you?" Sadie asked, shaking her head. "Because I'm so scared to lose you."

"Really?" Surprise flashed in Valerie's eyes, softening her face.

"Of course." Sadie looked away, feeling awkward under her mother's stare. She took a deep breath and tried to formulate the right words to convey how she felt. "I realized when I came back here that I've wasted so much of my life being scared. I was scared of fame, so I only sang in secret. Scared of confrontation, so I stayed away from you. Scared of interfering, so I gave Dad his space. And scared of what happened to me here, so much so that I did all I could to pretend it never happened. But it did, and last night was proof that running away from it didn't protect me. It didn't just go away, it came back and found me. And if it hadn't found me this time, it would find me next year, or in five years. I had to face my fear, and now that I have…"

"You're free," Valerie supplied, reaching for her hand. She squeezed it tightly. "I have my own fear to face, darling. I think I've waited long enough."

"What is it?" Sadie brushed away more tears as she met her mother's eyes.

Valerie took a deep breath, releasing it on a slow, calming exhale. "The night that Lee hurt you, I lied to the police. I told them I was downstairs when it happened. I wasn't."

Sadie's brows furrowed. "But I saw you in the kitchen with your friends. You'd just taken a hit of cocaine. You were high."

A soft laugh escaped Valerie's lips. "I know you stay away from the stuff—and I'm glad you do—but if you think the cocaine made me oblivious to what was happening around me then you're mistaken. It only made me more aware."

"I don't understand."

Valerie continued. "Well, I told the others I was going to the pantry for more vodka, but on the way I noticed I'd chipped a fingernail. I decided to run upstairs to fix it first, so I went through the dining room to the stairs, avoiding the party. As far as I know, nobody noticed me. On the way to my bedroom I heard strange noises coming from inside your room. I opened the door and saw Lee on top of you, and I panicked. I couldn't believe he would do something like that. I shouted at him and saw his gun on the dresser." She paused, her eyes glassy as the memories came back to her. "I don't know what came over me. I guess I was being the protective mother I should have always been. I didn't even think twice about shooting him. By the time my brain could process it, it was done. He was dead."

Sadie couldn't breathe. Her lips parted in stunned silence as her brain tried to piece together the remnants of that night. She recalled the shouting, remembered Walker rising away from her and the horrid sound of the gunshot. Had she seen the woman in the doorway, clutching the gun just as she had done the night before with Drew?

Her mother's face. She did vaguely remember seeing the mortified horror contort Valerie's beautiful features. But she'd always thought that was afterward, when her agonized screams echoed throughout the house.

Maybe, after all this time, she was wrong.

"But…Tommy," Sadie said weakly.

Valerie nodded. "He found me with the gun and asked me if I'd done it. If I'd killed him. Then he ordered me to wipe it clean and leave it on the floor before anyone else could see."

The memory Sadie had of Tommy asking that very same question resonated through her. So he hadn't been asking *her* that question at all, she realized. He'd been asking her mother.

"Why would he do that?"

Regret flashed in Valerie's eyes. "You have to understand, darling. Things were so fragile between all of us at that time, especially between me and Georgina. She'd already suspected us of having the affair. If she'd found out that I shot Lee, despite the reason for it, she would have accused me of staging the entire thing and killing him out of jealousy. So Tommy made the decision to take the blame for me, but by the time the police got involved everything got so muddied that neither of us were willing to say anything. To our surprise, you didn't seem to remember what happened at all, which I suppose was a blessing. We got in over our heads so quickly and the lie just grew bigger and bigger until we started to convince ourselves that what happened hadn't actually happened. It was a mess."

"But it was justified. You had every right to shoot him," Sadie argued.

"Did I?" Valerie mused, avoiding her daughter's eyes. She stared down at their joined hands instead, pressing her lips together in a sad smile. "I suppose a jury may have found me innocent, but the truth was I didn't even give Lee a chance to back away from you. A chance to stop. I just shot him. And from the confused terror I saw in his eyes the moment I pulled the trigger, I know he would have if I'd given him the chance. But I couldn't. I wouldn't. He was hurting my baby and all I could think about was destroying him for it."

Sadie's mind reeled from this new information. She stood up, unable to sit any longer. As she began to pace, she twirled a strand of her hair around her finger. "I saw the police reports. They tested for gunshot residue and found nothing on you."

"Tommy bribed the officer who swabbed my hands. He happened to be a big fan of Albatross, so he agreed to swab someone downstairs, label it as mine, and then dispose of the real test."

Sadie stopped pacing, eyebrows raised. "That was all it took?"

Valerie shrugged. "Sometimes it pays to be a celebrity, darling."

"What about the new lead the police had? What was that about?"

"Tommy had a guilty conscience," Valerie replied, her voice taking on a bitter tone. "With you coming back to town, he knew the entire mess we'd buried would be dug up again. I didn't help when I exposed you, of course, but he went behind my back to the police and told them the truth. I met with Mr. Odell and we worked something out with the DA. A fine for obstruction of justice or some such thing, and no charges filed for the shooting. Anyway, the case is about to be closed and I'm sure it'll only be a matter of time before the word gets out on what we did. Max tried to get a court order to seal the records, but the judge refused."

"I can't believe this." Sadie sat back down, stunned. "So all this time it was you. Why didn't you ever tell me?"

"I didn't want to burden you with the lie. It was a bad enough one for Tommy and I to share, much less you. You were just a baby."

"I was fifteen," Sadie corrected, looking at her mother. "I deserved to know."

"What you deserved was a better life, which you got the minute you left me." Valerie's eyes misted, her lips curving. "I didn't realize that until last night when I found out you'd been hurt again. This world of mine isn't good for you. It never has been."

Anger bloomed within Sadie. "You don't think I'm strong enough to handle being famous?"

"I don't think you're foolish enough to want it when you've seen what it does to people, what it did to me and your father. What it's done to you already."

Sadie's temper deflated, her heart aching. "We can fix it. I want to stay and record music with you. I want to be a part of your life."

"You do?" Valerie brightened, a pleased look crossing her face. "Well, if that's the case then maybe we should practice."

Sadie nodded, emotion tightening her throat. "I would love to."

Chapter *thirty-seven*

"WHAT DO you mean she's gone?" Brody asked, concern tightening his face.

Tess crossed her arms. "Her car's not out front. She must have taken off."

Tommy, Isaac, and Ben came inside from the patio, hearing Tess's words.

"Maybe she just ran to the store for something," Tommy suggested hopefully.

Isaac nodded, pulling out his cell phone. "I'll call her."

"Tried that," Tess told him with a sigh. "Her phone's turned off."

Brody cursed under his breath, wondering what the hell Sadie was thinking. Sure, Drew was at the hospital in police custody, but the press would be lurking around the area, hungry for a glimpse of her. She could get bombarded by paparazzi in the street.

Ben cleared his throat, earning the attention of the others. "She's probably at Val's."

"You're right. I don't know where else she'd go," Brody agreed, running a hand over the back of his neck. "I'll go check on her, make sure she's okay."

"I'll join you," Ben said, already heading for the front door.

Brody's eyebrows rose. "You sure that's a good idea?"

Ben gave a curt nod, then stepped outside.

Brody shot a curious look at the others before following him. Ben climbed into his rental SUV, prompting Brody to hop into the passenger seat. He buckled in, eyeing Ben warily. "Just so you know, if you and Valerie go to blows I'm stealing your car and taking Sadie with me."

Ben chuckled as he started the car and retreated down the driveway. "What makes you think I'd leave you the keys?"

Brody popped open the glove box and pulled out the spare key enclosed with the rental agreements, holding it up with a grin. "Got that covered."

A wry smile softened Ben's face. "Val and I will be behave. If we don't, there's a paparazzi in the room who might catch it all on tape and make fools out of us."

Brody grinned. "The tabloids would pay big bucks for that."

"I'm sure they would," Ben agreed. His humor faded as he glanced at Brody. "What are your intentions for my daughter?"

Brody snorted. "We've reached that point, huh? The part where you start acting like the concerned dad and I'm the asshole asking for your daughter's hand?"

"No matter what kind of relationship we have, she's still my daughter," Ben argued. "And you're still a shamed journalist-turned-paparazzi that for some reason has it in his head that he's worthy of her."

"I never said I was worthy." Brody stared out the passenger window, feeling irritated. "She knows the truth about what I am and so far she's been cool with it. I think you should worry about winning her trust back yourself before you start judging me."

Ben let out a quiet sigh as he turned onto Valerie's street. "Maybe you're right."

They drove up her driveway and hit the buzzer. After Brody spoke briefly with Carla, the gate opened and they were welcomed inside. Ben pulled in behind Sadie's car and shut off the engine.

Brody turned to him with a tight smile. "We're on the same team, Ben. We all want her to be happy. Keep that in mind, okay?"

Ben gave a quick nod, saying nothing as he exited the car. Brody followed him up the path to the front door.

When Carla answered, her lips parted in surprise. She stared at Ben, looking unsure of what to do.

"Mr. McRae, sir. We weren't expecting you," she stumbled, a hint of defensive anger in her voice.

Ben bowed his head in a sign of humility. "We're looking for Sadie."

"She's with her mother." Carla's eyes shifted to Brody, watching him thoughtfully. "Come inside."

She brought them through the parlor toward the music room, where they could hear the sound of the piano and light, beautiful voices singing. They came to a stop just outside the door, pausing to take a look inside.

Brody grinned at the sight of Sadie seated beside her mother at the polished grand piano. Valerie's hands were busy working over the keys, creating the tune of one of Albatross's most famous love songs. Sadie's face was lit with a brilliant smile as she sang, and Brody felt the pull of her beauty tug on his heart. She was magnificent, and the woman beside her was still every bit the goddess she'd always been.

He chanced a look at Ben, curious to see what he thought of his daughter and ex-wife singing together. He'd expected irritation, maybe jealousy. Instead he saw surprised wonder that softened the serious lines of his face and brightened the blue-green of his eyes. He looked like a man who'd just stumbled upon a pile of glittering gold in the middle of the desert, sticking unexpectedly out of the sand.

Sadie spotted them first. She flushed with embarrassment and placed her hand upon her mother's, urging her to stop playing. Valerie looked to her in confusion, before also shifting her gaze to the door.

Ben and Valerie met eyes for a long, quiet moment. Brody could feel the tension and electricity humming off Ben and hoped the man kept to his word about behaving.

Brody caught Sadie's gaze and shrugged. When she still didn't move, he decided to take the first step.

He patted Ben on the back and slipped on a cheerful grin. "So this is where you ran off to."

Sadie stood up from the piano bench, her hands bundled together in front of her. "Sorry, I should have told you."

Ben stepped forward, approaching the piano with a strained expression. His eyes went from Valerie to Sadie, then back to Valerie. He nodded and shoved his hands into his pockets, then glanced around the room. "Place looks a lot different since the last time I was here."

Valerie bristled, her eyes not leaving Ben. "Better, you mean."

He shrugged. "It suits you, Val."

She tilted her chin up, her lips curving. "Yes, it does."

Sadie stared back and forth between the two of them, a riot of nerves. She was shocked they hadn't started fighting yet, but knew better than to assume they could be civil for long.

It had been over a decade since she'd seen the two of them in the same room together. The feeling was surreal; they had always been two separate parts of one whole that couldn't exist in reality. Yet here they were, face to face. Her parents, the people who made her, brought together now because of her.

"Um, anyway, I was just going to hang out here for a bit longer then head home. You guys don't have to stay if you don't want to," Sadie stammered, running a hand through her hair and wishing she knew better how to handle the situation. She looked to Brody pleadingly, but before he could intervene, Ben spoke.

"I'm in no hurry." He walked to Sadie and placed a hand on her shoulder, his eyes warm. His other hand fell to Valerie's, like it had always belonged there. Sadie marveled at the rush of pleasure she got from seeing it.

She looked at him and smiled. "Would you like to hear us play some more?"

He nodded, still keeping his hand on her shoulder as she sat back down on the bench. She shot her mother an excited grin, and Valerie beamed with pleasure. She tilted her head back to look at her ex-husband, one eyebrow raised.

"What song should we play, darling?"

A smile bloomed over Ben's face. "How about the first song we ever wrote together."

Valerie nodded. "Excellent choice."

She started to play, her fingers sliding expertly over the keys. Sadie's heart filled, tears welling in her eyes. When they began to sing together for the first time in over fifteen years, her eyes went to Brody and she mouthed 'thank you.' It was the greatest gift she could have ever received.

He grinned, pleased to see her get her wish after all this time. God knew she deserved it. It had him thinking of his own family and the patching up he still had to do. Realizing it was better late than never, he ducked out of the room and called his brother.

"Hey. I want you and Dad to meet me at that Irish pub on Sunset for lunch today."

"*Sure, what for?*" Chase asked.

"It's time we had that beer."

"I REALLY am losing my touch," Brody lamented, shaking his head. He shot Sadie an amused look. "I never would have guessed Valerie had it in her to go all mama bear and shoot someone. Much less partner up with Tommy for one of the greatest cover-ups in L.A. history."

Sadie laughed, curling her legs beneath her on his sofa. Until the police were finished gathering evidence from her father's house, she was staying at his place. "Well, from the sound of it the press hasn't gotten a hold of the information yet. You could break the story, maybe get your reputation back."

Brody considered it for a second, then shrugged. "Honestly, I don't care about my reputation or getting the next hot story. It's probably time I got a real job."

Surprise flashed in her eyes. "But you love journalism."

"God knows I do." He chuckled, knocking back his beer. "But I had a good run with it. I saw things most people only hear about in history books. I also got shot at a few times, saw a spider as big as your head in North Africa..."

Sadie shivered. "Ew."

"Yep, good times." He sighed, part of him desperately missing those days of constant danger and intrigue. "But this is home. And now with you here, I have even less of a reason to get my old job back."

She smiled and reached for his hand. "I'll support you, whatever you decide to do."

"Gee, thanks McRae," he joked, squeezing her hand and leaning in for a hard and fast kiss. He met her eyes and grinned. "So if I take up a job as a male stripper, you'll come cheer me on?"

One of her eyebrows rose. "Only if I get half your tips."

"Ouch." He winced playfully, tweaking her nose. "Not like you need the money."

"Not like you need to strip," she retorted, smiling. "You know, my dad has some connections within the media, he might be able to get you a job. It probably won't be glamorous, but at least you'd be reporting."

Brody nodded, giving it some thought. "I guess there's worse things, right?"

"Not many, but some."

He elbowed her in the ribs. "Not all of us were made to follow in our parents' footsteps. I'd be a god-awful lawyer."

She leaned into him, resting her head on his shoulder. "You don't have the patience for it."

"Whereas you have all the right ingredients for a rock star, you just didn't know it," he told her, pulling her in close. "It was cool seeing the three of you together today. Kind of weird, too."

"I know," Sadie mused, smiling at the memory. "They didn't argue once. It was bizarre."

"For the first time they care more about you than their feud."

"I wish it hadn't taken them so long to figure it out," she said quietly, regret in her voice. "But maybe it had to happen like this. I'm just sad we may not have much time to enjoy it."

"Is she not getting better?"

"She seems okay on the outside, but I can tell she's tired. I'm going with her tomorrow to her chemo appointment. Dad's coming, too."

Brody's eyes widened. "Really?"

"Yeah. Told you it was bizarre." Sadie shook her head, still in disbelief over it all. "But they care about each other in their own way."

"He's just trying to win points with you," Brody decided, humor in his voice.

"Well, it's working."

"I'm glad." He pressed a kiss to the top of her head, happy for her. "So, what do you want to do tonight?"

"Isn't there a Dodger game on?" Sadie asked, lifting her face to meet his eyes.

His teeth flashed in a grin. "Girl after my own heart."

epilogue

BEVERLY HILLS, CALIFORNIA
SEPTEMBER 2014

THE SMELL of burgers and hot dogs on the grill wafted across the backyard, joined by the sound of laughter and good-old classic rock. Late afternoon sun spilled across the grass, the heat softened by the summer breeze that blew in from the sea.

Sadie smiled as she stepped onto the patio of her father's home—her home now—a bowl of strawberry and spinach salad in her hands. She stared around at her family and friends, humbled they all showed up for her birthday. Just over a year ago she wouldn't have imagined they'd ever be together like this.

Happy, safe. Alive.

She went to her mother, who was seated regally at the outdoor dining table, telling some tall tale of her days with Albatross to Tess, Chase, his wife and baby Charlotte. Tommy and Georgina sat on either side of her, filling in the details and calling out the boldfaced lies with big grins on their faces.

Though there'd been times over the last year when Sadie was sure Valerie would give up, she'd pushed through chemotherapy and the surgery to remove the remaining cancer. She'd lost some of her vitality in the process, her hair just now starting to re-grow from the places it had thinned and her face lined with the tired stress of treatment. But on this day, her spirits were high. She was officially in remission, which was more than any of them could have hoped for. What had seemed so bleak an outcome at the start had turned into a miracle.

She survived, at least for now. And that was enough for Sadie to hold onto.

Setting down the salad, she smiled at her mother. They were the closest they had ever been in her entire life. And although things would never be entirely without drama—it *was* Valerie—at least it was better than not having the woman in her life at all.

Her eyes went to Georgina, who laughed at something Tommy said and tossed back her fiery, shoulder-length hair. She reached for Valerie's hand and squeezed it affectionately, something that still took Sadie by surprise. After the truth of Lee Walker's death had come out, everyone had expected Georgina to lash out at Valerie. Instead, the woman hadn't seemed fazed by the news. It was as if she'd known the truth all along. And in the end, it appeared that the bonds of Albatross were stronger than any of them knew. The death of the scandal brought the band back together for a reunion tour the world had been waiting decades for.

A shout and breathless laughter came from the grassy yard, where Brody was busy throwing a football with Ben, Isaac, and Glenn. Sadie's grandparents and stepmother Paulette were watching from the sidelines, cheering on Ben with hoots of laughter. Sadie waved to Brody, grinning when he blew her a kiss. She caught her father's eyes, pleased when he nodded at her with a warm smile. He then tackled Brody for the ball, and Sadie giggled at the resulting scuffle in the grass.

Valerie spotted the brawl and pursed her lips, whistling to get their attention. "In case you've forgotten, Ben, we have a show to do tomorrow night. Don't break any bones. If you do, I'm still making you go onstage. The show must go on, darling."

Ben chuckled and rose to his feet, holding his hand out for Brody. Both men brushed dry grass off their jeans.

Ben shot Valerie a good-humored look. "All in good fun."

He grabbed the football from Brody's hands and tossed it to Isaac, who caught it and tried to dodge around Glenn. Sadie's grandparents burst into laughter as Glenn snatched the ball from Isaac only to lose it to Ben seconds later, allowing him to run past Brody and score a touchdown. He threw the ball into the grass in triumph and went to his wife, giving her a quick kiss. Paulette blushed and fixed her chin-length dark hair, a hint of a smile curving her mouth.

Brody chuckled and left the game, wandering over to Sadie. Her slender body was draped in a pretty floral sundress that left her lightly freckled shoulders bare.

She smiled as he approached, eyes dancing. "Having fun?"

"Always." He pulled her in close for a kiss, his lips teasing hers.

Behind them, Tess groaned and Chase whistled.

"Get a room!" Tess called out, laughing.

In response, Brody lifted Sadie over his shoulder cave-man style. He shot a triumphant look at the others. "Don't have to tell me twice."

"Brody!" Sadie laughed breathlessly as he hauled her inside the house and into the kitchen. He set her down on her feet and cornered her against the kitchen counter, kissing her again. She let out a long exhale, her hands cruising over his chest as her heart began to race.

When he broke the kiss, he grinned at her. "I was going to wait till tomorrow night after the Albatross Reunion show to do this, but you know me. I'm impatient."

Sadie blinked. "Okay…"

He reached into his back jeans pocket and pulled out a photograph, handing it to her. It was the same one he'd found over a year before of the two of them as teens, smiling with the sunlight glowing in their hair and the naivety of youth so clear on their faces.

"Remember this?" he asked.

Her lips spread in a warm smile as she nodded. "Wow. Yeah, I do. God, we look young."

"We *were* young." He watched her closely as she admired the picture, enjoying the flash of nostalgia and humor in her eyes. "You were the best friend I ever had. You still are. I think it's time I made my best friend my wife."

He slipped a ring from his pocket and slid it onto her finger before she could even process his words. Her lips parted in surprise as she stared down at it.

"Oh," she whispered, inhaling sharply and covering her mouth with the back of her hand. She looked up at him, speechless.

Brody brushed aside strands of her hair, his eyes searching hers as he smiled. "Well, McRae, what do you say? Will you have me?"

She nodded and threw her arms around his neck. When she pulled away, she stared down at the simple white-gold band topped with a sapphire surrounded by glittering diamonds. "It's beautiful."

He wrapped his arm over her shoulders and led her back to the patio door, kissing the top of her head. "We can wait to tell everyone if you want. I know how you hate being the center of attention."

"Are you kidding?" She shot him an excited grin, her arm winding around his waist. "I suck at keeping secrets and you know it. Best to get it over with now."

He chuckled, opening the door for her to step outside. "Good point."

She turned to face him and gave him a slow, tender kiss. As she pulled away, she grabbed his hand and dragged him with her onto the patio.

"Come on. Let's tell everyone the good news."

"*I will not die an unlived life. I will not live in fear of falling or catching fire. I choose to inhabit my days, to allow my living to open me, to make me less afraid, more accessible, to loosen my heart until it becomes a wing, a torch, a promise. I choose to risk my significance; to live so that which comes to me as seed goes to the next as blossom and that which comes to me as blossom, goes on as fruit.*" – Dawna Markova

ABOUT THE AUTHOR

Katie Jennings is the author of the popular fantasy series The Dryad Quartet as well as the award-winning romantic family drama series The Vasser Legacy. Her paranormal romance, *So Fell The Sparrow*, won an Honorable Mention in the 2014 Readers' Favorite International Book Awards.

She lives in sunny Southern California with her husband and cat, who both think she's the biggest nerd ever. She's a firm believer in happy endings and loves nothing more than a great romance novel.

www.ingramcontent.com/pod-product-compliance
Lightning Source LLC
Chambersburg PA
CBHW020229180626
46810CB00006B/2095